Murder at Conundrum Creek

A Nika McGuinness Mystery

Murder at Conundrum Creek

Joan Harvey Monroe

Writers Club Press
San Jose New York Lincoln Shanghai

Murder at Conundrum Creek

Writers Club Press
an imprint of iUniverse, Inc.

For information address:
iUniverse, Inc.
5220 S. 16th St., Suite 200
Lincoln, NE 68512
www.iuniverse.com

ISBN: 0-595-20914-9

Printed in the United States of America

To Dick, whose support and patience made this book possible. And to Kris, David, Nan, Geof, and Emma Jane who would always rather listen to my stories than have me read them books.

ACKNOWLEDGEMENTS

I wish to thank all members of Penpointers and especially Jan, Cheryl, Sue, Bryan. David, and Aaron. Honest gals and guys, I included most of your suggestions in this book.

Prologue

Rain drummed on the roof as thunder rolled. I sighed, this was the usual Memorial Weekend weather in Minneapolis, Minnesota.

I called to Kassi, busy unpacking, "See who's at the door."

"Why?" Kassi yelled back.

I waited. Eventually my sister would grow curious and check the door. Besides, nothing short of a cataclysmic event would move me. Two months after pneumonia put me in the hospital, I'd learned when my body said, "sit", to sit.

After banging on the door, the old man whined, "O.K. girls. We have to talk."

Hands raised in exasperation, my sister emerged from the bedroom and said in a stage whisper, "You're the scariest person I know. How did you know someone was at the door, and why didn't you open it?"

My body wanted nothing to do with opening doors. I stayed lazy in the old armchair, legs dangling over one arm, head snuggled into the wing-back. "It's our landlord," I ventured,"He wants the rent money."

With blond hair swinging out in wings, Kassi swirled the through living room, just missing the bag of barf basins, mouth wash and junk hospitals give you to take home and throw away in your own garbage can.

"Why me? Why not you?" Kassi sassed in my direction.

I said,"Because, you have the money."

She swung open the door and very nearly took a rap on the tip of her lovely tilted nose.

"Oh dear," Mr. Swazy said as he sneezed into a big red handkerchief. "I almost hit you. Oh my." His voice was muffled, his eyes shut ready for the next sneeze.

"Pay him," I mouthed to Kassi.

"I can't," she mouthed back.

The storm paused, and another sneeze erupted through Mr. Swazy's red kerchief.

In the sudden quiet I said, "Gesundheit, Mr. Swazy."

A splat sounded as rain dripped through the roof into a pan positioned under a predictable leak.

Our shy landlord's inability to demand rent often gave us the slack we needed. He deposited his sodden kerchief in a back pocket and drew out a fresh blue one from inside his jacket. "I'm sure sorry I nearly hit you."

"Nika. Come here." Kassi demanded.

While Mr. Swazy closed his eyes and shuddered in a fit of coughing, I mouthed, "Where's the rent money?"

For an answer, Kassi shrugged one shoulder and rolled her clear blue eyes as if to say, "How should I know."

Well that was just great. The rent money that I'd carefully placed in a sealed envelope and entrusted to her was gone. Damn and damn! I glared at her, but called up sufficient energy to drag my scuff-clad feet over to the door.

Semi-recovered, Mr. Swazy warmed to his mission. "Now you know well as I do, that you owed a month's rent when you got sick and then run off to Rochester. Well, you're both home, and Mrs. Swazy says after three months we can evict you." His voice trembled. "I want Mrs. Swazy's money. Now."

Thank God, Kassi at least had a vacation check coming. "Mr. Swazy, we appreciate your patience, and if you held our mail, there should be a check in it that will more than pay the rent."

"Really? A check? To tell the truth," he said earnestly, retrieving a box from the floor, "Most of this stuff looks like bills and junk mail. But then again, I could be wrong."

I accepted the box, "Thanks Mr. Swazy. We can always count on you." I palmed the letter from the law firm in Magdalena, Colorado, guessing it was about Kassi's fender-bender.

His foot prevented me from shutting the door. "When exactly will you pay me?"

"Let's see. This is Sunday, tomorrow's Memorial Day and the banks are closed. How about Tuesday?"

"Oh, that'll be good. I don't want to get tough with you girls, you're so pretty and all," he tipped back on his heels to look up into my face, "but Mrs. Swazy says it's the rent or else. Now, maybe you don't know, but Mrs. Swazy can be a very determined woman."

Kassi asked, "Mr. Swazy, your wife won't really evict us?"

"She sure will." Like he was ashamed, he ducked his head and a rivulet of rain ran down his pink nose. He sneezed.

"You better go downstairs to your own place and fix a hot toddy or you'll be very sick," I advised, seeking to distract him.

"A hot toddy? Really? Well, you're a nurse now, aren't you? So's you'd know. Mrs. Swazy always insists hot lemonade's best. But I'll tell her you recommended a hot toddy. Maybe she'll let me have one." Still holding the handkerchief wadded over his nose, he eyed first Kassi then me, comparing us. "You say you're sisters, but you sure don't look alike. Kassi's so pretty and blond, and you having such black eyes and hair."

I resented that. My eyes were dark enough to pass for black, but not my hair. It looked auburn in the sunlight, and lay in thick, determined waves. Really, it was my best feature.

Mr. Swazy held his finger under his nose to stop another sneeze. "I'd better go."

I shut the door and called to her retreating back, "Okay Kassi, what happened to the rent money?"

"Look. When the doctors sent you to those specialists in Rochester, I went with you. You needed family, and we're all the family we have."

Dripping sarcasm I said, "Yeah right, and a vacation for you."

"That's not fair. I went along to take care of you. When I thought about losing you, money didn't seem important." Her lips were trembling, a tear slid down one perfect cheek.

Rochester was what, an hour away from Minneapolis, with daily almost hourly bus service. I hadn't needed her. However, there was no good in arguing with Kassi, so I dumped the mail on the gray Formica table that stood near the dingy refrigerator and yellowed stove at the end of the room.

"What check were you expecting?" Kassi, still sniffling, wanted to know.

"Not me. You. You said your boss would mail your vacation money, that we'd have it when we got home."

Kassi ducked her head. "Oh, that."

"Yes. That. Is he going to mail the check?"

Silence.

"Well, is he?"

"Not exactly."

"Not exactly? Come on, Kassi, do we have money coming or not?"

"Not really."

Kassi was still wearing her brilliant colored, multi-stripped full skirt and matching fitted jacket. She stood with her back to me looking at the dreary view of roofs and chimneys out the narrow window that stretched up toward the leaking peak of our ceiling. It was a constant dilemma for me, her loveliness versus her need to face the seriousness of our situation.

"Kassi," I said so sharply she jumped, and turned to face me. "The money?"

She answered, "He gave me the check before we left. We spent it."

"Kassi! We were by ourselves for a month in Rochester, and in all that time you couldn't tell me we were spending our rent money *and* your vacation pay?"

"You get so upset." She dabbed at her tear-filled eyes.

"Aren't you upset? We're broke. Bottom-of-the-barrel flat broke. The Swazys *will* evict us."

Kassi tossed her blond head in defiance, "Mr. Swazy likes me, he'll never evict us."

My sister believed if you were really sweet to your creditors, they let you owe them money indefinitely. Her attitude made problems for us and was the reason I'd handled the checkbook and credit cards since Mom died. That is, until I got sick. She must understand this was as critical a time as we'd ever had. With hands on hips and feet spread apart, I yelled, "Kassi. Think. The Swazys live on the rent money from these apartments. They pay *their* bills with it."

"Well, they have two other apartments, and the other renters are always moving. And every time they paint and fix them up, they redo their own first floor place. Have they ever painted this one? Or moved in better furniture? No. It's going to cost them a bundle to fix it up once they kick us out. Mrs. Swazy's just acting mean to scare us. Mr. Swazy will never evict us."

Kassi had a point, but so did our landlords. "Look," I said, "the Swazys play good guy, bad guy. The one you talk to always quotes the absent one as demanding this or that. Make no mistake, Mr. Swazy may not evict us, but Mrs. Swazy will. We're in real trouble here."

"I'm hungry and all you can do is scream at me. You don't know how hard it's been for me since you got sick. I've had to do everything. And you don't even appreciate it. You're so crabby and unreasonable...."

A search of the cupboards produced a nearly empty bag of flour, a hard lump of brown sugar, and a portion of stale Cheerios. Luckily, the refrigerator yielded a lonely TV dinner sitting among the frost in the freezer compartment. I heated it up and divided it while I mulled over our problem. Finally, I asked, "When are you supposed to go back to work?"

Kassi looked at me with surprise, "Didn't I tell you? I got fired. Because I spent to much time with you, at the hospital"

"Ohmagod—they fired you? You didn't talk it over with me? Couldn't you have gotten a part time waitress job?"

"Well, you said when you finished college, you'd support us and I should take some time off and get a better job, or maybe go to school, or…," She shrugged those lovely shoulders again.

I had said that, but it was before I'd been sick. Before Kassi took charge of the checkbook and credit cards. Before we spent the rent money and her vacation pay.

"But Kassi, the hospital refuses to hire me until I get my nursing license, and it will only be on-call work until September. I want you to have a skill, I'll pay for your education, just as soon as I have a full time job."

My sister was crying again. "How was I supposed to know?"

"We talked about it, remember?"

She had taken the last paper towel off the roll and was crying into it. "You know Mom said you were to take care of me. You know she said that."

Kassi was twelve when Mom was killed by a hit and run driver as she crossed the boulevard in front of our house. Instead of getting the license number of the van that hit her, I'd run to Mom in time for her to ask me to take care of my sister. I was seventeen. Without a license number, and only the sketchy description of a hysterical girl, the police made no real search for the van or its driver.

The previous year Dad tried to save people who had fallen through ice on a frozen lake. When help arrived, he was half dangling in the water, caught by his jacket which was frozen to the ice. Dad never regained consciousness and lay comatose in a nursing home, a vegetable, they said.

I was five years older than Kassi, who had always tagged me everywhere, idolizing me, imitating me. At Mother's funeral we clung together, each fearful of losing the other. Kassi looked to me for strength while I looked to her for unquestioning love.

A teenager myself, I tackled the task of raising my teenage sister. Since I was interested in her continuing to idolize me, I made all the tough decisions without consulting her. Although, it was true there were few decisions left to me, because so much was taken care of by court appointed guardians, elderly men who represented themselves as our parents' attorneys when the only legal act they'd done for them was to prepare their wills. They'd told us our house had to be auctioned to pay taxes. We believed them and didn't ask why the taxes hadn't been paid, but moved to the first of our several apartments and continued working while going to school.

My college loans saved us from starvation and things looked brighter when, because of extenuating circumstances, the university allowed my mid-term graduation, using as credit, experience while working as a nurse technician summers. Had I insisted Kassi pay her share, we could have subscribed to health insurance, but it was the one place where healthy young women could cut expenses. We very nearly made it, would have made it, but pneumonia caused by a hospital-mutated bacteria, put me in intensive care and on a long-term recovery program. I could only imagine what my total medical bills would be.

Kassi was blowing her nose and wiping her eyes with the back of her hand.

"Yes, Mom did ask me to take care of you, but she didn't say you shouldn't grow up. Now tell me, are you saying this situation is my fault or my problem? Which?"

"Maybe the nursing license is in the mail," Kassi was hopeful.

Guess that answered my question. It was my problem.

While I wondered how many hours I could work with such shaky legs, we divided the mound of mail in half and began sorting it. Junk went into the empty box, bills were piled in the middle.

We'd been through the mail twice, but there was nothing from the Minnesota Board of Nursing, and the stack of bills was formidable. I leaned back in the wobbly chair and looked around.

Our furnished apartment began life as an attic and was little changed from its origins. The roof slanted, there was one ill-fitting long lean window at each end and a dormer off the only other room, our bedroom. The garage-sale furniture was mis-matched and threadbare. If there was a color scheme, it was drab. Even if we could find another place this cheap, there was no way we could pay two months rent up front to secure it. This apartment had nothing to recommend it. It was cold in winter, an oven in summer, but without it we'd be on the street. Somehow, we had to find the money to pay at least two months rent.

"Kassi, why don't you call your boss? Maybe he'll give you back your old job." Reluctant at first, I finally convinced her.

While she was on the phone, I pulled the official looking letter from Colorado out of my pocket. It was from a Randall McClean, Attorney at Law, and post-marked Magdalena, Colorado. I speculated, how much are damages for a whiplash?

Kassi turned from the phone and gave me a high five, "He's desperate. The new hostess quit. I can start tomorrow."

"That's wonderful," I said.

I was preoccupied sliding a knife under the flap of the envelope. The sneaky thought had occurred to me that if the envelope was undamaged, I could print, "Not at this Address," and slip it into the corner mailbox.

"Gees, how about a little more enthusiasm," Kassi complained.

"Do you remember the fender-bender we had last February?"

Kassi nodded.

"Wasn't that kid from Colorado?"

"Think so," she nodded again.

I handed her the envelope, flap open. "Well, we have a letter from a lawyer out there."

"What does he want? Didn't we agree it was the kid's fault as much as ours? He'd fix his car and we'd fix ours?"

"Apparently he changed his mind."

Gingerly, like it was explosive, she laid the letter on the table in front of me. "You read it."

"No. You." I handed it back to Kassi.

"It's addressed to you."

Disgruntled, I slid the letter out. Why, when Kassi was driving, was it addressed to me? I read it slowly.

"Nika, what does it say? Tell me, I can't hold my breath any longer."

"So breathe."

I read it again before I said, "This has nothing to do with that accident. It's from an attorney who says I'm heir to a Sapphira Domino's estate."

"Oh wow," Kassi said, "that's so wonderful! Who's Sapphira Domino? I never heard of her. How did you meet her? Was she a patient?"

I was rereading the letter, "It says that she's our aunt."

Kassi groaned, "I knew it was to good to be true. We don't have an aunt."

"That's right, Mom was an only child. The only other relative I remember is Grandma Ann. Remember her?"

"Grandma Ann? Yeah, some, but no aunts." Kassi said.

"No, no aunts. Unless Dad had some we didn't know about, but Mom always said his parents died in Ireland and he was an only child."

"Would be nice though," Kassi was wistful

"It sure would be, but if we can't pay the rent, I can't go to Colorado anyway. Besides, bet it's a scam."

"I think we should call Phillip. He knows about scams and stuff. He's a lawyer and he'll help us." Kassi said.

"He's not a lawyer yet. He's only a law student. And I don't want to call him."

"Oh yeah. You're currently mad at him, but so what? He's more apt to come if I call him anyway."

Phillip Sym was my off and on boyfriend, something we'd fallen into because it was convenient. We grew up next-door neighbors, walked to school together and went to parties together. We'd drifted apart once he graduated from high school a couple of years ahead of me, but still called each other when we needed a date and didn't have one. This had gone on until about a year ago, when Phillip began calling me often and telling me he wanted ours to be a permanent relationship. I wasn't in love with him, but it was a comfortable arrangement. Comfortable that is, until he grew careless about being on time for our dates, or forgetting them entirely. Finally, he stood me up once too many times. "Enough," I'd said and meant it.

That's why this was one of the off times, but desperate times call for desperate measures. Or something like that.

When he arrived, Kassi let him in and he greeted me carefully, "Hope you're better, Nika." He listened to me seriously, before he studied the letter. Then he said, "Wow. How about a lifetime commitment?"

"No. We tried that Phillip. Your idea of a commitment is for me to sit around while you date every woman you meet."

Phillip held out his right hand palm up in a beseeching gesture. "Come on Nika. That was one time. It was a business thing." His gray eyes gazed into mine, with a puppy's soulful pleading. "I couldn't get out of it." A lock of black hair slid down to obscure the widow's peak, which outlined his forehead.

"No Phillip. It was more than once. You're only counting the last and final time. And if you don't want to give me advice I'll understand."

"Of course I'll help you. Don't I always? When the McGuinness girls call, I'm Phillip on the spot, like right now."

"Depends," I said, standing my ground. "But anyway, this is a joke, isn't it?" I asked.

Phillip gave a short, derisive laugh, "Put stuff like this in writing and send it through the United States Mail as a joke? No way. That'd be a federal offense."

"So what does it mean?" I asked.

"You Nika, are named in your aunt Sapphira Domino's will as the sole beneficiary of her entire estate; ranch, house, furnishings, money. All you have to do is go to Colorado and collect it."

Kassi said, "We never heard of an Aunt Sapphira. Besides, if she was our aunt, I'd be in the will too."

I added, "I think it's a mistake."

Phillip shook his head, "I doubt it. Lots of people have relatives they never hear from until they die. Just because you don't remember an Aunt Sapphira doesn't mean she didn't exist, and the law doesn't state all heirs must inherit equally or at all. Don't worry about any of it. Apparently, she knew you. Go and collect, Nika."

So he lent us money for the rent and gave me a hundred for the trip. No discussion, no signing of notes, just a handful of money. Odd behavior for a penny-pinching guy, I thought as I thanked him.

He held me off by the shoulders and said, "I'm not giving up, you know. I *will* marry you. It's just a matter of time."

Chapter One

I'm not a woman who weeps at disaster. No way. Disaster has been my companion for the six years since Dad suffered brain damage trying to save Grandma Ann and a neighbor from an ice-encrusted lake. The next year I watched a hit-and-run driver kill my mother, leaving Kassi and me orphans. Oh, I knew disaster well, so well I should have known good fortune wasn't for me. How could I have been duped by the lure of an inheritance from an aunt we sisters didn't remember? Truthfully, I'd known from the beginning, this trip might collect a hoax instead of riches.

Yet, just this once I'd hoped for an easy way out of our problems. It took six years of working while going to college to get my degree in nursing. I'd battled pneumonia to find a pile of bills on the kitchen table, an overdrawn checking account, and a savings account with a zero balance. Not a risk taker, I took this risk.

Now, after driving five days, sleeping on the ground and eating nothing but granola bars, I was down to my last maxed out credit cards. Worse yet, I sat stranded on a high way, packed with vehicles streaming by at seventy plus. Except for the multitude of RVs, the traffic resembled any Minneapolis rush hour more than the Colorado wilds.

The grade had grown steeper as the summit of North La Veta Pass loomed ahead. I'd down shifted to grind another thirty feet, but I'd asked too much of old Bertha, my pickup truck. The engine coughed, and smoke spewed toward the brilliant blue Colorado sky. I'd given the steering wheel a hard right and felt the wheels slide into the shallow ditch, stopping the backward roll. By then steam, like beads of sweat, ran down the windshield and smoked on the hood. I turned off the ignition, then swallowed a sob and thought, *well at least it's not an engine fire.*

Opening the protesting door, I climbed out, my legs trembling and my stomach a tad queasy from too little to eat. The cool air, which had breezed through the cab of the moving pickup, deserted me on this sun blasted pavement.

Arching my back to ease stiff muscles, I looked around. When I'd read the borrowed travel book, (like I had money to buy travel books?), I'd wondered about a pass. No wondering now. This pass was a road up and over foothills that were part of the mountain range named the Sangre de Cristos by Spanish explorers. The name meant "The Blood of Christ," said the travel book, because they looked red in the setting sun.

To the right of the ditch, where Bertha rested, the unfenced foothills stretched steeply upward, to backbone ridges at the top. The sparse grass was dotted with gray shrubs and dusty looking bushes. It was not the lush green scenery I was used to. "Ah Bertha," I said sadly, "we're not in Minnesota anymore."

Not one to take risks, I was not one to give up easily either. Somehow, I must make it back down the pass for water at the gas station in Walsenberg.

Before leaving home, I tossed my beloved dirt bike into the pickup bed for just such emergencies. I felt the nubby tires to see if they were still inflated. They were. I looked back down the crowded highway and wondered what chance I had of riding my bike down that hill and arriving in one piece at the gas station. Not much, I guessed, unless I waited until traffic slowed, perhaps at sundown. I watched cars climb to the summit. Only another fifty or so feet and it'd be downhill. Damn and damn!

Well, I'd wait then. I went back to the pickup, found a bottle of Evian and my last Snickers. Sitting in the shade of Bertha, I sipped tepid water and munched candy. There were plenty of amused looks at us, until a midnight blue BMW slowed and pulled over to stop in front of us.

The gorgeous hunk who unfolded from behind the steering wheel called out, "Car Trouble? Need help?"

Even standing, I still had to look way up at him, unusual since I'm five foot, ten inches. His sandy hair sparked red lights back at the sun, and when he smiled his sapphire-blue eyes made my already shaky legs weaker still. I checked his license and sure enough they were Colorado plates. Just my luck this guy lived fifteen hundred miles from my home in Minneapolis.

It finally dawned on me,that he was looking at me quizzically; waiting for an answer. "Well, yes. I've got car trouble, I guess. Bertha boiled away all her water."

"Bertha?" He asked.

"That's what I call my pickup," I answered. There was no reason to confide that Bertha Svensen was the name of my clinical instructor in E.R. No longer young and built like a battle ship, she was as reliable as tomorrow's sunrise. Just like my pickup.

"Your name is?" He let the question hang and waited for my answer.

My credentials were none of his business, but I told him anyway. "Nika. Nika McGuinness. And yours?" I also let my question hang, but he ignored me.

"Let me have a look." He found some heavy gloves in the trunk of his car, and raised the hood without effort.

I watched him with misgivings, hoping he didn't harm Bertha's inner works. It was too much to expect a man as handsome as this guy had mechanical knowledge too. Besides, wearing light tan chinos and a matching knit shirt, he wasn't dressed for real work. Once he brushed up against anything under Bertha's hood, he'd be smeared with grease.

It happened to me every time I checked the oil, but *I* still checked the oil, and *I didn't need* his help now.

"I was just waiting for the traffic to clear some, before riding my bike back down to a filling station in Walsenberg."

No comment.

"It's really not a problem for me to take care of this myself," I offered. "I'll just get my water."

The attendant at the Walsenberg gas station had advised me to buy water, but with my money nearly gone I'd decided against it. Besides, Bertha never had radiator trouble. Never before, that is. "Yeah I know. Only greenhorns don't carry extra water."

He chose to ignore my comment, "You just hop in and start the engine," he called from the depths of his trunk.

"Start the engine? It's pretty hot."

He ambled back toward me. This man did not hurry. "That's why you got to idle the engine while I trickle in the water. Don't want to crack the block."

"Oh sure. I knew that," I said. *Heavens! Bertha had* a *block*?

I ground the starter with no luck, gave it a rest and ground away again. "Won't start," I said.

"Here, let me have a try."

Go ahead try, I thought, *but Bertha won't start for anyone but me.*

I watched, praying the unreliable spring in the seat cushion didn't decide to poke its head up into the seat of his immaculate, pressed slacks. He stomped on the gas and turned the ignition key. The engine came to life. Bertha betrayed me? Well, why not? What woman wouldn't respond to a guy like this one?

Poor neglected pickup, I thought. Some previous owner had spray painted the original blue with black. Where the black had flaked off, the blue showed through. Poor old black and blue Bertha.

I watched him trickle in the water, while I kept the engine running. With the radiator filled, the cap back in place and the engine rumbling away, he slammed down the hood and said, "You're camping I see. There's a great camp ground, called Elk Creek, about halfway up the next pass. I'll probably be around to help you out again." He smiled and it was like a blessing. I admit it, I was mesmerized.

When he turned back to the BMW I called out, "Thanks. Thanks very much. I'd be here until dark without you."

He smiled again, flashing white teeth, "You're welcome."

"Wait a minute," I called again, "What did you say your name was?"

He called out an answer, but it was lost in the noise of Bertha's engine.

As Bertha mounted the pass, the BMW was no longer in sight. For a moment I felt relief until I remembered he had said he'd "probably be there to help me out again." What did that mean? He's watching me? Stalking me? So frightening!

Frightening? He'd only helped me, had done nothing aggressive, and paranoia is not one of my character flaws, but I caught myself checking the traffic frequently for a midnight blue BMW. Why couldn't I just be grateful? If not for him, I'd still be languishing on the hot pavement. Yet I fretted, he hadn't asked how far I was going, but recommended a campground that was on the road to Magdalena. He couldn't know where I was going, could he? "Stop this," I scolded myself. "Speculation is a no win exercise. Deal only with the facts."

Then a Porsche whizzed by nearly colliding with an oncoming station wagon, bringing my attention back to the road. "Smart ass," I yelled out the window.

By the time we'd come down the pass, the afternoon sun boiled down on my arm where it rested on the open window. I was driving across a flat valley with only an occasional house on either side of the highway. In the distance the mountains climbed to snow-capped peaks. A sign had read, "Sand Dunes," and off to the right, I could see huge drifts of sand snuggled against mountains. While heat waves rose from the pavement, a dry wind blew dust into whirling columns rising from nearby fields.

The comparison to the cool rainy Minneapolis weather I'd left behind, probably made it seem warmer than June should be, but I was hotter than I'd ever been in all my life. With envy, I thought of my sister Kassi, working in that posh Minneapolis air- conditioned restaurant. She begged to come along at the last minute, and it was a temptation. She's irresponsible and unpredictable, but she loves me. I love her too and she's right, we're the only family we have.

Or thought we had, until the letter from Sapphira Domino's attorney came. I was still bewildered. I still questioned its authenticity. *Imagine having an aunt you never knew? Imagine our being the only family she had.* Unless, and the unsettling thought occurred to me that if her deceased husband had relatives they were also hers. And ours. Maybe the BMW driver was his relative, and wanted the inheritance. Maybe there were others. There could be dozens even. *All of them wanting me out of the way.*

"Stop this," I said. "You're borrowing trouble. Ask yourself, are there other relatives? Possible? Yes. Probable? No."

She'd have left her estate to them instead of me, I reasoned. Wouldn't she? But if she cut them off, they'd be petty mad, wouldn't they? Suddenly, hot as it was, I shivered. Someone had walked over my grave.

* * * * * * *

I saw the recommended state park, but decided against staying any place that isolated and lonely, just in case he lurked somewhere near. Exhaustion plaguing me, I drove on, wanting a safer campground. When we passed the sign announcing Magdalena, the rim of the Western horizon still glowed red, but it was way too dark to find the city park. I needed directions, and the all-night doughnut shop just off the highway, seemed a good place to get them. I parked Bertha close to the entrance, where lights glowed from the windows and a lone waitress was wiping off the counters.

The air had turned chill as the sun descended, and the warm sweet smell of the doughnut shop was comforting. I carefully laid two quarters on the counter and resisted asking for more than coffee. I was here for information, not food I couldn't afford.

In a series of fluid motions, the waitress held the mug under the tap, turned the spigot and placed the steaming mug in front of me before asking, "You been driving long? Where you headed?"

She wore a crisp, yellow uniform, her pleasant face was framed by tightly waved brown hair. Neither smiling, frowning, nor overly curious, she just wanted to fill the lonely night with conversation, I decided.

I sipped the coffee, "Here. That is to Magdalena. I have some business in the morning, then I expect to leave right away."

"Hmmm, not hanging around longer than you have to, huh? Well, I don't blame you, not much going on around here for a young girl."

This was the first coffee I'd had since I left home, and I drank deeply. It tasted wonderful, rich and hot. "The coffee is good. I'm kind of surprised. That is, usually it's not too good in one of these doughnut places."

"Glad you like it. Here, have some more," she said refilling my mug.

"Thanks," I said. "I'm sure the people who live here really like it. What with the mountains that are so beautiful and everything. But my home is in Minneapolis."

"Excuse me?" The waitress said, "What did you say?

I took another gulp of coffee. "Well, you said there was nothing to do around here, for a young girl, and I was saying that if they grew up here, that couldn't be true."

She had taken a chocolate frosted doughnut from under a glass dome, cut it in fourths with a knife and put one piece in her mouth. "Yeah, I know," came the muffled answer.

Her spare angular body in no way reflected her motherly personality. "Well, I wanted directions to the city park. I thought I could camp there for one night. It wouldn't offend anyone would it?"

"Who's to offend?" She asked. "You like to camp"?

It fascinated me to watch her put the last piece of doughnut into her mouth. I salivated, my stomach cramped and would grumble soon if it didn't get fed.

With an effort I brought my attention back to her question, "Yes. My sister and I camped regularly with my parents in Minnesota." I thought to add, "Oh, that's where we live. They were great on enjoying the outdoors."

"You're experienced then. That right?" She asked.

"Yes, I'm pretty good at it. And since my folks died, (Dad wasn't dead, but how did you explain to a stranger, that he was only a breathing vegetable?), my sister and I go camping every summer."

The waitress lifted the glass dome again, and I watched hungrily to see what she'd eat next. She used the tongs to disengage a custard filled doughnut, put it on a plate and placed the plate in front of me. I started to protest, because buying a doughnut was not in my budget.

"Now listen here," she said, "I hafta toss all this stuff out in the morning. Can't sell customers day old products. But I can give it away to a thin hungry young thing like you. Eat."

I took a bite and closed my eyes to enjoy the flavor of powder-sugared pastry mixed with sweet custard. Heaven. "Mmmmm. This is so good," I said. "Thanks."

A partial smile tilted her mouth up toward one ear. "You like jelly filled ones? Here. Try this one," She plopped another one on my plate not bothering to replace the glass dome. "Now tell me all about camping. You enjoy it?"

"I'm really hungry," I said, "but I don't want to get you into trouble with your boss or anything."

She chuckled again, "I am the boss. Do this here in the summer and go back to A Z to do it in the winter. Easy to hire day workers, but no one wants to work nights. You know?"

"Yes I do know," I said around a mouthful of raspberry jelly. "I just got my Bachelor's degree in nursing and I'm determined to never work nights."

"See how you are?" She said, with another chuckle. "But you were telling me about camping."

"Well, our parents loved the out-of-doors, and we learned to camp with them on once-a-year camping trips."

She asked, "Minnesota's mostly Scandinavians, isn't it. You don't look Swedish, I always thought they were blond."

I sipped coffee, "I'm not. Swedish, that is. Dad came from Ireland."

"Well, you don't look Irish either," she pronounced, "The Irish have blue eyes and your eyes are darker than your hair." She pointed the tongs, still held in her hand, at my hair, "I like your hair though, sure wished my hair waved like that. It's natural isn't it?"

I had to smile. Nice lady, I thought. "Yes, it's natural. My mother's family came from Greece. They all had black hair and brown eyes." I didn't really know that. Except for Grandma Ann who'd drowned, I didn't know any of Mother's family. Her eyes had looked black, I remembered, surrounded by lots of white wavy hair.

"Irish and Greek." The waitress shook her head in disbelief. "Boy how'd *they* ever get together?"

"At the University of Minnesota. They were both professors."

She was still holding the tongs battle-ready to pounce on another doughnut. I thought I detected sympathy in her steady gray-blue eyes. Damn and damn. I wasn't asking for anyone's sympathy.

"You were going to tell me about camping."

"Well, last summer, Kassi and I set up camp in a lonely wooded bluff above the Mississippi River."

"Kassi's your sister? Younger than you?" She asked, with another sympathetic look.

She was being very generous. I could keep her company, it wasn't like I had hotel reservations or anything. I nodded, "She's five years younger than me, and is phobic about bears. Won't go too bed unless I get the hammer." I began to laugh. "Everybody knows you bang pans together to scare off bears, but she won't let me bring pans in the tent because their racket keeps her awake."

I laughed until tears streamed down my face. The waitress joined in, handing me extra napkins to mop up the tears.

I ate another doughnut, before I asked for directions again.

She told me how to find the park and hugged me. "You take care now, you hear?"

I thanked her, and left with a warm feeling, generated as much by the conversation as the doughnuts. Still, when you've eaten nothing but granola bars three times a day for five days one more isn't very appealing, and that would have been my dinner.

The city park was easy to find, and I drove Bertha in behind the rest rooms, close to the ladies entrance, where the only light in the park burned dimly above the door. I changed from jeans and T-shirt to sweats after a quick wash-up in an unusually clean city park facility, and believe me I'd seen a lot of them this past week.

Not missing the forgotten tent at all, I unrolled my sleeping bag and crawled in. What a beautiful night, I thought. If the million or so stars didn't give much light, they did shed a glow better than candles.

If Aunt Sapphira left me enough money, say maybe five or six thou, we'd take a better camping trip this summer. Maybe buy a camper top for Bertha. After I paid the bills, of course. Thinking of Aunt Sapphira's legacy must have soothed me to sleep.

* * * * * * *

I washed in the rest room, even shampooed my hair, before changing into my one and only *power suit*. It was dated and wrinkled, but this was Colorado. Who would notice?

Shaky and nauseous from too many days without real food, I parked in front of the 'In Towne Cafe.' I needed to eat a substantial meal, and reasoned it was not a luxury, since Mr. McClean's letter said any business could direct me to his office. He was probably some old guy who worked out of his home, which might be open at six-forty five, but difficult to find. The aroma of coffee and bacon drew me inside where I sat at a back booth with a good view of the street and the other diners. If the 'Hunk' meant to see me, as he said, I intended to see him first.

A no-nonsense waitress brought me coffee in a sturdy brown mug and a glass of ice water. She recommended the number two which included bacon, eggs and toast, at only a dollar ninety-nine. While I waited, I sipped coffee that I'd cooled from boiling to hot with ice. Men and women entered the cafe wearing cowboy boots and hats, which they preferred to keep on their heads while they ate. My handsome mechanic was not among them.

The steaming food arrived with a bowl of salsa. We had Mexican restaurants in Minneapolis so I knew enough to ladle the salsa over the eggs. After the first bite, I sputtered and fanned my mouth to the amusement of the other diners.

My outlook much improved by the intake of fat and cholesterol, I found the rest room, washed up and went to the counter to pay my bill. I asked directions to the McClean Law office and learned to take a left turn, then up two blocks and across the street.

The street had several businesses; a shoe store called, "The Shoe Shoppe" a bakery and a fabrics store called, you got it, "The Bake Shoppe," and "The Clothe Shoppe." Should make walking your fingers through the yellow pages easy. I parked in front of "Legal Services Office," a storefront building with a door to one side where a half window was covered by a shade. I waited until the shade flipped up before I tried the door.

I was greeted by a guy about my age, five or so inches taller than I, which is rare since I'm five-ten..., by Jingo, it was the BMW driver. Except today he wore a light gray suit, conservative blue tie, and looked as though he'd forgotten to comb his sandy colored hair. I'd imagined a rheumy-eyed, ancient cowboy type, not "The Hunk." I wondered if he'd remember me? Nah. After all, yesterday my sweat-soaked T-shirt and jeans were the same ones I'd worn for five days. Today I was dressed in my best. Besides he was probably only the attorney's assistant, I thought.

I casually held out my hand to shake his, "I'm Nika McGuinness. Although I wrote that I was coming, I don't have an appointment." He raised his eyebrows in a non-verbal question. "I'd like to see Sapphira Domino's attorney, a Randall McClean." Then in my most respectful manner, "Will he be in today?"

He shook my hand as he spread that unforgettable smile from ear to ear, showing white even teeth and crinkling the skin around his truly beautiful dark blue eyes. "Yes, I remember. That's me. Your letter hasn't arrived yet, but please come on in."

From the look of him, I'd rather expected him to say 'Aw, shucks.' Instead, pulling my arm through his, he led me into his office and indicated a chair. I nearly lost myself in a worn leather wingback which reminded me of the ragged one in our Minneapolis apartment. I yearned for blue jeans and the freedom to hang my legs over the arms, but my tight skirt demanded a more demure posture.

"Well," I began clearing my throat, "You may remember that you wrote to me about my aunt Sapphira Domino? I have the letter in my purse...,"

"Oh sure. You're...,?" He was smiling, he'd said he'd remembered me.

"Look, I told you my name back on the pass and I just repeated it. Nika McGuinness." Gees. What a dim bulb.

He asked, "You have some identification?"

An easy question since there's no one alive today who doesn't have identification. "Will my driver's license do?"

Still smiling his great grin, "Have a credit card, too."

I gave him my poor exhausted credit cards and my driver's license. He took them saying, "I'll just be a minute." I heard the hum of a copy machine. If this was a scam, he'd be disappointed in the available cash on the credit cards.

I studied the office, which seemed to have been, at some previous time, a store. The still intact display window that opened on the street seemed lonely without apothecary jars or some such merchandise enticingly arranged. Bookcases covered the sidewalls and were stuffed with huge volumes, probably law reference books. Dark wood paneled the wall behind the huge Danish-modern desk, its light finish a jarring contrast to the eighteenth century surroundings.

Randall returned with my cards and interrupted my daydreaming. He said, "Ms. McGuinness, I'm due in court in an hour, and I'll be there the whole day. Suppose I give you the key to your aunt's house and directions to get there. The place should be clean enough to occupy. There's a couple, the Sanchez's, who live on the property and do the cleaning. I'll call and ask them to have the place ready for you to occupy."

He walked over to the floor to ceiling bookcase on the left and rummaged around in back of the books, dust motes flying in a shaft of morning sunlight. Occasionally, a passerby stopped to rap on the window and wave. He waved back.

"Had to hide this. Been a lot of interest in your aunt's place. Didn't want the curious wandering around uninvited."

I thought, *that's a hiding place? In full view of anyone walking by? Yeah, right.* "Excuse me. Do you hide many things there?"

"Well, occasionally," he said, holding out a three inch brass key to me. "Actually, no one saw me put it there."

"That's good," I said agreeably.

Mr. McClean smiled and nodded.

Was he laid back confused, or just very clever? I'd figure that out later, but now I wanted the facts. Dad, the family fisherman, had often said, "fish or cut bait." So I fished by coming to the point.

"Mr. McClean…,"

"Please call me Randall."

"And you call me Nika," I said warmly. So far this game may have been confusing but not difficult. "I've driven over fifteen hundred miles. I need to get on with this…, I'm sure you understand."

He nodded, "You have a question?"

"It'll wait until you answer the phone," I said.

He was momentarily puzzled. The phone rang.

"The phone?" I asked.

"Oh, sure," he smiled, "Good guess," he added. He excused himself to answer in another room, but first slanted me a quizzical glance.

I waited, wondering what was the matter with the one on his desk. Randall's deep baritone murmured from some back room, with periodic pauses for the caller to respond. Men and women in jeans walked by, stopping long enough to look in the window and stare in surprise at me. I smiled gamely back. Randall seemed popular, judging by the number of smiling faces that peeked in.

"That was Mom on the phone. She says to tell you welcome and as soon as she's back she'll throw you a party."

"That's very sweet of her," I answered. What made him think I'd stay long enough for a party? "But, tell me, how long before we can complete the transfer of property?"

His head down as he concentrated on the map he was drawing, his voice became terse, "We have to meet the terms of the will."

I stood up next to the desk to watch the drawing take form. "And when will that be?"

His head was still bent over the drawing, "This isn't an ordinary situation, you can understand that. No one out here ever heard of you until your aunt died."

I was suddenly tired of whatever charade he played, "Look. That letter of yours brought me out here. Believe me, I never before heard of Magdalena, you, or my so-called aunt, and your letter didn't fill me in on lots of important facts. I don't know if Sapphira Domino is related to my mom or my dad, and they can't tell me. I don't know how she lived, and I don't know how she died. When do you plan to tell me?"

My outburst surprised him. Finally focused, Randall met my gaze and answered, "I can answer all of your questions…, in due time, but as to how she died…," He paused and shook his head, "It's just such a shame you didn't know your aunt. She was a fine person, the kind who lives only to help others. All she asked for herself was to enjoy the trees, the mountains and flowers on her property. She even built a brick path along a little stream called Conundrum Creek. Everyone in town knew she walked along that path every day. One day, she went for a walk, and someone shot her. Shot her and left her there, bleeding to death."

Chapter Two

"If I leave you," the masculine voice asked, "will you stay right here? Don't try to get up, or anything?"

I nodded. Try to leave? While on a merry-go-round? He was out of his mind.

It seemed he was right back. "Here's water or tea. Which would you like?"

"Water first, I think." I shut my eyes again. How the books stayed on the shelves and revolved at the same time, I'd never know.

His arm went under my shoulders, lifted me and held a glass of cold water to my lips. I sipped, but not fast enough, and water dribbled down my front.

"Oh sorry," he said and patted my chin and neck with a tissue. "Here, let's try tea, a spoonful at a time."

The tea was strong, hot, and very sweet. I nearly gagged. "I like my tea with just lemon, please. No sugar."

"You just fainted. You need both the sugar and tea. When you're better, I'll give you some with just lemon."

I sipped the tea, marveling at my compliant behavior, but I did feel better. First I opened one eye and then the other. The bookcases held still. "I'll take the cup now," I said. When the man looked doubtful, "I'll drink it all, I promise."

"Okay, I'll sit right here on the edge of the desk."

I sipped the tea and studied him.

He said, "I'm Randall McClean, your aunt's attorney. You fainted."

I sipped the tea. "I remember who you are. And I don't faint."

He looked uncomfortable, like he was about to speak, but thought better of it and kept his silence.

He sat arms crossed over his chest, studying me as I sipped tea. It was disconcerting. To distract him, I said, "I Drove all the way out here in Bertha."

He raised an eyebrow, "That so?"

I finished the tea, "Now, I'll take some with lemon."

I straightened my skirt and looked around. The sun still shone through the window. It was a beautiful day.

He came back with a fresh cup of tea that smelled of lemon.

"Tea with lemon, just like you ordered," he said handing me the tea. His smile was so warm and sincere.

What a nice guy, I thought.

Wait a minute. He's an attorney? Attorneys are the ones who took every dime we had, sold our home, our furniture, and forced Kassi and me into that horrible attic apartment. They are *not* nice, but they do have power.

"Thanks." I said thinking his white, even teeth must have cost his parents a fortune, and they certainly enhanced his smile. His eyes were still a beautiful, honest dark blue. Just remember what Phillip said, I told myself, all this he learned in *Put the Client at Ease 101*. Thinking of Phillip gave me a warm fuzzy feeling. He lent us money to pay the rent and buy the gas for my trip out here. I smiled and looked up at Randall, who watched me with an alarmed expression on his face.

I sat up straighter. "What were we talking about?" I asked.

"You're sure you're up to this discussion now?"

I nodded, "Yes. I need to wrap this whole thing up as soon as possible." Didn't I have bills to pay? Didn't I have to pay off Phillip's loan? Of course, no way can I confide that to any attorney. He'd take advantage of the knowledge.

Looking doubtful, he crossed his arms on his chest in a determined stance, "I don't think so. Not today."

I said, "I believe I asked you how my aunt died, and you said she'd been shot. Isn't that what you said?"

"You remember?" He asked.

I was puzzled, "Of course I remember. Why do you act like I don't? You are not putting this client at ease." I took one hand from the tea mug, and shook my finger at him. The mug tipped, the tea nearly spilling. I steadied it with both hands.

"Actually, you're right. I had told you about your aunt's death," he said the worried frown returning to his forehead.

"Yes, you had," I said. "Is there more I should know?"

"Really, we can discuss this tomorrow," he said. "I have to be in court, and you need a good night's rest. I'll call the Sanchez," he reached for the phone behind him.

"No. You said she was left to bleed to death. That's murder. Isn't that it?" You don't want to talk about her murder? I covered my eyes. The mug teetered again.

"You O.K.?" He asked.

"What do you think? You wait 'til I get here and then dump this small detail on me. *Oh by the way, Nika, you're aunt was murdered.* Couldn't you have mentioned this in your letter? Told me who did it?" I sipped the tea. "Who did do it?"

An unsmiling Randall still sat on the corner of his desk, his arms folded across his chest, studying me. A Regulator clock hung on the wall and tick-tocked away with all its might.

I finished the last of the tea, feeling a great deal better, in very nearly full fighting mode. "Who murdered my aunt? I demand to know."

Randall took the mug, placing it on a small table in back of his desk where he sat down. "I didn't say she was murdered, I said she was killed."

"You said she was shot, but I'll go with killed." I thought well, being killed is not always murdered. "When was she killed? And by whom?"

"Mrs. Domino left the Sanchez a note, asking them to leave her dinner in the refrigerator. The next morning, when it was not eaten nor her bed slept in, Sergio Sanchez went looking and found her body. That was March tenth."

I was trembling, "Oh, then was it accidental?"

"Well," Randall's intense gaze studied me.

"First it's killed then it's shot. Make up your mind." Unless he was hiding something, why did he tell different versions? "But it happened three months ago, and you still don't know how or by whom she was shot?"

"There's some speculation it was done by a skeet shooter or a hunter, but she was on her land and it's posted. We've also thought about a transient. We'd like to know what you were doing on March ninth and tenth. Do you remember?"

Then she *was* murdered, and they suspected me? I breathed deeply, fighting for control. Me, who had not known about an aunt in Colorado, nor a Magdalena. I hugged myself to stop the trembling. Did I remember? You bet. "I was an attendant in a friend's wedding on the ninth, and went to the hospital the next day, with pneumonia."

What I didn't tell him was that Phillip had promised to escort me to the reception, but instead ate dinner with a gorgeous redhead at Kassi's restaurant. Had a reservation even. And I'd just been remembering him as 'good old Phillip.' He was a loser. A big lawyer loser. A big 'L' for a Big Loser. I tried to stifle a giggle.

His hand poised over a yellow pad, "That can be checked. You friend's name is?"

I didn't believe this. "Aren't you supposed to be on my side?" When he didn't answer, it confirmed my suspicion that he was not for me, but for himself. So what was different about this, from the way it had been since Mom's death? Not one thing. Well, I'd learned to be assertive, even aggressive when necessary, so here goes.

"Your friend's name?" He prodded.

"Her name is Nancy McCall now. It was Nancy Sorenson. You'll have trouble finding her, they're still honeymooning in Europe."

"She has parents?"

"No. She hatched from an egg. Of course she has parents. What do you think? Their names are Susan and Nels Sorenson. They live in St. Paul, but I don't know their address."

"That should be easy to find."

"Don't count on it. He's a senior, has a son who's a Third, and brothers like you can't imagine. They're one of those families who like the first name of all their kids to begin with the same letter, in this case with 'N'. Besides, Minnesota is loaded with Scandinavians and many of them are Sorensons. Of course, you could check the hospital's records." I could feel my face flush, my anger building.

"Of course. That's the thing to do," he was smiling again, "and that's the much easier course of action."

"Maybe. Except you'll need *my* permission to access *my* medical records, they're confidential." I spit out the words.

"Let's see," uncertainty clouded his smile.

It was fun to watch his confidence disappear. He wasn't as much in charge as he thought. On the other hand, I needed to clear this up, collect the money and go home. "You have a fax machine?"

"Yes."

"Then give me a piece of paper, I'll write the permit to release medical information. You can fax it to the University Hospital. Ask them to fax back the information you need."

All smiles again, he took the permit. "I'll just give you the key and the map, and explain the directions. It's not hard to find. Sure you're okay to drive?"

"Not so fast, Randall," I said, still furious with him. "You know where I was and what I was doing on March ninth and tenth. How about you? Do you have an alibi for those days?"

His sapphire blue eyes had turned to steel, "I was in Denver and can prove it."

I nodded, "Just checking." So he didn't like it, so too bad.

He walked me out to Bertha. "Hard to believe you drove all the way out here in this," he said with distaste. "At least the engine's still running, didn't stall on the next pass, I see."

I answered politely, "Yes, this is Bertha, best pickup ever built. Not to worry, you don't have to ride in her." In fact, I thought, you'll never be invited.

He opened the door, "Here's my phone number. Please call me when you get there."

"You'll still be here?" I asked.

"It's only fifteen miles. I won't leave for another hour or two. There's plenty of time." He was grinning that toothpaste smile again, holding out the key.

I'm sure he'd said, "he had to be in court in an hour," but maybe my memory's is out of sync, like he keeps inferring. "I'll call. There's only one key?"

"That's it. Can we meet at ten in the morning? To go over the will?"

"Ten it is," I said backing away from the curb.

* * * * * *

It was eleven forty-five by my watch as I waited for service at a fast food restaurant. The sign on the window listed the special and I decided I could spare another dollar ninety-nine from my flattened billfold. I wasn't particularly hungry, but I planned to take the hamburger with me and warm it up when I reached Aunt Sapphira's cabin. While I waited I wondered, did he seriously think I drove out here, killed an aunt I didn't know, and returned to Minneapolis in order to collect an inheritance I didn't know about? How could he believe so bizarre a tale?

Although his map was easy to follow, I was so preoccupied that I took a wrong turn and got lost. Finally, after much backtracking, I turned onto a county road, just as his map said to do. When I saw a rest stop, I pulled in and turned off the engine.

I took the sandwich and got out of Bertha to wander over to the lone picnic table where I sat on the table, my feet on the bench. There were shaggy looking pine trees at irregular intervals around the small park's perimeter. The amenities consisted of one outhouse, and a rusted pump. Well, I didn't need to go and I didn't need a drink. What I did need was to gather my scattered thoughts, while I nibbled the hamburger.

The first meeting with Lawyer Randall hadn't gone well, not well at all. No matter how I felt about any attorney, I had to build a working relationship and I didn't have much time.

But come to think of it, who was he to question me? Wasn't that a job for the police or sheriff? Sure. What was really going on here? Were the sheriff and Randall good buddies? Why?

"Because stupid," I said aloud, "there's money and property to be gained, and all it takes for the county to foreclose is back taxes." Kassi and I'd learned that. It seemed to me the pattern was always for the law and the lawyer to plot for their personal financial gain. Would they commit murder? How could I tell? What I did know was that an auction would bring a pittance of the real property value of not just another house, but someone's home.

Remembering how things had been when Mom was alive, and when Dad was healthy, made me suddenly lonely for Kassi. Now just a minute, I thought, of all people, I wanted Kassi? That queasy spell had really messed up my thinking. She's the one who spent every last dime of what little money I'd managed to save. She's the one who maxed out our credit cards, and, except for human companionship, how she'd help me I really couldn't imagine.

I took a deep breath of cool, pine scented air and looked up all around me, at trees marching to the tops of mountains whose sturdy backbone knifed the brilliant blue sky. The only other living things were three deer, grazing on leaves in a meadow, and a couple of gray jays.

Maybe Aunt Sapphira wasn't as eccentric as I'd thought. Maybe she was happy in her one room cabin, with a wood stove, a pump out back, and a privy. I could sympathize with her.

* * * * * * *

A few miles later, I turned onto a narrow, gravel road, and carefully aimed Bertha around curves that wound between pine covered hills, but generally westerly as near as I could guess from the sun which was beginning to slant. I checked my watch and saw it was three fifteen. It was too late to call Randall, he'd be in court. That took care of that obligation.

We came out of a narrow cut in the hills and onto the broad floor of the valley. We crossed a sturdy bridge, high above narrow stream, labeled, "Conundrum Creek." At the far end of the valley, I saw a turreted red brick house nestled against low hills that rolled upwards toward far away mountains. When I saw nothing like a cabin, I decided to drive to the house and ask for directions.

The valley floor was covered with long waving grass and dotted with groves of birch, and a few shaggy pines. With the car windows down, I inhaled the wild, sweet aroma of grass and flowers. Beautiful, but lonely. Who would build a mansion here? What if this was Aunt Sapphira's? Nah. No way.

I drove ahead to the gated driveway, stopped and read 'Domino' on the mailbox. This *was* the place. Unbelievable. Intimidating. My expectations of a rough cabin were reinforced by the rest stop. That I could handle, but this?

I parked Bertha nose to the gate and got out to open it. The fence, made of barbed wire, was fastened to posts set in the ground, and enclosed all the land as far as I could see. There were frequent "Private Property" and "No Hunting" signs hanging from the fence and posts. The gate had three wooden posts, one in the middle and another at each end, and was somehow hooked to the end posts in the fence. Since how it opened was a puzzle, I turned off the engine, gathered up my purse and duffel bag to crawl under. Then I discovered the trouble with a power suit is, the long narrow skirt is no good for climbing over or crawling under fences.

After checking the surrounding countryside for humans and seeing none, I changed into jeans and flats. I crawled under the gate, and thankful my skin was still, trudged up the hill, along a barely discernible circular driveway. Made of bricks, it was overgrown with grass so that an occasional brick had buckled.

The front door was a long walk across a brick terrace and up several wide, deep steps. The size of the key fit the massive door. It was wide and high enough to accommodate a horse with rider, if the rider crouched low over the horse.

I set my things down, and laid my shoulder against the door as I turned the key. The door swung inward so easily that I staggered into the entry, wondering if someone hadn't opened it. A chill crept up my spine. I teetered, saved from falling by my grip on the sturdy key. I called out "hello" and heard only my own voice. I forced out another trembling "hello" hoping I could hear an answer over my thudding heart.

After a long moment passed and there was no answer, I assumed I was alone and slowly walked in on red tiles each a foot square, worn in places, but polished to a rosy glow. A series of windows to the right of the front door stretched from floor to a distant ceiling and lit each turn of the open stairs, which zigzagged up three floors. The walls of both entry and stairs were paneled in dark wood and hung with signed prints. The fresh, cool air smelled of flowers and peaches, maybe a potpourri. I breathed deeply and without the constriction around my chest that plagued me since my bout with pneumonia.

Somewhere in the distance, a telephone began ringing. I tried the door to the right of the towering staircase and found it opened on a hall. A flowered carpet runner that padded the same red tile back to a sun filled kitchen muffled my footsteps. I traced the ringing to a small desk just inside the kitchen door.

"Hello, Kassi?" I said.

"Nika? Nika? Is that you?"

"Of course it's me. How'd you find me? Is anything wrong?" I asked.

"How'd you know it was me?" Kassi asked.

"Who else would it be?" I answered with a question.

"You're the scariest person I know. How do you do that?"

"Do what?"

"Know it's me on the phone, when I only just got the number? My friends all think you're crazy, know that? And why didn't you call me like you promised? It's been seven days."

"Is something wrong, Kassi?" I asked.

"Not with me. With you. Where've you been? Why haven't you called me before? You said you would."

Some people have hobbies. Pleasant, absorbing interests to keep them occupied. I have my sister. My beautiful sister whom I love and who operates on the principle that if anything can go wrong she'll help it along.

I dodged her question with one of my own. "How did you know to call me here?"

"You gave me the attorney's number. I called him and he said you were staying at Aunt Sapphira's house. How'd she get to be our aunt?

How long have you been there? Didn't you know I'd be stressed out? My stomach has hurt for two days."

"Kassi, I just this minute got here. Bertha's old and can't go very fast." I sighed remembering the cars surging past me on the interstate, swerving in and out around Bertha, sometimes dangerous, always frightening.

"And?" Kassi wanted to know.

"I didn't make as good time as we'd planned," I said, "and there was a problem with the engine overheating that took some time to fix. It's a miracle that I'm only two days late."

"Is that all?" Kassi's voice became petulant. I could see her, lower lip stuck out over the upper one, pouting.

"Let it go, Kassi, it's enough. I'm tired and dirty. What I need is a bath and some sleep in a real bed. What I don't need is your criticism."

"I guess what you're saying is that it took you longer to get there than you planned. Why don't you just say that?"

I let it pass. "Right. I got in last night and saw Randall this morning."

"Randall?"

"The lawyer." Anyone but Kassi would have picked up on the exasperation in my voice. "He's in court all day, but I have an appointment with him in the morning."

"Where did you get that idea? He's not in court. I talked to him just before calling you. He gave me this number and said he'd be in his office all afternoon, and if you didn't answer the telephone to call him back he'd get out a posse." She giggled. "He sounded young. Is he cute?"

"All day? Are you sure?"

"Of course I'm sure. I know what I hear. Are you in the house? What's it like? Is it big? Is it haunted? What's the address?"

"I don't know what it's like. I just got here. I went from front to back, a fairly long walk so I guess it's big. It doesn't seem haunted. There's no street address, it's in the country all by itself."

"I don't like your being way out in the country by yourself. I think I should fly out to take care of you."

The picture of Kassi taking care of me was downright scary. "Kassi, give it up. If we could afford a plane ticket, I'd have flown. We're broke. Remember?"

"Well, you don't have to be so crabby. How much money is there?"

I could detect the catch in her voice. I'd hurt her feelings. "Kassi, don't cry. I don't know. Look, why don't I call you tomorrow, when I know more?"

"Sure. You have the number?"

"Yes Kassi. Unless you changed it, it's been our number for several years. I only drove to Colorado, not to outer space."

"You're really bitchy. Just because I missed you and wanted to know if you were all right."

"Sorry. I really will call you tomorrow."

"Oh and Kassi, did you mail my letter to Randall? He hasn't gotten it yet and I wondered," The phone clicked. Kassi had hung up.

I got my things and left them in the entry while I found a suitable place to sleep. The stairway stretched up three floors and wasn't too inviting. An archway to the right of the front door opened onto a large living room, complete with baby grand piano in the turret window, and fireplace with a rounded opening where a fire was laid ready for a match. Two couches faced each other with a love seat across the end to form a rectangular 'U'. What did one woman do with all this room?

Opposite the living room and across the entry, was a door with a ceramic plaque on it announcing, 'Welcome Guests.' I swung open the door on a large bedroom. Off the long hall to the kitchen there was another bedroom that seemed to be the master bedroom. Across from it, was a comfortable, light-filled room that could be a sitting room or a sunroom? I really wasn't up to speed on mansions. There was another arched fireplace at the far right side, ready for a fire, the wood already laid. This room looked lived in.

Down the hall another archway opened on a dining room with china and crystal sparkling behind glass-fronted cabinets built into the walls. The kitchen at the end of the hall was a huge room, with an island in the middle and counters and cupboards on three walls. It was made sunny and bright by two extra large un-curtained windows above the sink. To the left of this, in a generous wood paneled alcove, were a table and six chairs. Two steps down was a rich woman's idea of a family room, furnished with burgundy colored leather chairs, walnut tables and facing a giant TV screen. To the left, double doors opened on an overlarge brick terrace. A back entry hall held a sink, above which were glass-fronted cabinets holding glasses. Across from the sink there was a door that must open on the basement, and to the left, another dead-bolted one that probably went outside. They were locked and I left them that way. I hate basements and the one key I'd been given only fit the front door.

I found tablets and pencils in the telephone-desk, and chose one to list questions for Randall. First on the list was, 'where are the rest of the keys?' I was jotting down number three when the quiet I'd gotten used to erupted with the racket of an engine protesting the grind of shifting gears. Company? Maybe Randall? A car door screeched. Bertha! Only Bertha's door sounded like that.

Automatically, I reached for the keys and found my rear jeans pocket empty. I had left the keys in Bertha.

Chapter Three

Stunned, my heart stuttered against my ribs. I watched the driver's side door slowly open. A small wiry man, with shoulder length curly gray hair emerged and carefully closed the door. With a smile that included his chocolate brown eyes, he mounted the long, low steps.

He bowed, "Patrona," he said and placed the keys in my hand. "I help with gate. All time." The smile grew broader, if that was possible.

"Thank you. Thank you very much." I said.

"Si," he bowed again and backed down the stairs, before turning to walk out of sight around the house.

That must be Mr. Sanchez, I thought as I locked Bertha up tight, reentered the front door, closed it and locked it. No way did I want to walk into Magdalena in the morning, and as nice has he appeared, I disliked the idea of people taking care of my truck or anything else that belonged to me. I shoved both Bertha's keys and the three-inch house key into my pocket for safekeeping.

The guest bedroom, the one with the 'Welcome Guests" plaque on the door, seemed to be the best choice for my limited stay. I unpacked my belongings, hung my few things in the humongous closet, and stowed others in the drawers of a chest. The bed was canopied in an unlikely burgundy and pink floral print that matched the quilted spread and the heavy drapes at the windows. Pale blue velvet wing back chairs were placed, one on either side of a fireplace that was centered between the overlarge windows and dominated the wall opposite the bed.

When I finished my unpacking, I filled the huge sunken tub in the bathroom adjacent to the bedroom. A long bath would ease the ache in my bones. I'd dug deep into my duffel for a Jan Elliott mystery novel. It was her first published book, *Murder on the Rocks*, loaned me by a friend who was addicted to crime fiction. I settled down to soak and read.

I'd finished the first chapter and was half way through the next when I began to smell a delicious odor drifting through the open door. Because breakfast and the hamburger had been ample, I'd thought I wasn't hungry, but the cooking smells brought me out of the tub. I toweled and dressed and followed the aroma to its source.

In the kitchen, I found a man and a woman. He was opening a bottle of red wine and she was stirring something on the stove. *I thought Randall said there were no other keys.*

"Hello," I said, my heart bounding.

Smiling, they answered in unison, "Hala!"

"I'm Nika McGuinness."

"Juana," pointing first at the woman and then at himself, "Sergio."

Of course, Sergio had rescued Bertha. Juana and Sergio Sanchez, the couple that lived on the ranch and took care of the cleaning and cooking. Randall said he'd call them about my staying here. "I'm pleased to meet you," I said.

"Si, si. We too," Sergio said. "You sit. Your food soon ready."

The table was set, the wine opened, and Juana began to ladle food on a plate. But there was something wrong. Where did Juana and Sergio sit?

"Please," I said, "sit. Eat with me."

Sergio talked in rapid Spanish explaining to Juana. Shaking her head and pointing, Juana said, "No. No, no. Patrona."

Apparently Sergio spoke some English, but Juana either didn't or didn't want to. So who was Patrona? Me?

"I'm Nika. Please eat with me." They were bewildered. Had Aunt Sapphira made them eat elsewhere? I got up from my seat and hunted through cupboards until I found china, glasses, napkins and silver. I pulled out the chairs and indicated they should sit down.

"Si patrona," Juana, was smiling and dishing up food.

I tried to carry on some kind of conversation, but finally gave it up. I didn't understand Spanish and their English was limited. They did a lot of smiling and nodding though, and it was pleasant to have their company.

After we'd eaten, I brought up the subject of keys by holding up the one I'd been given. "Do you have keys?" I asked much too loudly and with much finger pointing at the key.

"No. No," Juana answered.

Clearly, play-acting was the best way to communicate. I pushed back my chair, descended the two steps, and went to the patio doors. I opened the door and stepped outside. My plan was to demonstrate the use of a key, by pretending to open it with the only one I had. However, a huge green-eyed animal charged out of the dark, rose up and pinned me against the wall. The animal's breath was hot on my face. I began screaming and screaming.

The patio door opened and Sergio said, "Perro. Down. Sit." The animal got down and sat to Sergio's left. Then Sergio said to me, "Perro, he must know you."

"Sure, I see." I was pretty shaken, but, until he invited the dog inside, I thought Sergio was at least rational. I backed up to the TV set, the dog nuzzled Sergio's hand.

"Is good dog. He protect you. He needs know you." His brown eyes pleading, Sergio nodded his head affirmative with each statement. "Miz Domino, she 'fraid. She *like* Perro, she no be shot."

All I could think was, this is a dog? I said a timid, "Si."

From my left, I heard an emphatic, "Si." Juana, standing by the table, hands on her well-padded hips, her generous bosom heaving, was looking at me intently. "Si?" She asked.

They couldn't both be wrong, could they? "Si," I said with as much enthusiasm as I could, and smiled.

When I sat in the leather chair Sergio indicated, he brought Perro over and ordered him to sit in front of me. Perro's coat was the color of a deer's, his chest was white and his tail curled up on his back. I'd never seen a dog like this, and no one I knew kept a dog in the house. But, this *was* Colorado after all.

Sergio took my hand and moved it over Perro's neck and back, nodding for me to continue.

I did as told. Hadn't Sergio said that Perro would have saved Aunt Sapphira's life? I could be friendly with a bear for that kind of protection. Perro sat patiently allowing me to stroke his coat, his forehead wrinkled, his intelligent eyes watching me. I'd noticed when Sergio spoke that Perro cocked his head as though waiting for a command. This is a smart dog, I decided, and I sure need the help of a smart friend.

With the dishes stowed in the dishwasher, we sat back down to finish the wine. Sergio ordered Perro on an inspection tour of the house. I could hear his toenails going up the steps and after an interval, coming back down to rejoin us in the kitchen.

"All is well," Sergio beamed.

As they were leaving, Sergio brought a ring of keys from his pocket, and locked the patio door after them. They did have keys, then. He waved with a shy smile as they turned away to go home, which was somewhere on this property, according to Randall.

As I brushed my teeth, washed my face, and got ready for bed, I felt a friendly, approving presence in the house. Aunt Sapphira must have been a nice person to leave such vibes behind. I don't know if it was the excellent wine or the secure feeling Perro's search had given me, but I slept for ten hours and woke dazzled by sunshine.

I stretched lazily under the comforter and let my mind wander. I wondered, *did the sun always shine in this mountain country*? Some difference from where I lived. I loved everything about Minneapolis, except when spring came the clouds opened up to rain for weeks, and water dripped constantly through our roof. I hoped Aunt Sapphira left me enough money to pay the bills and to rent an apartment with a roof that didn't leak.

Those bills we must pay were bills Kassi ran up, when I was too sick to handle our finances. I shook myself, that's enough thinking in the past. This was the day I'd learn the facts of my inheritance. Then I'd go home. Except, I should stay long enough to insist the authorities find my aunt's murderer. That's certainly my responsibility as her only heir.

After my shower, I wrapped myself in a huge, soft burgundy towel, thinking what a gorgeous room. A sunken tub and Jacuzzi fit into the round turret, where privacy was assured by opaque shades that drew up from the windowsill. A generous, enclosed shower stood in the opposite corner, with a double lavatory between the two. There was a large separate room for the toilet, complete with a now empty magazine rack. In Minneapolis, our apartment bathroom was so small you had to leave it just to change your expression.

Thinking that one power-suit-day a week was enough, I dressed in white long sleeved cotton shirt and pressed jeans. In the kitchen, I measured out water and coffee and turned on the coffee maker before pouring cereal into a bowl and juice into a glass. The patio doors unlocked from the inside, so I took my breakfast out on the brick patio, and sat in a wrought iron chair to eat.

Dominating the view on the east was a half mountain. The whole part was covered with splashes of several shades of green from a variety of trees, but the south end appeared to have been hacked down by a giant hand intent on sculpturing a second inscrutable sphinx. Barren of trees, the cut had gone deep and straight. The morning sun was merciless and spotlighted the raw rock, bereft of spring green.

I sipped coffee and watched three hawks circle in the sky. Suddenly, one dived to the ground. I held my breath, surely he'd killed himself, but in a moment he flew into the air with a snake, caught midway between head and tail, hanging from his bill and writhing as it was carried through the air. I watched the other two circle away to better hunting grounds.

Everyone wants a Shangri La, and it seemed that Aunt Sapphira had found hers. Until she was murdered, that is. I shivered, and then yelped as a cold nose found my hand.

It was only Perro who wanted to be petted. Close behind him were the beaming Juana and Sergio. "He like you," said Sergio.

Gamely, I smiled back. "I like him too," I lied.

Sergio's smile was broader, "Juana cook. You eat."

"Ah…, no," I apologized, "I've eaten."

Many Spanish words poured from her mouth, some of them sounding amazingly like expletives. Sergio said a few soothing phrases, and she finally said, "Si."

She soon returned with a mug of hot cocoa. I started to decline, but one look at her stern expression and I decided that I could drink cocoa if Juana wanted me to. I used the spoon she handed me to sip rather than trust my tongue to test the temperature. It was hot, but surprisingly good. It was a wonderful sweet, thick chocolate drink. "This is delicious," I said.

A smiling Sergio said, "Si," and gave Juana a triumphant look.

So the cocoa was his idea, and Juana must have wanted to feed me a big breakfast because she shrugged and threw up her hands. When I asked them to sit with me, they both shook their heads, and went to work, Juana in the kitchen and Sergio disappearing around in back of the house. I soon heard the sounds of a motor and eventually caught a glimpse of him on a riding lawn mower cutting the grass on the driveway. Only the lower portion of the drive was visible from the patio, but the sounds of the mower indicated that it went back and forth on the north side of the house.

When I glanced at my watch it was nine-thirty. I had to beat it down the road. No time for make-up or anything. I managed to do the lipstick thing, grab my bag and keys, and urge Bertha to life. I waved good-bye to Juana and Sergio who made signs of the cross, blessing me on my way. They didn't know how reliable old Bertha was, but it was nice to have people concerned for my safety. Sergio had reopened the gate, and since how it closed or opened was still a mystery to me, I left it that way.

I arrived at Randall's office just two minutes after ten and offered my apologies for being late which he discounted, "We're not too punctual out here. Mostly anytime within a half hour is fine."

Yeah right, I thought, and of course I should believe you, even though I know you lied to me about being in court yesterday and ignored my mention of your help on la Veta Pass. I know schemers like you, I thought, you'll charge me from the appointment on. Betcha. Well, you'll not pad my bill.

"Now if you're busy, I can make another appointment. When it's more convenient."

He treated me to his dazzling smile, "No way, I've set aside my whole morning just for you."

The whole morning could stretch into all day around here, and at a hundred bucks an hour, cost me upwards of six hundred dollars. Of course, he set the whole morning aside. I scooped up newspapers, piled them neatly on the floor, and sat down on the edge of the straight back chair angled in front of his desk. The client's chair, I figured. I'd leave the wingback reserved for heiresses and *their* money. Maybe he had all morning, but I couldn't afford it. We kept eye contact and continued smiling.

"Now," he said, "should we get to the business at hand? Your aunt Sapphira's will?"

"Let's do," I answered.

He fished around in his pockets for keys, selected one, and unlocked a desk drawer. He pulled out a legal size manila folder, opened it and began scrutinizing the pages. "Your aunt's will may seem complicated, but it's fairly simple and straight-forward. I'll read it to you and you can jot down questions as I go."

He handed me a lined, yellow pad and proceeded to read in his deep baritone voice. As he read, he occasionally swept his fingers through his hair. No wonder it looked like he never used a comb. I made notes and wondered if these lawyer types would have to close up shop without these extra long legal pads.

When he finished he asked, "You have questions?"

"Just want to be sure I understand everything. I'm given a year to locate money and jewelry. I'm to live on the ranch for that year, and if I maintain the property in its present condition, *and* find the money and jewelry, I may then take legal possession of it?"

"Right."

"I understand there are other known assets, including money?"

Randall nodded, "That's correct."

"I'll need money to maintain the place. Where's the money?" A little blunt, but money was what this was all about.

"That's a fair question, but I don't know the answer."

Money was the only reason I'd driven Bertha this far, borrowed from Phillip, slept on the ground across four states, and gone hungry. Now some jerk, who happened to be Aunt Sapphira's attorney didn't know where the money was? This I didn't believe.

"Let me understand this. You are Aunt Sapphira's lawyer, you wrote her will, witnessed her signature, and declared her sound of mind?"

Randall was uncomfortable, "Well, not exactly. Dad drafted the will. I took over when he retired. I, along with two others, witnessed Mrs. Domino sign it."

"Isn't that a little strange? Write a will and before it's signed, then just go ahead and retire?"

Randall, loosened his tie, cleared his throat, and studied the telephone, willing it to ring. When it didn't, he said, "The circumstances were unusual."

"Yes. I'd say so." I watched him closely while I let that hang in the air.

He cleared his throat again, fussed with the place where his tie used to be knotted, "If you remember in clause 32, the deceased mentions boxes that contain money and miscellaneous valuables. And in clause 48 near the end, she states her beneficiary must locate these boxes to claim the contents."

"They're not deposit boxes?"

"They could be, but usually the executor in possession of the will has the key with the name of the bank, as well as a list of contents. I don't, so we assume the boxes are somewhere on her property. The best thing for you to do is to start looking for them."

Disbelief filled me with fury. My voice trembled, "That's preposterous."

"Look, we believe Mrs. Domino intended to leave a letter to her heir that described the location, but before she could write it, she was killed."

"To her heir? She didn't know it was me? Is the will valid? Or should I say legal? You addressed your letter to me as the heir, but Aunt Sapphira didn't know I existed?"

"I'll try to explain, Dad drew up the first draft, and instructed me to find the heir. We didn't know if Mrs. Domino's sister, your grandmother Anastasia, had a living descendant. We learned she died in an accident, and we discovered her daughter was killed by a hit and run driver, but we didn't know if her grandchildren survived."

"How is that possible?" I asked.

Ignoring my question, he continued. "As stated in her will, the eldest female descendent was to be her heir. Mrs. Domino had been adamant about it and said this was a Greek tradition. By the time we learned your name and that you were the oldest granddaughter, she was dead. We still didn't know you, how reliable you were, that kind of thing. You never wrote to her."

The hurt flooded back. While fishing through the ice, Dad, Grandma, and a neighbor had fallen into the icy water of a lake. Dad suffered irreversible brain damage from exposure. Grandma and the neighbor drowned. Mom had continued teaching, but was killed by a hit and run driver one December night. Her insurance was in trust for Dad's care. There was nothing for Kassi and me. We'd been broke ever since, Kassi was twelve and I was seventeen.

Now this rich kid, whose college was paid for, whose law practice was inherited, who never knew hardship was trying to lay a guilt trip on me for not writing to an aunt I didn't know existed?

I studied the yellow pad and fought back tears. When I could trust my voice I said, "I'll need money to live on…, in the meantime…,while I'm treasure hunting. Is there an allowance?"

"None, I'm afraid."

"But there's an annuity for Sergio and Juana. It doesn't seem fair."

"No it doesn't. But you'll manage. You're a nurse? An RN?"

I'd thought this was the boonies. He'd probably checked me out yesterday instead of spending the afternoon in court. Did he also know about the maxed out credit cards? "Well, yes almost but not quite an RN. I don't have my license."

"But you've taken your board exams?"

He knew that too? "Yes."

"A nursing home just opened a month or so ago. I'm sure you can get work there."

"Ah…, thanks." My mind was working overtime, making plans. I'd have to call Kassi for my license. I needed legal advice and Phillip was a law student, I'd better call him too. Maybe I could contest the will. After all, if he expected to get his money back right away, the inheritance had to be mine in a hurry. "May I have a copy of the will?"

"There's really no need. You can see it anytime you want, just by stopping by the office here."

Be sweet, be dependent, he'll love it. "Yes, I know. But this whole thing is difficult for me to comprehend. I'll have to study it to come up with anything close to an intelligent question. Then I could stop by to ask them. I'll try not to make," how did Kassi do this? I needed a word, a nuisance…, that's her word, "a nuisance of myself."

"You'll never be a nuisance to me."

Why that jerk, he was studying my boobs.

When he saw I was watching him, his cheeks flushed. "I'll just make a quick copy of this. Want to come along?"

"Sure."

I tried to seem interested in his conversation while I scanned each page as he handed it to me hot off the copier. He was talking about his mother. "Mom is planning a party for you, as soon as she and Dad get home. Can you come?"

I was reading the will and only half listening, "Love to. Do I dress up?"

"Yep. She likes everyone to look pretty."

Now I knew I didn't have any party clothes with me, but did I decline? Not me. I'd just noticed the will was dated March 3, this year. Six days before Aunt Sapphira was killed. "Randall, this is a very recent will."

"Yes. Mrs. Domino had a previous one, but she wanted to leave everything to you."

I felt a chill, "So someone else was previously her heir?"

"Apparently so."

I asked, "Who was that person?"

Randall was busy putting more paper into the copier, "I'm afraid I don't know. Dad was her attorney, and he destroyed her old will."

In response to my raised eyebrows, "…, at her request, of course."

"Don't you think you should ask your father? The previous heir may be the person who shot her."

"We've thought of that, but I haven't been able to talk to him."

"But you've talked to your mother."

"That's true, but they're on vacation, and I don't like to bother them with business."

We were back in his office, Randall assembling the will. He glanced at his watch, "I'd like to take you to lunch. It's after twelve, you must be hungry."

Just look at those steady blue eyes and that sweet smile.

He added, "I'd like to get better acquainted with you, Nika, tell you about the town and everything."

In your dreams Randall baby. In your dreams. "No thanks, the Sanchez fed me too well this morning."

"Well, we need to talk about the party Mother's planning. Did you say there was someone here that you'd like to invite?"

"Not a soul. Heck, not even a spirit," I said.

At Randall's quick frown, I realized that was not the most thoughtful thing to say. My aunt had been murdered after all. I shivered convulsively. Someone walked over my grave again.

Chapter Four

Maybe the altitude did this to people out here, and maybe I was immune to its effects, but ask me for names of local friends when I'd only been in town one night? And why focus on a party that may or may not be given by his mother who was not here, but who was vacationing somewhere with his father who apparently was not available to discuss the will of a wealthy client? If this was business as usual, it was monkey business, as the real Bertha would have said.

However, before I blurted out my thoughts, I remembered in time, that being an attorney, he'd argue. Also being an attorney he'd expect to win, just as I hated to lose. That was one of the problems with Phillip's and my relationship, I won arguments. Many times he stormed out of my apartment in a rage when I showed him proof that I was right. The more he stormed, the more I liked being right. It was the same with Randall, I could argue with Lawyer McClean or I could skip it. I chose to let it go. What mattered was my legacy, why argue? I held my tongue, smiled sweetly and said, "I'm sure by the time your mother is ready to give the party I'll know some people to invite. Hopefully, they'll be acceptable people." Acceptable meaning worthy of association by the McCleans.

Randall had a sweet smile too, "That's just one of the reasons you have an attorney. I'll take care of everything for you."

Sure you will, I thought. Aunt Sapphira's estate must be worth a bunch. My smile became what I hoped was demurely grateful. I'd play this game until all the money and property were mine. Then I'd be out of here.

Randall looked at his watch, "I'd still like to take you to lunch. It's after one, you must be hungry."

Just look at those steady blue eyes and that sincere smile. I bet Randall wouldn't stand a girl up. "No thanks," I said.

"Maybe a rain-check? Another day?"

"Perhaps," I said.

He was escorting me to Bertha, "I've taken the liberty of renting you a Post Office Box. The Post Office is just around the corner on a side street." He handed me a key and a slip of paper, "Here's the key and I wrote down the number for you."

Liberty is right, I fumed, but held onto my smile and grateful manner, "Thanks. That was awfully nice of you."

"You're entirely welcome. I want to make everything as easy as possible for you," he smiled back.

* * * * * * *

This should be Kassi's day off, and as soon as I got back to Aunt Sapphira's, I telephoned her. She was home, and I filled her in on the will and the murder.

"Murdered right there where you're living. I just knew it," said my suddenly prescient sister. "That place is haunted. Nika, take yourself out of there. Go into town and stay at a hotel. I can't worry about you and these bills too."

Kassi worried about bills? That's a new one. "What's going on? You had money to pay rent and buy groceries, and you got your old job back. What bills are you worried about?"

"Credit card bills. You charged stuff on them, didn't you? I got a call that we are over-extended"

"Just gas, as we planned. They can't be over-extended."

There was a long silence before I asked, "Kassi did you buy something?"

I heard a long tremulous sigh over the phone, "Just two outfits is all. It's summer and I have an image to keep up, at work. You know that. Everything can't always be for you. Except, I do insist that you check into a hotel."

What was the use? "If I stay at a hotel, there'll only be more bills to worry about. Besides the money is hidden here somewhere. I've got to find it. And Kassi, has my RN license come yet, in the mail?"

"I don't know. I haven't picked up the mail in a couple of days. It's so depressing to get only bills."

"Well, go look."

"Now?"

"Yes. Go. Hurry. I'll hold." Our mailbox was one of four at the front of the house. It would take awhile for her to make the trip down the three flights of stairs and back.

In minutes a breathless Kassi picked up the phone. "Yes. There's a letter from the Minnesota State Board of Nursing."

"Now listen Kassi, this is important. Mail it to me right away. Priority Mail or Fed Ex. Before you go to work." I gave her my box number.

"Honestly Nika, you make more trouble. It's always something I have to run and take care of immediately."

She had conveniently forgotten that our financial problems were a direct result of her spending money we didn't have. If she were standing in front of me, I doubt I could resist shaking her. Right after I talked to Kassi, I dialed Phillip's number.

After listening to my questions, he said, "Nika, your aunt Sapphira had every right to hide *her* money and make *you* look for it. Besides, what can you do? Sue her?"

When I confessed I had no idea what, besides the house, comprised her assets, he said, "You'd better get looking. Remember you owe me money. Try for a safe in the back of a closet, or in a bookcase. Wish I could be there to help my future wife. Sounds like fun. Have a ball." He was still laughing when I hung up.

I swore I'd never call Phillip for advice again. When he lent us money, he'd acted so sweet and concerned, but he'd just demonstrated an about-face back to his old arrogant ways. If he thought my affection could be bought, he thought pretty poorly of me. I wanted the man I married to love me, and me to love him.

The house felt chilly, so I changed out of my good stuff into sweats and sneakers. When I was discharged from the hospital, the exhausted resident ordered me to stay warm and dry, because, "…, anymore these pneumococus lay dormant until the body defenses are down, and the second time around are harder to knock out." Once dressed for the hunt, I began a search of the mansion.

By mid-afternoon, I'd ranged the first floor front to back looking for a concealed safe. As I'd seen done in a movie, I searched the bookcases in the living and sitting rooms, by comparing the outside measurements against the inside depth. There were no false backs here, or in the guest bedroom where I slept. The master bedroom seemed the most logical place to hide something, and I searched it exhaustively. I checked the closet, drawers, and furniture for false backs or bottoms. Nothing. There were still the fireplaces, china cupboards, and the whole upstairs to search, but I decided to leave them for another day.

I climbed the stairs. The fatigue came suddenly these days. I sat down on a mid-step to rest, chin in hands supported by elbows on knees, and waited for the vertigo to hit. Sometimes it did, sometimes it didn't. While waiting, I studied the newel posts, an unusual three for each flight of stairs, which were solid rectangular hunks of carved wood.

Each post had a base relief decoration of some improbable animal or bird. Quite ugly, really, but this was Aunt Sapphira's house. Who was I to criticize her taste in art?

The second floor opened on a long hallway where the odor of mothballs tickled my nose into a series of sneezes. I pulled the sweatshirt up over my nose and quickly walked from front to back, opening doors as I went. There were four bedrooms, two on each side of the hall with connecting bathrooms between. The closets held only wire hangers, the kind that always tangled. The bathrooms were furnished in freestanding sinks, toilets, and bathtubs. There were shallow linen cupboards in the bathrooms, but measurements proved disappointingly accurate. At the far end of the hall, a closed door seemed promising, but I decided to check the third floor before investigating what lay beyond that door.

The corner of the second floor landing was directly over the guest room bathroom, yet it had no turret window. That was strange, because I knew from studying the front of the mansion, that both turrets rose to include all three floors. I studied the intricately carved paneling. Vines and flowers competed with birds and squirrels on the heavy dark wood. If there was a closet or storeroom behind that paneling, there was no door that I could see. I glanced at the opposite end.

That portion of the second floor landing that was directly over the living room, was furnished like an elegant doctor's waiting room. It was paneled with the same lighter oak as the entry, and prints of the same type were hung at eye level.

The stairs to the third floor ended at a landing that encompassed the whole front of the house including the sunny turret windows on each end. Midway of the wall and parallel to the stairs, oversized double doors stood open on the ballroom. The north end of the hall, held a large open room with shelves on two sides and rods underneath them. A rack, I thought, for the coats and hats of guests attending parties. There was even a desk and chair for the attendant. Wow. I was impressed.

The ballroom itself was huge, but well proportioned. There was a platform-like small stage at the far end that held an upright piano with plenty of room left over for a small band. The floor of the ballroom shone from careful waxing and polishing. Cushioned straight chairs were arranged along the sides. Huge dormer windows beamed sunshine across the narrow floorboards. The stage floor was also made of narrow boards, but none of them were loose or hinged. I found nothing in the piano or piano bench that didn't belong there.

There must be clues somewhere, but this was discouraging. If she didn't hide her wealth in banks, where would she put boxes? I decided to see what lay on the other side of the closed door at the end of the second floor. I held a tissue across my nose and mouth to ward off as much of the mothball odor as possible. The closer I got to the far end, the colder it got. When I touched the doorknob, a draft of cold air swirled around me. I felt vibrations through the door, and turning my back on it, I saw mirage-like waves in front of each bedroom door. My instinct was to run, but my hand was frozen to the iced doorknob. I couldn't move. Terror filled me.

I took deep even breaths to calm myself, "Stop it," I said. "Whoever is doing this can just stop it. Now."

There was the click, click of sharp heels on the stairs. I held my breath and watched the corner of the stairs I was able to see. Two sharp ears appeared, followed by the long head and short body of Perro.

"Perro," I croaked, and he came running down the hall. I knelt and put my arms around his neck and closed my eyes, not believing how secure he made me feel. The cold draft stopped, there were no waving mirages in front of the door, and when I stood, he circled me and urged me back down the hall.

Before descending the stairs, I looked back to the end of the hall. Where before there had been waving mirages, there now were just ordinary doors, mocking me. Something had obviously been wrong, but was it wrong with me, or these doors?

Perro sat at my feet, watching me carefully. "Sorry, Perro, I can't seem to see what's wrong here." He watched me with such intelligent eyes, I almost expected this intuitive animal to solve my dilemma.

Juana was dusting the living room, and she looked up and smiled at me and Perro.

"Bein," she said nodding as though her child had done well.

"Si," I said fondling Perro's ears.

After retrieving the will from my purse, I went to the kitchen and poured a cup of cold coffee, which I zapped in the microwave before going to the patio. The sun was hot, so I chose a wrought iron chair and end table that were shaded by several birch trees. Once I was settled, Perro lay down at my feet. His deep brown eyes watched me as I sipped coffee.

"I don't have anything to give you, Perro. Tell you what, I'll get some dog biscuits next time I'm in town. Promise."

When I talked, he tipped his head, as though waiting for my instructions. This was one smart dog.

"Sorry fella, I've got to read this dull will. Maybe there's a clue to the fortune in here. If I find it, you get a steak." I promised opening the folder.

Perro settled down, his head on my foot. Birds flitted about the tree branches busily carrying grass for home building, while others cheered them on with chirping songs. A lone cottonwood across the way, its new leaves a bright waxy green, seemed to be a launching pad for the nesting birds. They made a comforting ruckus and dispelled my lingering chilled fear.

In the event of the death of the eldest daughter of my great-niece, I read, or *should she be unable to find the treasure or maintain the property, said property is to revert without restriction, to Sergio and Juana Sanchez for their lifetime of service. At the same time, Antonio's great-nephew Anthony Paul P. S., or his descendants, are to be given a year to find the money and jewels. If they fail, any eventually found belong to Sergio and Juana Sanchez.*

The will made me vulnerable. If Aunt Sapphira was murdered for her money, those clauses set me up as the next victim. I shivered with the same fear I'd felt in the upstairs hall, knowing there was no one to protect me. I was on my own.

Who knew I was Aunt Sapphira's heir? Kassi, Randall, and Phillip. But what of her husband, Antonio Domino's descendants? Not Phillip Sym, who was dark as any Italian, but our families had once been close neighbors and friends. In fact, Philip was the only survivor of that ill-fated fishing accident. Not hardly Randall, who with his blue eyes and sandy hair, looked less Italian than any of us. Or could he be? Would he or any of them kill for money? Absolutely not the afraid-of-her-shadow Kassi, who knew I'd share anything I gained with her. Sergio and Juana? Come on, not those sweet people. But back to Randall? Thinking he's Italian is a stretch, but I'd had bitter experience with lawyers who took, no, stole my home. He said he was in Denver at the time Aunt Sapphira was murdered, but I couldn't trust him. He'd already lied to me when he said he'd be in court all day yesterday, but was, in fact, in his office. Some people lied for no reason at all, was he one of those? Or did he have an agenda of his own? Even if I satisfied all the requirements of the will, would he validate my claim? Or would he use every excuse to disqualify me? One thing for sure, I'd have to be very careful, see that all bills were paid until I found the money. Then what of Antonio's nephew? Anthony Paul P. S. Paul as a last name was a new one on me, but what did I know? Anthony Paul Post Script, if that's what the P.S. meant, was a very strange name. Where was he? Did Randall know where this nephew was, but wasn't telling me? Are Randall and Anthony Paul working together to gain everything?

I'd been lost in thought, but suddenly I became aware of my surroundings. How long had everything been so quiet? There had been sounds of birds chirping, and the occasional shifting of Perro trying for a more comfortable spot. Now, everything was still. Dead still. With a whine, Perro stood, hair on his back standing straight up. I tensed, not knowing what to do, what to expect.

Then I heard the scream.

Chapter Five

I heard the rush of wings as a bird, big and black, dropped from the sky and snatched a small animal before flying up into the heavens. Watching the sky, Perro pushed back against me, a low growl rumbling in his throat. With awe, I watched too, because it was a bird with a white head. An eagle. This morning a hawk pounced on a garter snake and now an eagle carried off a plump brown puppy-size animal. What a brutal land. Perro stepped back to my side and I smoothed down the ruffled hair along his back, "Nothing we could do to save the animal, Perro," I said.

The open expanse before me didn't end until it reached the mountains. The sun's rays slanted across the meadow, and the flowers previously hidden by long grasses became visible. Their colors ranged the spectrum, red to yellow. Small brave flowers with short stems and single petals, blooms that must be the source of the sweet scented air. Such a peaceful scene to disguise such terror. Terror for the small animal. And terror for me?

A movement off to the left caught my attention. For a moment I thought an intruder was near by, and the will crackled in my hands as I clutched the papers tighter. A head appeared around some bushes, and Sergio approached lugging a toolbox.

"*Observar*?"

This was going to be tough. Either I had to learn Spanish or he had to pick up more English. '*Observar*' as in observe?

"Bird?" He asked.

Oh. Okay. He was asking did I see the eagle. "Si," I said.

"*Si*," he said, "he eat. Like we?" The smile, fringed by a hedge of a mustache, cut across his face and included his chocolate brown eyes. His thick hair had been trimmed to just below his ears.

I'd been wondering if perhaps there was a place to hide a fortune besides the house. If so, Sergio would know.

"Sergio, is there a garage?" Blank looks. "Well, a house for cars." More blank looks. What was the name for house? Testing my memory bank I came up with hacienda.

"Sergio, a hacienda for cars? For auto?"

After a moment, Sergio seemed to comprehend. "Si, si. Come."

Folding and stuffing the will into my jeans pocket, I obediently followed, tagged by Perro. Around the mansion and up a slight hill stood a two story barn-like structure built of the same brick as the house. The newly mowed brick driveway led up to a double hung door plus a single overhead door. Were there three cars, one behind each door? Were they operable?

Pine trees rose protectively on either side of the building. A stone path led to a small stream that sparkled intermittently beyond the trees to the north. Must be Conundrum Creek, I thought.

Two pairs of broad windows formed deep bays on the second floor. Below them, the double garage doors sagged with old age despondence, and the middle edges once intended to swing open, were now imbedded in gravel. The gap above had been closed by the simple expedient of nailing plywood over it. It had been a long while since those doors were opened. To the right, the ramp slid under the single overhead door. It must be the only one used, I thought. There was just a hint of green around the outer edge of the bay windows, otherwise every bit of wood trim was bare of paint and bleached to silver-gray. The roof was gray slate, the same as the mansion's roof. I guessed the garage needed some fixing up, but was structurally sound, and what a great hiding place. I wanted to explore it. There was a single door on the left of the garage doors, with a four-paned window in the upper half. This seemed the most likely access.

"Sergio, can we go in?" I gestured as though to enter.

"*Si, si*," Sergio smiled. He felt along the top of the door for the key. He turned the lock and pushed the door open, then gallantly bowed and held his hand at arm's length indicating I should go ahead of him.

I'm not fond of dark, dusty, spider infested places, but if I inherited all this I'd be boss, so I better start acting like one. I stepped gingerly over the threshold. Sergio, who was right behind me, switched on a light, and the dim interior became brightly lit.

Not a spider web showing. Gesturing and speaking mostly in Spanish, he proudly showed me a workbench that ran the length of the garage on the left side. His possessive manner told me that this was his own workplace. Hanging above the workbench were more guy toys than I knew existed. The floor was made from slabs of stone, a tad uneven, but swept clean. An open door onto a single car garage, beyond a separating wall, showed it was empty. There were no cars parked in this part either, just a large tarp covering a lumpy object in the middle, and a smaller tarp-covered object next to it. The garage was used for storage. Suddenly, it came to me. I could store my bicycle in here.

"Sergio," I began, "I have a bike…, out in Bertha 'er…, my pickup. Can I bring it in here?"

"Bike?" Sergio said, "Si. I help."

A miracle. Sergio understood right away.

He wouldn't allow me to do a thing. He lifted the bicycle out of the pickup and rolled it up the hill to the garage. Before taking it into the garage, he got a cloth, dipped it in some solution that smelled a lot like gasoline, and wiped it down.

I stood waiting, until I noticed a path worn in the grass around the side of the garage. I strolled over and looked up a hill covered with brush. I started to follow it when I heard Sergio call me.

"Patrona. Patrona, non. Mal." He came running. "Mal, bad," he said. "Is mucho bad. Big hole. Shimley. To breathe. Wildcat. No go there. Si?"

A shimyey? Maybe a chimney? A big cat? A wild cat? I definitely would not go that way. "Si. Si," I said. "For sure si."

"Is good," Sergio said as he went back to his polishing.

I asked, "Sergio, how far does Mrs. Domino's land go?"

He paused, puzzled. I tried to reword my question thinking he didn't understand, when he spoke, "Mucho way. Very far. My girl say, me, Juana too, need have some of land. We work very hard, very long."

Oh dear, I thought, he's not satisfied with only the annuity. "Yes. I agree," I said. He smiled, but was he capable of murder?

While he busied himself, making the bike clean enough for his garage, I looked around inside.

To the left of the outside door another door opened on stairs leading to the second floor. Soiled windows climbed upward with the steps, and allowed only a diffused glow to light the way. When I asked if I could go up, Sergio seemed doubtful, then shrugged and indicated with a hand wave for me to go on, but commanded Perro to stay. Either Sergio wasn't allowed up there or he didn't like it. It made this an ideal place to hide boxes, especially if no one ever went up there.

The stairs opened on a long hall. I followed the hall through an open door at the end, into a living room. This was an apartment. It was devoid of the common smells of living, cooking odors, furniture polish, cleanser. Who had lived her and how long ago? It ran parallel across the front taking advantage of the bay windows, and was furnished with easy chairs and a sofa that looked like it could become a bed. All were covered in chintz that was imprinted with unlikely blue poppies on a blue background. Hugging each piece of furniture like quotation marks, were end tables of some dark wood layered with dust. I sneezed and fished a tissue from my pocket to cover my nose. Dominating the center of the room was a huge coffee table that guaranteed bruised shins to anyone crass enough to sit on the sofa. The walls were covered with pale blue striped wallpaper. Darker squares and rectangles indicated pictures had once hung there, but had been removed. There were no books, no TV or radio. There were no cubbyholes, or drawers, in which to stow boxes of money. The bay windows were partially covered with scalloped shades edged with silky fringe. I felt the deep emotions of anger and grief, left behind by whoever had lived here.

I shivered the fear away and retraced my steps along the hall, opening a door to a bedroom on what must be the north wall. Another pair of generous windows looked out on tall shaggy pines, and the silver sheen of a creek that appeared intermittently between their lower trunks. Water seemed so foreign to this arid, dusty land that I longed to explore that creek soon. With a sigh I stepped back from the windows and studied the rest of the room.

The same scalloped and fringed shades curtained these windows. The same blue fabric was continued in the bedspread and cushioned chairs. The same wallpaper covered the walls and again any pictures that once hung here were only memories left by squares of darker wallpaper. It was furnished with twin beds, a dressing table, chest of drawers, bedside tables and a chaise lounge.

I felt someone behind me, and chill fingers crept up my back and across my shoulders. "Sergio, is that you?" I whirled around, but no one was there.

A faint odor of mothballs permeated the room. Fan folded doors lined one wall, which might be the hiding place. I opened the doors to discover the source of the smell, and a neat and tidy although shallow closet across the end of the room.

Completely filled with boxes of shoes from end to end, a shelf hung over storage bags, hanging shoulder to shoulder along the wide expanse, with zippers to the front. I pulled down a shoebox. Inside were pale blue sling-back pumps, wrapped in tissue and stretched with shoehorns. I checked the size, seven and a half narrow. Gee, my size. Resisting the urge to try them on, I returned them to the shelf. All the other shoeboxes, held shoes the same size. How strange that whoever lived here took the pictures, but left these clothes. I'd found boxes all right, but no money or jewels.

Well, that would have been too easy anyway. If Aunt Sapphira didn't trust banks or safety deposit boxes why would she trust a bunch of shoeboxes?

At the far end of the room, beyond the closet, was another door not at first apparent, because it had been papered to match the walls. Oh gees, maybe the sound had come from here. I listened for any small noise, a scurry,...an indrawn breath. When I heard nothing I flung open the door on a full bath. Blue tiled walls, gold plated fixtures, even a whirlpool. Talk about lavish, for an apartment above a garage.

The end of the hall widened into a dining room with wide dormer windows on the west and a pass-through into the kitchen on the north. There was a built-in china cupboard flanked by deep drawers that held plastic wrapped linens. A quick search turned up only table linens and an empty silver drawer. The table and six chairs were made of the same dark, heavy wood as elsewhere. The walls were covered in the same wallpaper and the chairs were upholstered in the same blue flowered fabric. You'd think at some point, whoever had decorated this would have gotten tired of the stuff. The kitchen was small but had everything from a compactor to a dishwasher. A food processor, a blender, and a toaster were spaced along the counter. A garbage disposal opened from one of the sinks. There was even a small breakfast table tucked into a single bay window that looked out on pine trees. The cupboards contained a few everyday dishes and pots and pans. The refrigerator stood unplugged with doors ajar. No one lived here now, although someone had. Who? What kind of people? Without pictures or books it was difficult to get a feel of what they'd been like. Except why had they had left the dresses.

I made another quick stroll through the rooms, with a proprietary attitude. This apartment was bigger and better in every way than the apartment we rented in Minneapolis. Could I turn this into a source of income?

Although it was only cold, water gushed forth when I turned on the taps. There must be a hot water heater somewhere, and there must be heat because otherwise the water pipes would freeze. That had happened to us the first winter in the apartment. I opened the doors under the sink to check for traces of leaks, but it was all spic and span. A wastebasket was unlined, but when I tipped it to look inside, I saw a scrap of paper. A quick glance told me it was a flight invoice, with the upper corner torn off. I crumpled it into my jeans pocket, thinking it was heresy to spoil the sterile quality of the kitchen with discarded paper. I noted what looked like panel heaters along the lower walls.

A creaking floorboard made me jump. Again the icy fingers crawled across my shoulders and down my arms, making me shudder. The sun was no longer filtering through the pine trees, and it had grown dark in the apartment. "Sergio? Is that you?"

No answer. Moving carefully, I came out of the kitchen, through the dining room and into the hall. The hall door was ajar. Had I left it like that? I checked every shadow, but nothing moved. The stairs were solid, not a creak or squeak.

Downstairs, my bike was propped against the back wall. Sergio was nowhere to be seen. Maybe he'd been upstairs and gone on to other duties. I leaned out the door, but Sergio was gone. Did people in this part of the country have a habit of leaving in a hurry without an explanation? In answer, thunder rolled across the valley. The sky was ominous, dark clouds were tumbling over and over each other.

Well, as long as he wasn't around, there was no reason I could see why I shouldn't look under the tarp. I had a right to know what it hid…,maybe covered was a better word. Another clap of thunder sounded, closer this time. If I was going to snoop, I'd better be about it. I lifted one corner, and slid the whole end up to expose a car. I was so riveted, the will fell from my pocket unnoticed. There stood a pale blue car with chrome fins and a Chevrolet insignia on the radiator. A little dust had accumulated on the hood, the axles rested on cement blocks. It hadn't been driven in years. It was in perfect condition, in mint condition.

I opened the passenger door and found a purchase receipt made out to Charles Raymond, for a 1957 Chevrolet. I replaced it and shut the door, wondering why Mr. Raymond's antique car was stored in Aunt Sapphira's garage. Then with a sigh, the tarp slid back in place, like unseen hands had covered a beloved child. A chill snaked up my spine ending in a shiver that shook my whole body.

"Stop this nonsense," I said out loud, "You don't believe in ghosts so stop acting like this place is haunted."

Yet, inexplicably I felt as though I'd intruded, pried into what was none of my business. I was little surprised that a voice out of the rafters hadn't rebuked me. Since I'd already peeked where I shouldn't, I decided to look under the other tarp. After checking for witnesses, I lifted it and found an engine. I pulled back the tarp covering the car again and opened the hood. It was empty. Someone was saving this car, but whom?

Again, I heard a soft sigh and again unseen hands slid the tarps back in place. Footsteps sounded overhead. Floorboards creaked. Outside, the thunder began to roll in earnest. I'd better get out of here. My heart fluttered against my ribs as I turned out the light and locked the door. A big drop of rain landed on my nose as I raced for the house, and then I remembered the will had fallen from my pocket. Reluctantly, I turned back, unlocked the door, felt for the light switch, which I flipped on before leaning through the door to look around.

I half expected to see Sergio standing at his workbench, puzzled that I'd left him locked in. Whatever I'd anticipated, the garage was empty. I called out, "Sergio, Sergio are you in here?" No answer. "Who is in here?" The last raised goose bumps on my arms. But there was no answer. No creaking floor boards. Just Aunt Sapphira's will on the floor.

I folded the crumpled pages of the will and tucked them under my sweatshirt. As I locked the door and deposited the key above the door jam, thunder cracked and giant raindrops splattered against the dry wood. I couldn't shake the feeling that someone was watching, and stood rooted to the spot getting wetter by the second. Silly, when a dry haven was just beyond the locked door. Reaching for the key, I glanced up at the bay windows just as a shade dropped to the sash. Someone *was* up there.

Thunder and lightning crashed open the heavens and a deluge obscured the mountains and veiled the house. Never would I go back into that garage. I willed my legs to run, but they felt like iron weights had been strapped to my feet and took more strength to lift than I had in my shivering body. I stumbled down the sharp hill, sliding and slipping on the wet grass. By the time I made it across the patio to the kitchen door, I was soaked and chilled to the bone. I began coughing. Dreadful, racking coughs that tore at my lungs. Oh no. Not the pneumonia again, I prayed. But another fit of coughing began and I started to cry, tugging at the patio door, which stubbornly refused to open.

Then Juana was there, opening the door. As I stumbled through, she pulled me to her generous bosom. A flood of Spanish words tumbled out faster than the falling rain. I caught 'Sergio' and 'Por Patrona' as she patted my back with one hand and shook her wooden spoon emphatically. I understood nothing except the effect on Sergio who stood with his head sunk on his chest, apparently guilty as charged, with Perro whining at his feet.

He hustled away and returned with a thick towel, which Juana wrapped around me. She led me into the master bedroom and pulled a thick terry robe from a closet. She began to pull off the sweatshirt, but I waved her away telling her I could do it myself. She must have understood, because she nodded and backed out.

I stripped off my clothes and tossed wet sweats, underwear, socks, and sneakers into the tub. I took a second bath towel from the free-standing brass towel caddie and rubbed my body until the shivering stopped and I began to feel warm. I rinsed my face in warm water from gold taps, like the ones in the garage apartment. Then I put on the beige robe and padded out to the kitchen.

"Gracias Juana, gracias," I said.

Juana held me away and looked into my face. A new flood of words tumbled forth and she clutched me back to her bosom, now damp from the previous hug, and lovingly patted my back. I caught 'por patrona' said enough times to make me think that Sergio should not have taken me to look at the garage. One thing for sure, Sergio wouldn't *dare* shoot anyone, Juana would beat him to death with her wooden spoon.

She escorted me to the table and sat me down. She gestured to Sergio shouting, "de vinos, de vinos," loud enough to deafen him if he weren't already so afflicted.

I guessed 'de vinos' meant wine. "Good," I nodded as Sergio unlocked the basement door, turned on the light and disappeared down the staircase.

Juan picked up a knife and began chopping onions, which she added to a skillet before picking it up and swirling the butter and onions around. She chopped and seeded thin peppers, adding them to the onions, and then added chopped tomatoes and turned the flame down. She gave me a despairing look and called out, "Sergio," who appeared with Perro almost immediately bearing a bottle of wine and two bottles of beer.

I rose and put the bottles on the table, but pointed to the wine. I caught Sergio hungrily studying the beer. Gees, I'd been so sorry for myself, I hadn't thought about Sergio and Juana, and Juana was cooking my supper while Sergio was fetching my wine. Quickly, I got out two more place settings of china, glasses and silver. Juana saw what I was doing and tried to protest, but I pointed to myself and said, "I insist."

Sergio nodded appreciatively and Juana looked flustered. "Please," I added.

Juana and Sergio ignored the glasses and drank the beer from the bottles. We ate cheese and beans wrapped in tortillas and drenched in a wonderful sauce. When I could eat no more, I tried to thank Juana saying the only Spanish I knew, "Gracias, gracias." She waved me away when I tried to help clean up the kitchen, finally escorting me to the guest room where she dismissed me for the evening, but not before refilling my wine glass.

I could get used to this, I thought, as I lay stretched out under crisp sheets and a down comforter. I could get to really *like* this. Comforted by the house made warm by loving people and safe by Perro who had gone on his inspection tour just before I went to bed, I closed my eyes and allowed myself to drift into a deep sleep.

When I opened my eyes, the red numerals on the clock said, two-thirty. Why was I awake? It was hours until morning,…real morning, I didn't have to get up, not yet. Did I? Where was Kassi? "Kassi? Are you home yet?"

Then I heard it. Soft music accompanied gentle singing, "It had to be you,…"

I switched on a light to see not our apartment, but Aunt Sapphira's guest bedroom. Someone was close to my bedroom windows, playing a guitar and singing.

Forcing myself out of bed, I grabbed the straight chair and propped it under the doorknob. I tested it and felt the door give. Pushing it tighter, I watched the chair legs mar the parquet floor, and prayed the carved, fragile looking chair would hold. Then I crawled shivering back under the covers, waiting for the shove that would splinter the chair and allow the singer entrance.

Chapter Six

The next thing I knew, I opened my eyes to a phone ringing somewhere far away. I stumbled out of bed and tried to open the door, but the chair blocked it. The chair screeched as I yanked it away from the door and ran down the long hallway to the kitchen phone.

It was Randall. He cheerfully wished me a good morning and accepted my report that I'd slept well, chuckling when I admitted that I'd just gotten up. The clock on the kitchen wall said ten-thirty. Gees, I really had slept well. He allowed as how he'd made a couple of telephone calls and had found me a job at the nursing home. I refrained from saying I'd much prefer to find my own job, gritted my teeth and thanked him. I was, he said, to keep an appointment at three that afternoon to get my assignment.

"I've also made luncheon reservations for us at twelve-thirty. I'll acquaint you with the details."

There went all my resolutions to never spend time with him. "Luncheon? Well sure, we have to eat. You don't have to be in court today?" I asked as sweetly as possible.

"No, I took care of that the other day."

"Yes. So you say." Liar, liar, pants on fire, I thought.

"Well," Randall said into the drawn-out silence, "Well, gotta go, and I'm sure this is a good job for you."

"Oh, absolutely," I answered as he hung up.

"I do need a job. Like I have a choice?" I said into the buzzing phone. I was grumpy.

It was pretty hard to stay grumpy and look at the beautiful panorama of the 'half mountain' and lower valley to the east of me. The rain had settled the dust. The sun filled the valley with golden light and warmed the brick patio. When I went for a coffee refill, I also got the telephone book from the small table and returned to the patio with it. Under hospitals, I found Lady of Guadalupe, Acute Care Facility, 625 beds. I decided to get dressed and run over to Magdalena for a look. If I had my druthers, Dad's expression, I'd rather work in a hospital than a nursing home.

Not until I'd gotten back to the bedroom and saw the chair skewed across my path did I remember the guitar singer of last night. As scary as it was having him right outside my window, my falling deeply asleep was even more frightening. He could have walked in here, and smothered me with my pillow. I'd need to secure the locks on the windows and find something sturdier than a fragile chair to keep the door closed. I'd do all that tonight.

Getting dressed should have been easy, but the power suit was soiled from my attempt to crawl under the gate the day I arrived. No amount of brushing got the clay out. From my duffel bag, I dug out some underwear, another pair of jeans, and a black cotton sweater. A couple of gold chains and gold loop earrings added a nice touch, I thought. I pulled on a clean pair of white socks and looked for my loafers. No loafers, anywhere. No sneakers either. The only footwear I had were black high heels, bought to go with the power suit. That would have to do, I thought as I pulled them over the white socks.

* * * * * * * *

The hospital was a four-story brick affair with wings pointing to the four directions. A workman was riding around on a tractor-mower trimming grass within an inch of its life. Shrubs and trees, planted without design on the generous grounds, were leafed out. I parked in the section for visitors, and entered via double doors underneath an arched niche that protected the statue of a blue-eyed woman with hands outstretched to all. The walnut paneled lobby was paved with green marble and decorated with statues of saints displayed in niches that were lit by recessed lighting. *I* was impressed!

I walked as sedately as possible toward a white haired lady in a pink smock, sitting in the center of a raised, octagon shaped walnut desk polished to a high gloss. The telephone was glued to her ear. A nametag pinned to her smock identified the lady as Mrs. M. Padilla, volunteer. She covered the mouthpiece with her hand and said, "Yes?"

"Ah…, Mrs. Padilla." Padilla, I pronounced as though it rhymed with armadillo, the anteater. From the death-wish look in the lady's eyes, I guessed that was not the way to say her name. "I'm looking for the Nursing Service Office?"

She pointed over her shoulder to the back of her desk where two red velvet upholstered benches were positioned across from two elevator doors. "Go past the elevators and to the left," she said, "you'll see the sign."

Once past the lobby, I smelled the hospital aroma I loved. I'd worked summers as a nurse tech to earn money while I was in college. Two summers I'd been assigned to a busy emergency room. I know most people wrinkle their noses in distaste, but man,…I loved that mixture of anesthesia and antiseptic. I slipped along a highly polished corridor, inhaling and hoping I could find work here. That's what I liked. Give me an emergency room full of accident victims and I purred. I came to double doors with frosted glass windows that were stenciled in black letters to read Nursing Service Offices.

I opened the door on the outer office where a formidable broad shouldered woman sat at a desk with earphones on her head while she hammered away at an electric typewriter. Ever so often, she backtracked the carriage, hit the error key and retyped a few letters. The band connecting the earphones bunched her hair up and ruined what was probably a proper 'do' of tightly curled snow-white hair. Her glasses were resting halfway between the bridge and tip of her narrow nose. With each back tracking her head wagged and the glasses slid down a millimeter more.

I restrained the impulse to reach out and push them back in place. Her preference for the electric typewriter when a covered computer and printer rested on an adjoining desk, revealed her clout and a steadfast refusal to learn new tricks. It was probably earned by years of guarding the inner sanctum. Guard dogs are stubborn. I'd have to approach her carefully if I hoped to get in to see the Director, today or ever.

At last she saw me, pressed the stop button on the dictating machine, removed the headphones, and fixed me with a cold stare. After pushing her glasses up on her nose, she looked me up and down. So far I hadn't opened my mouth. What could I say, 'Hey, my power suit was wrinkled and I'm too poor to have it cleaned or buy a new one.'

"You," she said, "must be that niece of Sapphira Domino's. You don't look a thing like her. I suppose you know that. You're much too tall. Except, of course, your black hair and eyes. I'd say they're like hers. Hmmm. The same square jaw, too."

I wondered what she'd say if I told her I hadn't the faintest idea what my aunt looked like? The nameplate on her desk read, 'B. R. Smyth, Sec.'

"Ah, Ms. Smyth," I stammered, "I'm Nika McGuinness. I graduated from University of Minnesota with a BS in Nursing. Who do I see about applying for a job?"

"Got your license?"

"Well, actually I don't have it with me, but my sister is forwarding it. It will be here any day."

"That's a Minnesota license, right?"

"Yes." She didn't have to know that it was brand new, so I didn't enlighten her. "I hadn't planned on staying here and I didn't come prepared to apply for work. However, my circumstances have changed,…"

She interrupted my explanation, "I dare say." She was flipping a pencil end over end on a nearby ashtray full of paper clips; clack-thump, clack-thump.

I continued as though she hadn't uttered a word, ",…and I've decided to stay…,for awhile…,probably a year. Maybe longer."

"Humph. Well, there's no use in your trying to get on here with a Minnesota license. You need to be registered in Colorado to work in *this* hospital." She began assembling the headphones, "Come back when you have a valid Colorado license."

I started to protest. I knew that couldn't be true. Most hospitals only ask to see your current license and know you've applied for licensure in the state where you're seeking employment. I knew I was right, but the earphones were back on her head, her fingers already skipping over the keyboard, keys hitting the paper rhythmically.

I shrugged. For all I knew, Randall had already talked to these people. Damn and damn. I swallowed my pride and went back to the pickup to drive to his office. It was a little early, but his office had chairs to wait in.

The McClean Law Firm door was open, so I quietly walked into the office and sat down. In a back room, Randall's voice rumbled with intermittent pauses. On the phone again, I guessed. This went on and on while I studied book titles without moving from my chair. There was still a gap where he had moved books to reach the key he'd given me. What could it hurt if I felt around just to see if there were other keys. It was an easy reach; being five ten had its advantages. Nothing there, but I slid several books at a time, closing one gap and opening another. Nearly to the end of the shelf, I felt a cord with keys tied at intervals and pulled them out. A luggage tag with 'Sapphira Domino' printed on it was strung on the cord. A smaller tag on each key identified the doors it opened.

"How did you find those? I've looked everywhere."

It wasn't clear whether Randall was angry or curious. "I thought whoever hid the front door key, your father I guess, hid others in similar places and I got lucky."

"Good for you. They're yours, of course. I'd have given them to you right away, but I didn't know where they were." He was straightening his desk, shutting drawers, and turning out lights. "What say we go to lunch?"

Dropping the keys into my bag, I watched him shrug into a suit coat and lead the way to the door, which he held open. That's all? No surprise that I'd search his premises without permission? Go figure, I thought.

"No reason to take both cars," he said eyeing Bertha with a frown, "we'll take mine."

"Sure," I said.

We got into a very nice midnight blue BMW. His I wondered? "You have a very nice car."

"It's Dad's. They took Mother's for their trip."

"She has a BMW too?"

"Mother has a van. More room for luggage and souvenir stuff she'll bring back."

"I'm sure that's true," I said, "but you were driving your car, when you stopped to help on that pass? Same as this one."

"Yes. But Dad's is a newer model," he answered.

Since he didn't seem to mind my questions, I blundered on, "Is your mother's van midnight blue too?"

"No." He turned and smiled at me, "No, her van is more a silver gray, sometimes looks blue though."

He guided the car to the edge of town, which wasn't far, and pulled into a parking place at a restaurant called 'The Pines.' Built of natural wood and stone, it nestled among trees that grew along a river.

"Is this the same river that forms a boundary for the park I saw as I drove into town?" What I'd done was sleep in the park, but Randall needn't know that.

"Yes it is. That's very good of you to notice."

Oh pa-leaze, I thought.

While we waited for a table, an older man paid his tab and was about to exit when he saw us, "Randy," he said, "good to see you. Miss your Dad. How's he getting on? Any improvement?"

"Mother calls nearly every day. She's very optimistic, says he's making great progress. Thinks they'll be home soon."

"Good. Good. Still paralyzed?" The man was taller than the tall Randall, his hair a bristly shrub of gray, cut a close inch from his scalp. His dark brown eyes were a little too close together over a hooked nose.

Randall's cheeks were pink as he shot me an embarrassed glance. "Mother reports he's much improved."

"Glad to hear it," the man said as he opened the door. "Good day to you, young lady. Big place in this community for you to fill." Then he was out the door without waiting for an introduction to me or me to him. He was impeccably dressed in a tailored cowboy suit, but looked more like a gentleman cowboy, than a working one. What a rude dude, I thought watching him leave.

Our table was next to a window overlooking a gully filled with birch trees growing along a river, which shot over a tumble of rocks.

Randall opened a menu and handed it to me, "Their pan fried trout is excellent, but so is most everything on the menu if you don't like fish."

"We have fish in Minnesota, too. And I do like it."

"You'll have the trout then?" When I nodded, he ordered trout for both of us and a bottle of chardonnay.

The long silence thundered. He hadn't been honest about his dad, and I resented it, but in a way I understood. Figuring it was no one's business, I told very few that my father was comatose in a nursing home. Randall might very well feel the same.

"Look," I said at the same time he said, "I know…, "

"Please," I said firmly, "I'm sorry your father's ill and I know how difficult it is for you."

"Thank you," he said, pain in his dark blue eyes. "We, Mother and I that is, thought it was better not to tell you about Dad's sudden stroke. We thought you might lose confidence in our ability to execute the will."

Touched as I was by the grateful expression on his face, I thought he should have leveled with me from the beginning. "But I'm not sorry I found out. It explains so much."

"Explains? What?"

"That you are executing a will you hadn't written and weren't privy to the reasons behind it," I said.

"That's what we feared, but that's not entirely the case." He pushed his disheveled hair back. "I was doing the leg work, finding out your name, and all that. There's much I do know."

"And a lot you don't." In moody silence, I stared out at the birch trees and the sparkling water splashing over rocks beside them.

Finally, "You ever see aspens before?"

"Aspens?" I asked. "Oh, you mean the trees? Sure. They're birch trees."

"They may be birch trees in Minnesota, but in Colorado they're aspens. We're pretty famous for them."

I commented, "Famous for trees? Well, why not."

"So what is it you think I don't know?" He asked.

"Well, don't know or aren't telling me. Like who is Antonio's nephew? This Anthony Paul P. S. Is his last name Domino or Paul, and is he maybe a grandson of Uncle Antonio's sister? If not, how exactly is he related to Aunt Sapphira? Where is he now? Is he the one Aunt Sapphira was afraid of? Or is there someone else?"

I refused to be treated like an incompetent twit. I'd been in charge of my life for over six years..., ever since Mom was killed. I'd earned respect and if this son-of-a-lawyer needed reminding, I could do that too.

"Antonio Domino was your uncle's name," Randall answered, "The great-nephew is Anthony Paul, P.S. Or so it states in the will."

Then I understood, "Is your father's speech impaired too?"

Our wine was served and Randall poured some for us both and sipped a little before answering. "It's true Dad hasn't regained his speech, and becomes very agitated when we ask him to write answers. But I'm trying to locate the nephew, in case sometime in the future he needs to be contacted."

"That's if I don't find the valuables and money, and can't maintain the property? Right?"

"Partially, but also as a suspect in Mrs. Domino's murder, as far fetched as that may be."

"I'll admit it would be nice if you had a viable suspect in case I get shot."

"Look Nika, can't you let me do the worrying for you?"

"No, I can't. When I trust someone else, they always let me down. It's not going to happen this time. Dying of a bullet wound is not in my plans."

The waitress brought our food, and we ate in silence, until Randall said, "You've met Juana and Sergio Sanchez?"

Sure, change the subject, I thought. "Yes, they're wonderful."

"Aren't they? Has Juana cooked you a meal?"

I swallowed a bite of fish and followed it with wine. "This is very good," I said, "the wine too. And yes, I've met the Sanchez' and yes, Juana has cooked me a couple of wonderful meals."

"They're fine people," Randall said.

"I agree and their dog is something else. I've never seen a dog like that before."

"She's a mix." Randall became enthusiastic at the lighter conversation. "Mostly Dingo, the vet said. The Sanchez found her in a ditch, badly beaten, near death. They carried her home and nursed her back to health. She's been there ever since."

Perro was a she? You could fool me. How was I to know, Sergio called her him, and I hadn't *looked*. "She looks like a deer. The right color, white chest, white rump, but a curly tail? The Sanchez bring her into the house. I think Aunt Sapphira didn't approve of that, but Sergio indicated Perro would have saved my aunt if she'd liked her. So, I'm trying to be friendly."

Randall watched me with steady, sapphire blue eyes. Naturally, he enjoyed talking about something besides his culpability, and I could ease up on him temporarily. He seemed to be truly interested and was smiling, the kind of warm sincere grin that was meant to be disarming,...and was. I'd have to watch myself around this guy. I didn't plan on being shot and I sure didn't plan on falling for some lawyer or anyone else in the near future.

"Good for you," he said, "getting along well with the Sanchez' and their dog is great."

"No thanks," I said when he offered me more wine. "I am making a job application. Don't want to smell of too much wine."

"Another wise move. It'll be a pleasure to represent you," Randall said.

Stuffy, stuffy! You'd think he was ninety. Maybe I'd already had too much wine, but he had such an attitude, "Represent me is one thing, but organizing and planning my life is another."

"I'm not doing that," Randall said.

"Yes you are. For example, making me an appointment today. I could do that myself, you know."

"I just thought, you didn't know anyone in town, you needed a job. And I could help." Randall's excuses made a long list.

When I didn't answer, he said, "I'm sorry. Truly. I only wanted to help."

"Apology accepted. Don't do it again."

It was a relief when, our lunch finished, he took me back to Bertha and I drove to the nursing home.

Magdalena Nursing Home looked new. It was designed with twin wings, which angled away from the central building. A nursery truck was parked in the middle of the unpaved parking lot. Workmen were planting spindly trees and leafless shrubs in lumpy tan colored soil. I parked Bertha where I thought she'd be out of the workmen's way and entered the lobby. It was carpeted from wall to wall in thick, beige Berber carpet, and furnished with several groupings of chairs suitable for visitors. There was no receptionist, so I went to the back wall where the frame of a door sported a doorbell under a card that said ring for service.

I did and waited. I rang again. When no one came, I pushed open the door and entered a central hall. Here the carpet was forgotten in favor of terrazzo. The door of an elevator at the back was locked open, and the odor of antiseptic soap clued anyone interested that it had just been scrubbed. Next to the elevator, a stairway led down to a lower level. There were four doors to the left of the elevator labeled, *Occupational Therapy* and *Activities Director*, *Social Services* and *Administrator*.

Randall hadn't said whom I was to see, just apply at the nursing home, but the administrator was a good bet. I walked across the hall and knocked on the door, waiting until I heard a gravely voice, female I thought, shout "Come in."

I did as bidden and walked into a room with an empty chair behind an empty desk on which sat a covered computer. A door at the back was partly ajar allowing cigarette smoke to drift out. Well, I could stand here and wait until the smoker called me back or I could rap on the door. I opted for the latter and an exasperated voice croaked, "Come on in."

I did as told.

The woman behind the desk had tawny golden hair done in a low bun at the back of her neck. There were two piles of manila folders on her desk. As I watched, she closed the one she was reading and put it on the smaller pile to her right plunking down a jagged reddish rock on top, before opening another folder on the pile to her left. Her hands were square with short square fingers and bright red painted nails clipped square across the ends.

"Well, what do you want?" She spoke with a cigarette bobbing up and down between her lips, which were painted to match her fingernails. As I watched, a long ash fell from the end of the cigarette and littered the front of her red plaid jacket. "Well," she repeated finally focusing on me through tortoise shell glasses, "are you looking for someone?" Her eyes were a startling amber with gold flecks. Stress had left a furrow between dark eyebrows. Clearly, I was an unwanted distraction. "Unless…, are you applying for the secretarial opening? I'm sorry, I've just been so busy with all of this…." She waved her hands indicating the piles of files. "Can you start today?"

"I'm Nika McGuinness. Randall McClean called me to say I had a two thirty appointment to apply for a job here as an RN. There's no one out in front, and he didn't say who I was to see."

Was it 'who' or 'whom' and why couldn't I ever remember?

"Oh well, I live in hopes. Don't we all? You're to see me. You start tonight. I'll call someone to show you around."

I gulped. Nights? I hated nights. "Well, I'd rather work a day shift. Randall said the nursing home was new, so surely you have some kind of a day opening. Anything."

"Wouldn't everyone! But nights are all I have. I understood that you'd take anything I had to offer. If that's not the case,…" She shrugged her shoulders and stubbed out her cigarette in an ashtray already overflowing.

Ah gee, Randall had agreed to a night job for me? And he claims to be representing *my* best interests? Well, I am desperate and I have little choice.

"Yes, that's okay, I guess. It's that I don't sleep well during the daytime and I'm just getting over pneumonia and I thought…,hoped actually, I could get something on days."

She pulled out a drawer, "Here's the forms for you to fill out. You can use the desk in the outer office and just leave them there. I'll call someone to show you around." She lit another cigarette as she began studying another file.

Well, maybe I wasn't a secretary and maybe I wasn't important, but she was downright rude and I was sick of it. Keeping my voice low and words measured to contain my fury, I said, "Excuse me." When she neither looked up nor spoke, I said, "Will you look at me? I have some questions. How much will I earn? How many hours will I work each week? Will I get paid vacation? Holidays? If I'm to work nights, what time do I report for duty? And if I'm asked, who the hell do I say hired me? Or should I be seeing someone else?"

Chapter Seven

Instead of kicking me out as I expected, she laid down the folder, and took off her glasses to reveal large amber eyes rimmed with black eye liner. Her brows were black and slanted up at the outer edges, but there her Cleopatra look ended, because her tawny hair was winged up on both sides of her head. Then it hit me, her resemblance to a cat was incredible, and she stared at me unblinkingly, as though ready to pounce.

For a moment I felt dizzy. To steady myself, I put my hands palm down on the desk and glared back. This hard-assed woman was not going to spook me, not if my thundering heart would cooperate. "Is this a nursing home or a mental hospital?"

She gave me the kind of long hard look I'd only read about. I was thinking, oops, I just lost my one and only job.

So, did I care? Well, no. I turned toward the door to leave. She didn't care if I worked here, so fine. Neither did I. I'd chuck the whole thing, ranch, money, and mansion…, the works. Who needed it? It was just too much trouble, with no guarantee I'd get anything when the dust settled, except lots of effort and no reward. The story of my life, exactly twenty-three years, this month. I'd pushed the door all the way open when I heard a chuckle behind me.

"Hey, wait a minute. Yes, this is a nursing home."

I whirled around intending to look as angry as I felt, but my heel slipped and my ankle turned under lowering me two inches on the left side. I corrected my foot, but had lost any advantage I might have gained along with my dignity.

The pain must have shown in my face, because she didn't look amused, but rose quickly, scooped the files off a chair and dragged it around to my side of the desk. "Sit," she commanded, returning to her seat. I sat.

"My degree is in hospital administration earned at the University of Nebraska. This is my third job. The others were worse than this, if you can believe?" She lit another cigarette, drew deeply, and exhaled a long uninterrupted ribbon of smoke. "Could I ever use someone like you. This place is a disaster. We've been opened two weeks, have a total of seventy beds, have admitted forty-five patients and still have over a hundred applicants to review. All are relatives of local people who want their *greats* close by. It's chaos."

"Sorry. I can't help you with all of that. I'm an RN."

"Want to apply for one of the other positions? Are you computer literate? We've got one out there and another in here. No one to install all this information, and I sure don't have time. If you want it, the job's yours. Money's no problem. We're endowed up to kazoo! Some local woman, a Mrs. Domino, set the whole thing up and then got herself murdered. Can you believe? Would you at least try it?"

Aunt Sapphira did all this? My aunt was an incredible woman. "Yes, I'm able to operate a computer, but I'm an RN. I can't help you." After all, I had problems of my own.

"Yeah, well. Too bad for me." She fished around in her drawer and came up with a second set of forms. "Here fill these out, use the desk out there, as you can see there isn't a spare surface anywhere in here. I'll call someone to tour you around."

"Excuse me," I said, "I'm at a disadvantage here. Could you tell me who you are? I mean, you know I'm Nika McGuinness, but I haven't a clue who I'm talking to."

Then she began to emit large guffaws of deep down throaty laughs. I watched her, wondering again if I'd wandered into a mental hospital by mistake.

She grabbed some tissues from a box on her desk, wiped her eyes smearing mascara and eyeliner. She shook her head. "You know, I'm considered a formidable person; no one, but no one talks back to me. Hell fire, I'm an administrator. I get paid to be formidable." She shook her head again.

The air was fogged with smoke. I began to cough. Finally I choked out the words, "What's formidable is that cigarette you're smoking. It'll kill you and anyone working near you. If I were qualified, I wouldn't touch a job in your office. Now tell me, do you have a name?"

She stubbed out the cigarette, "Ah,...sorry. My name is L.L. Eugenio. You start tonight. The hours, salary and benefits are in the booklet. It's yours." Her tone was serious, but her eyes were golden sparks of mischief. "You're pretty formidable yourself. Know that?" She was shaking with laughter.

This is a laughing matter? I defended my position, "It's just that I can't believe anyone in the health care industry hasn't heard that smoking is perilous to *your* health and the health of *those around* you. Well, I'll just fill the forms out. Don't want to keep my tour guide waiting."

"Just close the door after you," she called out in drill sergeant tones. "Ah..., if you please." As I closed the door, I could hear her throaty laughter.

Thankful the cushy chair behind the desk wasn't occupied, I sank into it. Standing was out of the question, because my ankle had begun to throb and the pain migrated to my head. I held my head in my hands and I wished the ache away. This may be a nursing home, I thought, but that yellow-eyed witch is nuts. I would try the job for a month, no longer. I should be able to get my Colorado license by then and get a job in a real hospital.

I filled out the forms and detached my copy, which I folded and tucked into my purse just as the outer door opened and a plump-bodied woman entered. "Hi. I'm Rosie. The boss wants me to show you around."

"Sure," I said. I laid the papers in a neat pile and started around the desk slipping and sliding all the way.

"Why don't you take those heels off and carry them? This floor is murder unless you wear rubber soled shoes."

I did as she suggested, carrying my shoes like a husband sneaking up the stairs after a late night out. Her round face was crowned with snowy hair, pouffed out around a bun on top of her head. Her white hair was premature, I thought, as her face was pink cheeked, wrinkle free, and her eyes were a lively dark blue.

We stopped outside the Administrator's door, "My name is Rosie Beneditto. Did I already tell you that?" She didn't wait for me to answer, "I'm an RN, night supervisor at Loopys, but Ells pleaded for help and she's a friend of my boss so I got loaned out. I work at Loopys, but I'll sometimes come in on days -depending on if they need help."

"Loopys is the hospital?" I asked and when she nodded I asked, "And Ells is?"

"L.L.Eugenio. You know, the Administrator who just hired you," Rosie said.

"Oh. You call her Ells. I see." Ells was not a terribly respectful name and I wondered who thought Ms. Eugenio was formidable. On the other hand, Ell rhymed with Hell.

Rosie stopped at a linen room and brought out a pair of stretch-knit booties, the kind they give patients in the hospital. "Here, put these on so you don't go skidding around."

While I was pulling them on, I asked, "You don't seem to resent floating between the hospital and the nursing home."

Rosie gave a jolly laugh that shook her barrel shaped torso, "Naw, I'm paid the same rate as I get at the hospital and we're not too busy there. Our hectic season begins with hunting and then skiing. You know, bullets and arrows gone astray and skis that ram tree trunks."

"Oh sure, I see," I said. We were still standing at the linen room door, which was located across from the elevator. It was more or less central and shared by both wings.

She led me down one of two corridors that angled away from the central hall. When we arrived at the nurses' station she said, "We're not full here yet, but busy. This wing has thirty beds and a hospice unit of five private rooms at the end. Some of the equipment still isn't here, but we're catching up. We're short bedpans and hospital gowns right now, although we manage well enough since so many beds are empty."

We were walking in front of the nurses' station, which was on a continuation of the central hall and faced the long corridor of patient rooms. A raised counter hid all but the bent heads of nurses who sat making notes on patients' charts. Drawn up to the desk between two nurses was a wheeled cart where the charts hung. It could be wheeled along by the nurse making rounds, I knew, except at night, when the noise might wake patients. There was also a medication cart, with drawers for each patient and a stainless steel dispensing tray that resembled a small muffin tin.

Rosie led me to the back of the nurses' station into a large room that she called a treatment-drug room. The smell of strong coffee suggested no one had had time to make fresh coffee, since early morning. Floor length windows and a broad glass door opened off the nurses' station and gave a clear view of the whole corridor. A full size refrigerator stood in a break in the counter to the right. The counter extended along three walls, and at the back, above the counter, a pair of broad windows looked down one story on the parking lot.

We began walking down the corridor toward the end, which, widened into a day room. It was furnished with a TV, a couple of chairs and tray tables. Several patients were sitting listlessly in wheel chairs, heads down, in no way enjoying the view of the trees that climbed the hills just beyond the front lawn and visitors' parking area. Although I realized the patients on this wing were more dependent than those on the other wing, it was depressing to watch the total lack of interest I saw on these down-turned faces.

Rosie noticed I was looking out the windows. "I don't know where you parked today, but employee parking is down in back. There's an entrance though the basement. You can either come up the stairs or the elevator."

"These stairs?" I asked, indicating a door next to the day room, with a glowing 'EXIT' above it.

"There's a stairway next to the elevator in the center hall. This is an evacuation stairway. It's one reason we have only five private rooms here. The stairs were built extra wide, so one person could help two patients exit in case of emergency. Fire or flood, I suppose."

I lowered my voice, "These patients don't seem able to negotiate stairs."

"Good point," Rosie said, "and I agree. It's something about the building code for any patient care facility."

"I think I'd get them out to the main lobby," and as I said it, I knew one person could not save thirty wheel chair patients.

Rosie gestured toward the nurses' station. "The sicker patients are on this corridor. All are double rooms except these five at the end, the hospice rooms."

"Hospice patients? Terminally ill with what?" I asked.

"We're licensed to accept cancer, Alzheimer's, and any other terminal disease you can think of. Personally, I don't think five is enough beds. You'll be stationed on this side because of complications that could occur with any of the terminal patients, but you'll be responsible for the other wing as well."

She continued, "The room numbers on this wing start to the left of the nurses' station, with Molly's room, and continue consecutively around the end and back to the nurses station. We call the patients by their first names or nick-names, never Granddad or Mom. Unless they ask us to."

"Yes," I said, "I learned that when I worked one summer in a nursing home." I added, "That was back in high school." I was watching a tiny hunched man make his way down the hall, by grasping chrome railings that were fastened along both sides of the corridor.

When he reached us, he leaned way back to look up into my face, smiled a big toothless grin, and said, "Will you marry me? My kids are grown, I don't have any pets you'd have to wait on, and I own all of this." He waved his arm around to encompass the whole hall, teetering out of balance at an alarming angle.

I reached out both hands to steady him as Rosie said, "Come on Dad, you're already married. You want to be a bigamist? Now come along and I'll help you into bed for your nap."

"I'm not your dad," he snapped.

We lifted him onto his bed, pulled his slippers off, and covered him with a crocheted afghan. "You said you were this morning."

"Changed my mind."

We toured the other wing, a mirror duplicate of the first one, which Rosie said had only fifteen patients as of now.

I tried to look nonchalant, "Who works this wing."

"Not to worry, you'll have a first rate orderly. His name is Rocky Ostrum. I've worked some nights with him, he's good. Been trained, but I don't remember where."

Rosie was a well of information. She directed me to a store where I could buy white jeans and T-shirts and said the home furnished lab coats. For shoes she suggested I get white sneakers, "They're as good as anything else, and by the way, if you're short of cash either store will charge until pay day."

I noticed she wore white gabardine pants and a white T as well as sneakers, and I guessed she must meet the dress code.

"I can't think of anything else you need to know. You better be off to get some shut-eye so you can be wide awake tonight."

* * * * * *

I stopped at a women's wear store and bought two pairs of white gabardine slacks, four T-shirts that were nicer than the kind I'd ordinarily wear to hang out. They charged my purchases without question. Next-door was the shoe store Rosie had told me about. I bought a pair of white leather sport shoes that made my feet look like freighters, but cost less, so the salesman assured me, than sneakers and wore better. Also picked out several pair of white socks in case it took me days to find the courage to tour Aunt Sapphira's basement hunting up a washer.

The salesman was cute. He had blond curly hair and a beard to match. He also had the most intense green eyes I'd ever seen. Nice voice too. He asked, "Where you from?"

"Minneapolis."

"Minnesota?"

When I nodded, he said, "You'll like this country. We have lots of snow in the winter, but it's not cold like Minnesota."

"How do you know?"

"My folks moved out here from Mankato, because Dad has asthma. The air's really good here. You got a place to stay? My folks run a Bed and Breakfast, and I know they'd give you weekly rates until you get settled."

I said, "I'm staying at my aunt's house, north of town."

"Oh wow. Sapphira Domino? That rich woman who got herself murdered?"

"The same." Everyone in town knew about that. This could get tiresome.

"Are all the things you hear about that place true?"

"Like what things?" I asked.

"It's rumored that people, men, I think, used to drive through town in long black limos and never drive back out. People say ole Tony shot 'em and buried 'em in that ole mine out there."

"Well, I haven't heard anything like that," I said. What had I gotten into? "Sounds more like Halloween stories to scare kids than anything else."

"Come to think about it, you never hear those stories until around Halloween. Hey, know what? I've got a small band and we play for 'events'. That house out there has a ballroom, right?"

"Yeah. Right." I was trying to leave, but he kept tagging along.

"Tell you what, I'll make you a deal. We'll play for nothing for your first party. Just for the chance to have a gig in that ballroom. They say it's awesome."

"Well, that's very nice of you, but I haven't met enough people yet to give a party." I had the door open and was about to walk out. "Nice to meet you, and thanks for everything."

"Hey, just a minute. I almost forgot, I got something for you." He raced back to the cash register and hurried back extending his hand, "Here, this is for you. It's a give-away. The promotion's over, but we have some left. Take it. You can never tell when it'll come in handy." He handed me several small white flashlights along with a business card. "And this has my name and number when you decide you want to take me up on that party. Don't forget."

According to the card his name was Jamie Ferguson, "Fine Jamie, I'll remember that."

His eyes pleaded with me and I knew he wanted a commitment from me, but my ankle had begun to ache, "I'll sure keep you in mind," I said and headed for old Bertha, and the drive back to the mansion.

I stopped at a pet store to buy Perro some dog biscuits. I'd promised him,…'er her,…hadn't I? When I got home, I put Jamie's card in the telephone table drawer in the kitchen. I laid out the clothes I'd wear tonight and hung the rest in the nearly empty closet. It was four and I had to be at the nursing home by ten. I slid off shoes, jeans and sweater before crawling into the bed. I never could sleep during the day, but I had to try, I thought snuggling down under the comforter and pulling the extra pillow over my head to shut out noise. I was too exhausted to get back out of bed and check the locks on the doors.

Chapter Eight

I woke up facing the glowing red numbers of the clock radio on the bedside table that seemed to be saying it was five thirty. I heard muffled voices, of two or maybe three people, rising and falling somewhere in the distance. They were having some kind of discussion that occasionally turned argumentative.

I turned over and rubbed my eyes. Sunshine was poking around the edges of drapes that were splashed with flowers in shaded burgundy. Oh yeah. I was not in our bedroom in Minneapolis, but in Aunt Sapphira's guest room in Colorado. And, ah gee, I had to start work tonight. Damn! Damn and damn!

Reluctant to get up, I lay trying to identify the speakers. One was a man, I was sure. Then a rapid jumble of Spanish identified Juana, but there was another one. Another man, not Sergio. Who were the two men? Who had let them in? Then I remembered. I hadn't locked the doors before lying down.

I threw back the covers, and stumbled into the bathroom where I ran cold water into the sink and splashed it on my face. Cripes, this house was like a bus station. Anyone who wanted to could enter. Had Juana let a bunch of guys in without my permission? I'd have to lay down some rules.

I dragged my last clean pair of sweats from the duffel bag. These were oatmeal gray, decorated with splotches of paint left over from a decorating binge of Kassi's. Her contribution was wanting our bedroom to look more cheerful and choosing the paint. I did the painting. I padded barefoot down the thick-carpeted hall toward voices coming from the kitchen. A twinge of pain darted up my left ankle, reminding me that I'd twisted it.

Randall sat on the leather couch in the sunken level. Juana was at the stove stirring something that smelled heavenly. A homey scene, spoiled by a red faced man standing just inside the patio door, his plump left hand holding papers. His right hand was clenched in a generous fist he shook at Randall. He wore blue coveralls with 'Bud' embroidered on his pocket. At the sight of me, his mouth dropped open sagging his several chins into facsimiles of smiles. He looked like a clown, his rotund body stretching the coveralls to the maximum, his tufts of bright red hair standing at attention.

Surprise modified the fury on his face, as anger suppressed my laughter. I'd laugh later. Maybe.

"I guess there's an explanation for the racket, entering my house without invitation and invading my privacy."

I stood on the upper level with Juana. I had the advantage of two steps up that required both men to look up at me. I said, "I'll hear you first, Randall," with exactly the same tone and inflection my fifth grade teacher used when she caught me whispering to the cute boy next to me.

Randall looked grave, "I stopped by to give you some papers. This is Bud from Magdalena Car Sales."

I'd deal with Randall later, but what was a garage man doing here? "And you?" I asked 'Bud.'

In spite of his awkward body, he took the two wide steps in one long leap and shoved the papers in my face, "Look, little Ms. Domino, you owe us big time, and we want what's coming to us."

Luckily, I'd raised my arm up to deflect whatever blow he aimed, because his saliva sprayed like water from a lawn sprinkler. I pushed him away and he stumbled backward down the steps and into the coffee table, which screeched across the tile floor.

Rescuing his mug of coffee, Randall quickly rose to his feet.

Juana put her arm around me, and threatened Bud with a spoon. "Go. Go." She took a step toward him and shook the spoon, which was dripping tomato sauce, in the direction of his face, "Go."

Eyeing her bulk, Bud retreated behind Randall.

Juana kept her arm around me and repeatedly called, "Sergio" until he appeared from the basement. He was holding a bottle of wine in one hand and three beers, separated by the fingers of his other hand. Perro bounded up the steps, flew between his legs with teeth bared, and the hair along her backbone straight up like a Mohawk cut. Sergio stumbled and would have fallen except for Randall's intervention. Bud put his fat hands up in surrender, but Juana wasn't finished. She continued in Spanish what had to be orders because as soon as Sergio deposited wine and beer safely on the wet bar, he marched up the steps and stood on my other side fiercely glaring at Bud, his hedge-like mustache quivering.

Barefoot, with paint smeared sweats, I couldn't look quite their patrona, but it was easy to be brave with two such loyal defenders. As sternly as possible, I said, "My name is Nika McGuinness, not Ms. Domino, and you can't collect money I don't owe. You've made a bunch of mistakes here, but I'll accept your apology and you can leave if you don't give us any more trouble."

I seriously wondered if Bud would explode with fury. He seemed to expand and his face got redder still as he tried to put his anger into words. Finally, "Why you little rich, lazy bbii…., some of us have to work for a living. You come out here and take over that wonderful woman's home and money and ignore…," His tirade slowed, but shaking his fist at me, he took two steps toward us and would have mounted the steps again, but Perro stood with front paws on his chest and growled saliva on his uniform.

Randall gripped Bud's arm. He spoke to Juana in Spanish before turning back to Bud, who reluctantly agreed to leave. Randall went with him, latching the patio door behind them.

Relieved, I let out a long breath before giving Juana and Sergio each a hug and saying, "Gracias" to them both.

"He bad hombre?" Sergio questioned, rolling the 'bre' on his tongue.

"He sure is a bad hombre," I agreed although the way I said hombre didn't sound nearly as evil as the way Sergio had.

By the time Randall returned, I was sitting with Sergio and Juana at the table sipping wine while they drank beer. Our dinner was simmering on the stove, and spicy aromas wafted our way. There were four places set at the table, one for Randall.

"Won't you join us," I said. Not a question actually, since I was certain the decision for him to eat with us had been made while I slept and before Bud came on the scene.

"Yes, thank you," he said taking a seat with an air of ownership and pouring himself a glass of wine.

I tried to regain the authority I'd momentarily had, but Randall seemed to be the Sanchez' fair-haired boy figuratively as well as literally. I set my Greek jaw and firmed my Irish temper, determined to change that. Eventually.

Juana rose to tend her cooking and called to Sergio for help. I said to Randall, "I assume Bud has made a mistake, and it's nothing I need to be concerned about."

He said, "Your aunt owed him money he wants to collect."

"Well, he can bill my aunt's attorney."

Juana served each of us a wonderful concoction of chicken and rice covered with green chili. The conversation, in Spanish of course, flowed around me while I ate without asking the questions still bumping around in my head. I must buy a book on Spanish. After I'd eaten Juana's powdered sugar coated puff, slathered with honey, I began questioning Randall.

"Why does Bud think I'll pay him money Aunt Sapphira owed?"

Randall glanced at me, but continued using his pastry to wipe up the last bit of honey before swallowing it.

What an annoying man! "Just because I am Sapphira's niece doesn't,…"

Randall held his hand up, "Nika, I'd have explained about the bill earlier, but this is the first I knew there was a problem. Bud is part owner of the Magdalena Sales and Service here. They'd not ordinarily go to this length to collect from an heir, but they've lost money recently, because they failed to expand their line in time to cash in on SUVs. The bill is for some service on a Reatta that Mrs. Domino bought from him several years ago. It comes to five hundred ninety dollars and he needs the money."

"But it's Sapphira's car and bill, not mine," I said.

"True. But it's yours as part of her estate that you've inherited. The car and the bill."

"He can have the car," I said.

"Not really. It's not yours to give him until you meet the terms of the will, which are,…"

"A rest, please. I know the terms of the will. I also know that five hundred and ninety dollars is a big repair bill for a new car. Is it a lemon?"

Randall handed me the bill, "It's all listed. Four new tires. Wash and wax, change oil, and storage."

I took the statement, glanced at it, "He can repossess it for the amount owed. I've got a car and I don't have five hundred and ninety bucks." Closing that subject, I looked at my watch, "It's nine. I've got to shower and change. I begin work tonight. Hope you don't mind my rushing off like this…,"

"Not in the least. We can meet for breakfast."

"That's necessary?"

"I have these papers to go over with you." When I hesitated, "This is information you need."

Juana had tidied the kitchen and gone home with Sergio, and after Randall left I made a pot of strong coffee to counteract the effects of the wine. I sipped it while I got ready. I knew I should have called Kassi, but it was ten in Minneapolis and she was still at work. I'd have to call her in the morning.

After checking the locks on all doors and windows, I switched on the outside light and looked about for anyone with a guitar. Not seeing anyone at all, I locked the front door after me, and descended the steps into a magical moonless night. The blue-black sky was so close I felt I could touch the huge stars hung like prisms. Their glow cast soft shadows on the mountains and dispelled my fear of last night's singer. I'd never be afraid of the night again, I thought as I started Bertha and headed down the road. How wrong I was.

A soft breeze blew crisp air through Bertha's open windows. Although I met no other cars, saw no one, my aloneness was comforting rather than frightening. Even after reaching the town itself, the air was clean. No exhaust fumes here, only a hint of pine smoke from someone's fireplace.

The front of the nursing home was dark, but several cars were parked in the back parking lot close to a well-lit entrance. I added mine. From here I could see that the building had two stories, and I wondered what was housed on the lower floor. I was early, but needed time to find a locker room or someplace to put my purse and jacket.

I'd already entered the door marked employees when I realized this was the basement. I hate basements. They house mice, rats, and spiders, and are not fit places for humans. If the locker room were down here, I'd take my stuff upstairs to the nursing unit and find an empty chair or something.

Across from the entrance, a door had STAIRS lettered on it. I hurried the fourteen feet or more to the door, dragged it open and climbed the steps to the central hall next to the administration offices, dark at this time of night. I was pleased at being a half hour early for the shift change.

A nurse sat at the desk, writing on a stack of charts. I put my purse on the desk and hung the jacket on the chair back.

The nurse looked up, "Hi. I'm Billy, and you're Nika?"

I nodded.

"Just finishing up here. Grab a cup of coffee from the back and I'll give you report."

The next fifteen minutes were a confusion of patient names, room numbers, and an introduction to the LPN, Sarah, who worked with Billy on the relief shift. An RN named Jane had gone home to care for a feverish child. Billy used a cardex to give me her jet-propelled report. When they left at ten forty, the only things I remembered was that Molly in the first room down from the desk, had been restless and I had no meds to give, because they were always given by the day and relief shifts.

I read through the cardex, which was a contraption that held five by eight lined cards, one for each patient, with diagnoses, medications, and level of activity orders. Each card was slipped into a holder that laid fan-folded flat, one on top of the other with just the room number and name showing at the bottom. I decided to use it to make rounds of the patients. I found a note pad in a drawer and tore off a sheet for each patient, slipping one into each slot. I intended to make notes as I made rounds, I'd worked with an RN who did that.

Skipping the empty private rooms, I began at the far end, zigzagging back and forth across the hall. Including the man who had proposed to me that afternoon. A few of the patients were sleeping comfortably, but the others were lying awake, their sheets twisted, an odor of urine permeating the room. They were grateful to see me, saying they thought I'd forgotten them and gone home. Had no one checked them on the relief shift?

I bathed them, rubbed their backs and buttocks with lotion and changed damp sheets and smelly gowns. Once, as I was dumping soiled linen down a laundry chute, I thought I saw someone at the far end going from one private room to another. It was just the shadow of legs and what looked like a guitar crossing the windows. And a cowboy hat? My heart jumped, skipping a beat. I couldn't tolerate this. I hurried down the hall, heart thudding, and swung open the door of the empty room the man had entered just moments before. Flipping on the lights I said with as much severity as possible, "Okay. I know you're in here. You have to leave." There was no movement, no response. There was no one in the bathroom, under the beds, or in the very small closets.

It must be one of the other rooms, I thought, so I searched every empty room, but found no one. Perhaps it was a reflection, maybe my own on the black windows at the end of the corridor.

I retraced my steps and began the washing, back care routine I'd started. With three down and seven to go, I decided grimly that this was going to be a long night, very long indeed. However, the door pushed open and in walked a white clad guy.

"Rocky Ostrum, need some help?" he asked.

His teeth were white and even, his smile was nice, and he had bright red hair cut conservatively, hazel eyes, and freckles. It was hard to tell how old he was; he could be seventeen or thirty.

"Do I ever. It looks like most of the patients were never cleaned up for the night."

"Figures. The evening shift was manned by the team from outer mars." Rocky was deftly changing the gown and linen of the in the next bed.

"Mars?"

"Yeah. Or Krypton."

"Krypton?" I said.

"Sure. You know, where Superman came from. That crew must be able to see through walls, because they never enter a room, just use their x-ray vision to check out patients." He cocked an eyebrow, "If you're going to retain your sanity, you're going to have to read the comics. Like really."

Like really? Subtract ten years. Maybe twenty.

By the time we got to Molly, she was awake and restless. We repeated the same routine, washing, changing linen and gown, and using lotion to rub her back.

All the time we worked with her, Molly talked to us, "I worried you'd left me all alone"

I tried to reassure her, "We'll never leave you, Molly."

"I haven't seen my love in such a long time," she said sadly.

I plumped her pillow and slid it under her head. "I'm sorry about that."

"You're new. I've never seen you play blackjack. Not ever." Rocky was waggling his eyebrows at me. He waved his hands like wings and mouthed, 'out in the ozone.'

I couldn't suppress my laughter.

"Did I say something funny?" Molly asked. "My husband, that's him in the picture with me, always said I did that and never realized it. Imagine." Her voice grew slurred, her eyelids closed. When her breathing became regular, I knew she slept.

Not for long, though, as soon as we left the room with soiled linen to put in the laundry, I heard her plaintive cry, "Please don't leave me. No one's ever nice to me, anymore."

Rocky and I had a hasty conference, "I promise to report the poor care to the day shift, Rocky," I said, "but I have to go back and comfort Molly now."

Rocky saluted and said in a whisper, "Like absolutely."

I sat down in the rocking chair next to Molly's bed, "I'll stay with you a little while, Molly. Is this your husband?" I asked holding up the silver framed portrait of a bride and groom.

"Let me see," she said. "Yes, and wasn't he a handsome man. There's another one in that drawer over there."

I found a framed snapshot of the same couple, a little older and standing in front of a car. "Is this it Molly?" I asked, holding the picture out to her.

"Yes. That was taken on our way out here. I think it was 1960. Our car was nearly new. It was a beauty."

Molly's eyes closed and when the picture slipped from her hands, I placed it next to the other one on the bedside table. She was immediately awake.

"How can I be sure you'll stay with me?"

"I give you my word," I said taking her hand.

I'm lonesome for my love, he doesn't come to visit anymore."

After awhile, my presence soothed her and she slept, but like a cranky child, as soon as I stood to go, she woke and started her rambling talk again. I began rocking the chair to the rhythm of gentle music and soft singing. Rocky must have a radio.

I didn't realize the night was over until a hand shaking my shoulder brought me out of a sound sleep. "Miss McGuinness, it's five thirty and the day shift will be here in an hour!"

I opened my eyes and looked up at the red haired Rocky. I struggled out of the rocking chair, and glanced at Molly, who seemed to be sleeping soundly. Once in the hall, I gave as sincere an apology as possible while standing on my swollen, aching ankle. It seemed that Rocky had watched his corridor as well as mine while I slept. If one of my patients pulled their light cord, it lit one on the panel at my desk and also on his. When the lights stayed on for several minutes, Rocky answered it for me. I owed him.

"Gees. Thanks. Oh, and Rocky did you bring in a radio? The music finally put Molly to sleep. Me too," I added sheepishly.

"No." He shook his head, "Mine's in for repairs. Want me to bring it when it's fixed?"

I almost said yes, but visions of music played at a high decibel stopped me. “No. No never mind Rocky. And thanks again.”

I managed to limp to the treatment room and make a fresh pot of coffee. I sipped a mug as I noted something on each chart. I drank the second one as I gave report to the day shift.

* * * * * * *

Next thing, I was standing on Main Street, supported by one hand on Bertha’s fender and staring at a gorgeous red sports car on display in a show room before I remembered that I’d forgotten to register a complaint about the evening shift.

“Damn and damn.” I’d half a mind to go back to the nursing home when a firm hand on my shoulder startled me.

A voice said, “A beauty isn’t it? It’s your car.”

Chapter Nine

I glanced up at Randall. "Yes. It's a beauty." Then pointing to the sign, 'In Towne Café, "Is this where we're to have breakfast?"

"Yup, unless you'd first like to check out your car. They made these just a couple of years. Only collectors have them now." He was beaming at the car, in that besotted kind of way men have.

Just like their fixation for curvaceous women, infatuation with cars was a guy thing I'd never understand. Why they spent lots of money on automotive magazines, lots of time waxing and polishing their latest acquisition, and then expected us women to be thrilled just to ride in one, was beyond my comprehension. I believed that a car was for transportation. Period.

"Look, I've been awake all night. The car may be part of my aunt's estate, but it's not mine and I see no reason to look at it. I'm here because you said you'd just found important papers, and I should have them. Otherwise, why don't I go home and get some sleep?"

"Sorry. Really! The cafe is open and the food is good. Let's eat before I show you the papers."

The aroma of frying bacon and coffee was more than I could resist, besides he had said he was sorry. I limped into the restaurant and sat down at the closest table. The waitress aimed her generous bosom like a slip covered freighter at our table, bumping into my chair. She giggled airily as she fussed over Randall and took his order before mine. She eyed me suspiciously, but when it was my turn, I ordered the number three special anyway.

Randall asked. "You were limping?"

"No kidding."

"Hurt yourself?"

"Twisted my ankle some." I answered in a tone meant to silence any more questions. My ankle was not his business.

The waitress brought us a thermal pot of coffee, and I no sooner drank a hot mug full, than our food arrived. I scarfed up hot-off-the-grill bacon, eggs and hash browns, while Randall forked in measured bites of his two-egg omelet filled with vegetables and made with yellow tinted egg whites. "Heart healthy," the motherly waitress had said, smiling. Some honest-to-goodness physical labor would take care of his heart, I thought.

Finally finished, Randall tried to pour more coffee into his mug, but I'd emptied the pot. He didn't have to ask for more because the waitress was there with another pot. She scowled at me, refilled his cup and told him how happy it made her that he ate all his breakfast. I nearly barfed.

"I guess you'd like to go over those papers I spoke about? There are two separate documents," he continued not waiting for my response, "or rather copies of two documents, that you should review. The first is called, *A Memorandum of Personal Property*."

"I see." I'd need more coffee to understand lawyer speak.

"A Memorandum Of Personal Property is an addition to the will, written to dispose of personal property. As long as the existence of such a document's in the will, it's legal and binding. It lists personal items that the deceased wishes to bequeath to a specific person or persons."

I picked up the sheet of paper. "I gather that as soon as you, " I emphasized the 'you,' "locate this person or persons they can have the personal items."

"It's not that simple."

Not that simple, huh? Why was I not surprised? "If you need a release from me, draw it up, I'll sign it."

Randall refilled my mug first and then his own. "You see, the will must be probated first."

"In that case, I fail to see why I'm sitting here listening to this."

"Because...,"

Was Randall at a loss for words? "Yes? You were saying?"

"Well, I realize you'd never participate in any illegal actions."

"You'd better believe it," I said, but thought, many more six hundred dollar bills like that car repair one, and I could be tempted. I asked, "What illegal actions?"

"Like selling some of the personal items before they are properly yours."

"Selling?" I asked, raising the one eyebrow again. "What an interesting idea."

"No. It's not interesting. It would be stealing. You'd be prosecuted and could serve time in prison."

I said, "I supported myself pretty well and made it through college without help from Aunt Sapphira when she was alive. I don't need or want her personal items now."

"Look," his hand firmly on my arm, "this is a bad time to discuss these papers. Why don't you take them home, get some sleep and then read them over?"

The man was good, no doubt of that. He asked questions that were, in reality, orders. I very nearly told him to shove the whole thing.

I picked up my purse to go, "I think I'll skip all of this and go back to Minneapolis. We have problems there, but nothing compared to what crops up every day here."

He put a detaining hand on my arm, "You are between the rubber and the road. The bills and problems are yours whether you're here or there, and it will be costly to manage everything from Minneapolis.

However, if that's what you wish, I'll do my best to hold down expenses."

"Yes, I imagine you will. Tell me, would those costs be charged to the estate or paid up front?"

Randall was thoughtful, "Well, I could charge my time to the estate, but day to day expenses will have to be paid as we go along."

I stood, "That's an interesting idea. I'll sleep on it, then call Kassi before deciding what to do."

Randall paid the tab and walked me out to Bertha. Before I drove off, he handed me a manila envelope holding the papers. "This was a bad idea to discuss business when you're so tired, but take a look at these after you've slept."

I took the papers, "O.K. By the way, I've forgotten where the post office is. Could you direct me again?"

He shut the pickup door, "Around the block. I doubt you'd have mail yet, maybe in the morning." He had an analytical way of watching me do everything, and winced along with me when I depressed the clutch with my left foot to shift. "You'd better do something about that ankle."

What an easy man to hate. Who knew more about the treatment of sprains, Randall or me? "It's just a slight sprain. You use a sprain, not bandage it."

"I was thinking along the lines of elevating it and applying ice," Randall had to shout above Bertha's engine noise. He frowned and shook his head, "You need a new car. Want me to look for one for you?"

"No. Bertha's sounded like this since I've had her and she hasn't died yet." He'd have to get used to it, unless of course, I did return to Minneapolis. "Well, thanks again for breakfast," I said backing out.

Ignoring his advice, I drove around the block and entered the post office. I found the box number without difficulty, opened it and pulled out the envelope. It was overnight mail, an envelope from Kassi with my Minnesota RN License. Bless her, for once she'd done something right.

I backed out and headed for home and sleep. All the way to Aunt Sapphira's house, I thought about how much more I'd like to be going home to our attic apartment, drab as it was. At least in Minneapolis, people were friendly, and glared only when I took their parking place. Only thing was, I had to earn some money and the E.R. job I'd been promised at City General didn't open up until September.

I tried the door before turning the key, and yes it was locked. I supposed most of Magdalena knew I worked last night, and although Randall had assured me this was the only key, how could I be sure? Once in, I shut the door and turned the lock. My clean, dry sneakers were parked under the dresser. My clothes were also clean and folded in a neat pile on the dresser. All Juana's work. Bless her. Under a flat, polished-stone paperweight, I saw the flight invoice I'd found in the garage apartment on top of the will. Bless Juana again.

I took off the whites I'd worked in last night and pulled on the paint stained sweats. Except for his allusion to 'my' car, Randall had said nothing about last night and Bud's visit. My ankle was badly swollen, but a good day's sleep would fix that. I checked the kitchen, patio and basement doors. All locked. Might as well crawl into bed and get warm. I felt chilly, the after effects of being up all night.

I'd had too much coffee and was pretty wired, so on second thought, I'd have a glass of milk out on the patio before going to bed. While I warmed up in the sun, I'd give a quick read of the papers Randall had said were so important.

Heading the inventory of furnishings, each bearing a number, was a statement that 'Photos tagged with matching numbers are in the file cabinet in the upstairs den.' The inventory went on for five pages. I'd skip reading the inventory until I had the pictures in hand, I thought as I flipped through the pages. However, the end of the last page I read, 'the key to the file cabinet is taped under the shelf in the master bedroom closet.' Now we were getting somewhere.

I fast-limped to the master bedroom and flung open the closet door, which turned on a light, just like the closet in my bedroom. Aunt Sapphira's dresses, slacks, and suits were carefully spaced along the rods in the walk-in closet. Even so, I had to push each hanger aside to look. I found the key at the far back corner where the shelves made a right angle. Not hard to find, but not in her purse or a desk drawer where a thief would probably look first. My aunt Sapphira was one smart lady.

Still energized by all the caffeine, did I think even once about sleeping for another night of rubbing backs and changing beds? Nope. From the decorative holder in the front hall, I chose a cane, the one with the snake's head carved in the handle, and without hesitation trekked upstairs.

The scent of mothballs was as strong as before, so I pulled the sweatshirt up over my mouth and nose. I went down the hall, opening bedroom doors and turning on lights as I went.

At the end of the central hall I stood looking at the door to what must be the den, waiting for the icy draft I'd felt before. If I doubted my courage to open the door then, how would I do it now? I retraced my steps back down the hall and would have descended the stairs except that I heard, "There's nothing to fear." Not spoken really, but felt by a burning place in my mind. It wasn't the words so much as the strongest feeling that I was loved and safe. So strong that I whispered the childish, "Mama, are you here? Oh Mama, I've always loved you. I thought you'd live forever, Mama."

My heart hammered and tears streaked my cheeks as I returned to the den and gently pressed against the door. Easily, it swung inward, to a welcoming room, where there was no mothball odor. South facing French doors could open on a broad balcony. Floor to ceiling windows dominated the western wall and opened on a breath taking view of hills rolling upward to distant snow capped peaks. The wall opposite the windows was covered with shelves filled with books interrupted only by the door where I was standing. An over-large walnut desk stood perpendicular to the windows. A cream leather pencil-holder, containing an assortment of pens and pencils sat at the left edge of a large matching leather frame, which held a desk-size blotter. A slim phone stood to the right. The opposite side angled across the windows to accommodate a computer, printer and scanner.

Aunt Sapphira could sit in either leather desk chair and gaze at the magnificent scenery to the west, or toward the balcony through the French doors in front of her, or swivel her chair to watch anyone approaching down the hall.

The computer was tempting, but would have to be plugged in before I could open any files on it. Besides, I must check any photos in the file cabinet. I'd check the computer later. The desk drawers were not locked and didn't qualify as a 'file' anyway. What I held was a key that unlocked a drawer in a *file* cabinet. Where was it?

I returned to the door and viewed the room again. The left side of the room was large and held lamps, and leather recliners next to the bookshelves. The right side of the room was shorter.

I studied the perfectly matched walnut paneling on the wall behind the desk. I moved to the opposite side of the room and eyed the wall. At first, I saw nothing, but by squinting, I could see the wood grain pattern changed at regular intervals. I limped back, concentrating on one spot, more clearly visible than the others. Partway up the wall, were two very shallow finger holds, and when I pulled, fan-folded doors swung open.

Inside, a liquor cabinet was between a selection of glassware, plates, and munchies. Another double door opened on a small sink and refrigerator. Wow! My aunt knew how to live!

On second glance, another fissure in the wall showed. It was an indented line in a discolored spot. I inserted the key, and the door swung open to reveal the file cabinet I was hunting. There were three file drawers. After checking each drawer for boxes of money and finding none, I opened the bottom file, which said, *Picture and Picture Records.*

I pulled out an accordion pleated file and took it to the desk. The first pocket of the file held a slim album labeled *Memorandum*. From each of the next two envelopes, I pulled out a file marked *Inventory* and an envelope marked *for my dear friend, Maureen*. Three sets of photos to match the Memorandum.

This could be a thirsty job, I thought, and opened the refrigerator to find something to drink. No cans of pop, but an assortment of other bottles. I decided against Bristol Cream and Marsala, however there was a clear liquid that smelled like licorice and was labeled *Ouzo*, a product of Greece. I poured a little into a glass, and after a taste, I added ice and topped off the small narrow glass. I carried the glass back to the desk and selected the memorandum list from the papers Randall had given me. The matching photo envelope contained pictures taken in the garage apartment. A page labeled living room focused on prints or maybe etchings. The dining room walls held watercolors. I turned to the typed list and read,

The Memorandum;

1) garage apartment, and all furnishings—Juana & Sergio
2) prints in apartment—McClean Law Firm

The list went on, but I stopped reading. There were no pictures on the apartment walls, only brighter rectangles in the faded wallpaper where pictures had once hung. Randall had warned me it was a felony to sell any of the mansion's furnishings, so had he or his father taken those prints?

I pulled open desk drawers and found a Magdalena phone book, lifted the receiver, and dialed his number. If we met for breakfast in the morning, I could ask him then, but I chose not to wait. Whoever took the prints might also have shot Aunt Sapphira. Randall answered on the first ring. "Randall, I have questions about the memorandum. Where are the prints from the garage apartment?"

"Is this Nika? Can I put you on hold? I have a client in my office and can't talk just now."

I heard music and fumed, this was only one kind of harassment businesses foisted on customers. Another was menu options from which you chose one in hopes a live operator answered. I took a pencil and tapped it on the desk, as someone changed the tape and the minutes seemed to tick by. "O.K., anytime like right now," I said but Randall didn't answer.

The glass of Ouzo was nearly empty when Randall said, "What pictures are you talking about?"

"The ones Aunt Sapphira left the McClean Law Firm in the Memorandum. There aren't any pictures in that apartment, only the shadows where they hung. I was all over that garage yesterday and any pictures, once there, are gone."

"Who was with you?"

So that was his plan. His word against mine. My elbow slipped tipping over the glass, "Damn and damn."

"Nika, have you been drinking?"

"Not really. I was thirsty and helped myself to a little Ouzo. Aunt Sapphira keeps it in her refrigerator."

"Nika, Ouzo's one of the most potent liquors in the world. And what are you doing up? You should be in bed. It's after two."

"After two." I parroted in my lovely low slurred voice. Hey I thought, that's pretty good, as good as Kassi any day.

"Go to bed, Nika. I'll meet you for breakfast in the morning." Randall hung up.

I tried to hang up my phone, but missed. "Naw, I'm not drunk. Tired maybe, but not drunk. I'd just replace the pictures in the envelope and put them in the file cabinet, which I'd then lock. All of a sudden, it seemed complicated. That's O.K., I'd just do everything very slowly. Very, very slowly. I finally locked the file and pocketed the key, only to find I'd left the envelope marked 'For Maureen' on the desktop.

I tried to balance it *and* the file key, but the envelope opened and pictures slid out into my hands. The first five or six were Polaroids and showed a slender middle-aged lady sitting in various rooms around the house and in the garage apartment. She was lovely, a smiling, rather grand-duchess-looking lady. She wore flowing dresses or severe slacks, her hair fanned in waves about her head. Most were taken in daylight although some were in pools of lamplight.

The only unique thing about them was they all showed a shadowy substance encircling her in a protective way. On the back of the first one was a note. "The ectoplasm," it said.

An ectoplasm? A ghost!

Ohmagod.

Chapter Ten

Juana urged me awake with a mug of strong coffee in one hand and another mug of her warm thick cocoa in the other.

I mumbled, "Gracias."

She returned a shy smile, gave me a quick hug, and went out the door sending Perro on his inspection trip.

Perro's nails clicking up the stairs reminded me to give thanks for her watchfulness. I drank the coffee and made it into the bathroom to swallow three aspirin with a giant glass of water. My equilibrium was out of sync and my hands were slow to cooperate. Heck, even my eyes didn't focus.

After a hot shower, I sat in the wing back chair and slowly drank the cocoa. Gradually my head cleared. Even my ankle was less swollen and painful. This stuff, I decided, should be available to the masses. Juana should patent it, she'd make a fortune! It gave me strength to dress and quietly go upstairs to tidy up the den.

I only hoped that Juana hadn't already found the disorder I'd left. The telephone was buzzing away unhappily, and I replaced the receiver with the command to "shut up."

The prints were scattered on the carpet. To be certain I'd not imagined the ghost figure, I studied each one as I replaced it in the envelope. The Polaroid shots were as I remembered them, taken of the regal lady with the wraith circling her. Had the photographer expected something like this? Was this the force that kept me from opening the den door that first time? Was the woman Aunt Sapphira? As nearly as I could tell from a black and white Polaroid, the subject was fair skinned, with light hair. Most Greeks were dark, I thought, but I'd never seen a picture of my benefactor. Besides the envelope was labeled *For Maureen*, whoever that was.

After I retrieved the empty bottle and carefully cleaned up the sticky area where I'd spilled Ouzo, I headed downstairs and to the kitchen hoping there was something to eat. Juana and Sergio had long ago gone home, and although there was no supper waiting for me, there was a pan of that wonderful cocoa which I drank greedily, wishing I had a thermos to take it with me to work.

* * * * * * *

The charge nurse handed me a sealed envelope addressed to me. When I asked what it was, I was told it was one of Ells' FYI messages, followed by much giggling. I tore open the envelope and read, "I misspoke this morning, I need you to work a month of nights without time off. Otherwise, same deal a week off with double pay."

The laughter had subsided and all three were watching me intently. Finally Billy said, "Wants you to work a bunch of nights without time off, doesn't she?"

"That's right," I answered.

"If you do it, only do it this once, then put your foot down. Think she cares how tired you get?"

"Thanks, that's good advice," I said.

Although, I hadn't seen her this morning and Ells had never asked me to work extra hours, a month would bring it to July tenth. Could I do it for double pay and a week off? Could I ever. Yes. Oh yes.

After the relief crew made their hasty report, Rocky stuck his head around the treatment room door, freckles afire in the strong florescent lights, "Hi, my bunch are all sound asleep. Want me to help with yours?"

"I'd like that," I answered and we began as we'd done last night, changing, washing and rubbing. With both of us working, the patients were settled by midnight.

"Guess your complaint didn't do much good. What that relief shift needs is a month of nights."

"Umm, Rocky, I forgot to say anything. I'll be sure to see Ells in the morning, though. I'm sorry. And you are great to help me anyway."

"Hey, no sweat. Probably wouldn't have done any good anyway." With a wave, he went back to his unit.

I turned to the half full coffee pot. A cup would be nice, wouldn't it? Sure have a cup, I nagged myself, have a potful. Then you can stay up all day tomorrow. You really like that? You've been there, done that, and you don't need to repeat it.

I took the pot and upended it into the sink watching the dark brown liquid circle down the drain. I'll really be organized tonight, I thought, I'll measure out water and coffee for the morning crew. I puttered around, washing out the pot and making the coffee right up to the point of plugging it in and turning it on. Tonight was going to be different.

I sat down at the desk, and flipped to the top card in the Cardex. I needed more information about the patients. Stuff like: diagnoses, allergies, medications, and next of kin.

However, the name and telephone number of the next of kin were missing from each patient's card. What was I to do if an emergency came up? Call Ells? I couldn't imagine doing that. No way. Were there more detailed records somewhere?

"All still quiet?" Rocky, his freckles pale and red hair darker in the muted light, was cradling his chin on crossed arms resting on the high counter, which formed a barrier in front of the desk. He was grinning.

"Seems to be. I'm trying to learn more about the patients by reading the Cardex, but there's not much here," I said, "and nothing in the charts except the usual 'patient resting,' 'patient eating,' you know, meaningless stuff."

"Like what more do you want to know?" Rocky asked.

"There's only first names on the cards, plus meds I don't have to give and admitting doctor whom I'm not supposed to bother. Not even a next of kin. Are yours the same?" I asked.

"Yeah. I guess. Pretty much."

I couldn't fault him for not being more interested, but I absolutely had to get over to Rocky's side and check patients. First I had to learn about these sicker ones.

"There must be more, but where? In Ell's office?" I asked.

"See that big drawer with the lock on it?" He pointed to a series of drawers under the kitchen counter. "One of those keys they give you fits it, I think. I'm only an orderly, so I don't get keys, but if you're really into boredom, one of yours should open it up."

I said, "Thanks."

"Is it okay for me to go down for a candy bar?" Rocky asked.

"Sure it's okay. Down where?"

"The basement," he said with a puzzled look like anybody would know that much. "Round the corner from the elevator, in a vending machine. Want me to get you one?"

My stomach grumbled, a candy bar sounded wonderful. Could I afford it? "No thanks, I don't have any change."

"Not a problem. I'll get you one and you can pay me back tomorrow night," Rocky offered. "What do you want?"

How could I refuse? Imagining the creamy delight of fudge, caramel and nuts. I asked, "A Snickers?"

I was finishing the notes for each patient when Rocky came back, "No Snickers. Here's some change, the machine is next to the laundry room door. I'll watch your lights while you get something else." He walked off munching a mammoth Baby Ruth.

My stomach growled. Well, why not. I'd brave the basement tonight and pay Rocky back tomorrow. Surely there wasn't anything dangerous down there, nothing had happened to Rocky. But in case the elevator stalled, which they all do sooner or later, I'd take the stairs.

I studied the stairway. Wide and bright at the top, it narrowed and became dark at the bottom and foretold a dark foreboding basement. "Forget this," I mumbled as I turned back to the dimly lit hall, "I don't need a candy bar this bad."

"Hey," Rocky said from the linen closet, "something wrong?"

"No. Yes. I hate that door. It's so hard to open, and the stairway is steep and dark. It's dangerous."

He came over to the where I was standing, arms burdened with stacks of fresh linen. His hair bristled like antennae as he shook his head. "No it ain't."

"Isn't. And yes it is."

"Well, take the elevator. It works fine."

He could be so difficult, "I don't do elevators. One got stuck in the IDS Building in Minneapolis when my grandmother and I were close to the top. That will never happen to me again."

Rocky hid a smile, but not quite fast enough. "Well, this elevator only goes one floor up or one floor down, and the basement door's a 'fire door'. Didn't Ells tell you about it?"

When I shook my head no, he continued, "Man, you got out of orientation, too?"

"Yeah, I guess. Rosie gave me a tour of the units and told me where to buy my clothes."

"Figures," he sighed. "Well, I learned all about that door before I started." He drew himself up to his full five eleven and mimicked Ells, "This door has a resistant hinge that forces it closed. Never prop it open, Fire Marshall's orders. Never."

He relaxed into his normal slump and sneered. "The boss is unreal, I mean she's out in the ozone. You think?"

"She's different," I said, trying to be neutral.

"No hey. But the stairway's okay. Look, somebody painted the ceiling white, and then somebody else came along and put that barf linoleum on the rest of it. It's supposed to look like brown marble. They must have ordered too much, because they plastered the whole lower part of the stairs, even around the door, with that stuff. Think it'll ever wear out?"

He did always cheer me up. "Nope, never. Okay, I'll go down the stairs. What are you doing with all the linen?"

"Sorting it into separate piles that I can deliver to each patient ready for morning cares. You know, wash cloth, towels, sheets. You don't have to do that?"

"One of the aides does that while I give report."

"Gees, you have all the luck," he grumbled.

"Yeah, right," I said to his retreating back as I started down the stairs. He was right, they were just ordinary stairs, and the lights were recessed and pooled at the bottom where it was actually brighter than the top. So bright in fact, the basement was clearly illuminated as I shoved open the metal fire door struggling against the 'resistant hinge'. I lost the struggle, and just before crushing my ailing ankle against the doorjamb, I stepped out of the way and the door clicked shut. I was standing in complete darkness. I tugged at the door, but it was locked.

Damn and damn. How could this happen to me? Rocky told me in detail about the door, why didn't he tell me the lights were off? My chest tightened, I struggled for air, terrified.

I'd experienced the same terror as a kid when Kassi told me, just before she turned out the lights and locked the door, there was a demon in our basement that only Daddy could get rid of, and if the demon didn't get me, the rats would. I'd seen a mouse there once, and I believed her. I screamed and cried until I fainted. Mother eventually found me and Kassi was punished, but the phobia had taken root and couldn't be exorcised.

Now, my back against the door, I sank to the floor, my legs too weak to hold me. I crossed my arms, hugging myself against the creeping chill.

I'd sit with my back to the stair door and, if one of my patients turned on a light, Rocky would answer it and realize I was missing. He'd come looking for me.

I heard a hum. Quietly the elevator door slid open. It had to be Rocky, there was no one else in the building.

A gnarled hand held the door open. Backlit, an immense figure filled the elevator door. A huge head sat directly on broad shoulders, which tapered quickly to narrow hips, a nightmare with no neck. I curled my feet and legs beneath me and pushed back against the stair door. With luck, he wouldn't notice my pounding heart or my rasping breaths.

Cursed exclamations erupted, "Yegodsamighty. What in hell's going on around here?"

Then he moved down the room and at the sound of a click the basement was flooded with blue-white fluorescent light. I saw not a demon, but a man dressed in a brown sweater over striped overalls and wearing a matching stripped cap. His white hair curled around the cap and straggled down his forehead. The most frightening things about him, were his barely visible dark eyes, shadowed by bristly white eyebrows.

He saw me pressed against the stair door, "I saw these windows all black when I drove by and came down to see the trouble. This light is to never be off! You remember that, you hear?"

"Yes, sir." I shook with tremors, my voice cracked. "But,...I didn't turn out the light. I was locked down here and I didn't know where the switch was."

"I'm the custodian here, it's my responsibility to see that everything in this building is done right. *Day and_night.* That's my job. Don't mess with anything down in this basement. Never turn the lights out again. You hear?"

"Yes, sir." He was bear-like with broad hunched shoulders and long arms. His brown sweater, knit of thick yarn grown fuzzy with age, hung limp about his big-boned frame. His white brows were drawn together in fury.

"What you want down here anyway? You supposed to be in this building?"

I scrambled to my feet. Better to face him than cringe on the floor. If he intended to assault me, he would see I could put up a fight. "Yes sir. My name is Nika McGuinness. I'm the charge nurse. I got hungry and came down for a candy bar, but the lights were out and the stair door is locked."

"It's not to be locked, understand? You got keys?"

"Yes. That is I've got some keys, but I don't think they're for this door, only for the locks upstairs."

"Let me see them." He held out his hand.

I reached into my pocket, but hesitated. These keys opened the medicine cart and presumably the narcotic drawer although I'd had no reason to find out. "I don't think I'm supposed to."

He hovered like a predator bird above me, but incongruously smelled of mint. He roared, "Give 'em to me, you hear now?"

Quickly I decided it wasn't worth a fight, and handed over the keys.

"See here? See this one right here? It's brass. This is the one to the stair door. You try it."

My fingers trembled, but the key slid into the lock and I heard a click as it unlocked.

"Now that was easy, wasn't it? What you doing down here again?"

"I was hungry and wanted to buy a candy bar." I showed him the change in my hand.

"Here, let me get you one." His broad feet took painful steps down a short hall to the vending machine. Inserting a key in the side, he asked, "What kind you want?"

"A Baby Ruth, please."

He took out three, "two for you, one for me," he was grinning. "No money needed. Payment for all my trouble and for scaring you to death." Blocking the hall, he roared a laugh.

Why didn't he move so I could leave. Did he want the keys? My heartbeat picked up, did he want drugs? Candy for drugs? That'd be a new one.

He peeled back the wrapper and took a cautious bite, "My name's Tim. Timothy Ryan. What's yours again?"

We were standing by the vending machine, his huge frame still blocking my exit. Thing to do was to make a friend of this 'custodian.' I smiled my biggest, and held out my hand, "I'm Nika McGuinness, Sapphira Domino's niece. Pleased to meet you."

When Tim hesitated, I thought I'd broken another rule, like *don't offer your hand to a real western fellow*. However, he put his hand out, but tears formed in his eyes and he winced as I shook it firmly. Then I understood and he became much less menacing. Osteoarthritis. So disfiguring. So painful. The wintergreen I'd smelled was from the ointment he used. The poor man.

"You're Sapphira's niece?"

I nodded, taking a bite of candy.

"She was a great lady. Built this place. Made sure I got this job—and that I kept it. You hear any rumors about people disappearing out there, ignore 'em. Nothin' bad happened once that fine lady took charge. But how'd her niece get an Irish last name? It is Irish, isn't it?"

"Sure is," I mumbled, my mouth full. The kids called me 'Mick.'

"Me too," he said taking another big bite, "but how're you related to Sapphira Domino?"

I swallowed and explained, "Well, my grandmother was Aunt Sapphira's sister. Her daughter was my mother, and she married my dad, an Irishman from Ireland."

His smile was broad, "From the old sod, yet. Can't get more Irish than that. I'm Irish too, and us Micks got to stick together, don't we?" He turned and started down the hall, but paused to ask, "Say, is that old pickup in the parking lot yours?"

I had to smile, he'd seen my pickup and knew it belonged to someone new. "Yep. That's Bertha, best pickup ever made."

"Well, it's not new, so it must be pretty good. Has Minnesota plates, so you must'a driven it all the way out here, right?"

"Right."

"I'm not being nosy, you know. It's my job to keep track of who's parked out there. Sapphira wrote it into my contract. During the summer and again while hunting season's on we have some weirdoes hanging around. Don't want 'em hiding their cars out there." Tim pointed out the windows where floodlights now illuminated the parking lot.

"I'm really glad someone is watching out for us. Working nights is lonely, and my imagination runs pretty wild. When I was locked down here, I didn't see any lights out there. Did you turn them on too?" I asked.

"Sure did. They're never to be turned off at night. Anyone down here before you?" Tim asked.

"Rocky. He works the unit down the hall from mine," I said.

"Think I've kept you long enough. You best be getting back to your patients. Ride up in the elevator with me, then I'll go talk to that what's-his-name about these lights."

I defended Rocky, "His name's Rocky, and he's a very nice guy. An orderly."

Tim's only response was to grunt.

"And Tim, that door is very hard to open and impossible to hold open."

"I know. It's a fire door." He said.

"I know that too, but you shouldn't have to fight against it, should you?" I asked. "That's why I got locked down here, I wasn't strong enough to hold it open and turn around."

"Well, I'll just fix it." Tim said, taking a screwdriver from his pocket. "Here, you help."

We manhandled the door open, and I braced my back against it while Tim reached up and released the spring. Then he skillfully tightened it back and instructed me to try opening it again.

"Much better," I said. "Thanks."

"You bet. Now let's take the elevator upstairs," he said, "easier for me than climbing stairs.

It seemed like I'd been gone for hours and I was surprised to find everything still quiet on my unit, but raised voices sounded from Rocky's side. Part way over I met Tim coming back.

"Can't believe it, that kid says he was told to turn out the lights as soon as everyone left the building. 'To save on the electric bill,' he said. Those fluorescent lights don't cost hardly nothin' to run. The patients and the help too, need the security of a well lit building." As he talked, he turned on lights in the entrance, "I'll talk to everyone tomorrow and see to it that this never happens again. You have a good night now." He grinned a big grin and added, "Irish."

I smiled back. Unexpectedly, I'd met a really nice man. Maybe things would get better for me from now on. Maybe I'd even get to like Magdalena. I walked down the corridor to return Rocky's money and found him heading in my direction.

"That guy, he went really postal," a subdued Rocky said.

"Postal?" I asked.

"Yeah. You know…,ballistic."

"You mean he lost his cool?"

"How old are you anyway? Yeah he got mad."

"Look Rocky, he was only doing his job. He says, for safety's sake, the lights are never to be turned off…,and he has Osteoarthritis. He's in constant pain. We can cut him a little slack if he's cross. O.K.?"

"Cripes, you never came off like a boss before. Sure. O.K. But they did tell me to turn out the basement lights and the parking ones, because of the expense."

"I believe you Rocky, here's your change. He treated me."

"He bought you a candy bar?"

"He's just a nice man with an odd appearance, that's all." I did sound like a supervisor. Maybe it went with the title, although Charge Nurse wasn't much of a title.

"Rocky, wait a minute. Want to share a candy bar? He gave me two?" I asked.

Rocky halted and whirled around, "He gave you two?"

"Yes, he did. Come on, let's go back to the treatment room and I'll divide it."

When I'd cut the second bar in sections and we'd eaten most of it, Rocky said, "That was sure good. I didn't have anything to eat last night."

"Neither did I."

There were two lights on the treatment room wall, one light for each wing. Rocky left to take care of his, and I turned to answer Dermet's light. He was asleep when I entered his room and his respirations were even, so I went back to the desk.

The night went pretty fast. I mostly stayed awake, but Rocky did find me, head down on the desk about five thirty.

Although the evening cares were better than before, I'd still make a complaint to the day shift in the morning. I decided to see Ells about that problem as well as her note.

I walked into the administration office, but knocked at her inner door waiting for her invitation to come in.

Something hit the floor with a bang followed by, "Damnitalltohellanyway."

A furious Ells swung open the door, her amber eyes shooting sparks. "You should know better than to knock, it ruins my concentration. Just come in."

"Sorry," I said.

Long strides took her back to her desk. "Well, out with it. What do you want?" Although smoke was curling from a cigarette burning in the ashtray, she tapped another one on the desk and hunted for her matches.

"No thanks," I said, "your office is hazardous to my health. I'll stay out here."

She put down the cigarette and picked up the smoldering one inhaling deeply. "So speak, cat got your tongue?"

"I've come to complain about the relief shift."

"So speak up." Ells exhaled two curls of smoke out her nostrils. "What don't you like about the relief shift?"

"They don't do their PM cares. The incontinent patients are left lying in wet beds. That's an invitation for decubitus ulcers. We, Rocky and I, have to change the beds completely, rub backs and make them comfortable for sleep."

"Hmm. I see," she said.

I watched mystified as she extinguished her cigarette and took the ashtray to a bathroom at the back of her office. I could hear the toilet flush before she came out wiping the ashtray with a paper towel. She then went to the large window and opened it wide. Fresh air blew through the room.

Hesitantly I asked, "You did hear what I said?"

"Yes, yes. I heard. Come on in. We need to talk," she said.

"O.K.," I said clutching the FYI note in my hand and wondering which mental illness she had and if she'd ever been treated. I walked in but didn't take the chair she indicated, preferring to stand looking down on her. Who could say I wouldn't have to make a dash for it? "What did you want to talk about?"

"Oh, Ms. McGuinness. I'm short staffed next week. Could you work some extra hours?"

"Sure. I guess so. I have your note here, so I was expecting to work a month without time off, but I guess you just want me to work 'some extra hours next week.'"

What I just said made no sense to me, but, I consoled myself, maybe this insane stuff was catching!

"When?" she asked, looking really confused.

"You asked me to work from now through July tenth. If you don't need that, it's fine, but I have to know."

She was studying the *Hours Book*. "Could you work a week without a night off?"

"A week?" I asked.

"Yes. Beginning June tenth, until June twenty-second. I'll give you a week off after that. That's a week off *with* pay. You'll double your check. What do you say? Can you do it?"

I couldn't help it. I looked at the big calendar hanging behind her. This was June fourteenth. I started June tenth and I hadn't a night off, so she was right about the dates, but wrong about the number of nights. "That sounds like twelve nights, not a week which would be seven nights, the way it's usually calculated." I said.

"Indeed. And it is. Imagine? Well, that's what I need, and I'll adjust your pay. "Upwards, of course. That, besides a week off with pay. What do you say?"

Still standing and ready to run, I took a deep breath of cigarette-tainted air before I said, "There was a note from you left at the desk of my unit. In it you said you'd meant to ask me to work a month on nights without time off. The double pay and week off offer is the same. Do you want me to work twelve nights or a month?"

She turned another page in the H*ours Book* and studied it intently. Finally, "Yes, that's precisely what I need. Well, don't just stand there, will you do it?"

What an arrogant witch, usually when people ask for help, they are a tad more humble. But a straight month with double pay would nearly pay off our debts and would be worth the exhaustion. "Can you put it in writing and address it to me, not FYI?"

She drew a piece of stationary from a drawer and wrote a few lines before passing it to me. "Will that do?

I studied the paper. It seemed fair enough. "Sure. If you need help that bad, I'll do it."

Chapter Eleven

Although I regretted agreeing to meet Randall for breakfast, I wanted to remind him that removal of the paintings, even though they were designated for the McClean law firm, was, in his words, " an act punishable by law." He could deny taking them but his reaction would tell me if he had them.

I parked Bertha and entered the cafe looking for Randall and saw him sitting at his usual table. He rose and pulled out a chair for me, as he motioned to 'his' waitress for coffee.

"If that's regular, I'd prefer decaf this morning," I said.

"That's not what you drank before," Phyllis snapped. "If you're not sure, it's a lot of running back and forth for people who can't make up their minds."

I bristled, "I'll take the decaf. I can also get it myself," I added half rising from the chair.

"That's not necessary," Randall interrupted, "Phyllis will get you whatever you want. Right?"

"Yes, of course, Mr. McClean." She turned to leave, but Randall held up his hand.

"Is this the day you have sour-dough pancakes?"

"Yes sir. It is." If she seemed a little miffed, she made sure I knew it was not at Randall, by gifting me with a glare.

"Nika, if you've never eaten sour-dough pancakes, I'd recommend them." Randall had covered my hand, with his.

"Whatever," I answered, pulling my hand away.

"Bring her a big glass of your fresh squeezed orange juice, too." When the waitress was out of earshot, "That'll counteract any lingering effects of too much Ouzo."

"A small narrow glass of Ouzo, diluted with ice doesn't qualify as heavy drinking. I feel fine." I answered. "But I am curious about the pictures or prints that are missing from the garage apartment. What do you know about that?"

Randall opened his mouth, but was interrupted by Phyllis who served my decaf and two giant glasses of orange juice. I sipped the coffee, which was surprisingly good. I suspected a switch, although the thermal pot she'd brought did have an orange lid. How, I wondered, did people like Tim, Jamie, and Rocky, who were as nice as anyone I'd met anywhere, relate to people like Phyllis?

"I guess you had an easier night last night. I'm glad. And don't let Phyllis trouble you, she has bad days and takes it out on everyone," Randall said.

"She especially seems to resent my presence," I began, "and I wondered why?"

"Mom worked part time in the Law Office once, and hired Phyllis to be my baby sitter. Mom paid her more than the baby sitters around here earn, and Phyllis started calling herself my Nanny. Even then she had problems with her men, and needed the extra pay."

"Men?" I asked with raised eyebrows.

"Her son is what everyone out here calls 'slow,' and her husband is an alcoholic." He answered sipping his coffee.

"I'm sorry about the son, that's a shame. But why not kick her husband out?" I asked.

"It's not that easy," he said. "She can't leave her son alone while she works, and her paycheck is the only income they have."

"That's sad, but how does she see that as my fault? Or does she still see herself as your Nanny?" I admit, I had trouble suppressing the giggle and couldn't suppress the smile.

Randall answered, "Because she's had a *hard* life, she may see you as someone who has an *easy* life, living on inherited money, no need to work for anything."

Like I never had to work for anything? If she only knew. "So, she's mad at me because I'm Aunt Sapphira's heir. Does she have a claim?" Should Phyllis be on my suspect list?

"Your suspect list? Absolutely not," Randall answered firmly. "No, not at all. It's unreasonable, I know. It's just that she's had to cope with terrible problems without help from anyone."

"Poor thing," I said, meaning it, "but in Minneapolis, we have group homes for retarded children where they can learn skills and be with others like themselves who can't achieve at a very high level. There must be something like that here."

Randall again took his time before answering, "Mom's been trying to find places like that here in Colorado. A rehab for the husband and a group home for the boy. In fact, she thought she had everything worked out when Dad had his stroke." When he did look at me, there was sadness in his eyes.

"Look, Randall, now that I understand Phyllis, I'll not let her get to me. And in time, your dad will get better, okay?"

He nodded, "I hope so."

"I have another question for you," I said.

"I'll try to answer any questions you have," he said with that wonderful smile of his, the one that spread slowly over his face, touching his eyes last.

I looked away to remember what else I wanted to know, "Oh yes, I've heard from several people about some illegal activities that went on out at the ranch. People arriving in Limos, but never leaving. What do you know about that?"

"Only that those stories always surface around Halloween. There was an investigation once, long time ago, but they never turned up any incriminating evidence."

"That's all?" I asked. "Nothing more?"

Randall sighed, "Mom always suspected it was because of the mansion. No one here understood how people who didn't work at anything could build a house like that. Some shrewder ones thought old Tony did hold gambling weekends because guests did drive up in Limos. That doesn't say they didn't drive out again. There is an access road to Wolf Creek Pass from the house."

"I don't believe I crossed that pass on the way here," I ventured.

"No? You may have come over Cumbres Pass, but no matter, I'd ignore the rumors, if I were you. Mrs. Domino was a wonderful lady, liked by everyone."

"Not everyone. Someone shot her," I said tersely. Then I changed the subject, reminding him, "You were going to say something when our coffee arrived. About the lost prints?" Couldn't let him think he'd gotten out of answering that one.

"I've never been up in that garage apartment. I've no idea what prints were hanging on the walls or where they are now, but I assure you that neither my father nor myself took anything. I'd also like to know how you got up there." Randall's sapphire blue eyes were neutral, neither angry nor pleading.

"Easy," I answered. "Sergio unlocked the door with a key that's kept above the garage door. Anyone, even you, can go in there anytime."

Randall digested that, and then asked, "Did Sergio go upstairs with you?"

"No. He pointed the way for me, but I think his domain is the first floor workbench."

"Ah," Randall said. "That explains why Sergio knows where the key is. Is there a second key? Another one that Sergio carries on a key chain or something?"

"Not that I know of," I said. Boy, I thought, talk about changing the subject.

"After we've eaten, I'll drive out there, talk to Sergio and check the apartment. That all right with you?"

"Sure," I said just as our sourdough pancakes arrived.

There were four dinner-plate sized, crepe-thin cakes, with crisp brown edges. Besides butter, we were served honey, maple syrup, and a bowl of brown sugar. Randall skipped the butter, but poured on the honey. I opted for butter, lots of it, and sprinkled brown sugar generously covering the pancake to the edges before I took the first bite. They were heavenly. Absolutely.

I was suddenly fatigued, but sipped my orange juice in lieu of the suspect coffee. When the juice glass was empty, I rested my chin on my fist and shut my eyes, I thought for just a second. The next thing I knew, Randall was talking.

"Just keep the change," he said to Phyllis, "I'm going to drive Ms. McGuinness home. She's too tired to drive herself."

"I'm fine," I said, standing up and knocking the chair over. "I'll drive myself."

Phyllis was looking at me like I was a worm on a salad, and Randall was setting the chair upright.

"Sorry about that," I said. "I admit I'm tired, but I'm capable of driving home. After all I have to work tonight, and I'm sure you won't be around to drive me." Randall was steering me toward the door, hand on my elbow, "This is the job you set me up for, as you know," I continued, "and I'll handle it, without your help, if you don't mind."

I was still babbling as he handed me into Bertha. "I'll follow right behind you," he said shutting the door. "Keep your windows open. The fresh air will help you stay awake."

"Yes, I know," I said defensively, "and I'm stopping at the post office, so don't wait." Why did he always use that parental tone? I'd been independent for years, and I didn't need supervision now.

I opened the post office box and drew out an electric bill, which I tore open and gasped in surprise at the amount. It was nearly seven hundred dollars. I'd never pay everything off. Maybe I *should* sell something. Why not, someone else had taken the prints and sold them. There were prints all over the house. No one would miss one here and there.

I stashed the bill in my purse and went back out to Bertha, while still mulling over the missing pictures. What if his father took them, stashed them in a hiding place just before he had a stroke. If he never learned to talk again, the prints were gone for good. Well, that was not my problem, it was Randall's, I thought as I started Bertha and headed toward home with Randall close behind. I glanced into the rear-view mirror after I hit the gravel road and smiled at the sight of Randall's BMW barely discernible in Bertha's billowing dust.

With Randall watching, I took my time unlocking the front door and did my usual check of the other doors to be sure they were still secure, as I'd left them last night. Then I invited him to have a chair in the living room while I changed.

I found him leaning on the grand piano and looking out the bayed turret window in the living room. "Studying that half-mountain?" I asked.

"Yes. It's a lovely spot for a house, isn't it?"

"Yes. Very." And you're not going to get it, I thought. "You wanted to see the garage apartment?"

"First, those keys you found the other day, does one of them fit the garage door?"

"I don't know, but I suppose we could check."

With Randall tagging along, I went back into the bedroom and opened one of the small drawers that adorned either side of the dresser top. The keys were still on the string as I'd found them. I read each tag: basement, patio door, back door, wine cellar, storeroom. "No garage door here," I said.

"I'll take them along and try them. Just to be sure," Randall said.

No you won't, I thought. "I'll just go along, try them myself. Just to be sure." I mimicked.

Of course, none of the keys fit the garage door and also of course, the real key was above the door as I'd told him it would be. The garage apartment was undisturbed, with only the clothes bags in the closet and only the dark patches on the lighter walls where pictures had once hung.

I watched Randall adjust the shade that had fallen the other night. Then I looked out the bedroom windows at the stream visible beyond the tree trunks, while he checked the apartment as I'd done and then said, "Why don't you go on to bed. I want to talk to Sergio before I go back to town."

"Actually, I'd like to talk to him too," I said. I was being stubborn, but until my year was up, these people worked for me. We followed a path that lead upwards to the left of the garage. Once over the crown of the hill, I saw a rusty-pink cottage made of brick-like material. The cottage was shaded by round-topped willows, and instead of a lawn, neat gardens were laid out row after row, glowing in the mid-morning sun. Perro saw us and came bounding out from the shade of the tree where she'd been lying. She came to me first and I knelt to hug her around the neck and slip her a dog biscuit I always carried now.

Sergio came from the cottage at a run, spoke to me and then to Randall. What followed was unintelligible gibberish, at least to me, but resulted in Sergio returning to the garage with us. After much discussion, Sergio pocketed the key and turned back up the path to his little house.

"Sergio says as far as he knows, the key has always been kept there. He thinks Mrs. Domino had another key, but he doesn't know what happened to it." Randall laughed, "He's never been upstairs, because Juana believes it is haunted."

"You mean haunted as in ghosts?" I asked, thinking of the Polaroids of a lady and ectoplasm.

Randall pulled my hand through his arm, "Precisely. She also thinks Mrs. Domino's den is haunted."

"Haunted? Just since Aunt Sapphira died?" I asked.

"He didn't say. You don't believe in ghosts, do you?"

"Not if I can help it," I answered. Another thought came to me, "Randall, didn't you tell me that Aunt Sapphira was shot on a path along Conundrum Creek?"

He nodded, "Yes I did. That's where Sergio found her."

"Is that the creek over there?" I asked, pointing to the stream showing beyond the tree trunks, north of the garage.

"Yes. Want to see it?" He asked.

I nodded my answer and we strolled between pine tress to a brick bench, shaded from the sun on the banks of the stream. I sat down and Randall joined me. The stream tumbled and sparkled down the hill, where rocks formed a miniature waterfall. A solidly built brick path led out of sight up and over the hill.

"Dad told me once that Mrs. Domino was fascinated with this little creek, especially its name." Randall said, "He said she asked him to explain what conundrum meant several times."

"It is unusual," I said. "A creek that's a riddle?"

"When she understood the meaning, that was Mrs. Domino's reaction, Dad said. She spent many mornings walking over the path to where the creek rises out of the ground in the foothills."

Of course, "Randall, was she shot here?"

"No. "Up higher, you can't see the spot from here.

We sat there several minutes, before Randall broke the silence, watching the water in silence. "You're tired. Let's get you to bed. We'll come back here another time, I promise."

On the way past the garage, I looked up at the windows checking the shades. I shivered. "Juana believes in ghosts. But you don't?"

"I've never seen one, and the problem with Juana's theory, is that ghosts don't steal things, only real live people do that. I'm glad you lock your doors. Keep doing it."

"It's a habit I got into living in a less than savory section of a big city." He was so close I could smell the clean fragrance of shampoo and shower soap. I stared into his gorgeous blue eyes, dark and deep like sapphires. The sun picked up coppery lights in his sandy hair. What a shame, I thought, that a lawyer is so great looking when there are so many guys..., Without warning, Randall bent and kissed me lightly on the lips.

"Now go in, lock the door, and go to bed. I'll see you for breakfast."

"For breakfast?" I asked weakly.

Randall nodded and walked around the corner of the house. I went inside and to bed. I was instantly asleep, waking only once to hear soft guitar music. How nice, I thought, turned over and went right back to sleep.

* * * * * * *

That night went better. I'd slept well and my patients were clean and sleeping. That and the cool reception I got were evidence that Ells had reprimanded the evening shift. After I made rounds on my wing, I went over to Rocky's side for a report. We'd gotten through the cardex, when a call light went on.

I asked, "Want help?"

"Nah, that patient's no problem. Wants hot milk to help her sleep. We do this every night about this time."

"Flip the desk call button if you need me, okay?"

"Will do," Rocky whispered as he hurried down the corridor.

When I returned to my wing, I found Timothy sitting at the desk and drinking a cup of very black coffee.

"Hi Timothy," I said in a hushed voice, so as not to wake the patients. "I wondered if I'd see you again."

"You weren't here so I helped myself to some of your coffee. Hope you don't mind. Wish you'd call me Tim, though. We're friends now aren't we?"

"'Course we're friends. I don't mind you helping yourself to coffee, but that stuff should come with a warning label, 'may cause severe insomnia.'"

"Can't sleep when you get home?"

"Right," I answered. "Then I come back to work so tired, I can't stay awake. I usually throw it out when I get here."

"Don't throw it away. I often make my last checks this time of night, and if there's coffee left, I'll drink it. Nothin' keeps me awake. My wife used to complain about it."

"You're married. That's wonderful."

"My wife died three years ago. Miss her."

"I'm sorry. Do you have children?"

"One daughter. She lives in Fort Collins. Teaches grade school while her husband finishes up at the State University up there. They've got a new baby girl," he added proudly.

I remembered seeing the sign that said, 'Fort Collins' and 'stadium' when I drove down I-25, but I had no idea how far it was. "Have you visited them, since the baby was born?"

"No. Probably won't. Almost have to go by bus, 'cause I don't drive that far any more." Timothy said, "But let's talk about you. How are things at your new house? How come you gotta work? Sapphira had plenty of money. If you're her heir, you should have it, that's all there's to it."

"It's strange," I answered. "It seems Aunt Sapphira thought only someone smart enough to find her fortune was wise enough to have it. Ever hear of such a thing?"

"She did huh? Hid it I guess?"

I nodded and he continued, "That's not like her, being so generous and all. That young lawyer, he have any ideas?"

"Randall McClean, you mean?" I asked. When Timothy nodded, I said, "He's about as much help as any attorney I've ever seen. Mostly they're in it for money."

"Well now, he's as nice a lad as can be, altogether. He studied law 'cause his daddy had his heart set on it."

"He didn't want to be a lawyer?" I asked.

"Nope. Wanted to study computers, learn what makes 'em tick. Got two degrees, he did, one in jurisprudence, I think they call it, and the other in computer science. Had a job too, in Denver, but when his Daddy had that stroke, he came back to take over the practice. He's a lawyer out of love for his daddy, not fer the money in it. You can take my word on it."

"I wouldn't have guessed," I said.

"No, maybe not. Some lawyer give you trouble?" He asked.

"You could say that," I answered. He waited for me to continue and I found myself telling a shortened version of Kassi's and my problems after Mother died.

When I'd finished, Timothy sat silent a moment before removing his cap and scrubbing his fingers through his thick white hair. I saw him turn his face to one side and quickly wipe his eyes.

"Ah gee, things are better for us now," I said hurriedly, not wanting his sympathy. "I have my degree and my license, and we're going to be all right."

"I bet so," Timothy said, "but Sapphira hiding her money like that?" He shook his head in disbelief.

"Excuse me, Tim," I interrupted. "I have a light to answer."

It was Dermet, who wanted a drink, which I gave him and then pulled his covers over him."

Tim was smiling at me when I got back to the desk, "Did you know you had a light to answer before it went on?" he asked.

"I did?"

"Yep. And I'll bet you know when phones are going to ring, and when someone's comin' to visit before they knock on the door."

"Well, Kassi complains that I'm weird. So maybe I do."

Tim shook his head. "You're not weird. You have the *gift*. Only some of the Irish have it. You need to cultivate it."

"If you say so Tim," I said doubting it was much of a gift, if it didn't tell me where Sapphira stashed her money.

"You say Mrs. Domino hid her money? And you have to find it?" He continued without waiting for me to answer. "It's hard picturing her doing a thing like that, not like her. I bet it was her husband's idea. He was I-Tal-inn, wasn't he?"

"Now that you ask, I seem to remember hearing that Uncle Tony's last name, Domino, was Italian." I said.

He continued, "You know I grew up in an I-Tal-inn neighborhood, and those old time Dagos…, oops, if my wife was here, she'd scold me like the dickens, saying that's not a nice thing to say."

"It's O.K. Tim," I said, "I imagine they're the ones who called you Mick. Right?"

"Yer right, they was the ones. Anyhow those I-Tal-inns were always hiding their money around the house 'cause they didn't trust banks any more than they trusted their own kin."

"You're serious?" I asked.

"Yep. I remember one time, a poor widow woman needed money and sold her house. The guy who bought it was doing some repairs and replaced some of the stair risers. Boy, he was surprised when money came fallen' out like water." Timothy chuckled.

"Shame the woman didn't know where the hiding place was. She couldn't claim any of it, I guess."

"Didn't have to," Timothy said, "The widow was pretty near destitute, but the guy was a real decent sort of a fellow. An Irishman, don't ya' see.

Generous to a fault." He nodded at me like I knew all about generous Irishmen.

"He didn't give her all the money, did he?" I asked.

"No, but nearly as good and lots better than most would've done. He split it with her. She was mighty grateful, I'll tell you. Kept him in homemade tomato sauce and lasagna for as long as she lived."

"He found the money in the stair risers?" I asked. "What's a stair riser?"

"It's the front part of the stair step. He had to replace the step itself and took the risers off first, for some reason. There, behind each riser were hundred dollar bills, stacked clear to the top. Was the talk of our neighborhood, let me tell you."

"Yes, I can imagine. So you think I should take a riser off and look behind it?"

Timothy took his billed cap off again and combed his fingers through his already disheveled curly white hair. "Before you do that, if the basement stairs runs under the other ones, or lots of time there'll be a closet next to the stairway, you can see the way its built by looking at 'em from below"

"I don't quite see how...," I said in puzzlement.

"See, if you can see the back of the steps there'll be nothing' hidden inside. But if a board's been nailed along the back of the steps, why then there's room to hide money between the riser and that piece of wood. Get what I mean?"

"Yes. Yes I do. That's really interesting. Thanks."

"You're welcome little lady," Timothy had rinsed his cup and was about to leave, "By the way, if'n you have to take a step apart, just let me know ahead of time. I'll be out to help."

I glanced at his swollen hands, "Well," I hesitated.

Reading my thoughts, he said, "Yup, these hands don't have much strength anymore, but I can do a little and tell you how to do the rest. A bargain?"

"A bargain," I answered, tears in my own eyes. I watched out the back windows until he was pulling out of the parking lot. Then I heard guitar music and someone singing.

Grabbing my flashlight, I walked slowly down the corridor, listening intently. I should know who was visiting.

I didn't have far to go as the music was coming from Molly's room. I poked my head around the door and saw a shadow sitting in the armchair, with one hand twanging the guitar, which was propped against his knee, and the other holding the sleeping Molly's hand.

"You're not to be here at night. Visitors are allowed only in the daytime," I said as firmly as possible while speaking in a whisper.

"You're right," came the answer, "I'll leave right away." He moved past me, leaving a cool breeze in his wake, and was gone.

The rest of the night shift went so smoothly, that I was fearful I'd forgotten something, but report went quickly too. I had a very quick breakfast with Randall, and hurried home without even checking the Post Office box.

I was determined to sleep first and search later, but thoughts of Juana's questioning looks as I knocked on stair steps made me decide to search first and sleep later. After changing into sweats and sneakers, I studied the stairs. The back of the front hall stairs, shared a wall with the sitting room and was paneled in walnut similar to Aunt Sapphira's office upstairs. Since it was similar, maybe there was a way to slide open a door for a view of the underside of the steps.

The south wall was covered with drapes that were usually open just a little. I pulled the cord was treated to rainbows dancing everywhere. The whole south wall, floor to ceiling of the sitting room, was one long bow window made up of beveled glass. Every pane sent out its own colored lights. "Wow, what a house. No wonder Aunt Sapphira loved this place," I said.

After a moment, I turned my attention back to the paneled wall next to the stairs. Sure enough, there was a slight depression and close examination showed a keyhole. But what key?

The keys to the upstairs office were under my underwear in the bedroom. I fished them out and tried them all in the keyhole. No luck. Where was the key? I moved books back and forth on the shelves, stacking them on tables and the floor, but apparently only the McCleans used bookcases as a hiding place. Discouraged, I returned the books to their right places as near as I could remember. That finished, I lay down on the chaise lounge, propped a plump pillow under my head, and gazed at the panel hoping for inspiration. It was cool in the house and I covered myself with a throw folded neatly at the foot. This was luxury. All I needed was champagne and chocolates, I thought.

Then inspiration struck, and my fatigue dropped away. I glided effortlessly down the hall, into the guest bedroom where I opened the small drawer and drew forth the string of keys I'd found in Randall's office. Back down the hall I went and stood in front of the paneled wall selecting the storage room key from the others. I couldn't seem to lift the key. I struggled and groaned, but the key only got heavier and heavier. In a panic, I sat up on the chaise lounge, the throw sliding to the floor. My hands were empty. I'd been asleep and dreaming.

Why not try that key? I hurried to my bedroom, removed the string of keys and fitted the storage room key into the keyhole. With a slight shove, the panel slid open and a light came on in a good size storage room across one end of the sitting room. A quick look at the bottom of the stairs showed there was no place to store money behind the risers. Ah well, I thought, no hiding place there, but this room, kept secret by the lock in a camouflaged keyhole. This was not a room just anyone had access to and worth a look around.

The front wall was lined with shelves that held those hard cover caseholders Mom's lawyers used to store old files they didn't bother locking up. The contents of these were listed on the back. Income and

Expenditures was held in one box for each ten-year period. Family Photographs were in another, and Property Improvements was on the back of another. There was so much information that could be useful, but that miserable fatigue was building, first in my legs and then in my back. I knew I'd have to rest before sorting through all this, to say nothing of digesting the information. However, the box right in front of my eyes was labeled *Diaries*. I took it down and returned to the small writing desk before opening it. Removing the last diary, I sat down and opened the cover as a sheet of paper slipped out onto the desk. I picked it up thinking that I wasn't the only one who slid single sheets into books, must run in the family.

"My dear little Nika," it began.

"We can't locate you. We just learned that your beautiful mother was killed in a car accident, your father unconscious since the terrible accident on the lake. You and Kassi have been alone for six years. My poor dear little girls. What has become of you and why wasn't I told? Here I've been giving my money away and you've had nothing. My heart breaks. But I can't wait for Randall, such a fine young man, to find you. My life is in danger. There is someone who wants me dead, I know it. So I'm writing a conundrum for you alone. It will tell you where my fortune is hidden, as I want you to have it, don't you see? I'm sorry for my poor attempts as I'm not well taught in English and I fear you don't know the Greek. Am I right? But I try."

So much of my love to you and Kassi
Your grieving Aunt Sappy"

Chapter Twelve

Stunned, my hands were shaking as I fluttered the diary pages, hoping another single sheet containing the conundrum would fall out. This was the clue I'd been hoping for, the tangible link between Aunt Sapphira and me. Randall was wrong. She had known who her heir was, she'd meant her estate to go to me, and most important of all, she hadn't known about Mom's death or Kassi's and my financial problems. Tears flowed from my eyes and I wiped them away with my fingers.

Starting at the back cover, I began a page-by-page search, but in my haste, I dropped the book. Oh well, I thought, with the luck I've been having I'll probably never find it anyway. The book lay sprawled face down, on the carpet like a bird with one wing splayed out. When I picked it up a single sheet still adhered to the inside of the front cover. Printed on it was a short poem titled, 'Conundrum'. I sucked in my breath and read:

CONUNDRUM

Chatty ran up the oak tree,
but only acorns did she see.
Janie flew to the owl's nest,
but only peanuts gave her zest.
Daisy clung to the sunflower,
but only seeds will give her power.

Nika must remember the rest,
but only springs unlock the chests.

I grabbed a tissue from a flowered ceramic container on the desk, and blew my nose. I remembered we used to make up riddles when Kassi and I were kids, but nothing this complicated.

Chatty, *Janie*, and *Daisy* sounded like names in a children's book, but I couldn't recall the characters or the book. My head was beginning to ache and the back of my neck was stiffening. I must go to bed, just as soon as I'd tidied this room. I drew a sheet of paper from the desk and copied the conundrum to carry in my pocket and study tonight. I'd return the original to the diary and replace everything the way I'd found it. No one must know I'd discovered the secret storage area.

When that was done, I refolded the throw on the chaise lounge and closed the drapes. I hid the ribbon of keys by hanging them on a hook, behind some clothes at the very back of my closet. That had worked for the den keys and should hide these as well.

Most mornings, I had little energy for anything except sleep, but this morning I'd accomplished so much. I felt good. I crawled into bed and stretched out under the cool sheets. In spite of my excitement at finding the first significant clue, I was drifting off when I sat up with a start. How had she signed the letter? Aunt Sappy? Sappy. Of course, that's why we didn't remember a Sapphira. We'd called her Sappy. She visited us when we were small. I remembered now.

Throwing off the covers, I ran down the hall to the phone. I must call Kassi. A glance at the clock assured me it was a little after eleven here and Minneapolis was an hour later, so she'd still be home. I dialed our number and waited while the phone rang. "Come on Kassi, answer the phone." There was click and a recorded voice told me, "This number has either been disconnected or is no longer in service."

"Ah Kassi. Gees. You didn't pay the phone bill? Damn and damn."

Nothing for it but to go back to bed and get some sleep. I snuggled into bed thinking, "Aunt Sappy, Aunt Sappy. I remember you now." Smiling, I went soundly to sleep.

* * * * * * *

From far away, came a pounding, pounding, pounding. Ah damn, I thought, whatever is Mr. Swazy pounding on? Not the roof I hope. The stairs? Maybe. I covered my head with the pillow trying to drown out the racket.

"Nika. Nika. I know you're in there. Open up. I will not stand out here all day."

"Kassi," I groaned. "She's forgotten her keys. Again."

I shrugged off the covers and got out of bed, but not in our Minneapolis apartment, in Aunt Sapphira's guest bedroom. "Kassi? What's she doing in Colorado?"

I stumbled to the front door and opened it to Kassi's fists poised to attack the door again. "What are you doing here?"

"I came to see you," she smiled.

"Come on, you know what I meant." I scolded, "What are you really doing here?"

"Nika, can't you be glad to see me? I'm your sister, after all. While you're out here living in this mansion, you expect me to live in that awful apartment and work my fingers to the bone? How about sharing with your only relative? Invite me in."

Something was going on here, but as usual I'd have to wait until Kassi was ready to tell me. "Sorry Kassi, I didn't mean you'd have to wait outside. You're here for a visit?"

"Phillip," Kassi commanded, "bring in my things. Just set them in the hall."

I looked around the door and saw Phillip standing to one side, suitcases piled around him. Weakly, I asked. "How'd Phillip get all this in his Vette?" Then asked, "Phillip's here for a visit too?"

"A visit? Fat chance. As usual when the McGuinness girls get into trouble the first one they call is good old Phillip."

"Trouble? What kind of trouble are you in Kassi?"

Kassi stepped into the entry, "Wow, some joint *we* inherited. Why didn't you tell me it was this big, I'd have come out before."

I demanded, "What trouble, Kassi?"

Phillip dumped a suitcase, a cosmetic bag, a hang-up bag, and a wheeled carry-on at Kassi's feet, and stood gazing around, "This is quite elegant Nika. I must say I'm envious."

"You wouldn't be if you saw the overdue bills," I said.

"But Nika," Kassi gushed, "this is gorgeous! And after sleeping on rough blankets in the back of that delivery truck, I'm anxious to see my bedroom."

"Delivery truck? What happened to your Vette, Phillip?"

Phillip gave me his condescending smile, "Needed some minor repairs. Good thing I had access to another vehicle or your fair sister would be hanging out with the homeless." He laughed his gotcha laugh, and I had to hide a smile. Imagining my immaculate sister sleeping on the floor of a delivery truck was pretty amusing, after all.

"Nika," Kassi said, "It looks to me like our bad times are over. We'll find the money and you can pay off those mean old bills. Imagine our living in luxury!"

I'd noticed the '*we find the money*', '*you pay the bills*,' and '*our living in luxury*.' Being rich was the worst possible thing for Kassi, I knew, but it was twelve thirty, I'd slept one and a half hours. My disposition was at its worst.

"O.K. Kassi, now you listen. This is not our permanent home. We're here only long enough to settle Aunt Sapphira's estate. Once it's taken care of, I'm going back to Minneapolis, with or without you. You *know* that. I *told you* that."

"But you never told me how lovely everything is here. I think we should reconsider. After all you made that decision before coming out here. Now you have a job and a beautiful home."

"Kassi, my so-called job doesn't pay enough to keep this place up, it's not even enough to pay the electric bill."

"It seems to me that I've fulfilled my part of our bargain," Kassi said with a toss of her lovely blond head.

"Your part of the bargain?" I was stunned. "*Your* part of the bargain. What does that mean?"

Phillip cleared his throat, "May I interrupt this touching family reunion?" He was sitting on the bottom step, a pleased look on his face.

"O.K. Phillip," I said, "What is it?"

"While you're discussing bills, don't forget you wouldn't be out here enjoying all this if not for me." With a nod in Kassi's direction, "Neither of you! You can stall the electric company, but you can't stall me. I need my money. I'm a poor struggling student, not a lending institution. What say you?"

He said this with a mocking smile on his clean-shaven face, the lock of black hair, that I used to find attractive, had slid over the widow's peak. I caught the threatening glint in his dark eyes that sent a calculated warning.

"Phillip," I said, "I gave you every chance to back out of your offer, and you said, 'Not a problem. Pay me when you get your inheritance.' Well, I don't have my inheritance, and I may never get it. Until I get the money I'll pay you a little at a time, but not the whole amount. Clear? " Threaten me, will he?

His expression didn't change nor did he move from his perch on the bottom step, with the stairway climbing up behind him to the light filled upper hall. "You're a good looking broad when you're angry, know that? You'd look better, of course, in a sexy gown instead of those paint-smeared sweats you insist on wearing. Any woman of mine has to look good in bed."

"You understand this," I thundered, "I'm not your woman."

In one movement, he rose and kissed me hard on the mouth, "Unless Kassi still needs me, I'll be on my way."

I scrubbed my sleeve across my lips, "Ah gees, I can't handle this." I'd cope after I'd slept…,maybe tomorrow…,or on a day off sometime in the distant future. "Kassi, I have to work tonight and I'm going back to bed. You can sleep in Aunt Sapphira's bedroom, it's down the hall, first door on the right."

"Why not upstairs?" Phillip was looking up the stairway.

"No," I said, "the beds aren't made. But Phillip, if you're staying, Kassi will make up a bed upstairs. The linen is on the closet shelf in each bedroom. Now I'm going to sleep."

I went back to my bedroom, but Kassi followed, "Nika, I need a key to the door. The way you sleep, I'll never get back in."

"I only have one key," I said holding it out to her, "you can use it, but don't lose it. I'll need it to get back in tomorrow morning. And shut the bedroom door on your way out."

I fell back on the bed and was instantly asleep. When I finally woke again it was after five. I turned over and lay on my back staring at the impossible burgundy chrysanthemums glowing on the canopy. Every afternoon when I woke, I studied them and reviewed the progress I'd made. I'd reluctantly eliminated Randall as a suspect in Aunt Sappy's murder, and was left with the elusive nephew, Anthony Paul P. S. P.S.? Was he really an afterthought? Was Anthony the first name and Paul really his last name? I'd think about that in two weeks when I had a week off. If I had my paycheck tomorrow, I'd open a checking account.

Then why was I depressed? Why the feeling of doom? I puzzled a moment, before remembering. Kassi! Ah yes, Kassi had come to visit with Phillip along.

Visit? With the telephone at home disconnected? I don't think so. More likely she lost her job. Betcha!

I shoved out of bed and stumbled into the bathroom. Cold water splashed on my face and a comb pulled through my snarled hair, brought me as close to wide awake as I'd get this day. I needed a cup of coffee, just one.

As I shuffled along the hall, I heard merry voices coming from the kitchen. Yes, and in Spanish. My sister and Juana were at the stove, Kassi stirring and Juana gesturing. Juana was teaching Kassi to cook Mexican food? Incredible!

"Is there a cup of coffee in this kitchen that I could have?" My request was bitchy, but so was I.

Kassi spoke to Juana in Spanish then reached for a pan at the back of the stove and poured a mug of cocoa. "Juana says coffee's bad for you, drink this."

I took the mug down the two steps to the recessed sitting area, "You're getting pretty high-handed. You win the lottery or something?" Still bitchy.

"She says that you are to eat something, it's not good to work like you do without eating a real meal." Kassi didn't look at me, just continued stirring whatever was in the pot.

I took a sip of thick cocoa, "My, how do you suppose I managed for the last month without you?" My best bitchy.

"Drink your cocoa. There's more when you finish that. Your supper will be done soon. Go out on the terrace and relax?"

This was not Kassi. Some extra-terrestrial had taken over my sister's body. "O.K. Kassi, turn down the burner and come with me. We have to talk."

I led the way through the French doors to the terrace and sat down in one of the wrought iron chairs. Kassi joined me with another mug and the pan of cocoa. She pulled two keys from her pocket, "Here's your key, if that's what you're sassed about."

"How'd you get the extra key?"

"Easy." She looked up at me with guileless blue eyes. "Phillip took me into town to a place where they copy keys and gave me the money for a copy. If we're to live together, it seems only reasonable that we both have a key. I'm really surprised you hadn't already had one made for me."

"I've been in Magdalena for nearly a month and I've never seen a locksmith's place. How did Phillip find one?"

"He must have asked someone. I don't know. The locksmith is also the pawnshop owner. Makes sense, Phillip says, because people often hock boxes that are locked and when they're not picked up, a locksmith opens them. Sometimes there're valuables inside. Phillip knew a man who…,"

"Kassi! Enough. I don't want to hear it. Why are you here? What trouble are you in?"

"Why do you always expect the very worst of me?" Kassi sniffled into a paper towel she conveniently had in her pocket. "You always get so mad at me…,"

"I always have reason to. What's the story?"

"I got fired," she sobbed. "I couldn't find another job. I couldn't pay the rent, and that mean Mrs. Swazy evicted me."

"That's it? Kassi, how could you mess up so bad?"

She blew her nose, but tears still ran down her face, "It just happened, like things always happen to me. It's really scary to be out of work and hungry. You don't know 'cause it never happened to you. I'm your sister. You should care about me."

I put my arms around, "Oh Kassi, I do care about you."

"And you should listen to what Phillip says, he has a lot of useful information."

"Sure. Like how to find a pawnshop. Kassi, dry your eyes and listen to me. I'm living in this beautiful mansion temporarily. Aunt Sapphira's will says I have to find the fortune before I can inherit it."

"You already told me that. I'm not stupid. You just haven't tried is all." She hiccupped, and then offered, "A bank?"

"Randall told me she didn't believe in them, or at least her husband didn't." I finished the cocoa and refilled our mugs.

"Have you looked?"

"Have I ever. The only thing I learned is that we called Aunt Sapphira, Aunt Sappy when she came to visit. Remember?"

Kassi said, "No. And I don't see how that matters. What matters is the money. Tell me where you looked."

"I've looked for false fronts on bookcases and closets. I've looked in drawers, in the apartment above the garage, everywhere I can think of. No fortune." I didn't tell her about the conundrum. If she found the money before I did, no telling what she'd do. She was my sister, but I couldn't trust her with money.

"How long do we have?"

I took a long drink of cocoa, before answering. "A year. A year from the date the will was read to me. Next June eight."

"We'll find it. I'll look while you sleep. It'll be fun. How hard can it be? I'll begin in the garage apartment."

"O.K. Kassi, ask Sergio for the key, and have fun. Just remember, what you'll look for is a job. Any treasure hunting will wait until our time off from work."

"Nika, you're mean." She was weeping again, "You promised that as soon as you got your degree, you'd work and put me through school." She sobbed, "It's not fair."

Ah yes, that was our bargain. Kassi'd work while I went to college, then it'd be my turn. Except, of course, I'd worked *and* also borrowed money to make it. Yet, I had promised her she could go to college once I'd finished.

I put my arms around her again. "You're right, it's not fair. But this is an unusual situation. Aunt Sapphira was killed in March, and no one paid the utility bills or anything else all this time. I've been hit with a seven hundred dollar electric bill and I dread the day the propane tank has to be refilled."

"And you don't make enough money to pay these bills?"

"I get paid once a month, so my first check will be minus two weeks pay, a policy they have to prevent people from quitting without giving notice."

Kassi hiccupped before belligerently stating, "That's no fair."

I started laughing. Soon we were both laughing, tears streaming down our cheeks. Finally, I said, "Oh Kassi, when you're poor, nothing's fair. And we're poor."

"Well," she said staunchly, "we'll just have to find that fortune."

"Kassi, I love you and I'm glad you're here." I was too, but Kassi had never in her life been as determined as she could sound. I knew if anyone found the fortune it would have to be me.

"Is good," came Juana's voice from the door. "Good to make laugh and hug."

"Right!" We said in unison.

"Come. Eat. Is ready."

Sergio poured that wonderful red wine into glasses, and reluctantly he and Juana again ate with us. Surprised me when the Sanchez and Kassi exchanged toasts, but I touched glasses with them and said, "Cheers" to their "Oles." Why pretend?

When they quieted down, I asked Kassi, "When did you learn Spanish?"

"Oh, we had a kid from Mexico working as a bus boy. He was trying to get into the U, but his English was atrocious. So I taught him English for his Spanish words. I remember a little."

Surprised me. What a nice thing to do. I'd known Kassi to expect praise for not running the grocery cart into toddlers, but never, ever to be self-effacing. I watched the three of them chatter and laugh, almost like *family. Almost.* The lonelies hit me. *Almost*, because I was looking on, not participating and we had no real family left. At least, I thought, I'd told Kassi I loved her, something I'd never admitted to the rest of my family. Now, I'd never get the chance to tell them, they were all dead,

Aunt Sappy too. Tears escaped from my eyes, and I wiped them away with a napkin. The others didn't notice, because they were so engrossed in their conversation, in Spanish, of course.

Finally, when my watch said eight-thirty, I pushed my chair back, "That was wonderful. Thanks Juana. You too, Kassi."

Sergio stood and bowed. Kassi said, "Don't worry about cleaning up the kitchen. We'll do that, right Juana?"

Juana said, "Si."

Same old Kassi. She'd say *we*, but let Juana do it all. "See that you do your share of the clean-up," I said. "In fact, tell Juana to go home and you do it all."

"Sure," Kassi said with a dismissing wave of her hand.

"I mean it," I frowned.

Juana beamed, "Si. Is good to talk."

I took an extra long shower, to hell with saving propane.

* * * * * * *

I parked Bertha under a reassuring floodlight. The parking lot friendlier and the basement less intimidating since I'd met our protector Timothy. I was confident that he'd watch over us.

The evening nurses were cool, and emphasized how hard they'd worked to settle all the patients. I knew they were angry about my complaints, but I smiled, and wished them a good night's sleep.

I was definitely pleased when I made rounds to see all but Dermet and Molly asleep. I rubbed Molly's back and gave her a fresh drink of water. She seemed lucid tonight, even told me to go tend the other patients, but to come back for a visit later.

I was getting a fresh pitcher of water for Dermet when Rocky poked his head into the back room. "Hey," he said, "You must have lit a bonfire under those do-nothings. My evening shift was all sympathies for me having to work with such a tough boss."

"Yeah, well I tried, and they only just got the message."

"Need some help?"

"Not really, this side is pretty quiet, all clean and dry. The only wakeful ones are Dermet and Molly."

"Want me to settle Dermet down? If you rub his back, he'll insist that you marry him."

"How'd you know?"

"He even hits on old Rosie."

I was hesitant to ask him to do my job, but if I could soothe Molly, I could read the patient records. I didn't even know what health problems my patients had. "Well, if you don't mind,…"

"See ya later," he said, but turned back and added, "if you're not back at the desk, I'll stick my head in the door to

Molly's room to see if you need me."

"Great," I said handing him Dermet's water.

Taking another fresh pitcher of ice water, I hurried down to Molly's room, but stopped midway into the door to let a shadow-like wisp of chill air whisper by me. I turned from the doorway and said, "Is someone there?" My whispers were hoarse and sounded loud in the quiet hall. "You just go home and stay there."

I swear I heard, "Yes Ma'am," in a soft whisper, but I saw no one. I must be hallucinating. I had to get more sleep. But I was trembling when I entered Molly's room. She was resting in bed, pillows supporting her head and shoulders, as I'd left her. Ordinarily she'd be sleeping, but tonight her eyes were bright, her smile was for me rather than a distant memory.

"So Molly, what can I do for you? Want another back rub?"

"You're trembling dear. You mustn't let Charlie bother you. He's a harmless, sweet man."

"Harmless? Charlie?" I asked. Had she seen someone too?

"Of course. Go open that drawer and you'll find a picture of Charlie and me."

The picture was same one I'd taken out before, a black and white of two laughing people in front of a car with suitcases piled around them. "This is you and your husband?" I asked. Actually, if the picture had been in color, the car would be like the one stored in the garage, I though.

"Yes, just before we left for out here. Now you just sit in this rocker so we can visit."

I poured a fresh glass of water, and helped her drink some.

"Nothing's better than good, cold white wine, don't you think?" she asked.

White wine? Maybe she wasn't as clear as those bright eyes suggested. "I always like wine, too." I held the back of my hand to her forehead. "Molly, I'm going take your temperature."

"That's nice of you, dear. I always think a small piece of angel food cake's a delicious ending to a meal."

Then Molly was asleep. What to do? Did Molly sometimes run a slight fever that wasn't serious? What I'd have to do is watch her and try to find a medical history somewhere.

I turned off the bedside light, lowered the head of the bed, and quietly left her room just as Rocky was leaving Dermet's.

"I need some help," he said sheepishly, "they admitted a woman at change of shift this afternoon and it's just kinda strange. You have time to take a look at her?"

"Sure, no problem." This is the first time Rocky had asked for my help, and I prayed I'd know what to do.

"What's her diagnosis?" I asked.

"Like I told you," he said, "this lady was admitted this afternoon, change of shift. No doctor, no diagnosis."

"What?" I whispered. "That's unthinkable."

"Yeah. Would be anywhere else, but not here. Some rule made by the gal who donated this place. She set up a fund and ordered that no patient could be turned away. Ever!"

Oh great Sappy, I thought, but to Rocky I said, "She meant well, I'm sure."

"There you go, sounding like a boss again. Anyway nobody got around to getting a doctor to take her as a patient. Now guess who's stuck with the problem? The night shift."

"There's disadvantages to every shift," I said. Rocky just glared at me, disappointed that I hadn't agreed with him.

"Well," he said, "like I was saying. The lady was admitted this afternoon, change of shift. She's really thin and a little confused, according to the report I got, but she's been asleep all the while since I got on duty. I need to check on her, and I don't want to do it alone."

"What's her name?" I asked.

"Geraldine."

"No last name?" I'd hoped she'd be listed in the phone book.

"Nope. Just Geraldine. It was pinned to her night gown when they found her."

"Someone abandoned her. Where?" I asked.

"In a wheel chair in the lobby. Nobody else there, natch."

"Was it one of ours?" I asked, hoping we could trace her from the markings on the wheelchair.

"Yep. Left there by some dumb day person," he answered.

The wheelchairs were marked for each wing and the ones not in use, were kept locked in a storage room. Either someone had gotten one out for this lady, or one had been left in the lobby.

Our conversation had been in whispers as we walked soundlessly along the corridors to a room mid-way down the hall of Rocky's section and pushed open the door to enter the room. A woman dressed in a garish pink gown with orange ruffles around the neck sat upright in bed, her eyes bright.

"Hi, Geraldine," Rocky said, "what can we do for you?"

"My name's Tallulah and I'll thank you to remember, young man. Who's the woman with you, your ma?"

"No ma'am," A smile tugged so hard at Rocky's mouth that his freckles danced. "This lady," he continued, "is the charge nurse, an RN. She's my boss."

"Humph. No difference." Tallulah pushed the covers down to reveal thin legs from thigh down to her dirty feet. One of her legs, the left one, was wrapped in layers of faded material, stained with mud and perhaps dried blood.

She asked, "Is the doctor comin' to see this leg of mine?"

"Tallulah, how did you hurt your leg?" I asked checking her toes for circulation and swelling, the dressing for drainage.

"I tripped over a wrench that no good bum left on the kitchen floor. Fell down the steps. Scraped the skin and busted some bones. Lay there long 'nough callin' fer help. Where's the doc? That's why I'm here."

"How far did you fall?" I asked, carefully unwinding the makeshift dressings while Rocky supported the leg. They looked like strips torn from a flannel blanket. There was bloody drainage, still oozing from an angry cut on the upper thigh. The knee and leg were scraped and soil was imbedded in the wounds.

"Tallulah, what's the name of your physician?" I asked.

"Physician?" Came the quick retort.

"Yes. The name of your doctor," I explained.

"Name? I don't know no name. When the vet come out to look after the horses we asked him what to do if'n one of us was sick." Her alert, brown eyes, were the color of the dried blood. Tallulah studied me, assessing me, as I was her injured leg.

"Do you remember the name of the vet?" I asked.

"Naw. He come up from Farmington. Kicked the bucket about the same time my old man passed. I sold the horses, was too much work for one and I needed the money. And those two bums ain't goin' to find it no matter how hard they dig and spy." She cackled a laugh and Rocky shot me a 'help' look. "I'm tellin' you fer the last time, I need a doc right this minute."

"Tallulah," I said, "it's one in the morning, I can't get a physician, that is, a doctor out this time of night. With your permission, I'd like to cleanse this wound and redress the leg."

"Sure, if you say so. When will I see a doc?"

"Sometime tomorrow, maybe in the morning."

"Humph." she grunted as I helped her off with the nightgown.

I washed her face and upper body before helping her into a regulation hospital gown and easing her back down. I thought her ankle was broken since the foot was twisted, so I'd sent Rocky for a brace and dressings.

"Who found you and brought you in?" I asked.

"Nobody found me. I crawled up the stairs from the cellar, grabbed this here blanket out of the dog's bed, tore it up and covered my leg. It was bleedin' somethin' fierce."

"But you didn't drive yourself here."

Tallulah bristled. "Could've. I got out the door and into that red truck a his'n, had the engin' goin,' which musta woken them two up. They come a'runnin', and said I had to wear a decent gown to the docs and he'd drive me. Then they took off my good flannel shirt and put that itchy rag of her'n on me. Couldn't tell 'em anythin', but I was hurtin' by then and didn't care too much. Trash, that's all there is to it. Nothin' but trash."

Rocky was back and we went to work cleaning the wound as gently as possible. Tallulah yelled dag-nab-it, a curse I'd never heard and others I had. Using both hands, Rocky held the leg, careful to support it in alignment, while I applied sterile abdominal dressings over the open wounds, and covered the dressings with roller bandages. Rocky had also found a canvas splint that had stay-like supports on both sides. It held the leg from ankle to hip in a safe position. When we finished, Tallulah was white with pain and exhaustion.

"This happen to you early this morning?" I asked.

"It was dark, but I don't know the time. Thought I heard a noise and went to see what was goin' on."

"We're going to bring you some soup now and a pain pill," I said. "Then we'll move you to a different room."

Back in Rocky's kitchen we found an unopened box of instant soup and some crackers. While that was heating I used my drug key to open the cupboard and choose one tablet of buffered aspirin.

"Why the aspirin?" Rocky wanted to know.

"Because it'll prevent a blood clot from forming that could cause a stroke," I answered. "The buffered because she's not eaten in a long time, and plain aspirin might upset her stomach."

"Are we going to get into trouble for fixing her up?"

"Not as much trouble as the person who put her to bed. And Rocky," I added, "thanks for your very professional help."

"Ah, it was nothin'," he said, "that was fun. I mean, I learned a lot tonight. You're great." Then he blushed, a dark red flood that began at his neck and rose to his hairline.

We went back together, I not looking at him to spare his embarrassment. We gave her the buffered aspirin and got her started on the soup. I'd returned to do the charting when a low voice, asked, "Everything okay with you?"

"Well sure," I answered Timothy.

"You don't look like it's okay. Tell you what, I'll go help myself to some coffee, sit at your desk, and watch for lights."

"Tim, it's one thirty. Sure you're not too tired."

"Nah, when you get as old as me, you don't need the sleep that young ones like you have to have. I'll be fine."

I went back to the chart. The admission note had said, *Elderly confused female admitted via wheelchair*. The evening notes had said, *Patient resting quietly*. The notes were utterly meaningless. The patient's condition was outrageous. That poor old lady, I thought. Another visit to Ells was inevitable.

"What should I do with these things?" Rocky was standing at the desk with the orange gown held at arms length and a bag of dirty dressings in the other hand.

"Bag the gown and label it," I answered, glad I'd been an E.R. Tech two summers in a row and I knew the drill for this kind of situation. "We're going to move her to my side as soon as I chart everything. Then we'll lock the gown up in her closet and put the dressings in another bag to show the day shift.

"Sure, I can do that," he said shifting his weight from one foot to the other, nervously, "But what do I tell my day shift?"

"Tell them how we found her and what we did. Here," I said, handing him the chart, "I've written it all down."

Rocky, fiercely loyal said, "You're really smart, know that?"

"Thanks," I answered.

We pushed her bed to a private room on my wing and settled her for the night. I sent Rocky back to his side, but not before he whispered, "Do you feel someone out there watching us?"

"Out there?" I asked pointing at the front windows.

"Yeah. I can feel them boring a hole in my back. Can't you?"

I had the uneasy feeling that someone was watching us, too. "If someone is looking in those windows, they'll only see us taking care of patients. How exciting is that?"

"Yeah, Not very," Rocky said and went back to his unit.

Back at my desk, "Tim, you'll be beat tomorrow."

"Not me," he grinned, "I'm curious how your hunting went today. Were there any exposed stairs?"

"Better than that," I said and told him a very edited version of my search before showing him the conundrum.

"Now that's more like the Sapphira Domino I knew. She wanted you to have the money all along. But," he said, handing the conundrum back to me, "I'm not good at puzzles. Never was, or I'd sure help you. But why aren't you happy? Is it because she knew her life was in danger and nobody helped her?"

"Well, sure that bothers me, but my sister showed up today. She lost her job and was evicted from our apartment. She's just not very responsible."

"Probably been leanin' on you all her life. That about it?"

"Just about. She was twelve and I was seventeen when Mom died. I always let her have her way. It was just easier."

"You did good. Don't give it another thought."

Just then Molly called out, "I have to see about Molly," I said and left Timothy sitting at the desk sipping his coffee. I hurried to prevent Molly from waking up the whole floor. She had such a strong voice for such a small weak lady.

I opened her door just as she was about to call out again. Quietly shutting the door, I said, "Yes, Molly. Can I help you?"

"You can," she said. "Get me some fresh water and then sit down so we can have a chat."

When I came back with the water, I poured her a glass and helped her drink most of it. She was not feverish; her head was cool as were her hands. She held both pictures in her hands as if she'd been looking at them.

"Now," she said, "sit down and tell me all about yourself; your name, what you're doing here, everything."

"There's not much to tell. I'm Nika McGuinness. I came from Minnesota."

"Nika. Nika," Molly interrupted. "That's a Greek name, isn't it?"

"Yes," I nodded. "Yes, it is. My grandmother was from Greece. She came to this country to marry a man she'd never met. I think it was arranged by her family."

"That's so interesting, don't you think? I have a friend who came to the United States to marry a man her family had picked out, only she ran off with someone else. Isn't that fun?"

Now Molly seemed cold, her lips a little blue. I went to the closet and pulled a wool blanket off the top shelf. I tucked it around her and asked, "What was your friend's name?"

"Oh, that feels good. You're such a good nurse."

"I try, Molly," I said.

She patted my hand, "You are." She seemed to be nodding off, when suddenly she awoke, "What was it you were asking me?"

"It's not important."

"Of course it's important. You wouldn't have asked if it wasn't important. Let me think."

I felt her forehead, and found it warm again. "Molly, I'm going for a thermometer, I want to check your temperature."

"Whatever you say, dear."

"I'll be right back."

"Oh, and dear," came the faint words from the bed, "My friend's name was Sapphira. Sapphira Domino."

Chapter Thirteen

I turned back into the room, "Sapphira Domino? Are you sure? She's my aunt, my great aunt. My grandmother's sister." But Molly was fast asleep.

I had made rounds at least every hour, by alternately starting with Molly's room and ending there. This time, Molly had been last, and I could see Tim still sitting at the desk, still sipping his coffee. "Tim," I whispered, "Molly just told me she knew Aunt Sapphira. In fact she said they were friends."

"Your aunt was a friend with everyone. Couldn't think who'd want to kill a nice lady like her."

"Randall said it might have been a transient, if it wasn't me that is."

Heatedly, Tim asked, "Did that young man say such a thing?"

"Well, not exactly. He asked me where I was and what I was doing March ninth and tenth. It was easy to remember because I was a bridesmaid on the ninth and sick on the tenth."

"Robertson probably asked him to check on you instead of doing it himself. We need a new sheriff in this county. It's an easy job and people just get complacent, you know? "

I nodded.

"Anybody can see you didn't do it alibi or not. The Sheriff no doubt came up with the transient theory too, but it's hard for me to believe that. Weather up this high's not too friendly in March. No. I think it was someone who figured to benefit. I keep thinking, her husband musta had a relative none of us knew about, someone who planned to inherit. Her will pretty new?"

"Her will was signed just six days before her death."

"Six days huh? That young man of yours checking on the husband's relatives?"

I answered, "He's not my young man, he's Aunt Sapphira's attorney. And says he's looking, so far without success."

"He'll find them," Timothy nodded his head confidently, "I keep telling you, he was a good boy."

"A good boy doesn't make a good man," I said.

Tim smiled. "But somethin' else is bothering you. If it's still your sister, it's never too late to lay down the law. But I think it's more than your sister. Can I help?"

Should I confide in Tim? I would. He could know this woman.

"There's a new patient, admitted without a physician. She said 'bums' brought her to the nursing home. It seems, she fell down the basement stairs, broke her leg, managed to climb up the stairs, wrap her leg, and make it to a truck before the 'bums' woke up. She said they were living with her, while looking for her money that she hid around her place. Sound familiar?"

"Like you aunt, you mean? Where's she from?"

"We don't know. She said a veterinarian used to treat their horses and themselves too. He drove up from a place called Farmington. Do you know where that is?"

"Farmington?" Tim took off his bill cap and scrubbed his fingers through his tumbled white hair. "That's down in New Mexico. Not too far, but a ways for a veterinarian to drive. Her place must be on the border or just across into Mew Mexico. She didn't say?"

"No, she didn't," I answered, "but she was in pain and hadn't eaten since yesterday. Whoever put her to bed, didn't get any admitting information, as they should have done."

"You going to talk to the boss lady this A.M.?"

"Yes I am."

"That's the way. Your aunt'd be proud of you," he said.

I smiled, "Well, you're a good friend. I have to check on Tallulah again."

"See you tonight if you're working," he said.

"I was supposed to work a month without any time off, but according to the hours just posted, I work through the weekend and then get three days off. Hours keep changing around here."

He gave a snappy salute and turned down the corridor.

Tallulah's vital signs were still stable. Tough old lady. I'd tell Randall about her at breakfast. Maybe her 'bums' were Sappy's killers and had been about to kill again. When I swung back to the desk, Timothy was standing at the back window looking out on the parking lot.

"What's up, Tim?"

"Funniest thing. As I pulled out of the parking lot, a truck, lights off, pulled away from the curb and high tailed it out of here. Tried to follow 'em, but my pickup's built for durability not speed. They got away. Just used your phone to notify the sheriff."

"That could be the 'bums' pickup. Think we should ask the sheriff to post a deputy in front of Tallulah's door?"

"Yes, I do. And I'm sorta remembering a woman like that, a shirttail relative of my wife's. I don't know much about her, and it's maybe not even the same one, she'd be pretty old now."

"But, it could be, do you think?" I asked, hopeful we could give Tallulah a last name and a family to go with it.

"Might be, is all I can say. Anyway, the one I'm thinking of lived alone after her husband died, on a ranch that straddled the border of New Mexico and Colorado. They raised racehorses. Sold 'em for big money, because any animal from up here has bigger lungs than low land ones and can run longer without getting winded. So they say. When her man died, she sold 'em off. Some kind of trouble about it. I'll think on it, it'll come to me."

"There's the sheriff's car now," I said.

Timothy hurried down the stairs to the basement. I watched them standing by the sheriff's car, talking, before they both got in and drove away. I didn't see Timothy again that night, and wondered, when I had time, if they caught up with the 'two bums.'

Another check of all patients found them sleeping. All except Molly, who was contented because someone was strumming a guitar and softly singing. The singer I couldn't see was Charlie, she said. She was right, I couldn't see him, but I could hear the music. I needed a couple of good nights sleep, to stop hearing music where there was none.

So I smiled and said, "Just not too loud." Although the window was closed, it was chilly in the room, so I covered Molly with an extra blanket.

After morning report, I stopped at Ells' office to recommend that a watch be posted in front of Tallulah's door. A suggestion she negated, telling me I wasn't in a big city anymore. I also verified my days off at the beginning of next week and picked up my check…,minus the over-time, which she'd have ready for me Monday. I'd have breakfast at the cafe and then open a checking account at the bank. I'd been avoiding the cafe unless Randall made a specific date for us to meet there, but this morning I hoped he came in.

I was seated at the usual table, drinking decaf coffee before Randall arrived. On Tim's recommendation, I'd decided to tell him about Kassi's sudden arrival and about Tallulah's problems.

Watching him stride across the dining room, greeting each person as he made his way to me, my heart, that most treacherous organ, lurched. I couldn't be falling for a lawyer. Not that. But he was so handsome and he seemed so glad to see me.

"I was afraid to hope you'd be here this morning," he said.

"I'm glad you came for breakfast, because I need to talk over a couple of things with you, if you have the time."

"I always have time for you." His smile crinkled the corners of his eyes, those beautiful sapphire blue eyes.

Without meaning to, I sighed and gazed back at him. "It's business."

He covered my hand with his. "A lot of business is conducted in small town cafes, Dad always said." Randall was wistful when he spoke of his dad.

"He'll get better, Randall," I squeezed his hand to reassure him, "Truly. I know it seems slow, but, with therapy, stroke patients do make progress."

"Hope I'm not interrupting," Phyllis said, clearing her throat, "but if you'd like to order?"

"I've already ordered," I said.

"I'll have my usual," Randall added, not taking his eyes from mine, or his hand away.

"I'll try to remember what it is you usually have, Mr. McClean," Phyllis huffed as she turned away.

"What can I help you with?"

"Look," I said, pulling away my hand. "I have to tell you that I have no intention to stay out here once Aunt Sapphira's estate is settled."

"I understand," Randall said covering my hand with his again. "Is that what's troubling you?"

I removed his hand. "And I have to think clearly. So none of that," I said firmly.

"Yes ma'am," Randall answered.

I waited for Phyllis to serve our breakfasts, my egg on whole-wheat toast and juice, and Randall's heart-health vegetable omelet. "A couple of things, but I need to start with a lady that was admitted yesterday afternoon at change of shift." I repeated as accurately as I could remember what Tallulah had said and what Timothy had said. "He's a big fan of yours, by the way."

"I remember him," Randall nodded. "I used to see him in Dad's office a lot. They were friendly, but I think Dad did some legal work for him too. His opinion of me is a little slanted by what Dad said." Randall laughed softly, then added, "You probably know more about him than I do."

"He was in the service during the Vietnam war, has a daughter who lives in Fort Collins, a new grandchild he's not seen, and his wife died a few years ago," I said.

"That's a lot more than I know," Randall said. "He must be in his sixties. His health good?"

"He has arthritis, pretty bad in his hands. I think his pain keeps him awake, he doesn't sleep well. He's the custodian at the nursing home and says Aunt Sapphira got him the job. He's very loyal to her."

"Anyone who knew her feels that way," Randall said.

"Clearly, someone didn't. Speaking of which, you mentioned the theory of a transient shooting Aunt Sapphira, and Tallulah called the people who moved in with her 'bums.' They drove her to the nursing home in a truck and just left her in the lobby. And someone in a truck sped away from the nursing home last night. Tim tried to follow, but they were going too fast for his pickup. He called the sheriff and they went off together. Timothy said he'd ask for a deputy to be placed outside Tallulah's door. I repeated the same request to Ells this morning, but she said no. Could you back us up?"

"My pleasure," Randall said, "that's only one problem. You said there were a couple of things."

I debated, should I tell him about the conundrum? I'd told Tim, hadn't I? Did I trust Tim more than Randall? Maybe I'd tell him after I'd told him that Kassi needed a job. I explained briefly that Kassi had been evicted and arrived on my doorstep yesterday and that she needed a waitress job.

"How'd she get here?" he asked.

"A family friend, Phillip Sym, we've known him forever. He drove her out," I said.

"You date him?"

Randall's question was unexpected and put me on the defensive. "Yes some. Nothing serious," I answered.

"I see," Randall said. "I'll be out about five. I'd like to meet your sister and report what I've found out about Tallulah. That all right?"

"Sure," I said.

"Another thing, I think Phyllis has to take a leave of absence, to place her son in a group home and her husband in a drug rehabilitation place. I told you about that, didn't I?" When I nodded, he continued. "Maybe Kassi can fill in for her. I'll ask. If they can use her, they may even call her today."

"Thanks Randall. I'll see you this afternoon."

* * * * * * *

"Sooo, Nika? Where have you been?"

Kassi was dressed to go out, displaying her aggravation by tapping her foot on the red tile floor of the entry.

"Kassi, I stopped by the bank. It wasn't open so I had toast and juice at the Cafe."

"You got paid?"

"Yes, Kassi, I got my check and I opened a checking account."

"Then you won't mind writing me a check. I need some shoes."

I was too tired for this. "No Kassi I can't write you a check. I just opened the account. I won't get the checks for a week or so."

"But they gave you some of those temporary checks, didn't they?"

This person was my sister who opened new checking accounts like buying popcorn at the movie. When she'd emptied her latest account, she solved the problem by opening a new one. "Yes. They did," I said, "but I'd like the money to just wait for *me* to decide what bills I should pay first. And believe me, new shoes for you are way down the list of things to buy."

"Well, okay then. I can't accept my new job." The tears began their trail down her cheeks. "I thought you'd be so proud of me, I called the only restaurant in a hundred miles and got the only job they had, a waitress. But I don't have any low heeled white shoes, which I must have to work there."

It wasn't the only restaurant and I'd bet they called her. I asked, "In Towne Cafe?"

Kassi nodded.

"How much will they cost?"

Kassi sniffled, "I called the shoe store and the nicest man answered, but he can't charge them because *you* haven't established credit with them. So I have to pay in cash or by check."

"How much?"

"A hundred and fifty dollars."

I studied my sister before answering. Was this the time to put Tim's advice into practice? "I have breakfast often at that cafe, and the waitress wears black shoes, with rubber wedgie soles that elevate the heels. You will notice, Kassi, that I'm wearing sport shoes. I bought them at the shoe store next to a women's shop for seventy-nine dollars and, Kassi, they charged them. Now what do you really need money for?"

"I'm broke! I need some spending money after all."

I opened my purse and took out a ten-dollar bill, "This is spending money, not a hundred and fifty dollars. The waitresses wear plain black uniforms with 'In Towne Cafe' stamped on the back, so I assume they're furnished. I'd recommend you take off the high heels and put on those black flats you wore yesterday. It's a busy place, mostly men, and they tip generously. You should make enough in tips to have your own spending money and I'll expect you to pay room-rent here."

"Pay for my own room? You inherited this beautiful mansion and I'm your sister and your guest, too. And you want me to pay for my room? You never asked for rent before, you're being mean." For a change Kassi wasn't crying, but she was so angry she shook.

"No. I never asked you to pay rent, I paid it out of my school loans. It was a mistake. You're irresponsible, and it's my fault. Well, I'm correcting my mistake as of now. You will pay rent. If you run out of money, your clothes will be out in front, and if you can't stretch tips for pocket money, I'll not give you any. You Kassi, will grow up."

Kassi's lips trembled, her eyes filled with tears, which was her usual response when I was firm. Before, I'd always given in, but not this time. This time I would not relent. "It's no good Kassi. My mind's made up."

Her voice was meek when she finally spoke, "I paid for groceries."

"Occasionally! Occasionally and only when I got on your case, you did buy some groceries," I said.

Kassi's tears began to spill, "You're right. I know I'm selfish and I'll try to do better. Can I use Bertha?"

"Sure," I said handing over the keys, "but put gas in her."

She looked startled, "Nika, don't you love me anymore?"

Putting my arms around her, I gave her the best hug I knew how. "I love you very much, Kassi. Very, very much."

She hugged me back, "I thought maybe you didn't love me anymore."

"Not a chance," I said.

After she left, I cried a little myself. If this *tough love* stuff worked with Kassi, she'd be a great friend as well as a loving sister. It would be so nice if I wouldn't always have to be alert for disappearing money. I went to sleep blessing Tim.

When I woke, it was five and I remembered Randall said he'd be here then. I got up, found a clean pair of sweats, washed and went to the kitchen where I put on a pot of decaf coffee. I went to open the patio door and found Randall sitting in one of the chairs.

"Gees, I'm sorry I kept you waiting out here. Come in, please," I said.

"Good afternoon, or do I say morning?"

"Better say afternoon. I hardly know what day it is anymore let alone what time of day," I answered. "I put on a pot of coffee. Will you have a cup with me? It's decaf, I'm afraid."

He was standing over me, "Decaf's fine," he answered softly, "whatever you like is fine with me."

Looking up at him was like drowning, I thought, because nothing existed for me but his deep blue eyes.

He bent down and kissed me on the lips. It was not a kiss to greet a casual friend, but a full-on-the-mouth kiss that increased my heart rate alarmingly.

This must stop, I thought, but he pulled away first.

"Let me help you pour that coffee. I brought some cookies from the bakery; they make good peanut butter ones. Do you like peanut butter cookies?"

I was still standing in the patio door. "Ah, yes, sure I *love* peanut butter cookies."

"Good," he said stepping quickly back down the steps to stand beside me and cup my chin in his hand, "good, because I love dark- eyed girls who love peanut butter cookies." He pulled me close and we did a good job of it. No telling what would have happened, but the phone began ringing.

He pushed me away and said, "Why did I leave this number where I could be reached. We will finish this later."

He strode over to the phone. "Randall McClean here."

I didn't listen to his end of the conversation, because I was too busy stilling my hammering heart and carrying coffee, mugs, and a plate of cookies out to the patio.

I was nibbling a peanut butter cookie when a very serious Randall joined me. "Trouble?" I asked.

"The strangest thing," he said, "I tried all day to reach Ells, even drove out there, but I couldn't see or talk to her. She was always in a meeting. Same thing with the sheriff. I left word for both of them to call me either at the office or here. Was there a call for me before I got here?"

"If there was, I slept through it. There isn't a telephone in my room, and I might not hear the others. What's happened?"

"We'll get a phone in your room, I'll do it in the morning. Maybe a lock on your bedroom door too."

"You're making me nervous, and I've never been afraid in Sappy's house."

Randall asked, "Sappy? Who's Sappy?"

"Something I came across. By accident," I amended. I wasn't ready to tell Randall or anyone but Tim about the conundrum. "Anyway, Kassi and I used to call her Sappy. Aunt Sapphira was too long and too hard for us to pronounce."

"Was it a letter to you?" Randall was studying me sharply, like he was trying to read my mind.

"Well," I stalled.

"It was a letter, wasn't it?" Randall exalted, "She promised to tell you where the money was hidden. She did, didn't she?"

"She wrote a short note, addressed to me, Nika, proving that she did know who her intended heir was, the opposite of what you said when you read the will to me."

I smoldered, it was always the same. Every time he began to look attractive to me, he said some stupid thing that made me furious. He was a pompous jerk, who wanted to manage my life. I'd never tell him about the conundrum now.

"Whoa, sorry if I jumped on this piece of news. But it's so important. I'd like that letter," seeing my look of disbelief he added, "to make it part of the record, in the law firm's safe."

Not now, not ever, I thought. "Not to worry. It's in a safe place. But what, by the way, is the 'strangest thing' you were going to tell me. Something to do with Ells and the sheriff."

"Sorry. Just keep the letter in that safe place of yours. That was the sheriff. That woman you admitted last night?"

"Of course. Tallulah. I felt she was in danger and I reported this to Ells and to you."

“Ah, right,” Randall said. ”The phone call was from the sheriff. Your patient was dead when the day shift checked on her after you gave report and left.”

“Dead! What did she die from?”

“They’ll do a post. It’s pretty likely she was murdered. They couldn’t locate the truck Timothy saw. It was a gray panel truck. Another thing, they don’t know where her ranch is. He’s got someone working on it.”

“Are you telling me they will say this is my fault?”

“No, I’m not saying that. There are no suspects, he said, except perhaps these ‘bums’ she allegedly told you about.”

I asked, “She didn’t *allegedly* tell me, she told me about them at some length.”

Randall nodded.

“But he thinks she was murdered? How, does he know that? She couldn’t have been shot, someone would have heard that.”

“The physician who responded to Ells’ call, said it looks like she was smothered.”

Chapter Fourteen

A car door slammed in the distance. Not Kassi, a part of my brain thought, the door didn't squeak. Better get this said, before someone barged in on us.

"No way," I said. "She didn't smother. We positioned pillows to prevent her involuntarily moving the leg and forcing the broken bones though the skin. She had one pillow under her head. I checked her every half hour all night; she'd rouse, smile at me and go right back to sleep. Poor lady."

"Nika, no one is saying this is your fault," Randall said.

"Sure they're not. You know they're biased against me. Half the town thinks I shot my aunt. You know that, as well as I do. What they don't understand is that if Tallulah had been anyone of them, I'd have given that person best nursing care I know how to give. When I take care of a stranger, I am taking care of one of them." I'd jumped to my feet, spilling both mugs of coffee. "And I take that kiss back. I take both kisses back."

"Wait. Just wait." Randall put his hand out, "No one's accusing you. Sheriff said he *thought* she'd been smothered."

"This is the same sheriff who is still baffled by Sappy's murder? Now he has another questionable death under similar circumstances and he is baffled again. What a big surprise! What obscure bit of evidence made him conclude that Tallulah was smothered?"

Randall ignored the coffee spill and answered in lawyer-speak, which made me more furious than ever.

"They found her not breathing, a pillow over her face. It seemed reasonable to conclude she'd been smothered. No one, not anyone believes you smothered that woman."

"What kisses? Who got smothered?" Kassi stood with one foot on the brick walk and the other on the patio. Could it have been Bertha's door? "Nika," she said, "is this man harassing you?" She glared at Randall, "We'll sue!"

"Did you come home in Bertha?" I asked, visions of new car payments running through my head.

"Oh course, I came home in Bertha. What do you think?"

"But the door didn't squeak." I said.

"Oh that," Kassi said, "one of the guys in the cafe said there was no reason why I had to put up with that door. He got a can of something and sprayed the door. It doesn't squeak anymore. Funny you didn't have it taken care of yourself."

Knowing it sounded petty didn't stop me, "You've always had so much free time, it's funny didn't have it taken care of before this."

Randall ignored the blooming family row, "You must be Nika's sister, Kassi, that I've heard such nice things about," he smiled warmly. "I'm your aunt's attorney Randall McClean."

Without missing a beat, Kassi behaved in predictable fashion. "I'm so happy to meet you ah, Mr. McClean?" She asked, gazing up helplessly and holding out one delicate hand. "Do I call you Mr. McClean or should I call you Randall?"

"Randall, by all means," he said, surreptitiously appraising her luscious figure while shaking both her hands and holding them a tad too long. Only Kassi and I knew he'd just lost his scalp.

To tell the truth the only boyfriend I'd ever had who wasn't more enamored with Kassi than me, was Phillip, and he was no prize. Come to think about it, Phillip and Randall were a lot alike. Randall was an attorney and Phillip soon would be, and they both had the disgusting habit of trying to control me. "Randall," Kassi said gazing up at him with sincere blue eyes, "If Nika's in some sort of trouble *again*, I'm here to help-as always. Let me just wipe up this mess."

Oh pa-leeze Kassi, I thought. You help me? Never happen.

However, Randall was doing the wiping up and pouring fresh coffee, completely mesmerized by my sister. Like I cared?

We were soon sitting back down at the patio table sipping coffee and nibbling cookies, which had miraculously escaped the coffee spill. I ignored both Kassi and Randall, their conversation buzzing around me like a flock of Minnesota mosquitoes. If there'd only been a guard outside Tallulah's door. Maybe if I'd been firmer, or the sheriff had insisted maybe then Ells might have allowed a guard to be posted. But even without the guard, it couldn't have been easy for the 'bums' to enter Tallulah's room. Only Rocky, Timothy, and I knew which room was hers. How did they find her? Did they just ask someone?

Could they have entered the basement with the day shift, hidden until half the staff went down for breakfast, and then walked up the back stairs and into Tallulah's room? It was next to the exit-stairs, after all. Or maybe they'd eaten breakfast in the cafeteria which was open to anyone, visitor or staff, and had overheard the order to add a tray for a new patient and the room number. Even if they had been that lucky, they'd have had to find the room…,unless they had been part of the construction crew who built the nursing home. I needed to talk to Tim.

"Kassi, may I have the keys to Bertha?"

"Please," Randall said, "we need to talk. Privately."

"I don't think so," I said heading down the hall.

"Yes, we do," Randall was close on my heels.

"By jingo, you're a stubborn man," I said.

"Nika, please don't use that word. Everyone knows what you mean and it's not lady-like," Kassi's voice followed us.

"Stuff it, Kassi," I called over my shoulder. "Come on Randall, you can have five minutes."

I led him down the hall to Sappy's sitting room just as a phone began to ring. "That call will be for you too," I said.

He shot me a mystified look and started out the door. The ringing was muffled, but came from the desk. I pulled open an over-large drawer and lifted out a flowered ceramic phone, handing him the receiver. "Why don't you take it here?" I asked.

While Randall listened, I studied the phone book, also in the oversize drawer, for Timothy Ryan. If he remembered about where Tallulah's ranch was, maybe we could find it. I was writing down the listing, when Randall hung up.

"They've arrested a suspect," Randall said, "someone who had a motive and opportunity."

"Oh good," I said relief flooding me. "Could he have also killed Sappy?"

"The sheriff hasn't connected him to your aunt's murder yet, but he is considering it."

"Oh Randall, this is wonderful news, such a relief," I said, "Who is this person? Did the sheriff give you a name?" When Randall acted reluctant to tell me, "I have a right to know. If this person also murdered Sappy, I *should* be told who it is."

There was a soft knock on the door before Sergio opened it. He held a tray with a bottle of red wine and two wine glasses.

"Gracias Sergio," I said taking the tray and setting it down on a table in front of the draped windows. As I sat down, I realized this was one of the chairs shown in the Polaroids I'd found. I glanced around the room expecting a ghost to materialize. When one didn't, I gave an involuntary shiver.

I felt the feather touch of the soft throw around my shoulders, before Randall took the other chair and poured us each a glass of wine, "You're chilled," he said, "It's cool in this room. Want me to start the fire?"

"No thanks. Someone just walked over my grave," I said, as I shivered again. Someone had been doing that a lot lately.

"Drink some wine then, that'll help."

The wine did taste warm and rich. The shivering stopped and I came back to the person in jail on suspicion of murdering Tallulah. There were *two* bums Tallulah talked about, which one had the sheriff arrested?

"Randall," I asked, "did the sheriff tell you the suspect's name? Did he arrest just one of the bums or both of them?"

Randall topped off the wine in my glass. "It's neither of the 'bums.' He arrested Timothy Ryan."

Chapter Fifteen

"Tim? He arrested Tim? He's out of his mind. The sheriff has been bumbling around for five months without a clue as to who shot Sappy and in less than eight hours knows without a doubt that Tim murdered a woman he didn't know and had no reason to want dead? It's insane. He's insane. I want Tim out of jail. I want you to get him out. Now."

"Nika," Randall said, "I can't do that. As you said there are similarities between this and your aunt's murder. I can't represent Timothy because of possible 'conflict of interest.'"

"Then we'll get another attorney. You must know someone."

Randall reached for my hand, but I grabbed the glass of wine, gulped a mouthful, "I intend to get Tim out of jail. Will you help?"

Smoothly, Randall said, "There are other considerations."

"Oh yeah, right. You're wondering how I can pay for this when I can't pay the electric bill. Just understand this. Tim isn't guilty, he's my friend, and I intend help him."

"What electric bill?" Randall asked.

Damn and damn. I'd done it. It'd slipped out, and now Randall knew I had a problem keeping up the property, he'd never let it go until I told him about this bill and all the others. This man was worse than that puppy with my Mom's best slippers. Daisy chewed everything including the sunflower stem until it fell over and then tried to eat the seeds.

Daisy! Sappy remembered and was trying to tell me something. Without realizing I was speaking, "Oh Sappy, you dear sweet old thing."

"The electric bill is sappy?" Randall asked.

When to answer meant to confess I wasn't keeping up the property, I just took a long drink of wine. Then, to my embarrassment, I hiccupped.

"That's enough to drink," Randall said as he took the glass from my hand. "Now, what electric bill?"

"Oh, the electric bill," I said as off-hand as I could, "It came the other day. It's not been paid since January. It's several hundred dollars. But I finally got my check this morning and I'll pay a part of it."

"Give me the electric bill," Randall said, "I'll pay it."

"Uh uh," I said, wagging my head from side to side. "No thanks. Then I'll owe you which I refuse to do."

Randall gave a short laugh, "You're the stubborn one, know that? This money will come out of the estate account, which will be yours someday anyway. You won't owe me, you'll just owe yourself."

Stubborn? And take away my wine? I reached for the glass of and took a sip. "Now then," I said, "this is a new development. What estate account? What happened to the requirement that I keep up the property for a year?"

"You've only been here what, six weeks?"

"About," I said.

"Mrs. Domino's intention was that her heir pay her own bills, not hers. Since you didn't use the electricity until six weeks ago, you're only libel for the time you've been here. The estate account may as well pay the whole thing. As I said, it will be yours anyway," Randall explained in his most reasonable tone.

"Explain to me then, why I owe several hundred dollars for that Reatta," I demanded, "Explain that to me."

"I took care of that too. If you'd looked in the garage window you'd have seen it was gone. I'm storing it in my folks garage, for now."

"Why do you twist everything to be my fault, this time for not noticing the car was gone?" Fury made my voice tremble, "Why not just tell me you paid the bill? Or is that too straight forward and honest for you?"

Randall wasn't even embarrassed. "I saw it as just one more duty of your aunt's attorney."

So furious, I couldn't trust myself to speak, I drew deep breaths to calm myself. The important thing was to get Tim out of jail, as quickly as possible.

"O.K.," I said, trying to be as smooth as Randall, "then I may as well owe myself whatever amount it takes to get Tim out of jail and defend him on this ridiculous charge."

Randall was studying me. "Unreasonable too," he said.

"Those are only my good points, wait until you get to the bad ones," I said getting up. "I'm ready to go, are you?"

"Where are we going?" Randall asked.

"To the jail, you and I are getting Tim out."

"Nika, I can't represent Tim."

"Then we'll call an attorney who can."

Randall was uncomfortable, "The closest attorney's in Eldorado and today is Friday. It's impossible to get him here to represent Tim until Monday. At the earliest."

I challenged. "Just give me his name and I'll get him up here."

"There's a set protocol to referring a client to another attorney. I have to follow it," Randall said.

"Will you listen?" I demanded. "You just said you couldn't take Timothy as a client anyway. Just give me an attorney's name and I'll call him, leaving you completely out of it."

"His name is Roger Robertson, his office is in Eldorado. But it's not that easy." Randall said, "This is Friday, an attorney has to see the judge and ask him to set bail. Then we have to find someone who will go bail and be responsible for Timothy's actions until trial?"

"Is that all," I interrupted. "That's easy. I can do all of that. Let's go."

Confident that I'd won this time, we took off for the jail. Later, after Tim's problems were solved, we'd discuss the 'estate account' and I'd find out why Randall hadn't confided that bit of information to me before. I wanted to take separate cars, but Randall said he intended to install locks on my bedroom door when we came back and I could go on to work while he did that. When I asked 'who'd drive Tim home,' Randall, an amused smile tugging at his mouth, had agreed he would.

For security reasons, Randall said, the jail was centered in flat, spacious grounds. There were no shrubs or bushes to soften the tan brick structure, because they added hiding places for escapees. The only trees were mature deciduous ones, now fully leafed out and planted at the very edge of the grounds and along the walk, which curved up to a tall gate in a high fence.

"I suppose there are no trees around the building to prevent a convict from climbing out a window, down a tree and so to freedom," I said.

"Matter of fact, that's right," said Randall. "Very astute of you."

"Hmmm, a very high risk security prison. What kinds of inmates are held here?" I asked.

"Just locals who have too much to drink or a very occasional family quarrel when the husband or wife must be held over night to cool down," Randall answered.

"How very reassuring to know the county has gone to so much expense to protect the residents from themselves," I said.

The trees towered over our heads as we walked up the long curved walk to the gate where the sheriff waited for us as promised. His arms rested on his swollen belly, his holstered gun forced his left arm and shoulder higher than the right, and sweat stained the underarms of his tan shirt made official by the badge pinned just so over one pocket. The broad smile on his plump face should have been jolly, but the small, flat shrewd eyes held no humor so the effect was chilling.

"Good evening, sheriff," Randall said holding out his hand which the sheriff ignored, unlocking the gate instead and leading the way to the jail itself.

"We're here to see Timothy Ryan," Randall tried again.

"You said you'd be here," still smiling the sheriff turned to look us over. "You representing Tim?"

"No, that could be seen as conflict of interest," Randall said.

"Glad there'll be no trouble 'bout that," the sheriff answered. "What business do you have here then?"

Randall turned to me, "Ms. McGuinness wishes to see Tim, I represent her and I will accompany her. Ms. McGuinness, this is Sheriff Robertson."

"How do you do, Sheriff Robertson," I said emphasizing the Robertson. Was this man related to the attorney in Eldorado? How cozy.

"Sheriff," I said, finally taking his out-stretched hand, and squeezing it as firmly as years of playing softball made possible. "We came to get Tim out of jail. He's my friend and I know he had neither the motive nor the opportunity to kill Tallulah. So what do we do?" I crossed my arms, my right hand rubbing my sleeve to be rid of the chill dampness of his hand.

"You gotta get a lawyer for him. That lawyer has to see the judge and get him to set bail then find someone with enough money to go his bail. Can't do any of that until Monday, and not then unless he's been charged. Right now...,"

"Sheriff," Randall interrupted, "We'd like to see Tim, see if there's anything he needs, anyone he wants called."

"You said you weren't representing him, you got no right to see him." The sheriff crossed his own arms, and since only his fingers met, held them in place by locking his thumbs, inches apart, in the waistband. He stood sway-backed like a pregnant woman in the last trimester, a belligerent glare in his flat eyes.

Randall countered, "Ms. McGuinness wants to see him and since I do represent her, I insist on accompanying her."

"Don't you realize woman, Tim Ryan probably killed your aunt? It's not right for you to go seeing him."

"What's not right, is you holding Tim without charging him. That's what's not right. I know he didn't murder either woman. That you don't know it is, is…," I fought for words to express my fury, "shows lack of solid detective work on your part." I ended a little lamely.

"I'll take you back, but you remember, I'm the one with the badge and I'm the one with the gun. Those two things make me right. I have good reason to say that Tim Ryan's guilty." The sheriff turned and ambled his belly through another door, and down a hall where he stopped, unlocked the door, and gestured for us to enter. "This is the interview room. Take a chair and wait here," he said. His small eyes were dark buttons in his face. The heavy metal door thunked shut.

It was a gray walled room furnished with, a gray metal table bolted to the floor and four molded plastic chairs one on each side of the table. The two windows on one wall, were too high to see out of and too small to give adequate light. A high bare bulb hung over the table.

I shivered, "Well gees, where is the well-lit visitor room, with facing desks shielded by bullet proof glass?"

Randall had pulled out a chair and held it for me to sit, before taking a seat across the table, "Pretty bad, I admit, but it's what the city fathers thought a jail should look like when it was built back in the early forties."

The door was opened and a young acne faced kid pushed Tim through the door, unlocked the handcuffs and forced him to sit in a chair. Tim uttered a groan and I rose.

"That's no way to treat an arthritic patient."

"Patient? Ha, he's a prisoner, not a patient. If my old man murdered a helpless old woman I'd do worse than that to him. Well have a good talk." Laughing, he swung open the door and let it thunk shut.

"Randall, do something. He can't treat Tim that way."

"I'll go see the sheriff and then I'll wait right outside the door while you talk to Tim." Then he was gone and the door swung shut with another thunk.

Tim was wearing a thin, short sleeved, cotton shirt. There were goose bumps on his arms, his lips looked blue. He'd not last a week in here. I had to do something to get him out.

"Tim, how could this have happened?"

"It's sorry I am, that you have to see me like this," he said.

"But you had no reason to murder Sappy and you didn't even know Tallulah."

Tim looked down at the table, as though ashamed.

"You didn't know her, did you? You said you'd met her just one time," I reminded him, "or did you remember something?"

He shook his head, his shaggy white hair moving from side to side. Then he looked me right in the eye and sat up straighter.

"Who was she? Tim, tell me. I'll help you, I promise."

"She's a relative of my wife's, all right, just like I thought. That side of my wife's family we never had much to do with."

"How," I asked, trying to help him focus on his problem, "how were they related?"

"Somehow through my wife's mother, who was a shirt-tail cousin of Tallulah's mother, maybe by marriage, I don't know. They were the well-off side of the relations. I'd forgotten it, Mick. It never was important to my wife, nor to me."

"But that's such a distant relationship. That doesn't give you a motive for murder," I said.

"It's kinda a long story. We got time?"

"I'll get us time," I said, "Just tell me."

"Well some of it came out when Tallulah's husband died. They had a horse raising operation on their ranch. It was small and isolated, but made them enough money for their needs. Didn't have any kids, and kept to them selves. When he died real sudden, she found herself pretty broke and the horses too much for her to handle alone. So she sold the horses off, thinking they were hers to do with as she pleased."

"I don't see how that affects you," I said.

"Well, the stickler was that her husband had agreed to give a certain number of the foals to the owner of the stallion at stud. Some of the mares had dropped their foals and they were sold along with the mares, but there were a lot that hadn't."

"Wait a minute, wait a minute. You're way over my head," I interrupted. "What's a stallion, a mare, a foal, and a stud if it's different from the guys who hang out around Kassi."

Tim actually laughed. "You do me good, girl." He scratched his head in concentration. "I'm not good at explaining this stuff, 'cause I don't know that much about it, myself." He rubbed his head again, tumbling the thick, curly white hair still more. "A stallion is a male horse. The owners say the stallion is at stud, or ready to father a baby horse, the mare is the mother of the baby horse which is usually called a foal."

"Gotcha," I said, "I think."

"When a rancher can't afford to keep a stallion, he works out a deal with the owner of a stallion at stud to give him a certain number of foals instead of paying the usual stud fee. Most times there's a written contract, but if there was this time, the stud owner didn't have a copy nor did Tallulah. Or said she didn't. So the stud owner took her to court."

"Did he win his case?" I asked.

"Naw, didn't have any proof, he didn't. I think they settled, Tallulah talking the buyer into giving him a foal or two."

"But he didn't have any proof," I objected.

"Mostly, it's better to compromise out here, where there aren't many folks. You never know when you may need the other guy to help you out, and it's best to get along."

"But that still doesn't give you a reason to kill Tallulah."

"It's pretty indirect," said Timothy. "All of this was in the papers, but I never thought she had any money left after she paid the bills. They say she did, since none of her family's alive, it goes to my wife and says so in her will. This is the first I heard of a will."

"But, I thought you didn't even know her," I said

"We didn't, except when her husband died and it got in the papers, my wife wanted to go and express our condolences. Seemed like the decent thing to do. So she packed some of her home made bread and we set out for the ranch. It was a long drive and I don't know as we'd have found it but for a life size wooden horse up high on a hill the head pointed at the gate to the ranch."

"A horse? Life size?" I asked, "That's pretty unusual. How'd you find out about that?"

"It was in the papers along with her old man dying. Seems that horse was a land mark down there."

"Did you see her?" I asked.

"Yep. We did. At first she didn't want to let us in, but I reckon the smell of that fresh bread that'd stayed warm in the pickup did the trick. Tallulah asked us in and put on a pot of tea." Tim chuckled, "Served the tea with brandy on the side and insisted we add a little to the tea. The wife didn't like that, but it sure tasted better than weak tea. I ain't that Irish."

That made me smile. Tim liked his coffee and liked it strong. I supposed weak anything didn't suit him too well. "And because of that visit she named your wife in the will?"

"Must have, if I can believe the sheriff."

"But how did the sheriff know about the will?" I asked.

"Said he checked at the court house to see if there was a will on file and there was. Said it was normal in these cases to find out who benefited by the death. Unlucky for me, I was the only beneficiary."

"We'll get you out, don't you worry," I said laying my hand over his cold swollen ones. I believed it too, but my first concern was Tim's well-being.

There was a loud rap on the door just as the sheriff opened it. "Time. I've let you stay too long as it is. I'm not running a boarding house here."

Randall stood behind the sheriff, towering over him. Tim and I both rose, "Thanks for stopping by," Tim said, "I appreciate it."

"Excuse me sheriff," Randall said, "if I might give these things to Tim."

The sheriff slid his feet two steps to the side and allowed Randall admittance. "Tim, I brought a wool sweater, some wool socks, and a warm sweat suit for you. Although it's July, it's cold in here, and I thought you could use them."

Tim started to protest, but I interrupted with, "Of course he can. Weren't we just saying how you wished you had some warm things with you, Tim?"

Tim looked hard at me, but then smiled, "I can and I'm that grateful to you for bringing these. Your dad always said you were a good lad, and you are."

Once outside the jail, I noticed the moon was starting to show its face to the east. A glance at my watch showed me that I had less than an hour to hurry home, change my clothes and get back to the nursing home. "Gees. Randall, I've got to run," I said and hurried toward his car.

"Get in, fasten your seatbelt and I'll get you there in record time," Randall said.

Watching Randall skillfully navigate every curve and tight corner while checking the rear view mirror and every crossroads for other cars, fear gradually rose in my throat. That he believed someone would try to kill me next, was evident.

"It's too quiet, not even any lights," I said, when we got to the mansion.

He pulled up close to the patio. "There's a light in the kitchen, run on ahead while I lock the car."

Quietly, my throat tight and my heart hammering, I stepped onto the patio. Had someone entered and killed Kassi? Or Juana? Why didn't they lock the doors and pull the drapes like I asked them to do? I slid back the screen and walked into the wide-open patio door.

I needn't have worried; an oblivious Kassi was dressed for bed, but curled up in one of the leather chairs watching TV. How could she be so relaxed and me so worried about her? Randall followed me in and slid the patio door shut and locked it.

Kassi didn't flinch. As furious as I was with her, my empty stomach needed immediate attention. Scold Kassi or eat? The hunger won. I had to work tonight.

"Kassi, is there anything around here to eat?"

No answer, "Kassi, are there any left-overs?"

"Sure, but you better hurry or you'll be late."

Hands on hips, I was ready to vent my fury when Randall said, "Go change your clothes, I'll make you something to eat."

Still damp across my shoulders and back, I was dressed except for one shoe, which I couldn't find. Finally in desperation, I turned on all the lights and lay on my stomach searching under every piece of furniture until I spotted it under the bed. "Damn, how did you get under there?"

"Are you talking to yourself?"

I sat up and pulled the shoe on, but by then I was mad at everyone especially Kassi. "Kassi, you are never again to sit with the door wide open, in plain view of anyone who just happens to be passing by. Don't you realize you could have been killed? From now on, you are to lock all the doors when Juana and Sergio leave. Every single door. Do you understand?"

Hands hugging her shoulders, Kassi's face was shocked, her wide blue eyes gazed back at me.

"Did you hear me?" I asked.

"What's wrong with you? We're way out in the country. Who's to pass by?"

"How do I know? It's just not safe. Not anymore." Was my answer.

I followed her back down the hall to the kitchen, "As soon as I leave, lock this door and pull the drapes. Check all the other doors to be sure they're locked, even the basement. When you go to bed, lock the bedroom door and be sure the phone is plugged in. If it rings, answer it, but don't say you're alone. If someone does call, telephone me at work right away. Promise?"

"Is Randall spending the night?" Kassi asked hopefully.

"No," Randall, who stood at the kitchen door, answered. "I'll only be here long enough to install a lock on Nika's door."

"You guys are frightening me."

"That's our intention. You need to be frightened. Just do as I say. Want me to call when I get to the nursing home?"

"Yes."

It was a small yes, but I thought she'd do as I asked her.

Randall walked me out to the pickup that he'd pulled close to the patio. "Wait a minute."

I was ready to leave, the engine running and the lights on.

"This is the key to the new lock. I'll install it in your bedroom door tonight before going home. The other key will be on your bedside stand. Another thing," he said, "this is Dad's cell phone. I want you to have it, carry it with you at all times and take it into your room while you're sleeping."

"I don't know how to operate those things, and I don't need one," I answered. Would he ever stop trying to control me?

"I'm concerned for your safety. We both know Timothy didn't murder Tallulah, if she was murdered, nor did he kill Mrs. Domino. That means whoever did kill them is still out there, and as Mrs. Domino's heir, you're in danger."

"It's the money, isn't it?" I said, not so much a question as restating a basic fact I'd forgotten with this latest death.

“Has to be,” answered Randall, “and as word gets around that Tim is under suspicion for both murders, the real killer will get bolder and may try to hunt for the money while you’re asleep.”

“But if I keep the door locked, he can’t get to me.”

“True, but I want you to have a telephone to call for help. At least until I can get someone out to install a jack in your room. Now listen carefully, it works like an ordinary phone. Push this button to turn it on, dial like a phone, and then push ‘talk.’ If you’re in trouble…,of any kind, the number taped to the bottom is my cell phone number. I’ll have my cell phone with me at all times and I’ll know it’s you. All you have to do is tell me where you are and that you need help. I’ll get you help. I promise.”

“I guess I can do that.”

“No guessing. Just promise me you’ll do it.”

“O.K. Randall, I promise,” I said. He did look concerned. I thought maybe this kind of controlling was acceptable.

“Now, fasten your seat belt and drive carefully.”

”Ah gees, Randall, give me a break. I’m grown up and do take care of myself. You can be such a pain…,“ I revved the engine and shifted into reverse.

“But you aren’t a careful driver. You go too fast…,” His words faded as I shifted into first and gunned the engine. Bertha coughed once and took off spewing gravel and sand.

Chapter Sixteen

With Randall's warning echoing in my ears, I drove, checking the rear-view mirror and searching each cross road for signs of another vehicle. I'd reached the edge of Magdalena, my mind working on a plan to solve Tallulah's murder, when a phone began to ring. "What phone is ringing?" I asked stupidly and looked around the truck cab. The phone rang insistently.

"Damn and damn. The cell phone Randall lent me. He must be calling me." Guiding Bertha with one hand I searched the seat with the other until I felt the vibrating phone under the sack with my dinner in it.

"Hello Randall," I said. "What do you want?"

"What if it's not me?"

I sighed, "Who else could it be? This is your phone and presumably you're the only one who knows I have it. What do you want?"

"Just to know that you have the phone with you and that you're not in trouble," he answered.

I maneuvered Bertha into the parking lot behind the nursing home, with one hand, while holding the cell phone with the other. "I've managed my whole life without you, and I can manage now."

"You've never been the target of a killer before," he said, "I need to impress you with the seriousness of your situation."

"So I'm impressed," I shrugged, "but no one has threatened me, no one's lurking around the nursing home, and it just doesn't alarm me too much. Besides, I have to go to work. Good night!" I broke the connection as I parked Bertha behind the nursing home.

Now, I thought, he'll call me all night and I can't have that. What to do with this thing? What do other people do with them? Where do you store a cell phone?

Under the front seat, I thought. I stashed the phone and prepared to get out. Oh no, I remembered reading that police said, "That's the first place a thief looks."

So where then? There was a small space between the seat and the back of the cab, just about right for a cell phone, deep and dark. I dropped the cell phone and stuffed a newspaper on top, before locking up Bertha.

The nursing home looked unfamiliar, much like the first time I'd seen it. The dark central office rode in disembodied detachment atop the brilliantly lit basement. In contrast, the two dimly lit second floor wings angled away from the dark office suite. For a moment I panicked and very nearly returned to the security of Bertha and Randall's cell phone. In time I remembered the only difference between tonight and other nights, was that the reassuring presence of Tim wouldn't be here. He was locked up in jail for a crime he didn't commit, not in a million years. Resolutely, with heart still pounding, I entered and climbed the stairs to the second floor where my greeting was less that friendly.

"You're late," the three evening shift nurses said in a chorus, perhaps you forgot the night shift is supposed to be here and ready for our report by ten thirty."

I glanced at the clock, "It's ten forty-five. Unless there was a new admittance or major changes in the old patients, you can give me a brief report and be on your way home by eleven. The time I'm scheduled to take over, I believe."

She set a record for fast reports. Two of them were gone before the charge nurse Billy, finished. Not a great crew, but I didn't have to work with them.

"Ho Billy," I said, as she picked up her purse, "check the basement door to see that it's locked to outsiders as you leave."

"I've never done that before," she huffed.

"When you leave, there'll be no one here but Rocky and me. It'll save our time and assure the safety of the patients and us, if you check the door on your way out."

"But…," she began.

"Just do it. One unexplained death should be enough for you," I snapped.

"It's not unexplained. That Ryan man, he does the scut work around here, has been arrested. To think, he was always out there on the parking lot watching us leave." She shivered, "Gives me the creeps. Always thought there was something wrong with him. Thought he was some kind of a pervert."

I was putting together a suitable retort, when she said," I sure hate to go out on the parking lot alone."

"I can see the whole parking lot from the back window." I pointed behind the desk. "I'll watch you get into the car." This whole conversation had been about the evening shift being afraid to stay here. If they only knew what I knew, I thought.

"Thanks Nika," Billy said, "I'll check the door too," and ran for the stairs.

I watched from the back window until she came into view and turned to make an'O' with her thumb and finger to indicate she'd checked the door and it was locked to the outside. I watched her flashlight bounce along with her steps and I waved as she climbed into her car and drove away. Now it was just Rocky and me, I thought, and jumped at his cheerful voice behind me.

"In case you're wondering, I always check the front door to see if it's locked, and it is."

"I didn't know that was one of your duties," I said as I dumped black coffee down the sink. No Tim to save it for tonight.

"It isn't, I guess, but Tim showed me how and asked if I'd be responsible for it." He shrugged, "So I check it every night. We can get out and, if anyone wants to get in, there's an emergency bell by the door that rings on my unit."

I'd added water to the coffee maker and was measuring ground coffee. "I didn't know any of those things," I said. "Thanks."

"Do you ever get the feeling that someone's out in front on the parking lot watching us?" He asked. He'd asked this before.

I glanced toward the front windows which, during the day, filled the small lobby with sunshine, but which acted like a mirror at night, reflecting every move we made. "No, Tim used to check for cars in both lots. Doesn't seem to me anyone could see much of us from out there."

"I drove by tonight and you can see almost the whole of both wings from out there. Why didn't they hang blinds at those front windows? Someone out there can see everything we do. Don't you ever feel eyes watching you?" Rocky fidgeted nervously.

I'd better not admit that I had thought someone was out there watching us. "Look Rocky, I think Tallulah's death has us on edge. As long as I can turn on a light for your help and you can do the same for me, we'll be all right. The doors are all locked, and anyone who stands out there watching us do our boring stuff just doesn't have much to do."

"You're right," he said, sheepishly.

"Would you like us to make rounds together tonight?" I asked.

"Nah, that's okay, but say that emergency bell has never rung when I've been here, but if it rings tonight will you go along to answer the door?" He asked.

"Sure, and if we don't have a good view of who's out there, we'll not open the door. Deal?" I asked.

"Deal," he said as he started back to his unit, but stopped. "Say," he said, and he was grinning, "say, is it my imagination or did you jump when I came up behind you?"

There was no way to fool Rocky. "I jumped," I said, "but if the emergency bell rings, I'll go with you to the door. Promise."

Still grinning he said, "Thanks."

I opened the drawer for the flashlight I used to make rounds, tried it, and found it dead. "Damn and damn. How can that be?"

I carried the flashlight to the back counter and opened it under the fluorescent light. As I'd thought, there were no batteries. Someone took the batteries for their own flashlight, someone on the evening shift. Someone, who was afraid to cross the parking lot and get into her darkened car. Where were extra batteries? I rummaged through drawers likely to have batteries stored in them, but found nothing. Not light bulbs, not batteries, nothing.

I ran with rubber soled quiet to Rocky's unit where he was rummaging through drawers, "Rocky, are you looking for batteries?" "Your flashlight dead too?" He asked.

"It is," I said.

"Darn second shift took the batteries. They're such losers, can't think of us. Just them." His face was red with fury.

"Yeah, I think you're right. Do you know where they keep batteries around here?" I asked.

"Sure. Timothy kept them locked up somewhere. He got some one other time when the same thing happened. Before you started here. He didn't tell you?"

"I guess they're not available to us," I said.

Rocky shook his head, "No, they sure aren't. But we could turn the hall lights up to bright and leave the doors ajar while we make rounds."

But I was remembering the day I bought work shoes and the kid who wanted his band to play in Aunt Sappy's ballroom. He'd shoved a couple of small flashlights into my hand along with his business card. Now, if I still had them in my purse, we could get by tonight.

"Rocky, maybe I've got flashlights in my purse, let's go see," I said.

Back on my unit, I emptied my purse on the counter and shoved all the accumulated debris aside. Receipts, lipsticks, pennies, crumpled tissues so soiled looking only in an emergency would I blow my nose on one. But there were three small flashlights, each dangling on the end of key a chain. "Yes," I said.

"Find something?" Rocky asked.

I handed him one of the give-away-lights after depressing the button on the end. It lit up, with a small narrow beam, barely adequate to light up the palm of my hand.

"This is a flashlight?" He asked dubiously.

"Come on, Rocky, it's better than nothing. Shine the beam on your white shirt," I said shining mine on my own white coat. "See, it gives off a quite acceptable glow. It'll get us through the night. That's all we need."

He did as I'd told him and smiled a jaunty grin, "Say, you're good, boss." He was on his way back to his unit.

I dialed our telephone number, and the phone was picked up on the first ring.

"Nika?"

"Yes, it's Nika," was all I could say before a verbal deluge spilled out of the telephone.

"What took you so long? I've been sitting here thinking you were killed right out here in our own yard. I looked out front, but remembered you parked Bertha by the patio door, and I was afraid to go out there. I worry about you all the time. You just have to quit this night job. It's bizarre for you to work nights when you're an heiress. Really."

"Randall gone?" I asked.

"Hours ago," Kassi answered. "I don't like being alone here. You're supposed to take care of me, Mama said."

"Kassi, I called as I promised as soon after I got here as I could. How are you? Is the house secure? All the doors locked?"

"Yes, all the doors are locked, even the door to this bedroom. I'm cowering under the blankets, because I'm afraid to even have the bedside lamp on. Afraid someone out there will look in and see me. If I could have a lamp on, I could read a book and that'd take my mind off everything. But no, I can't even do that."

"Kassi, listen. There are wooden shades on your bedroom windows and lined drapes to pull over the windows. Why don't you get up, shut the shades, they work just like the Venetian blinds in our old house, next pull the drapes over the window. No one can see in, then."

"You think?"

"Yes, I think. I'll wait for you to do it."

She was back to the phone in minutes, "Nika, this is great. It's cozy. I won't be afraid now."

"I'm glad. Good night, Kassi."

It was after midnight when I peeked into Molly's room. She was sleeping so I decided to make rounds with Rocky to see if he had any surprises for me. He was glad of the company and together we checked each of his patients. The tiny flashlight aimed at my lab coat gave enough light. His people were all ambulatory, and one old gentleman was just climbing into bed after going to the bathroom.

He reached up his hand in a gesture to tip a cap, and apologized when there was none there to tip. "I keep fergittin' I can't wear the old cap at night, not while I'm in here."

"The gesture is all we need," I said, "You sleep well, now."

"Yes ma'am, I always do," he answered as he crawled into bed.

It was after one when I began rounds on my side. I was pleased. There was no smell of urine, and everyone was asleep, until I got to Molly's room, and she was wide-awake and bright eyed.

"Good morning, dear," she smiled patting the side of her bed. "Sit here, rest your feet and listen to the music."

"Music?" I asked stupidly.

"Yes dear. Charlie's going to sing for us. And play his guitar."

"Really," was all I could say. She'd talked about Charlie before, but I'd never seen him. Why must I meet him tonight of all nights?

"You look dismayed. Haven't you met Charlie?" she asked.

"Not really," I answered cautiously. Whoever he was, I couldn't let him wander around my unit playing and singing. How had he gotten in? Was there a window unlocked? My knees were refusing to hold me upright, and I sank onto the bed.

"That's right dear," Molly said, holding my hand in her very warm one. "You look a little peaked. If I just had some of Sapphira's Ouzo, just a thimble full would make things right for you. She brings it straight over from Greece, you know. There's nothing like it when you're not quite up to snuff, and I know it would make you feel good."

Oh you bet, I thought, it sure would, and you dear lady have a fever again. "I'm getting a thermometer," I said as I started to rise, "I think you may have a fever." At least this was a problem I could do was something about.

"Oh posh," she said, "who cares about a little fever. I haven't felt this good since my husband passed away. Now you just sit here beside me. Charlie promised he'd be right back."

I was checking her forehead with the back of my hand when I heard guitar music. It was playing softly, some gentle tune, but it was close by. I searched the room and there in a dim corner I saw a shadow of someone who sat on a straight chair, holding a guitar. He looked as though he wasn't going anywhere very soon, and a Stetson, that I assumed was his, hung on a corner bedpost.

"You're Charlie?" was all I could say.

"Evenin' ma'am," he said smiling. "Anything special you'd like me to sing?"

I gulped, "Charlie, you shouldn't be here. You must leave before someone sees you. How did you get in anyway? Everything's locked up."

"I can manage most locked doors." My eyes had adjusted to the dim light and he was more clearly defined.

Alarmed, I said, "I hope you locked the doors. This building is supposed to be secure."

"Now, don't you worry none. Ever'thin's shut and locked. No one will get in. Think I'd put my Molly in jeopardy?"

His Molly? What nerve. "Someone was murdered on this unit last night," I hissed, "and you have to go. Now."

"Please, dear," Molly was squeezing my hand. "Don't make him go. It's been so long and I do so love him."

In the distance a telephone had been ringing for sometime. It was distracting. Here I had Charlie, hanging around like he owned the place and refusing to do as I told him to. "Wish someone would answer that phone," I said to myself.

"You go answer the phone, I'll sing to Molly," Charlie said.

Of course, it was the phone on the desk. I'd better get it before it woke the whole unit. I hurried to the door, "You better be gone when I get back," I said to the corner.

"Yes Ma'am," I heard as I ran down the hall.

"Yes," I said catching the phone before it rang again.

"Nika, what took you so long? I'm terrified and I can't get you to answer the phone."

"I should have known it was you," I said. "Kassi, I'm at work, I'm responsible for the whole nursing home. Can't you take care of yourself? Just for one night?"

"Can't you wait until I've explained, just once? Until I've told you what's going on out here in the country where not another soul is within a hundred miles."

"It's nowhere near a hundred miles," I said. I could hear guitar music, persistent plucking and soft singing of words I couldn't hear and a tune I couldn't identify. Knowing Kassi, I'd have to solve her problems before taking care of my other responsibilities. "Okay Kassi, tell me what's bothering you?"

"Nika, someone's in that garage apartment."

"Maybe it's Sergio, he has the only key," I said while wondering what errand would take Sergio to the garage apartment at night. "It must be close to one."

"It's nearly one thirty and I haven't slept at all. I got out of bed to get some warm milk and happened to look out of the kitchen window, the ones over the sink, and there was this light bobbing around. Like it's someone with a flashlight. Nika, I'm really frightened." Her voice was shaking.

"I still think it must be Sergio," I said.

"Why would he go up there at night? And why wouldn't he just turn on a light? No Nika, it's someone who doesn't belong there. Wait, the light went off. What'll I do if he gets in the house?"

"If it's Sergio, you have nothing to worry about and I'll ask him in the morning what he was doing up there at night. I'm sure there's a logical explanation. Why don't you just go back to bed, lock the door after you. I'll talk to you in the morning."

"Wait, he came out the garage door. Now he's walking toward the house. Nika, what'll I do?" This time I heard pure panic.

"First turn off any lights." I tried to think logically while strains of 'It had to be you' came down the corridor.

"I don't have any lights on. Just the microwave."

"Hit the stop button, and head for Aunt Sappy's room. Go in and lock the door. Stay there, no matter what. I'll get help."

"Can I take my hot milk?"

"Just go. Now," I said. "Before he sees you watching him."

"Oh gawd, Nika, he just looked up at me. I saw him tip back his head. I can't see his face, but I saw his eyes gleam. And he's got a beard. He'll kill me. Oh Nika, if I die tonight, remember I love you."

"Kassi, do as I say. Run back to Aunt Sappy's room, shut and lock the door. Quick."

"I'm going. I'm going."

I heard the connection break. I'd better call Randall, he knew the sheriff and could convince him to check on Kassi. I pushed the jumbled contents of my purse around on the counter looking for the business card Randall had given me. The card lay at the bottom of the clutter, corners curled and dirty. It had both Randall's office number and home number. I dialed the home number and waited through ten rings for him to answer. When I finally heard his sleepy hello, I was shaking helplessly.

"Randall, Kassi just called. She's got a prowler."

"Nika? Why didn't you use the cell phone? I had mine with me like I promised."

"I've no excuse and no time to explain. This is an emergency and I didn't know who else to call. Kassi has a prowler and needs someone quick."

"I'm on my way," he said as the connection broke.

I sank down into a desk chair. I was trembling uncontrollably, tears stung my eyes, "Oh God," I prayed, "please help Kassi. Don't let her die in my place. Oh please, protect her. Please." I grabbed tissues from the box on the counter and tried to stem the flow of tears. From somewhere far away, soft music played and a voice sang words about falling in love.

"I must stop this blubbering," I said aloud, "I have patients to care for. Randall will get to Kassi in time." The tears wouldn't stop, and I finally went into a small bathroom that said visitors on the door, ran cold water in the sink and splashed my face until it stung. "Now, I'll get Charlie, or whatever his name is, out of here."

I started down the hall, but a voice came from the desk, "She's sound asleep and no fever. She'll be fine until morning."

"Charlie?" I asked searching the shadows for his figure, but not seeing anyone. "If it gets out that I allow visitors at night...,"

"And," he said as I heard the chair squeak, "Randall will take care of that prowler of Kassi's. He's a good lad. You could do a lot worse than picking him." I watched the cowboy hat move from my desk to what was no doubt his head. "Well," he said, "I best be gettin' on." I watched the cowboy hat move down the dark corridor above a shadowy form, before it turned and someone whispered, "And if anyone spills the beans and sez I was here, nobody that knew me will believe it anyway." With that the hat disappeared down the basement stairs. He must have made good time because I felt the small tremor that always came with the shutting of the basement door, but when I looked out the back window, there was no one to be seen.

Chapter Seventeen

Oh man! I need a good night's sleep, I thought. If anyone ever finds out I'm watching for a hat to walk out of the basement door, I'll be sent for a psychiatric examination.

"Did you hear the basement door shut?" Rocky was standing in back of me.

Rocky heard it too? "I thought I did but there's no one out in the parking lot, and the basement door *is* locked."

"Boy, this place is getting on my nerves," he said.

Remember, I told myself, you're in charge here. Act like it. "Rocky, we have to remember that it's the same place it was before Tallulah was murdered."

"Yeah. I guess. But it sure seems scary now," he said.

I vowed to chalk up the bouncing hat to loss of sleep, the door shutting to an erratic breeze. I had all I could handle worrying about Kassi.

* * * * * * *

Molly slept until a little after four when I heard her plaintive voice calling me by name. "Nika, Nika."

Alarmed, I ran silently down the hall and into her room. She'd never remembered my name before. She was either much better or a lot worse. In the light of the bedside lamp I saw her face was calm and her forehead and hands were cool to the touch. However, she was trapped in twisted sheets and blankets. This was unusual for Molly who had to be helped to change her position.

I brought lotion from the adjoining bathroom and helped her turn on her side, "I'm going to rub your back, Molly. That'll make you more comfortable, maybe you'll even go back to sleep." I was as cheery as possible, but my mind was on Kassi and the intruder.

I'd called her right back to let her know help was on the way, and called her again after Randall telephoned to say he couldn't find anyone on the grounds. He offered to spend the night on one of the sofas, but Kassi refused to unlock a door. She argued that for all she knew, Randall was a serial killer, and maybe it was Randall who had been searching the garage. "How do I know," she'd said. With Kassi I learned it's better to let her work out her periods of paranoia in her own way. So I instructed her to call if anything else suspicious happened.

After the back rub, Molly wanted me to sit with her and as she said, "Just visit, the only illness I have is being an old lady, and not worth much to anyone anymore." She sighed.

"Don't say silly things," I scolded, "you're worth lots to me."

I'd never known Molly to be so lucid, I'd brushed her hair and it lay fanned out on the pillow, no longer gray, but silver with the strands luminous and glowing in the soft light of the table lamp. Her skin was nearly free of wrinkles, her pale blue eyes sparkled with mischief, and knowing exactly which buttons to push. I thought, well, she's lived lots of years and if she wants me to pamper her a little, I can do that.

"Am I truly?" She asked, "How can I be worth lots to you?"

"Let's see Molly, well for starters, my own grandmother died in an ice fishing accident years ago, my father's been unconscious all this time from the same accident, and my mother died a year later. I didn't know Aunt Sapphira was alive, didn't remember her until I was summoned here in May. I'm kind of alone. I'd like someone to be my pretend Grandmother. Could you do that?" The words came easily, and surprised me with how much I meant every one. At that moment, I wanted a Grandmother more than anything.

"I'd love to be your grandmother," Molly said, "Charlie and I never had children. Oh, we wanted them all right, but it just never happened. After Sapphira and Tony lost their second baby, found him dead in his crib, just like the first one, we thought we should just be grateful for each other. And that's what we were, always together." I'd provided the hand she'd reached for. "I'd be proud to be your grandma. Such a kind, good girl."

I had trouble containing the tears brimming my eyes, but managed to choke out, "Thank you Grandma Molly, you're exactly the kind of Grandma I want. Exactly."

We sat a few moments like that, Molly's face full of love and my heart devoid of grief and guilt for the first time in years.

"Grandma Molly, I should probably know your last name, for real, that is. And if you have any other relatives." I knew she'd once said her name was Raymond, but I intended to take advantage of this clear moment and verify it.

"Why, for goodness sakes" she said, "didn't anyone tell you? My husband was Charlie Raymond. He died you know, but he still comes back to see me. He was a dealer for Tony, until Tony had to get out of the Cities because of something he'd done that was not quite legal." She squeezed my hand and smiled at me. "Isn't this nice now? Having a lovely girl like you pick me for her grandma."

"I wish I'd met your Charlie," was all I could say.

"Oh you've met him. Don't you remember?" She asked.

I had to bring her back to the present, "Molly, you were telling me how you happened to come to Colorado."

"So I was," she said thoughtfully. "Well to start with, you know it's hard to be exactly on the up and up when you run gaming houses for a living. And you make enemies."

"Yes," I said, "I can see how you would." That was the second time she said her husband was Charlie Raymond, and they didn't have any children. "Now if I've got this right, Tony was Sapphira's husband. Is that right?"

"Oh, you didn't know him, I suppose. But he was Sapphira's husband, all right. Let me tell you, her family was upset when she told them she loved Tony. They'd arranged for her to marry a good Greek man and they didn't like Tony's line of work, said it wasn't upright. There was particular Ned to pay, believe me, but Sapphira married him, she was that stubborn. He sold his businesses to his sister's son and came out here with his winnings. The two of them made a whole new life for themselves."

"That's so romantic," I said. I was excited. I hadn't learned this much from anyone else, not Randall, not Tim. If she was right, Tony's sister did have a son. I needed to know his name. If I could only keep her talking, "How did you meet her?"

"Well, we'd gotten to know each other after she met Tony. He used to bring her to the casino and we'd visit in our upstairs apartment while Tony and Charlie attended to business. No matter what the law says, people will gamble and Tony ran a respectable place. No drugs or drunks, and no loose women, if you know what I mean. Mostly nothing was rigged. Tony and Charlie always said that the law of averages kept them winning most of the time."

She was getting sleepy. It was harder and harder for her to keep her eyelids open. I didn't want to over-tire her so when her grasp on my hand went limp, I slipped out the door. There'd be other nights when we could talk, I thought.

It was four-forty. I had twenty minutes to get Molly's file out of the drawer and read it. I was given the narcotic and medication keys every night by the relief shift charge nurse. The keys to the file were kept on a ring in the narcotic drawer. I retrieved the keys, unlocked the file drawer, and went through the names as quickly as my trembling fingers allowed. Raymond was the last file in the drawer, and I took it to better light to read. Her first name was Maureen, nickname Molly. Her husband Charles Raymond was deceased and there was no next of kin. In a flash I knew that Molly was the Maureen in the Polaroids, and Charlie must be the ectoplasm. It wasn't lack of sleep. I'd been entertaining a ghost. That took a minute to assimilate, believe me. Then when I could read on, I gasped in surprise. Sapphira Domino had signed the admission form, which stated Mrs. Sapphira Domino would be responsible for any and all expenses incurred in the care and treatment of one Maureen Raymond.

I was stunned. Did that mean I was now responsible for Molly's expenses? Like the electric bill, the propane bill, and the storage of Aunt Sappy's car? Except Randall had paid those bills. Was he taking care of Molly's expenses too? No way could I pay for all of this, not on a night nurse's salary.

The minute hand on the wall clock made a kind of tick as it jerked to the twelve. Five. I had to have patients checked and charting finished by six thirty for report to the day shift. I hurried on my rounds, assisting some to the bathroom, to use a urinal or the bedpan. I straightened the sheets, handed out fresh water, and hurried back to do the charting.

After giving what I hoped was a credible report to the day shift, I hastily wrote a note requesting batteries for our flashlights and slipped it under Ells' office door. I'd made the same request to the day shift, but it never hurt to make a request to all the warm bodies around, especially on a weekend.

I'd decided to go directly home and ask Juana to make up a food package for me to take to Tim. The In Towne Cafe was closed on Sunday and I hated the thought of Tim forced to eat food provided by the sheriff. However, I saw Randall leaning on Bertha as soon as I walked out onto the parking lot.

"I'm taking you home for breakfast," he announced. "Got some of Mom's cinnamon rolls heating in the oven, and we can take some to Tim after we've eaten."

To go or not to go, was the question. However, I'd left my lunch in Bertha and refused to brave the parking lot during the night so I hadn't eaten since yesterday's cookies.

"I had no idea you could cook," I said.

"My skill is limited, but I talked to Mom last night. She suggested the cinnamon rolls and scrambled eggs," he answered.

I followed him to the outskirts of town, not a great distance, and to the top of a hill where the view was great if not as breathtaking as Sappy's. Shaggy pines stood in random groups of three leading in font of a forested areas to the south of the house. Low growing pine shrubs snuggled close to the house. We followed a circular drive past the three-door attached garage and to the front door. The house was built of field stone and dark-stained wood siding.

Randall saw me checking the garage, and said, "I'm storing your Reatta in the far stall, at least until Mom and Dad get back with the van. Want to see it?"

I started to deny it was my car, but I was too tired to argue, so instead I said, "Let's eat and take some food to Tim."

He unlocked the oak door, which was protected by a brass kick plate and swung soundlessly inward on well-oiled hinges. The aroma of warming cinnamon rolls directed our footsteps left of the entry to a family style kitchen. It was warmed by the morning sun streaming through the floor to ceiling windows that comprised the east and south walls of the adjoining great room. The great room was furnished, not surprisingly in brown leather furniture, grouped around a fieldstone fireplace where a fire was burning cheerily. The chairs were man-sized with the kind of cushions you sank into and fronted by tables just the right height to put your feet on. From the scars of heels left on the heavy dark wood that's exactly what was done.

"Impressive," I said, "but I don't know whether to praise the room, the view, or the smell of cinnamon rolls."

"Forget everything but Mom's rolls. They're the best,"

Randall said. He poured coffee and led me to a round table that shared the window wall. "Sit, sip the coffee while I scramble us some eggs. We can talk while I work."

"You didn't see anything when you searched the grounds around the house last night?" I asked.

"Only a kind of gray-blue van," he answered as he took packets of cut-up food and a bowl of eggs from the refrigerator.

"A van? What kind of a van?" A mini van?" I asked. Something tugged at my memory.

"No a big one. Know anybody who drives one of those?" He asked.

"No," I answered slowly thinking I had seen such a van. Somewhere. Maybe I'd remember later, when I'd had some sleep.

"Funny," he said, "I thought the license plates were from Minnesota. I could be mistaken. They were pretty dirty and the van was going really fast."

"You must be mistaken. The moon had set. And if they were dirty." I tried to recall that illusive memory, but it was gone. "They weren't parked in front of Sappy's?"

"No. Driving along that road that leads to her house."

"Now what would someone from Minnesota be doing driving fast along that road? It doesn't go anywhere, does it?" I asked.

"Eventually it connects to the paved road that goes over Wolf Creek Pass. Until then it's a bad narrow road with no houses along it, just an old camp site way off the road and up in the woods. Doubt if many people even know it's there," he said.

"Do you think it's significant?" I asked?

"It was the only vehicle that I saw on the road. It could be connected to Kassi's intruder. But that may be wishful thinking. Wish I'd gotten the license number."

The coffee was delicious, scalding hot and strong. "The coffee flavored?" I asked.

"Yes, hazelnut decaf," he answered. "Hope you like it."

"It's wonderful." I watched him break eggs into a bowl, whisk them and stirred in a bowl of cut up veggies and meat. "Those aren't ordinary scrambled eggs."

"I'm making a Denver omelet. Instead of folding the eggs over the ham and vegetables, you just mix it all together. Easier," he said.

"Sounds good," I said, as my eyelids closed.

The sound of plates sliding onto the wooden table woke me. "Sorry," I said, "This is so comfortable, the sun, and the fire, that I'm having trouble keeping my eyes open."

"Want a half a cup of leaded coffee?" Randall asked.

"Why not a whole cup," I said. "I'm thinking about visiting Tim when we were finished."

"Sure. How many more nights do you work before you have a night off?" He asked.

"Just tonight. I was supposed to work another week and then have a week off, but I got another of Ells FYI notes telling me my hours had changed. Now I'm supposed to have three nights off." I took a mouthful of omelet I had smeared with salsa. I shifted the hot food in my mouth and declared it was, "Excellent," watching Randall's anxious look turn into a big smile, before he dived into his. We ate in silence. I was buttering another cinnamon roll while Randall poured us both coffee, decaf again for me.

I said, "Tim told me last night that the sheriff checked county records and found that he was Tallulah's beneficiary as his wife's survivor. I wonder if that's correct? Can you find out?"

"It may be true. But ordinarily wills aren't a matter of public record until they're probated and that doesn't happen until the testator dies. It must have been Tallulah's husband's will he was quoting, which doesn't take into account that Tallulah might have had her own will," Randall explained.

"Tim said he and his wife visited Tallulah once, after her husband died. He said he thought her house was south of the Colorado border in New Mexico. If that's true, would her husband's will be on record in this county or in the county where they live?" I asked.

"Well," he said, "usually it's on record in the home county, but sometimes it's also placed in record in an adjoining county if some of their property is across the border."

"That makes sense. Also, Tim thought, Tallulah's husband owed other horse owners who had their male horses impregnate his mares on a verbal agreement to pay with a share of the foals."

"Verbal agreements in this country are often honored in court, but as nearly as I know, both parties are still living when a law suit is brought. I can look it up, see if a suit was ever brought, but not until tomorrow."

"That's soon enough," was all I could manage. I'd been trying to stay awake but I shook my head, "Sorry Randall, I've got to go home and get into bed."

"I'll follow you home," he said. "Can you wait for me to package those rolls for Tim and pick up some warm clothes I think he can use?"

"That I can wait for, and thank you," I answered watching him take rolls from the oven and double wrap them. He picked up a small suitcase at the front door that must have more warm clothes.

* * * * * * *

I parked Bertha in front of Sappy's and staggered up the steps to the door.

Randall was there before me, "Where is the cell phone?"

"Cell Phone?" I asked stupidly, sleep rapidly taking over any gray matter still functioning.

"The cell phone I gave you last night, the one I asked you to keep with you at all times." He was stern.

"Oh that one. I dropped it in back of the seat in Bertha."

He tore down the steps, wrenched open Bertha's door, and delved into the hiding place with one arm. He had the cell phone in hand by the time I got the front door unlocked.

"Here, put this on the bedside table. If you need me, you know how to dial and you know the number?" He asked this in a tone that discouraged smart-ass replies.

I'd hung my lab coat over the back of a needlepoint and hand carved chair without apology. I slid my shoes and stockings off and was ready to crawl between the sheets without thought of changing clothes.

"Nika, I'll wait in the hall while you get out of those clothes. When you're in bed, I'll set the phone and lights in a way that'll be safe for you. Just call out," he instructed.

Completely unlike my usual self, I did exactly as he said, even to calling out, "ready Randall" as I pulled up the sweet smelling sheets.

He entered immediately, checked the phone on the bedside table, and pulled the down quilt up to my chin before kissing me lightly. "Sleep tight," he said.

Later when I'd had twenty-four hours off and slept at least half that time, I'd explain to him that our relationship was a hands-off one. No more kissy-face and huggy-bear. But now I needed sleep more than anything. I hoped any murderer would kill me quickly without waking me, I thought as I drifted off.

I woke to the sounds of singing, but not, thankfully, "It had to be you" which I was getting sick of. This time it was something in Spanish. Kassi and Juana singing in parts? Maybe I'm still asleep. I groaned as I turned over. I was stiff. Every muscle in my body complained. The clock's glowing red numerals said five-thirty. I must have slept six or six and a half hours, I thought. We were home by eleven, and I was in bed at once. All I needed was a shampoo with my shower and some caffeine to start my motor. I'd be my normal self…nearly.

Throwing the cover back, I staggered down the hall in the direction of the kitchen from which the singing was coming.

"Nika, you look awful," came Kassi's critical words.

I gave Juana a hug, releasing her in time to pour a mug of her special hot chocolate.

"Thanks Juana, I'd die without this every afternoon." I was trying to ignore Kassi and her bitching. She hadn't asked for money or new clothes since the morning I'd tried Tim's tough love. I couldn't expect her to stop picking at me too.

"Really Nika, you're going to have to pay more attention to your looks." Kassi finally hit the wrong button.

"How about, 'Did you sleep well, dear sister? And 'thanks for getting me help last night when I was so frightened.' You know, something loving. Or is that too much for you to master this late on your day off?" I admit my remarks dripped with sarcasm, but I was barely awake, tired and gritchy.

Kassi burst into tears. "I was voicing my concern because you look so tired." She wiped her eyes, "You're working too hard. It's crazy. You're an heiress."

"Yeah, well you're the only one who knows that," I answered as I carried a mug of Juana's chocolate drink out to the patio. Kassi, of course followed me. I'd have no peace, until I reassured her.

"I'm sorry, Kassi. I really am tired. I've worked over three weeks without a day off. I'm a walking zombie." I rose and hugged her, "I'll have three days off starting tomorrow. Then, I'll rest up and be a different woman. You'll see," I promised.

Kassi gave a sobbing hiccup, "That's what I was trying to find out," she said, then smiled me the brave smile of a martyr and returned to sing and cook with Juana.

I angled a second chair out from the table and rested my bare feet on the seat. A wet nose nuzzled my hand and I fished a dog biscuit out of my pocket while I toyed with the idea of asking Sergio to leave Perro in the house when Kassi was alone. But that wasn't fair to he and Juana. They were both named in Sappy's will, and could be in as much danger as Kassi. I'd better rely on locks and hope they were actually locked. I'd remind Kassi again when I left for work tonight.

We ate together as Sergio, Juana and Kassi conversed happily away while I remained in ignorant lack of language skills. The thought of my new, English speaking, adopted grandma Molly made me smile.

After dinner, I checked the desk drawers in Sappy's upstairs office. When I found maps of Colorado and New Mexico, I removed them, leaving everything else undisturbed and quietly returned to my bedroom. I showered, shampooed and found clean whites for work. I wore the lab coat, which was relatively clean and had the mini flashlight in its pocket. There was no flashlight here and I had no faith that anyone bought batteries for us. All the while I was considering a plan that had entered my mind while we ate.

With Tim's description, I'd find Tallulah's ranch. If I could enter the house, I'd search for a will and clues as to the identity of 'the bums' and why they might want her dead. I'd slept well today, and could leave tomorrow after taking Kassi to work and be home by the time she needed to be picked up. I hid the maps in my ample purse where they didn't make a bulge.

After having my safety talk with Kassi, I left for work.

The cell phone rang as I pulled into the parking lot. I answered, thinking Randall must have memorized the time I left and the length of the drive. If he could do it, so could anyone else. I shivered.

"Hello?"

"It's Randall, how's everything look at the house and did you meet or see another vehicle on the way in tonight?"

"Kassi's all locked in and promises to stay that way. I didn't see anyone, certainly not a gray-blue van if that's what you had in mind." There was another question I'd intended to ask him. What was it?

"Good. Take the cell phone with you and call me if anything disturbing happens to either you or Kassi."

"I will. Do I need to worry about Juana and Sergio?" I asked as I maneuvered Bertha into a well-lit slot.

"I think they'll be fine. That dog of theirs will kill to protect them and just Perro's looks are a deterrent."

"Good, that's been on my mind," I said.

"Will I see you for breakfast in the morning?" he asked.

"Not tomorrow morning. I should get my overtime check and I need to deposit the money after I take Kassi to work." Too late I knew he wouldn't buy that, I could deposit the check on the way home. "I'll need to get some money orders to pay a bunch of bills we left behind in Minneapolis." At least that much was true, and I knew I didn't dare tell him about my planned trip.

"I'll see you later in the day then," came his disappointed response.

I was on the way into the nursing home when I remembered the question I hadn't asked. Did he know anything about Sappy paying Molly's bills and was I now responsible?

Chapter Eighteen

After the relief crew gave a record-fast report, the three of them grabbed purses and shrugged into jackets. Their shift was finished. They thought.

I held up my hand, "Wait," I said, "how about batteries for our flashlights?"

They traded uncomprehending looks, while poised to run for the stairs, "Batteries?" They asked in unison, "What batteries?"

"This morning I asked the day shift to get Rocky and me batteries for our flashlights. They said they would. I also wrote each of you a note and stuck them in your lockers. You had to find them when you picked up your lab coats this afternoon.

We need them because both the flashlights were emptied of batteries during yesterday's evening shift, most likely by you three. Now, one more time, where are our batteries?" I'd been running on nerves instead of sleep for weeks. I was tired and bitchy, and boy was I mad at these three.

They looked at each other taking a silent caucus before the charge nurse answered for them all, "Our flashlights were dead and we took the batteries so we could see to get to our cars. It's scary out there. You're here now and nothing can happen to you. I'll check the door to be sure it's locked, but we don't want to give up our flashlights. You want *us* murdered tonight?"

"Certainly not," I answered, "but remember, Tallulah was murdered, if it was murder, in her bed at change of shift. I doubt a flashlight would have saved her."

I let that hang in the air. There was no response from any of them. They gazed first at one another and then at their feet.

"But," I continued, "it's more reassuring to have a heavy lit-up flashlight in your hand than an empty, dark one. I'll wait one more night, if you promise you'll each stop by the hardware store tomorrow and buy batteries for your own flashlights *and* for these two that Rocky and I depend on. I'm sure you'd not want us murdered for lack of a flashlight, would you? No? Then promise."

With proper humility, each in turn promised before trouping out to their cars. I had them, and they knew it.

"I smiled at the black coffee circling down the drain and continued to smile while I prepared coffee for the morning crew. It was a victory, a minor one, I knew, but still a victory. I felt good and the smile would be pasted on my face all night.

"Say," Rocky asked, "what's to smile about?"

"They promised to buy us new batteries tomorrow."

"They didn't," he said.

"They did, and I'm going to smile all night. Even if they don't do it, they admitted they're our battery thieves."

"But for right now, tonight, we're still out of batteries?"

"That's about it. Does the little one I gave you still light-up?" I asked snapping the lid on the coffee maker and pushing it to the back of the counter.

He sadly shook his head, "Naw, it's dead."

I upended my purse on the counter, shoving the contents about with my fingers until I uncovered the third flashlight I'd been given. "Here's another one." I depressed the button and a bright beam came on, "Take this one, it'll get you through tonight."

"How about you? What're you going to do?" He asked.

I pulled my little white light from my pocket. When I depressed the button, a steady although dim glow resulted.

"You'd better take this one, I'll use yours," Rocky offered.

"No. I'll use this one," I said, "you don't have a night off until Friday, right?"

"Right, but the boss always gets the best stuff."

"The point is, that I'm off three nights, by the time I'm back to work someone will respond to one of my requests and provide us with real battery operated working flashlights."

"Okay," Rocky grinned, "If you say so."

The first part of the shift went smoothly. Everyone was asleep and there was no odor of urine in the rooms. Maybe the evening nurses were our battery thieves, but they had finished their work again tonight.

I sat down at the desk to do my first charting, automatic by now, and debated whether I should leave right after delivering Kassi to her job or take time to see Tim. An hour later, after my third hourly rounds, I still hadn't made a decision.

I was quietly pushing in the door to Molly's room, when the desk phone began ringing, and I saw a shadow, cowboy hat in place, poised on the arm of the chair while he strummed a guitar.

"Evenin' ma'am." I heard. "Come on in."

The phone rang insistently as I glared at the shadow. I pointed a finger at the hat, "I want you outa here. Now."

"Yes ma'am, one more song is all, then I'll be goin'"

I stared, trying to bring the shadow into focus. When it disappeared along with the singing, I shook my head, and vowed to never work this many nights again.

I shut the door and ran for the telephone, "Hello."

"Nika?"

"Kassi? What's going on?" I asked, my heart trying to get out of my throat. "Is someone in the house?"

"No," Kassi said and my heart receded back into my chest where it belonged. "Not yet," she said and my heart began its palpitating climb back out again.

"Explain," I ordered. I was in no mood for guessing games.

"I woke up about an hour ago and couldn't go back to sleep so I decided to warm some milk. The way Mom used to do?"

"Uh huh," I said.

"Well, while I waited, I went over to the kitchen windows and looked out. Honestly Nika, the moon is so big and bright, I can almost see the color of his hair. Except he has a bandanna or something tied over it, and he has a beard."

My heart was going to make it all the way out, "Then what, Kassi? Are the doors locked? Are you safe? You're not standing in the kitchen window where he can see you, are you?"

"Of course not. Juana and I made sure everything was locked up tight before they left last night, and I shut the drapes too. But do you know what he's doing?"

"Absolutely not," I said.

"He's going around trying all the windows and doors to see if he can get in. That's what woke me up. Nika, I'm scared."

"Where are you calling from?" I asked.

"I took the phone into the closet and dialed your number. The cord is a long one and there's a light in the closet that goes on automatically when you open the door," Kassi answered, proud of her resourcefulness.

"Is the bedroom door locked?"

"Of course it's locked. What do you think I am, some kind of an idiot?"

"Is the closet light still on?" I asked, wondering if I dare tell her the window locks hadn't seemed very secure when Randall and I'd checked them.

"Yes, otherwise I couldn't see to dial the phone. Honestly Nika, you'd think I didn't know anything."

"I'll call for help. Here's what I want you to do. Pull the closet door all the way shut. I think there're blankets or quilts on the shelf, pull them around you and get comfortable."

"I'm afraid of the dark," Kassi sobbed quietly. "I thought you'd be proud of me. I did everything like you asked me to do."

"I am proud of you, but I want to know you're safe and you'll be safer if there isn't any light showing anywhere. You'll be better off to stay quiet and locked in. I'll get you help and I'll call as soon as I know everything's clear."

"Okay Nika, I'll do as you say, but hurry."

Randall's sleepy voice answered on the first ring. "Someone's prowling around the house again." I said.

"I'm on my way," Came his alert reply. "The sheriff too."

I heard the click as he hung up.

I checked Molly's room to find her sleeping peacefully. I watched the rise and fall of her chest against the flowered comforter that covered her. She looked younger asleep than awake, and I could imagine she was still the lovely young woman in the pictures. I dimmed the table lamp and adjusted the head of her bed down, realizing that I loved this lady. What if Tallulah's murder was a random act, as it might have been? Suppose it had been Molly who had been smothered instead of Tallulah? I checked the windows, closing and locking one. It was on the front courtyard, and anyone could have cut the screen and climbed in. The killer could have gotten in this way. I shivered. Now that she was mine, my grandma Molly, I couldn't have anything happen to her.

I paced the floor in back of the nurse's station, willing the phone to ring.

Rocky came into the treatment room, "What's wrong?"

"My sister called. She woke up and saw someone trying to get into the house through a window. I've called for help."

"Happen before?" He asked.

"Yes. Last night," I said.

"Did the sheriff check?"

When I didn't answer because to be truthful meant admitting it was Randall who checked, he asked, "Find anybody?"

"No. Only someone driving a gray or blue van along the Road."

"Out on that road? At night?" Rocky asked.

"I know it's crazy," I said.

"Maybe he was trying to make a pizza delivery in fifteen minutes." He grinned his biggest.

The cell phone in my pocket began to ring. "All's okay," came Randall's voice, "Except this time we found tire tracks. Dual tires on back. I've persuaded the sheriff to post a deputy out here at least at night, and he's gone for plaster to take casts of the prints. I'll stay until he gets back."

"Thanks, I'll call Kassi and tell her to come out of the closet and go back to bed," I answered.

"See you in the morning?"

"No. Not tomorrow morning. I'll take Kassi to work and then I must go to the bank." I answered, amazed at how easy the lie came. "Good night and thanks for everything."

"I didn't know you had a cell phone. Impressive," Rocky said.

"It's not mine, it's a loaner. The cost terrifies me."

Rocky grinned broadly, "Glad your sister's out of the closet."

"Not funny," I said.

Rocky sobered immediately, "Have to admit though, it sure is exciting working with you. There's somethin' going on all the time. Call if you need help."

"I will, thanks," I answered as I dialed Kassi's number.

Kassi was relieved but doubted she could return to sleep, which I knew wasn't a real worry to my sister, since she slept better any time and any where than anyone else I knew.

I was going to hang up when I remembered to ask, "Kassi, was he searching the garage again?"

"I don't know, but the door is wide open."

Puzzled, I asked, "What does he want up there?"

"Nika, honestly, for someone as smart as you are, you're sure dumb sometimes. It's someone who knows our aunt hid her money and thinks it's up there."

"But it isn't. I've searched that apartment. There's nothing but some old dresses in garment bags. I've been all over it. Randall looked. You looked."

"Yes, I did, and it's the spookiest place I've ever been," Kassi said. "Nika, I'd like to go back to bed now, if it's safe."

"It's safe, the sheriff assigned a deputy out there somewhere," I said.

"All the time?"

"I wish," I said, "But only at night is all I was told."

I finished the rest of my work automatically. What did he expect to find in the apartment? There was nothing there. I'd searched it twice and again with Kassi. Nothing. Zero. Nada. Yet it must be someone who knew Sappy'd hid her fortune? The thought raised goose bumps on my arms and caused a shiver to travel up my spine. So few knew that fact and none of them had a beard. Even so, one search was enough to prove there was no money hidden in the apartment, why go again?

I'd finished the charting and flipped on the coffee maker switch, then started tidying up the treatment room and desk. I upended the two wastebaskets down the trash chute and stood balancing one on my knee to pull out a single sheet.

Then I remembered. The first time I'd searched the apartment, I'd found a single crumpled sheet in a wastebasket under the sink and put it in my pocket. It was part of a flight invoice. Could that be what the intruder was looking for? Was there anything on it to identify the person? Had a visitor been staying in the garage apartment, perhaps when Sappy was killed? Doubtful. Sergio and Juana would have known. Unless they hadn't seen him. Neither of them went up there. Maybe he only came out at night, like now. He could be the one who murdered Sappy.

The wastebasket, a metal one, clattered onto the utility room floor. Still I held open the trash chute, alarmed at the unknown danger lurking everywhere. It was suddenly clear to me that the person who shot Sappy and maybe smothered Tallulah was not someone who lived in Magdalena, but someone who'd visited often enough to know about the garage apartment. Who? If Uncle Tony nephew had died, who was this phantom person?

"You okay?" I jumped at the sound of Rocky's voice coming from the door where he lounged against the doorframe.

"Yes, I'm fine, just clumsy. You caught up over there?" I asked a normal question hoping the solid fear that had taken up lodging in my chest, didn't also show on my face.

"Hmmm, you look like you saw Dracula down the trash chute. Here, I'll finish. You get a cup of that poison you're brewing."

Rocky must know my imaginings had scared me silly. "I'm going to accept your help and take your advice," I said in as cheery a voice as I could muster.

"It's okay, you know. Your sister's out there all alone with prowlers around. That'd make anyone jumpy. For my money you're still the best." Loyal Rocky smiled, "Your fresh water passed?"

"Yes, thanks. Thanks for everything." I sipped coffee and felt the hot liquid warm me from the back of my throat until it reached my stomach. It gave me a lift too."

"You goin' to sleep today or do like I do on my day off and stay up until way late tonight?" He asked.

"I'm going to stay up, but not until way late. I've got a million errands."

"You're doin' errands on your day off?" That's bad man, really bad. How come you're doin' that?"

"Ells promised me an overtime paycheck today. It should be good-sized because I've worked three weeks without time off. She promised me double pay, and if I've figured it right, it'll just about payoff all the stuff we still owe in Minneapolis." I was talking too much, confiding too much in someone I supervised. Must be fatigue or stress. Or both.

"You know that's a bummer. You live in that mansion and still don't have any money. Me, I'd sell the place."

"Eventually, maybe I will," I said, "but you best get back to your unit. The day shift'll be here in ten minutes."

I was passing the desk on the way for another cup of coffee, when the phone rang, "Hello," I said snatching it up to prevent another ring.

"One of these nights, when you least expect it, I'm coming for a visit. An uninvited one."

I slammed down the phone. Got the coffee and took a long drink of the hot, strong liquid. Who was calling me? Who wanted to frighten me, or did he want me dead? What should I do?

After giving report, I stopped by Ells' office and picked up my check. I also told her about the flashlight batteries and got her promise she'd get us new ones today. In the meantime I'd ignore the caller, crank callers were harmless, weren't they?

I decided to drive home and change clothes before taking Kassi to work. Back in town, I could deposit my check; send cashier's checks registered mail to pay all our Minneapolis bills. I had the envelopes all addressed, the amount owed noted and postage all figured out. I watched other traffic for someone following me, there was no one. And no gray vans.

On the kitchen table at home, I found a note from Kassi, *Please don't wake me, as I am too tired to work today and want to sleep in. Please call the cafe.*

That made my escaping to the Colorado-New Mexico border easier, since I didn't need to make excuses to anyone. I changed into black jeans, T-shirt and loafers, called the In Towne Cafe from Sappy's private sitting room, wrote Kassi a note telling her I was off on errands that'd take until twelve or even one. In the meantime the doors must be kept locked at all times until we had the intruder identified and jailed. I was walking out the patio door when I remembered the scrap of paper and went back hoping it was still in my drawer. It was underneath a stack of underwear in the lingerie drawer. I took it into Sappy's sitting room and for the first time, really studied it.

The name of the buyer was completely torn off and most of the bottom. It was as though someone had folded it and torn it in smaller pieces, before throwing it in the basket. Perhaps the person tidied up the apartment before leaving and got only part of the invoice from the wastebasket. Perhaps he didn't realize that he'd packed only the upper portion, until he got home. Maybe he thought he'd be back and it didn't matter.

This was useless conjecture, I knew. If it were possible, I needed to trace the ticket holder. The airline running the flights from Minneapolis to Denver and back again was clear, as was the date of purchase, March 8, and the invoice number, 820222063. In the upper left corner, part of the agency was still intact, Twin...angled underneath it was Trav...Could I trace it with only that information? I puzzled a minute and then decided to ask my high school friend Jill, who worked in a St. Paul travel agency for help. I even thought it was called Twin Cities Travel.

With the aid of a helpful operator I got the travel agency telephone number. Still I was prepared for it to be the wrong agency, so it was a relief to hear Jill's cheerful voice answer. Could it be this easy? I wondered.

"Hi Jill," I said in what I hoped was as cheerful a sounding voice as hers.

"Who's this?" asked a puzzled Jill.

"It's Nika McGuinness, I'm calling from Colorado. Remember me from twelfth grade? We were in the same chemistry class."

"Oh sure. You're the pretty, tall one with dark wavy hair. Your sister has the baby blue eyes and was in my brother's class. He still sighs for her on occasion."

"She'll like to hear that," I said with no intention of telling Kassi.

"Where did you say you were calling from?" Jill asked.

"That's just one part of this complicated story, I'm out here in Colorado with Kassi to settle the estate of a distant relative," I answered.

"What a great place to be. I'm jealous and I hope you get to inherit big bucks," Jill said.

"I have a favor to ask of you," I said.

"I didn't think you'd call to chat after all these years. What can I do for you?" Jill asked.

I had remembered her correctly, always generous and helpful. Just the kind of trusting person I needed for what I intended to ask. Violate the privacy of a customer.

"There is a guest apartment in an separate building on my aunt's property. It looks like someone took valuable paintings from that apartment, but we don't know who. All I have to go on is a part of a flight invoice for a flight leaving Minneapolis airport bound for Denver and back again. I think it was issued by a travel agency which may be, 'Twin Cities Travel', or something close to that."

"You want me to go through the telephone book and list all the agencies with similar names?"

"No. I was hoping if I gave you the flight number, airline, dates and times, you could identify the name of the person. Is that possible?" I asked holding my breath. This was the part where I was asking her to go into the computer data bank and give me confidential information. Would she do it?

"I can try, but don't count on anything," Jill's calm voice came back. "You've got the invoice number, did you say?"

"Yes, I do."

I gave Jill all the information I had and my telephone number and thanked her for promising to try. I unlocked a panel to the storeroom off the sitting room and slid the invoice between files '96 and '97. The invoice had been safe in the dresser drawer for weeks, but I wanted it somewhere no one knew about except me.

Now to deposit my check, mail the payments, and then go hunting Tallulah's ranch.

* * * * * * * *

I followed the road southwest as Tim had described and then turned left toward New Mexico. It was a beautiful day, with a cloudless sky and a hot sun. I was alone on a road that seemed to be on top of the world. Most of the views were of distant hills, pine trees, even a spot of snow here and there shaded from the sun. I crossed Cat Gap Pass with Bertha wheezing a little and was thankful when I came to a rest stop.

I parked Bertha in the shade and took my breakfast burrito and thermos of coffee to a picnic table to eat and study the map. Unless it had changed a lot in the years since Tim visited here, I should find a road that went due south, crossing into New Mexico. I counted on the life size wood cutout of a horse to lead me the rest of the way to Tallulah's ranch, if a wooden horse could last, in this land of wind, snow and sun. I'd watched carefully for cars or trucks, but there had been none.

I took the first road south and drove about twenty miles before spotting a horse on the horizon. Although it stood upright on one leg, with most of its black paint and tail gone, there was no doubt it had once been a horse. My spirits lifted.

I rounded a corner as a bright red pick-up, with a scruffy dog riding in the back, passed going the opposite direction. I memorized what I could see of the Colorado plates for later reference, in case that was the 'bums' pickup.

Another mile and I came to small sign in the shape of a horse pointing toward ranch buildings. I turned into the driveway and drove down a long steep hill through a grove of silver leafed trees to a ranch house. There was no sign of life, no barking dogs, no other cars or pick-up trucks, certainly not a red one, or a gray van. But someone could be in the barn or behind a shed. I'd need to be watchful.

It was eerily still. It was a watching, listening land. No bird sounds, no bawling calves, like I'd heard at that rest stop, not even the wind reached these leaves. I shivered and very nearly turned Bertha around to run away from this haunted place.

"Now don't panic," I scolded, "you can go into that house for evidence that proves someone other than Tim murdered Tallulah."

I drove Bertha behind a thick stand of low growing pine trees. When it was hidden as well as possible, I decided to knock like any ordinary visitor, and if someone answered the door, I'd ask for water for my over heated truck, parked in the shade.

My footsteps were noisy on creaking floorboards of the porch. I rapped hard on the wood door with the knuckles of my left hand. In the right I held, my new heavy flashlight like a weapon. When, no one answered my knock, I tried the knob and found it unlocked, so I pushed the door open and entered a long shadowed room.

In the middle, a pot bellied stove ruled its mute subjects, the rocking chairs that circled it. A full and overflowing box of fore wood sat next to the stove. A long table, with plenty of carefully positioned chairs, was on the right. A sagging couch identified the left wall. A single end table teetered on uneven legs at one end of the couch, and an equally unsteady looking coffee table littered with yellowed newspapers and dog-eared magazines fronted the couch.

There was a door at each end. Although they both looked ominous, I reluctantly approached the one near the couch. I knew that anyone might lurk behind it, and cautiously slid it open.

Holding my heavy flashlight, I walked through the door and into a bedroom. A large bed sat against one wall where a green and orange night gown, similar to the one Tallulah had worn, lay crumpled on the pillow and a pair of not too clean jock shorts was tumbled onto the floor. Although the dresser drawers were empty, it wasn't hard to figure out that this was the 'bums' bedroom.

I retraced my steps and quietly opened the door at the dining room end. I entered a windowed hall that boasted an open stairway. At the end of the hall I found a giant kitchen and another stairway that led down to a musty smelling basement. Must be the one Tallulah fell down, I thought as I firmly shut the door. That was one place I'd not search. I felt the coffee pot on the wood stove and found it half full and still warm, as was the stove. This morning's breakfast coffee, I bet. The walls held open shelves with a few dishes and canisters of flour, sugar and coffee. The refrigerator was nearly empty. I checked the ice cube trays, since I'd read they were often used to hide valuables, but these didn't even have ice in them. I'd try upstairs.

Every step creaked, but by now I was certain there was no one but me in the house, so I thumped upwards. I opened the only door on the small landing at the top, opened it carefully, remembering a movie where a door like this opened on nothing but a drop down a cliff. So it was anticlimactic when I found only a huge room with double-hung windows on all three sides. There was a big bed at one end and an old-fashioned roll top desk at the other. I'd lucked out.

The air was stale, and dust motes floated along a shaft of sunlight from the south windows. I pulled curtains aside and tried to open first one window then another. It was no use. They were either painted shut or warped beyond my strength.

The desk was a mess, papers were stuffed into drawers without regard for alphabetizing or date. Tax receipts from '27 were tucked in next to tax notices from '98. I'd heard that everyone had a system, and the trick was to discover the system. With that in mind, I pulled out a chair and began organizing the papers, just enough to find my way through the desk. An hour and a half later, my stomach clenched in hunger grumbles, but I'd not stop to eat my remaining burrito now. I was down to the bottom drawer.

This one was organized, the one where I should have started. I pulled out an accordion-pleated file, untied the laces and found all the things I needed. The original sale to Tallulah and her husband, the plat of the property, Tallulah's own will, signed by her, and most puzzling of all, a promissory note dated August 18, 1973. It was for a loan of ten thousand dollars secured by the ranch, signed by Tallulah and witnessed by an attorney-at-law, a Mr. Robertson. The note was payable on her death by forfeiture of all properties to one Anthony Paul P. Simmons. Simmons? Was that what the 'S' stood for? Could this be Uncle Tony's nephew?

Talk about a motive for murder, I thought jubilantly, this will get Tim out of jail. I'd take the whole file back with me and copy the note for the sheriff and Randall, but hold the original in Sappy's hidden storage room.

Carefully, I returned the papers to the file and retied the laces. I was elated, hunger and fatigue forgotten. I planned a quick trip back to Magdalena and a celebration dinner for Tim at Aunt Sappy's. I brushed dust from my black jeans and started for the door. There, I froze, hair standing up on my neck. Someone was coming. If only I had time to get down those stairs.

The sound of creaking steps stopped me. Gees! Someone was on the stairs. And no place to hide. Even if I survived in one piece, the window couldn't be opened for a jump of forty feet. Under the bed was not an option; the springs were so sunken they rode on the floor. Only the edges of the springs hung to the bed frame, the thin mattress disintegrating into the coils. That left me with one choice, and into the bed I jumped drawing my knees up to my chin and piling quilts high over me. I rested my face on the file and clutched my purse to my stomach. I willed my breathing to be soundless and waited for the heavy-footed person.

Even so, I jumped when the door swung open and hit the wall with a shattering slam. I had a vision of an old western bandit standing legs apart, gun drawn, surveying the room. After moments of challenging quiet, a loud shuddering sneeze made me wince. I heard him walk over to the windows and manhandle two open with much grunting and cursing. Then he went hunting, and I heard drawers open and slam shut, the roll top pushed up in protest and finally papers being tossed about.

Did I dare a peek? If he were concentrating on the desk, he wouldn't notice if I moved the covers just a little. I did and saw a silent figure, back to the bed, bending over the desk.

It was a man dressed in jeans, dark T-shirt, and a bandanna tied over his head, a knot at the back. Like Kassi had described.

Just then, I knew the phone would ring. Damn, why hadn't I left the cell phone in Bertha. I ducked my head back under the covers and held my breath waiting.

A phone rang once, twice then four or five times. I stopped counting when I realized it was Tallulah's house phone ringing, not the cell phone in my purse, which was after all, turned off. The relief was momentary, as my stomach clenched up in hunger ready for another rumble. It'd be a loud one this time, giving away my hiding place.

The man voiced a round of curses. He slammed drawers shut and the old desk shuddered and rocked against the wall. He walked around the room, opened a closet door where only a dress, a couple of sweatshirts and a heavy jacket hung. There was no place to hide anything in there, I knew. I'd looked. He seemed to be going through pockets as I heard one hanger after another fall to the floor. This was lucky for me, because in the midst of his search my stomach uttered a low melodious complaint.

I could sense his pause as expectant quiet fell like fog. I stayed frozen, not breathing, just willing him to give up and leave. He walked around the bed and I could feel his eyes bore through the piled quilts, until the plaintive call of a dove came through the window.

“Shit,” he said with so much feeling I could smell the manure. I heard the stairs creak as he walked down them. He was leaving. I willed him to walk out the door and go without checking around and finding Bertha. I heard an engine start, but stayed hidden in the bed for long moments. Finally, I crawled from under the quilts, and ran to the window to watch a gray van pull up the hill toward the main road. Our intruder.

My heart pounded, bile rose in my throat. He’d been that close to me. If he’d known, I’d be dead, I had no doubt. The file gone, hope for Tim gone, and Sappy’s money to an impostor.

Oh thank you God. Thank you.

Best thing to do now, was to get back to Sappy’s where the will, note and I would be locked in and safe. I’d take care of the details later.

The ride back was easy and didn’t take as long as it did to drive to Tallulah’s. I hadn’t kept track of the time, but my watch read one thirty when I unlocked the front door, clutching the file I’d found. My biggest concern was how to get this past Kassi as I pushed open the front door.

I sucked in my breath. There on the entry floor, lay Kassi, a blue bruise on her left temple, her breathing ragged.

Chapter Nineteen

I was sitting by Kassi's cart in the Emergency Room of Guadalupe Hospital, holding her hand. I was sitting because I'd fainted, and this was my concession to the medical staff's orders to 'lie down' and 'get some rest.' They added the usual 'we don't need any more patients.' Like I didn't know that?

No problem. I'd no intention of being a patient. The discussion, that rumbled on and on over me, was whether or not to admit Kassi to ICU or wait it out in the ER. The majority thought she'd wake up soon and ICU was full, after all.

Kassi's color had improved, her blood pressure had stabilized and her pulse had settled down. She occasionally made sounds of waking, but hadn't managed to do so yet, and it was three-thirty in the afternoon. I had no memory of what I'd done after dialing 911 the first time. They told me, I dialed it again when I found Juana sprawled on the kitchen floor, blood congealing around a hole in her chest. They also told me I'd covered both with warm blankets, cushioned their heads, and elevated their feet. Juana was in surgery at this time, would come back much later today and go directly to ICU. I'd promised Randall, who was lurking around here somewhere, I'd go home as soon as Kassi woke.

It was not a good day to go looking for information at Tallulah's ranch, that much I'd figured out. Two people that I loved were close to death because I'd gone off instead of staying home and protecting them. Never mind that I'd found Tallulah's own Last Will and Testament and a Promissory Note that gave a Mr. Anthony Paul P. Simmons the best motive of anyone to smother Tallulah. The same Anthony was probably speeding around the area in a gray van. I'd not go home until Kassi woke up.

I'd laid my head down on her cart for just a moment, when a hand shook my shoulder and a voice said, "Ms. McGuinness, we're taking your sister upstairs where she'll be carefully watched."

"What unit," I demanded shaking the sleep out of my eyes.

"Second Neuro," the voice answered. "Mr. McClean is here to drive you home. It's four-forty-five and you may as well go on now."

"Four-forty-five?" I parroted stupidly, "How did that happen. My watch must have stopped."

"Nika, go home and get some sleep, come see me in the morning." Kassi's voice came from my sister who lay with blankets up to her chin, and only her left arm outside the covers where it rested on an IV board attached to the cart. Her blue eyes were bright, but the only color in her face was the big purple bruise on her right temple.

"Kassi," I squealed throwing myself on her, "you're awake. Thank God. That's what I've been praying for."

"You've not been praying, you've been sleeping. With your head on my cart. It was really uncomfortable for me."

I bit my lip to keep from an angry retort. Kassi was not only awake but also back in form. "Sorry Kassi, I hoped I'd hear you when you woke up. Do you know who hit you?"

"No, I don't. Do you think for one minute I'd have waited around for some goon to belt me on the head?"

Same old Kassi, "I'm glad you're better, just the same. I'm going home now, have the nurses call if you need anything."

She waved more weakly than necessary and was whisked off to the elevators. "Here are your things," a white suited male attendant said handing me my purse and the brown file folder I'd found at Tallulah's. I mumbled thanks wondering by what miracle that file folder had stayed with me through all this long day.

When the ER door closed behind me, I stood disoriented for a moment. Which way was out, how would I get home, and what was the condition of Sappy's house? Randall emerged from a waiting room, and said, "Let's get you home."

"Thanks, that's nice of you," I said, not arguing. He offered to take the file for me, and when I drew it close to my chest protectively, he looked puzzled, but didn't protest.

I rested my head back on the cushioned seat and must have dozed off, because the next thing I knew we were pulling up to Sappy's front door. I handed Randall the house keys and allowed him to lead me into the darkened entry where he turned on lights that chased away the shadows. He led me out to the kitchen where only a small smudge of dark brown showed where Juana had lain.

"Randall, I didn't ask about Juana. I have to go back."

"I visited her just before I came back to the Emergency Room. She's out of surgery, stable, and in ICU. The Doctors think she has an even chance of recovery." He was doing something with hot water and tea bags. "Sit," he commanded.

"If I'd been here, it wouldn't have happened," I said.

"If you'd been here you'd have been shot too." He brought teapot and teacups to the table. "Where were you by the way?" He poured scalding tea and offered sugar and milk both of which I declined. He had to repeat his question before my mind focused. "Mind telling me where you were today?"

"It seemed like such a good idea, and I was the only one who could do it," I whispered.

"And what happened?" He encouraged.

I laid the brown file folder on the table and began the story. I told it from the beginning, leaving nothing out, while Randall listened to every word without interrupting me.

When I'd finished, he asked, not what was in the file folder but, "How much of a head start did that gray van have on you?"

"I don't know. I stayed hidden for a few minutes, until I thought it was safe. When I looked out the window, the van was cresting the hill at the top of the driveway. It's a long way, probably took half an hour to leave the house and drive that far."

"Did you leave then?" Randall asked.

"No. I waited until I was sure he wouldn't circle back or still be able to see me from one of the hills that look down on the ranch buildings. At least another half hour," I said.

"Then he had plenty of time to get back here and surprise Juana and Kassi. I don't see any connection between your patient and Mrs. Domino, but there must be something."

"I think it's the money. Hidden money on both ranches. That's reason enough for some people to kill."

"But you didn't find any money."

"No, but I wasn't looking for any either. Do you think he was looking for the will and the promissory note? Could that tie Sapphira and Tallulah together?" I asked.

"What will? What promissory note?" Randall said.

"I found her own Will, a new one, signed by Tallulah. It leaves everything to Tim," I answered.

"That doesn't help Tim, does it? Randall asked.

I added, "I also found a Promissory Note. It gives the ranch to someone named Anthony P. Simmons for his loan of ten thousand dollars."

"That's a new slant," Randall said.

"Sappy's husband's first name was Antonio," I spoke as the knowledge suddenly came to me. "Antonio is a old fashioned name for Anthony, isn't it? This could be Antonio's nephew, the Anthony Paul P. S. in Sappy's will. I'll bet, he's the one who was searching Tallulah's house, and I'll bet he was looking for the documents I had already found."

Randall was lukewarm to the idea. "I've looked everywhere for a descendent of Antonio Domino, I'm convinced there's none of that family left."

"But you were looking for an Anthony Domino. This man's last name is Simmons not Domino. Maybe he's a sister's child?"

"There was a much older sister who is buried as Miss Domino, so we know she had no children. As interesting as your ideas are, no one like that person is listed in any records anywhere."

"Like there were no unwed mothers back then?" I flipped back.

Then another idea came to me suddenly, "Randall, could the prowler have had time to search the house or garage? Shouldn't we check the upstairs at least?"

So we did, through all the rooms and Sappy's office. Randall checked the deck outside the sliding door because the door was unlocked and standing open, but nothing was disturbed and it was a forty-foot drop to the ground with no trees to use for ladders. The computer was still unplugged.

There was nothing of value in Sappy's desk, but letter paper and envelopes were as neatly stacked as they'd been before.

Randall made toast and scrambled eggs for our late supper. We were both quiet while we ate. He seemed to be engrossed in his own thoughts, and I kept my mind blank. I'd done enough deep thinking for a long time. Suddenly, I remembered the file I'd found that Randall could use to get Tim out of jail.

"Randall," I began as I reached for the file. "I forgot to show you the evidence that links Anthony Simmons to Tallulah's murder if not to Sappy's. Let me show you," I said.

I pulled out the papers and spread them on the table. "Like I told you, this will and a promissory note were in Tallulah's desk. I took them. See, Timothy is her beneficiary, but the note says the ranch will go to this Simmons guy on Tallulah's death, in payment of the note. Doesn't that negate the will?"

That's interesting information," was all Randall said.

"Listen, a little enthusiasm is in order here. That's enough to get Tim out of jail and you know it. And look at the name of the attorney who wrote the will and witnessed the signing of the Promissory Note. It's 'Robertson,' a brother, cousin, or otherwise cooperative relative of the sheriff's, wouldn't you say?" I wanted Randall to jump up and call the sheriff who would release Tim. Why he wasn't doing it, I couldn't imagine.

Randall spoke logically, "The note is for ten thousand dollars in 1973. Twenty-nine years later, the same ranch is worth thousands more. It could be sold, the note paid off, and there'd be an ample inheritance left for Tim. It'll have to be probated and a judge decide which document takes precedent."

"But, the interest due all of those years?" I asked.

"The interest is listed here at two percent, but that plus the loan would in no way add up to the present value of the land."

"All today for nothing?" I said.

"No, not for nothing," Randall said. "You saw Tallulah's murderer, whether Anthony Simmons or someone else who drives a gray van. Now all we have to do is find him."

I was sneezing into a tissue, while Randall poured some red wine and sat down. "Hope you're not catching a cold," he said and then asked, "can you describe the man you saw?"

I shook my head, "I didn't see much of him, only his back. He wore the kind of boots sportsmen wear, heavy rubber soles and feet with leather uppers."

"How do you know what sportsmen wear?" Randall asked.

"Because they wear them into the ER when they get hurt. Do you want to know what else I saw, or question me about details?" He could be so picky.

"Sorry, go on," Randall said.

"He wore a blue bandanna tied gypsy fashion around his head that covered his hair although a fringe of hair hung below it. Oh, and his boots weren't muddy, just dusty."

"Color of hair, young or old, would you recognize his voice if you heard it again?" Randall asked.

I was thinking when angry barking and growling began and Perro raced across the patio and off toward the road. "Someone's out there," I said, "Is the house locked up?"

Quickly, using a panel of switches just inside the basement door, Randall turned on floodlights, from patio to back, north side, and front. Why hadn't I known they were there?

"Watch out the kitchen window for anyone coming around that way," Randall ordered, "I'll check the north side and the front."

I stood leaning over the sink, watching the well-lit path to the garage and garage apartment. I didn't realize I was trembling until Randall's warm arm and hand went around my shoulders.

"It's okay, I think. Everything's locked. I'm going out and have a look around." Randall was reassuring. "I think it may have been the sheriff's deputy, but I want to know if anyone else is out there. I'll call Perro in to stay with you."

"No. Take Perro with you," I pleaded. "Please."

"I can do that. Now go find a blanket to wrap around you. You had pneumonia a few months ago. You're not to get chilled, remember?" Randall sounded genuinely concerned.

Not get chilled, I thought? What a laugh. Lots of rest and no anxiety? An even bigger laugh. I picked up the down-like afghan from Sappy's chaise in her sitting room and pulled it around me. Warmth spread through me as I toured the house, the sitting room, the living room, her bedroom, the kitchen and back. Three trips later, Randall rapped on the patio door.

"Anything?" I asked, unlocking the door to let both Randall and Perro in.

"Not a thing. No vehicles, no tracks, no exhaust fumes. Unless you count this as something," He held up a scrap torn from faded blue jeans that included a portion of a pocket. "Perro dropped it at my feet."

I took the piece of material, turned it over to see a bit of bright red. "Well if we need to verify DNA, we've got a sample."

I kneeled to stroke Perro's head and neck, when a question occurred to me. "Randall, where's Sergio?"

"He's at the hospital, wouldn't leave Juana's side. They gave him a room right outside ICU and serve him trays."

"But Perro's not been fed."

"Don't they leave food out for him so he can help himself whenever he's hungry?" Randall asked.

"Sergio warned me about wild animals. Wouldn't they get it first? Anyway, neither one of us is hiking up that hill looking for his feeding dish, not at night with a prowler out there."

I got out two bowls and filled one with fresh cool water, then I looked in the refrigerator for dog food. "Didn't you ever have a pet when you were a kid? A puppy or a kitten?"

"No. Never did," Randall admitted.

"Your education's lacking, mine too. We had only one puppy who chewed up Mom's shoes until she found a home for it," I said. I dished out a cupful of cooked unseasoned beef. Perro was watching hungrily, but waited patiently for me to set down the bowl and invite her to eat.

"Now you're going to bed. I'm going to spend the night. Mind if I join you after I clean up the kitchen?" Randall asked.

"When and if any man gets into my bed, it'll be at my invitation. Understood."

"It seems kinda hard to expect me to sleep on a couch when your bed looks so comfortable." Randall followed me into my bedroom and leaned on the door.

"Forget it. The only one welcome in here is Perro."

Randall sighed, "You're a hard woman. So, may I ask if you have a safe place to put this file," he said, holding up the brown file folder, "somewhere just in case our prowler gets in, where he can't find it."

"Good thinking, the prowler would destroy it. But matter of fact, I have a couple of places. Just give it to me, I'll take care of it. Oh, and you don't have to sleep on the couch, you can change the sheets on Kassi's bed and sleep there."

"He wouldn't destroy is. If he's Anthony as you think, he'd come up with an air tight alibi and collect the money and the ranch. He wants money, but not a murder conviction."

I found Randall clean sheets, and left him with his promise to stay put until I came for him. I took the string of keys to Sappy's sitting room and shut the door. I carefully shelved the file next to the box of diaries, locked the storage room door and put the sitting room back to normal before I remembered a stash of men's toiletries in the bathroom cupboard of my bedroom. I chose a packet containing a razor, toothbrush, paste, and a hairbrush that I took to Randall.

"These are only the absolute necessities, but should help in the morning," I said.

"Thanks," Randall said, "and lock your door after you, and I'll do the same. Keep the cell phone with you and call me on that number if anything alarms you."

"Can Perro sleep in my room?" I asked.

"Be my guest," Randall answered.

* * * * * * *

I knew nothing until nine forty-five the next morning. This was my second of three days off. I visited Tim and tried to cheer him up, but it was easy to see that his arthritis was more and more painful. I told him to not give up hope, because Randall was getting him a super defense attorney and I'd figured out who had really killed Tallulah. Just a day or two more, I said.

Then I went to visit Kassi, where I was treated like an ordinary hospital visitor and asked to leave the room at every opportunity. Each time that happened, I made my way to ICU to check on Juana, but was not allowed to see her nor talk to Sergio. Back and forth I went from one floor to the other. I could never see Juana, but did meet her daughter and managed to slip her a note with my name and telephone number on it. These two days hadn't been restful, or productive, and another one would be a repeat. Tim was still in jail, and a murderer was still at large and since I was convinced the same person had murdered Tallulah that killed Sappy, this monster was a killer of elderly, defenseless women, a person to be despised who was probably looking for me. The thought gave me a chill and I sat huddled and shivering in the waiting room.

I'll go home, I decided. Where it was perhaps no safer than here, but at least where there were secure locks and a warm protective dog. I stopped first and bought Perro the most expensive dog food on the shelf, a box of treats, and a soft bed. At that moment, nothing was too good for Perro.

I was loading my purchase into Bertha, when the cell phone rang, "Nika," came Randall's voice, " I'm on my way to your ranch with food for a very good meal. Where are you?"

"Also on my way to Sappy's."

"Good, I'll meet you there."

A huge bellied man with a broad brimmed official hat stopped me at the gate. A leather encased revolver hung on his hip. I sputtered a little at having to prove my business here was legitimate, but soon figured out sputtering would get me nowhere and showed him the three identifications he requested, my driver's license, RN license and my check book, before he waved me on.

"Like the security measures?" Randall asked.

"It's inconvenient." I snapped, already bitchy because I had no influence at the hospital and because of Tim's slow deterioration. "Poor Perro won't know what to do, attack those guys or what. Are you responsible for this?"

"I called in the State Police," he said, "They made the decision to post a man at the gate. The local sheriff's an honest man, but this may be a little over his head."

"What gives you the authority to call in the State Police," I asked slipping the key in Sappy's front door and entering.

"The woman I plan to marry's in danger. All the reason I need," he said stooping to pet Perro, who was ecstatic at having company after a long day alone.

How dare he? "Marry you? Why would I marry you? You're so controlling. If you asked me to marry you, which you didn't, I'd say a big loud 'no'. Consider it said." I was steamed, "And stop telling me what to do. I can very well manage my own life."

"I'll just have to hope you change your mind," Randall said.

I followed him, trying to think of something so insulting it'd wipe the smile off his face. However, he put the groceries on the counter with instructions not to touch. "I'm going to take Perro for a run and introduce her to the State Trooper."

Randall had no right here, no right to have Perro respond to him instead of me, no right to bring food to cook for my dinner and no right to say he'd marry me. He and Phillip were so alike, both assuming I'd marry them. It must be a lawyer thing.

I washed the new stainless steel dog dishes, dried them, measured out dry food, and poured fresh water into Perro's gleaming new water dish. After first turning on the floodlight, I put the trash in the copious garbage can just outside the back door and carried the dog food to the roomy pantry.

Now what, I wondered. My anger at Randall was fast evaporating in his absence. Let him cook, let him call in the State Patrol, but I'll never marry him and that's final. I searched the refrigerator for an opened wine bottle, and found enough in two bottles to fill one wine glass. I settled down in the sunken family room, turned on the TV with the remote control, surfed for a news channel while I sat sipping and listening. The news was about the latest sex scandal in the capitol, and shootings in the work place.

When I noticed the shadows lengthening and darkness settling, I got up and opened the basement door far enough to turn on the rest of the floodlights, before shutting and locking the door. Then I toured the house, closing drapes and shades until I felt snug as a caterpillar in a cocoon. A warm feeling, altogether, as Tim would say. I took *Murder on the Rocks*, to Sappy's sitting room, turned on a reading lamp next to the chaise and settled down.

A tantalizing aroma of stir-fry beef and vegetables woke me. My book had dropped to the floor, but as I stirred, Perro's head came up level with the chaise and she nuzzled my hand. "Perro, about time you noticed your dog biscuit friend," I said stroking her warm back and burying my face in her soft short fur coat.

From the door, Randall said, "That dog adores you. I'm jealous."

Well, I thought, that's gratifying. "When we came in together, she never noticed me. Don't be jealous."

"Well, I am. Come and eat. The wine is breathing and our dinner is hot," Randall said.

The meal was good, and we ate in silence until I got up to answer the telephone. "Nika, Rosie has an emergency and can't work for you tomorrow night as we'd planned. I know your sister's in the hospital, but I'd count it as a personal favor if you'd come back to work a day early."

"I suppose I can do that. How about my regular days off, do I get them once a week like ordinary people?" I asked.

"Absolutely. I promise—after this week. I've hired an extra nurse who will work relief and nights for charge nurses." Ells sounded certain, but I knew that could change over-night.

"Ells, I'm taking my nights off whether you have someone to cover for me or not." That's the only real power I have, I thought as I hung up.

Randall had been watching me, "How do you do that?"

"Do what?" I asked.

"Answer the phone before it rings? You've been doing that since I've known you. Is my hearing bad or what?"

"I don't know. Tim says it has to do with being Irish, but I think maybe I feel the vibration before I hear it ring."

"Sure," he said, with sarcasm, "that makes a lot of sense."

We cleaned up the kitchen together, and while I was putting leftovers away, Randall asked, "Did you see anything of a red pickup truck at Tallulah's house?"

I shut the refrigerator door. I'd forgotten. "There was a red pickup going way too fast about four or five miles from the ranch. It was a sharp curve, but I memorized the first numbers," I said writing them down. "It was a Colorado plate, if that helps. The room I entered from the porch door was big, like a family room. A door at one end opened on a single bedroom. On the floor, beside the bed were a pair of jockey shorts—not too clean looking, and on a pillow was an orange and green nightie. The kind Tallulah wore to the nursing home. There was a half a pot of coffee on the kitchen stove that was still warm. An open stairway in the hall led to Tallulah's combined bedroom and office. That's were I found the file folder with the note and will inside."

A half smile tugged at his mouth, "That's a very good description given a day and lots of trauma later."

"Gee, thanks," I said, "but I'm not going to bed with you."

"Understood. Same rules as last night?" he asked.

"Same rules," I said.

After I introduced Perro to her new bed and she accepted it, I crawled into my own and slept soundly. I woke the next morning at eleven. I had needed that second night off.

There was a note from Randall on the kitchen table saying he'd gone to the office, but would have the cell phone with him all day should I need him. I didn't see him again until just before I went to work that night.

To my surprise, nothing had changed at the nursing home. It was as though I'd not had any time off at all. Only Rocky mentioned the intruder problem at the ranch.

"I was sure glad to find out you weren't home when all that happened. I didn't tell anyone that you had problems for a couple of nights, didn't think you'd want anyone to know," he said.

"Thanks Rocky, I think the less speculation the better."

"Yeah well, my folks are saying that old Sheriff Robertson needs to be replaced next election. He's not sharp enough to catch a real criminal. Look how long it's been since your aunt was shot. Bet they'd have got the guy in Minneapolis by now."

"Hopefully," was all I could say.

The night dragged. I called the hospital about two and asked how my sister and Juana were doing. Didn't learn much, except they had this telephone number for me at night.

About three-thirty, guitar music floated down the hall coming from Molly's room. I was on my way when the phone began to ring and I ran back to answer it.

When I picked it up, there was no answering voice just a trace of breathing. I hung up immediately, but it was unnerving. I debated calling Randall, and finally did, because maybe someone was trying to find out if the house was unoccupied.

"What's up," his alert voice came through the cell phone.

"I just had a breathing only telephone call. I'm concerned our intruder was trying to find out if the house was empty. I wanted to warn you."

"Thanks, I'll get dressed and watch. I'll call the sheriff too, and ask for a deputy to guard the nursing home," Randall said.

"Where's Perro?" I asked.

"Asleep on her bed in your bedroom," Randall answered.

His voice was loud and faint by turns with an occasional grunt added. I guessed he was trying to dress.

"Why guard the nursing home?" I asked.

"Your caller could have been finding out if you were on duty. You may be more vulnerable there than here," Randall said.

I gave a convulsive shudder. "I never thought of that."

"I have to go," Randall said. "You be careful."

I turned off the cell phone and went back to the desk as Rocky came jogging soundlessly down the hall from his unit.

"Your phone rang?" he asked. "Was it the hospital? Is your sister worse?"

"Nobody but a breather," I answered. "I called Randall to warn him and he will call the sheriff to send a guard to the nursing home."

"See? I told you someone was out there. I'm staying with you until a guard shows up," Rocky said as we walked to the back room windows to watch for an official car.

I smiled, gallant Rocky.

"So, you called Randall, huh?"

"Yes, I thought this might be the same person who killed my aunt, murdered Tallulah, injured Kassi and shot Juana. I didn't want Randall to be surprised if he showed up at the ranch."

Rocky eyed me with interest, "Randall staying at the ranch? With you?" he asked.

"Yes. He doesn't want to leave the ranch unattended as an invitation to our prowler, not when that prowler is probably also a killer," I said.

Instead of watching out the window, I could feel Rocky's eyes studying me. Oh, oh. I'd done it. Rocky's speculation was evident by the expression on his face.

"Now don't get any ideas. He has his own bedroom with a lock on his door and I have my room that also has a lock on the door. And the dog sleeps in my room. There's nothing between Mr. McClean and myself," I said.

"Sure there isn't," Rocky said.

"There'll be no talk about our conversation to anyone else, including your parents. I don't want anyone distracted from the crimes," I ordered.

"Sure, ma'am. Trust me, my lips are zipped."

Then he turned back to the window and said, "Look boss, there's a State Patrol Car circling the parking lot."

We watched as the officer parked his car and began a search of every car in the parking lot.

"Wow," Rocky finally said, "your Mr. McClean sure has influence."

"Rocky. Will you run to the front and look out those windows. I'm curious as to whether or not they're protecting both front as well as the back of the building."

"Done," he said jogging off.

"Don't go outside," I said and he turned and saluted.

He was back in minutes, "Yep, there's a Patrol Car outside the front entrance. Boy, is this exciting or what?"

"I find it scary," I said. "But it's nearly five and I have lots to do. You too."

"I'm off," he said.

"We both need to check the windows in the patient rooms. Be very careful," I said, "and Rocky if any of the windows close to the ground are open, check if the screens are in place and shut the windows."

"Sure, no problem," Rocky said.

"And Rocky, if you find any open windows with no screens, lock them, leave quietly and come for me."

Chapter Twenty

After a week without incident, the State Police stopped guarding the ranch and nursing home, saying the prowler had gotten tired of it all and left the area. Kassi came home from the hospital, which meant less sleep for me, deprived of his bed, Randall returned home. Juana opened her eyes and responded to stimuli, but didn't speak, either by choice or because her long comatose state had damaged a part of her brain. That she'd made progress was evident when she was moved out of ICU and into a step-down area. Sergio and his daughter began staying at the ranch, and Perro happily returned to her real home. I was left adrift, even Randall stopped coming around.

One night I was surprised to find I'd gone to work on my night off. I didn't want to go back home, my mind was in turmoil, working on first one worry and then another. I needed some non-stressful human companionship and the first person I thought of was the waitress I'd met on the way into Magdalena. I drove out to the edge of town and stopped at the doughnut shop.

Once again I was the only one there, and the warm moist smells of coffee and pastries welcomed me as I entered. I asked for decaf coffee and sat sipping it silently, wondering why I brought danger to everyone I cared about. Mom, Dad, Grandma Ann, Timothy, Juana, and even Kassi had suffered because of me.

The waitress broke the quiet. "My name's Clara. What's yours?"

"What? Oh sorry," I said, trying to bring my scattered thoughts back into focus. "My name's Nika. Nika McGuinness."

"The one whose mother is Greek and father is Irish? Am I right?" She asked.

"You're right," I said, "except they're past tense now. All of them dead."

Clara gave me one of her long steady looks and then lifted the lid on the doughnuts and used her tongs to place a custard filled one on a plate and set it in front of me. "You know, Nika McGuinness, you still look tired and hungry. Eat up. My favorite aunt always said, 'a trouble shared is a troubled halved.' So, if you feel like talking, go ahead. It won't go any farther than this counter."

"Did you ever lose anyone you loved?" I asked.

"Sure did. The best husband in the world and a son I loved more than anything."

"Are you all alone now?" I asked.

"No. I have another son, who's my own personal Rock of Gibraltar. Everyone else's too."

"Did you ever get over the sadness? I mean the death of your husband and your other son?" I asked. I could hear an engine idling out on the parking lot.

"Not really, but then, I don't want to forget them either. What I learned is that you have to walk through the pain, until it gets easier." Clara thought for a bit, "helps me to know I told them both I loved them just shortly before they died."

"You're lucky, you know that," I said as I paid the tab and started for the door. Just as I opened it, a van that had been idling in front, backed away and spewed gravel taking off down the highway. Was it gray? Did it have a Minnesota license?

"Do you know that van?" I asked.

"Never saw it before," answered Clara.

I used her phone to call the sheriff. I described the van, but not the driver, whom I hadn't seen. In fairness, all he could do was look around the parking lot and follow the road in the direction the van had taken. He didn't catch up with it, and the incident only confirmed that the person who watched me and who tried to enter Sappy's house, was still out there somewhere. The sheriff offered to follow me home and I accepted. As I was leaving the doughnut shop, I heard Clara call after me, "Come back so we can finish our talk." Everything was quiet at home.

* * * * * * * *

There were three weeks left in August when Kassi declared herself well enough to return to work. Tim was charged with murder and remained in jail, but everything else returned to as normal as possible. However, without Juana's invisible support the laundry piled up and the refrigerator smelled of stale leftovers. I'd gotten three nights off to clean up the mess, but I also had to work twelve nights in a row to get them. Ells drove a hard bargain. This was the tenth night. The result of this many nights without sleep, was always the same, so I expected to begin seeing and hearing things that had no right to be heard or seen. Although I heard no music, the last couple of nights, I had seen the cowboy hat hanging on the bedpost and a filmy shadow in the corner.

This night I picked up the picture that showed a younger happier Molly and Charlie standing in front of a new car. Even knowing that the substance in the corner was a result of extreme lack of sleep, I spoke to it anyway. "Molly's condition is deteriorating every night. I don't think she'll rally again." I drew a tissue from my pocket and wiped my eyes. "I've become very fond of my adopted grandma Molly."

I swear I heard, "She loves you, as do I. I'd like to be your pretend grandpa. May I?"

"That's so sweet of you," I answered, not feeling foolish in the least, "I'd like you for my pretend grandpa."

I went directly to the rest room to splash cold water on my face. The shock of it jolted me wide-awake. A good thing no one heard my conversation with a shadow, I thought, I'd be declared incompetent at the least, and lucky if not insane.

I'd finished my charting and plugged in the coffee maker thinking I'd have a cup, while giving report, but I must have dozed off sitting upright, because the ringing phone woke me with a start. I answered, to hear only heavy breathing and whispered words, "I'll getcha yet." The time was six thirty-five.

I pulled Randall's cell phone out of my lab coat pocket and dialed his number. When there was no answer after ten rings, I gave it up and went to the treatment room for coffee. I stood looking out the window and saw the bridal couple, the ones from the picture in Molly's room. The groom Charlie, opened the back door of his Chevy, identical to the one stored in Sappy's garage, and put the guitar on the back seat before helping a young lovely lady, into the front seat. They both looked up at the window and blew me kisses. It was Molly, and finally I knew for certain that Molly was the woman in the Polaroids. The ectoplasm was Charlie protectively encircling her.

I put down my cup and ran to Molly's room. She was lying as though peacefully asleep, but when I felt for her pulse there was none.

Chapter Twenty-one

Sitting straight up in bed, I clutched the comforter and fought a nightmare. It was ten-thirty by the bedside clock. I'd only been in bed an hour. I realized too that I was not dreaming, but reliving the events of last night. A sob caught in my chest, tears ran down my face. Grief knotted into a lump in my throat, and I wept into the comforter.

Charlie was the ectoplasm, the ghost in the Polaroid print I'd found. Of course. The way he appeared and disappeared, why hadn't I believed my eyes? What must it be like for two people to love each other so deeply that death can't separate them? Incredible that Charlie protected Molly, as she grew old, and when she died, led her away to a better, happier place. Charlie had been my grandfather; Molly had taken the place of my grandmother. Now, I'd never see either of them again. Would I always grieve for people I'd loved too late and lost too soon?

And the business of telling everything to Randall while crying in his arms, as he stroked my hair and finally found a boob to fondle, was juvenile. Transferring the desire for the kind of devotion Charlie and Molly shared to the first male who happened along was idiocy.

Get over it, Nika. Don't let it happen again!

I glanced at the clock. It was definitely ten-thirty. The sun sliding through the east side of the drapes, was proof the time was morning, not night. I disentangled myself from twisted sheets and comforter and made my way to the bathroom. Cold water splashed on my face should end the weeping. I was about to turn on the cold water tap when I heard a thump overhead.

Someone was in the house? Who? Kassi was at work, Sergio and his daughter were certainly at Juana's hospital bedside. There should be only me here, and I should be asleep.

Sure I should. If I ever slept again. In my life time!

With eyes blurred by unshed tears; I studied the door and windows of my bedroom. They were securely locked, just as I'd kept them since Randall installed new locks. Just as every door and every window in this house was always locked, since we had a gun-carrying intruder. I must be alone in the house.

Returning to the bathroom, I used a still damp washcloth to wipe the tears away and held a handful of tissues to my nose before quietly returning to the bedroom. The noise was my imagination.

There was a soft footfall. The sound was close, in the next room. Except the next room was the bathroom.

My heart throbbed, beating against my ribs. My god! I'd just come from there, how could anyone get into my bathroom? Cautiously, I looked. The bathroom was empty.

There was another footfall, louder still and this one came from my bedroom. This was for real. The sound an echo made by someone who had entered while I was asleep. If it was the same one who shot Juana and hit Kassi on the head, I was in danger.

I moved slowly, studying the walls for false panels. There were plenty of those in this house. 'Careful,' I warned myself, 'any sound I make will be carried to the intruder's ears as his footsteps are carried to mine.' A muffled sneeze warned me I was close. I looked up toward the sound and realized I was standing under a small grate that vented the area directly above this bedroom. The enclosed part of the second floor landing? The part I couldn't get into? Sure. What else? Another secret room that someone else had access to. Someone who could get into a locked house. Our intruder!

Our intruder, who murdered Sappy, shot Juana, hurt Kassi, smothered Tallulah, and searched Tallulah's house? The killer of elderly women. Oh my god.

Now easy. Maybe it was Randall or Kassi, and if it were either of them, their car would be parked out front. I moved to the front windows and parted the drapes. No Bertha. No BMW. I went noiselessly to the bathroom turret window and lowered the shade to see the side yard. No Bertha, no BMW. Maybe I imaged the noises. I'd done enough hallucinating lately to see hippopotamuses in the Jacuzzi. I couldn't help myself—I looked. When no beasts poked their heads above the tub, I began to laugh: silent, helpless, stomach-shaking mirth. A soft footfall above me acted like a slap in the face.

I had to get help. Thankful I had Randall's cell phone on the bedside stand, I gathered it and my list of telephone numbers, went into the closet, and shut the door. It locked. I'd deal with that later, now I needed a light. I found the switch and flipped it back and forth. No light. I tried again. Still no light and the door was locked. Damn! What to do?

The small flashlight was in the lab coat I'd hung on a hook. Where in this humongous closet was the hook? The dark was disorienting. By moving around the walls I found the lab coat hanging from a hook near the back. I felt for the pocket, but the coat just twisted on the hook, threatening to fall to the floor. I put it on. First getting it front to back and finally shrugging into it. Once on, I automatically reached into the right pocket, and retrieved the flashlight. I prayed it still had some small charge. It gave a dim light.

First thing I did was to slip the catch on the door to the unlocked position, opening it a crack. There were times when being locked in a closet might be the preferable option, but this wasn't one of them. Next I tested the bulb and found it was only loose. When I tightened it, the light came on. A relief. I slipped the small flashlight back into my pocket.

I punched in the numbers for Randall's cell phone and listened to it ring and ring and ring. Randall must have stopped carrying it, but it was nearly eleven, the sheriff and his cronies often had coffee at the In Towne. I dialed the number for Kassi's work and on the fourth ring her voice sang, "In Towne Cafe, how may I help you?"

"Kassi, it's Nika. Is the sheriff there?"

"No, he's not here."

"Are you sure?"

"Yes, I'm sure. Nika when you go this long without sleep, you do weird things. So what is it this time, you're imagining Randall is taking another girl out to eat, like Phillip used to do? Are checking up on your lawyer?"

"Why would I ask for the sheriff if I wanted to talk to Randall?"

"Because unless your lawyer is buying you breakfast, the two of them are in here huddled over a pot of coffee. I told you that. Just like I told you people are saying that you and Randall are a couple. Why you deny it, I don't know. Why don't you just ask for Randall? You're a devious person, know that?"

"Kassi, this is serious. At least look around."

"I have looked around. They're not here. Not the sheriff. Not Randall. Now I'm hanging up. Just because you're not working doesn't mean no one else is."

The receiver clicked. Kassi had hung up.

Maybe they were at Randall's office.

I checked the number list, punched it in and listened to the phone ring ten times before I hung up. Maybe they were in court? Then they wouldn't be out before noon, and maybe not available then. Well, I'd have to take some kind of action. I slid my feet into loafers and headed out of my room.

So what action? Undecided, I stood just outside my bedroom door, under the overhanging balcony, when the sound of a sliding door came from above me. I flattened against the stairway and craned my head up.

The paneled, intricately carved wall moved, exposing a room with a rounded wall and bowed windows. The turret. I couldn't find a panel that opened on the turret room, but there was one. Whoever was up there was searching for the money and jewels, and knew more about this house than I did. Even how to get in without a key. Who could it be? A softly spoken 'God Bless' answered a sneeze. A masculine voice. I sucked in my breath; there were two men up there! I silently went back to the security of my bedroom. What could I do against the muscle of two men? I leaned against the door; afraid to click the lock shut knowing the sound would alert the men up stairs. The house was eerily quiet, waiting. The house knew evil men were here. I must concentrate.

Who could *they* be? Everything had pointed to one man, one man named Anthony, if not him then who? The sheriff and Randall? I'd never liked the sheriff, but I'd learned to trust Randall, just this morning he was so reassuring about Charlie and Molly driving off in that Chevy. I wasn't hallucinating, no way he'd said. Just because I was on my tenth night and had gone to sleep sitting upright at my desk this morning and might not have been fully awake when I saw Charlie and Molly drive off, there was not one thing the matter with my powers of observation, not a thing. He'd said such nice things, even claimed he would marry me some day, if I'd only have him.

Well, guys have faked that before, I thought as a flash of Phillip's face went through my mind. Randall and Sheriff Robertson weren't anywhere else, why couldn't they be upstairs?

Another heavy footstep sounded over my head, a muffled curse. With my eyes shut, I sensed only one man move along the balcony and down the hall. If I was to prove Randall or the sheriff was in my house illegally, I had to see them.

I could hear someone searching the bedrooms. Now was the time to sneak up the stairs. A footstep came from the hall. My sense still felt just one person, but I grabbed the bandage scissors I always carried in the pocket of the lab coat. I flattened against the stairway with them held open, thumb braced on the flattened point and index finger braced against the opposite handle, ready to slice. Better than nothing at all. My raspy breathing was loud, my thudding heart like a drum beat.

I heard the click of a door. He'd gone into one of the bedrooms. This was my chance to sneak up the stairs and watch for him. If it wasn't Randall, if it was an older guy, or someone who was hungry or just down on his luck, maybe I could order him out. Or feed him, or give him some money.

In your dreams, you could, Nika.

I gripped the scissors and crept up the stairs until I could see across the hall floor. I braced my foot against the newel post and lay flat across the steps, waiting. Just as the phone rang once, a bedroom door opened and someone stepped out. I rose up to watch and gasped in shock. It was not a beggar, nor an old man, nor Randall. It was Phillip. Phillip with a bandanna tied over his unkept long hair. Phillip with a beard.

Oh dear God. Phillip? How could Phillip be involved? The phone began ringing again. It rang four or five times and suddenly stopped. I had to move, before he discovered me.

I ducked my head and began backing down the stairs, sliding faster and faster, all the while expecting Phillip to come into the hall and see me. I slid onto the tile floor with a soft thump, and scooted on my rear under the protection of the balcony. I couldn't open my bedroom door without exposing myself, so I'd wait until I heard him go back into a room before moving. I sat silent; concentrating on the carved posts that supported the stairway railing, still, quiet, not breathing.

The carved post closest to me depicted a blue jay on the edge of nest, holding a peanut in its bill. A fantasy. That's what Sappy, Grandma, Kassi and I had told stories about. We'd watched the squirrel run up the oak tree for acorns. We'd laughed at the Blue Jay hiding peanuts in the owl's nest. Sappy's conundrum ran through my head; *Chatty ran the oak tree, but only acorns did she see.* Chatty was the name we gave the squirrel. *Janie flew to the owl's nest, but only peanuts…,'* Janie was the Blue

Jay….,' *only springs unlock the chests.* Without thinking, I stood up, reached out and gave the peanut a little twist. There was a faint click and the side panel opened on a velvet box with rolls of bills stuffed next to it. I saw $100 on the bills. I'd found the treasure. Now of all times, I'd found it.

One thing, I couldn't let Phillip know. I gently pushed and the panel slid silently shut. It was then I realized I stood in full view of the balcony. I ducked down the central hall, hoping that Phillip was still searching the bedrooms. The phone, which had stopped ringing, began to ring again. I slipped off the loafers and ran barefoot along the carpet. "Hello?" My voice was little more than a whisper, my breath came in gasps.

"Nika? Hello, Nika. It's Jill."

It was my friend from the travel agency. "Yes it's Nika. Did you find out anything?"

"Can't you talk louder? I can hardly hear you."

"Yes," I hissed, "it's Nika."

"Boy, you sound awful. Well, I called to tell you that I traced the reservations like you asked. It was for a Phillip Symm. Isn't that the guy you used to date?"

"Phillip flew out here in March? What for?"

"He was there four days to be exact. Nika, customers don't have to tell us why they fly somewhere, they just have to pay for their tickets, which, by the way, he didn't. Or rather he did, with a check that bounced. And he's flown that route before, lots of times. Must have a relative out there, or given his reputation maybe a girlfriend."

"He never told me."

"Well, you two had broken up as I recall. Oh, and another thing, he also goes by the name of Anthony P. Phillip Simmons, jr. At least he's known that way at the District Attorney's office. We found out when we listed his bad check with a collection agency. Ever hear that name before?"

Phillip was Aunt Sapphira's husband's great nephew. The son of the man who'd loaned Tallulah money. Dear God, I prayed, help me. "No, I don't believe I ever heard that name spoken." "Well, I hope this helps. I gotta run. Nika, you'd better take some aspirin and go to bed. You sound really hoarse. You got a virus or something?"

"Something, I sure got something. Thanks for your help."

I checked for Kassi's work number she'd scribbled on the phone book cover and dialed it. "In Towne, how can I help you?"

"Kassi, it's me Nika. I must have help."

"Can you please speak a little louder?"

"No, I can't speak louder. I'm in serious trouble, here. I don't want Phillip to hear me."

"Phillip?"

"Yes. Phillip. He's upstairs lurking around, and Jill just told me he's flown out here lots of times and was here during the time Sappy was killed. His real name is Simmons. He's Aunt Sapphira's husband's great nephew. I need the sheriff. I need Randall. I need help. Now."

"Nika, what's the matter with you? We've known Phillip for ages. If he came to Colorado, he'd tell us. And how could Jill tell you anything? She's in St. Paul, with her handsome brother. He still at home? Did you ask?"

"I don't have time to explain now. Just believe me. It's Phillip and he's dangerous," I whispered.

"You've either lost it totally, or you've got the greatest imagination in the world, know that? You don't need help, Nika you need sleep. I'll tell you to do, the same thing you told me, go back to your room, lock the door and stay there. When and if the sheriff comes in, I'll tell him you need help."

"Kassi, I'm scared."

"Go back to bed, and who knows while you're sleeping maybe the bogeyman will let himself out the way he let himself in."

Kassi's musical laughter ended when she hung up.

I saw a movement out of the corner of my eye. Phillip was leaning nonchalantly against the doorframe. Smiling his easy smile, one hand in his trouser pocket, the other behind him.

"Well, thanks for telling me," I said into the phone. "I have to go now."

"Where are you going?" Phillip asked still smiling.

"Phillip, what a surprise. How did you get in?"

"It's time we leveled with each other. You've known all along where the money and valuables were hidden. Just as you've always know it was really mine."

I started to protest, but he held up his hand, "I'm through listening to you, tired of being the sympathetic friend in need to be discarded when a more affluent guy comes along. I resent your cavorting around with Randall McClean."

"I haven't cavorted around with Randall or anyone, and as for Aunt Sapphira's fortune, she left it to me in her will. I didn't even know she existed until I got Randall's letter. You know that. Nothing I had anything to do with."

"So you say."

My being on the defensive was exactly what Phillip, the champion debater, liked. How could I turn it around, put him on the defensive? Think, Nika, think.

"Take that misunderstood look off your face. You're a bigger schemer than I've ever been. Admit it. You nearly beat me at my own game here." Phillip still leaned against the doorframe, hatred in his eyes, still the superior male.

I stiffened, my own dislike for him boiled up. I lowered my gaze; it might be wiser to play the helpless woman. "I don't know why you say such mean things to me," I met his eyes, trying for my sister's best beseeching look. "How did you get in? Did Kassi lend you her key?"

He shrugged his shoulders and left his position in the doorway to take a seat at the table opposite me. He'd been clutching a gun in the hand he held behind him. Now he laid it on the table.

"Phillip, put that ugly thing away. I hate guns. They kill people."

"They do, don't they? They sure do," Phillip said.

At that moment, I was certain he'd shot Sappy and smothered Tallulah. I'd developed a huge dislike for Phillip, but to think of him as a murderer was a stretch. He couldn't be that evil. After all, he'd taught me to play softball.

"Why not tell you. You won't be telling anyone else."

That was a chilling thought, my not telling anyone, whatever else he intended, he meant for me to die. I tried to control a shiver, "You know you can trust me not to tell secrets. Remember that time on the lake when you pushed that kid and he fell through the ice? I never told."

"I pushed the kid? What baloney. You pushed the kid. You pushed him and ran. I stayed behind, found a stick, held it out to him while I lay on the ice and pulled him out when he grabbed it. Now you're turning everything around." Cunning replaced the hatred in Phillip's eyes. Insane cunning.

It had been exactly the opposite, he ran, but I stayed behind and helped the little kid out and back home. I told his Mom he'd had an accident. How could Phillip twist the facts? He was crazy. A sudden thought hit me, "Phillip, did you and your father went fishing with Grandma Ann and Dad that day"

"Now let's see. Did I go fishing and push them all, even my Dad, into the lake? Or did someone else, maybe you do that?" Whoever it was, they did Dad a service, he was dying anyway."

His smile was evil. He was certifiably insane. He'd kill me. I had to control my trembling and think. I had to keep him talking. I had to hope I could somehow get away from him. "Whatever. So how did you get in the house?"

"Why not? Might as well tell you everything. What can you do about it, any of it?"

"Sure, you do that. If it's a long story we might as well have some coffee." I was over to the stove before he could stop me, thinking a pot of hot coffee in his face would detract him long enough for me to make it back to the safety of my bedroom. I filled the pot with hot water, it would boil quicker, and was measuring out coffee grounds, before he was beside me, strong hands squeezing, pinching my neck. "You're hurting me, Phillip," I wheezed.

He propelled me back to the chair, "You just sit back down, and I'll stop." His breath was hot on my neck, "Man that's tempting, but not yet. Soon, but not yet."

Terrified, shaking, I rubbed my neck. No doubt he could kill me. If I stalled for time, maybe Sergio or his daughter would come home. They did sometimes, late in the afternoon, for clean clothes, or something. Yet it was only eleven-twenty. Late afternoon was five-six hours away. I stopped the sob in my throat, whatever he must not see how frightened I was.

"Are you going to tell me how you got in? Did I forget to lock something? Did Kassi lend you her key?" I asked.

"Not scared yet? You will be. Count on it. Let's see. How did I get in?"

He was at his best, condescending and arrogant. Briefly, I thought what a good trial lawyer he'd be, if he could be poor long enough to get his degree. He was thin, needed a shave, his hair a little too long, and was too emaciated to be as handsome as he once was. Thin, emaciated? Was Phillip on drugs?

"So, you were telling me how you got in. I have a right to know?"

"So you do, so you do. This ranch belonged to my great uncle Tony. Aunt Sapphira got it by default when the old boy died out in the mine. Took Charlie with him. They both drowned. Every time a hard rain hits, that old mine fills with water. The storm came up fast, caught in the far tunnel, they didn't have a chance."

"How awful."

"Yeah well, luck of the cards."

Luck of the cards? That was the other thing Phillip liked, poker. Was that why he needed money so badly he'd kill for it?

"When I was a kid, not in school yet, before Uncle Tony died, Dad brought me out here every summer. When Dad was so sick, at the last there, he told me I was Tony's only living heir. I'd inherit everything. The ranch and the fortune."

"Hmmm, I see." Let him tell a long story. As long as possible. "This is pretty interesting. Is there more?"

"Is there ever. I started coming out here every summer. Helping Aunt Sapphira, making myself useful to that old lady friend of hers Molly. Charlie's wife. The money she spent on that woman. She spent my inheritance on her."

"Well, they cared a lot for each other."

"Cared? She should have cared for me. I told her that. But all she ever did for me was pay my tuition to the U. Tuition and money to live on. Parceling out *my* money to me."

"I can see that."

"I bet you can. She finally said I was taking too long to get through law school. Cut off the money. Told me she was changing her will, making you her heir. I knew all along you might inherit something that's why I dated you, and that's why I came whenever you called. Everyone thought we were an item. That we'd marry. And so we would have, and the marriage would have lasted long enough for me to control all the money, then out you'd go. That's why I shot good old Aunt Sapphira. I didn't know she'd already changed her will. My timing was off, but you have to admit my reasons were right on."

Dear God. Phillip was admitting he shot Aunt Sappy. He was a monster. "Phillip, did you know Tallulah?"

"No, Dad knew her. After her husband died, she was broke, so he gave her ten thou and she signed over the ranch to him. She shouldn't have lived so long. I needed that money. So I held a pillow over her face, she was gone in seconds. Just like that." He snapped his fingers and laughed.

He'd killed them both and he'd kill me. I had to make a bargain. "Phillip, I can understand your disappointment. I'm willing to give you most of the money and the ranch. You were here as a kid, it means more to you than to me."

"Most of the money? How about all the money? It's rightfully mine. Everywhere in the world, except Aunt Sapphira's Greek family, the male inherits."

"All the money's good with me. I need enough to pay the bills, and move back to Minneapolis."

"I don't think so. I let you live and you'll tell your sweet Randall how I shot Sapphira and smothered Tallulah and the game will be up, for me. No, I think we've talked long enough. Time to jog on down to the mine. Come on."

Phillip gripped my arm, propelling me toward the patio.

"But you haven't told me how you got in."

"Easy," he said as he slid the door open and pushed me through it, "I've had a key since I was a kid. Uncle Tony wasn't nearly as stingy with keys as Sapphira."

The brick patio was hot, searing the bottom of my feet. "Phillip, if we're going to walk far I need my shoes. Let me run and get them."

"You'll not miss them for long. Walk fast, the heat won't bother you so much."

I could hear Perro barking. " Is Perro in the garage?"

"Yup. I put an old dead squirrel in the garage. When that mangy mutt went in, I locked the door. Been better if I'd shot her, but I figured the noise would wake you up. Might as well have shot the old mongrel and had it over with, you're awake now anyway. When I am through with you, I'll shoot her." There was that laugh again. "Plenty of time for that after I have you safely tucked away." Another laugh. "Tucked away, that's a good one."

I could hear Perro barking. She was frantic, nails scraping the door in an attempt to get out. Phillip would shoot her. I couldn't stop him.

I felt something burrowing into my back. "Whatever that is, it hurts. Stop it."

"Doesn't hurt as much as if I pulled the trigger. Just go to the right of the garage, up that little hill and right through the trees. We'll be in the mine before you know it."

It was farther away than Phillip said. A turn to the left would take us to the path and eventually to Sergio's adobe house. I started in that direction. Perro was barking frantically and jumping on the garage door. If she got out…

"Not that way, this way," Phillip said, pushing me ahead of him and to the right.

I'd never been this way. Someone, Sergio or Randall, had said this was a wild animal path. Wild animals? A cougar? Was Phillip afraid of cougars? "Have you ever seen that hungry mountain lion that comes around looking for food?"

"I ever see a lion, I'll shoot it and find out later if he's hungry. Now through these shrubs and down that hole."

He shoved my head down and pushed me into a hole. He flipped on a flashlight and shown the light around. We were in a fair sized cave. At the back were two tunnels. We took one, and went down step-like cuts for several feet.

"Phillip, I don't like this."

"Yes, I remember, you're afraid to go underground, refused to go into the basement at your house. Still don't, I'll bet."

"Yes, I do. I go into basements all the time. But my feet are bare. The rocks are cutting them and I'm cold, I'm freezing. Remember, I had pneumonia and nearly died. This is undoubtedly bad for my lungs."

"Yeah? Might be fatal, do you think? What a shame."

We'd turned into at least two other tunnels. The ceiling was getting lower and lower. It was claustrophobic. "Please Phillip. You've had your fun. I made a deal with you. You can have it all. Remember, you need me to tell you where the money and valuables are. I can't do that dead."

"We'll stop here. You sit on this boulder and I'll tie your hands to that post that holds up the overhead beam. If you struggle hard enough to pull the post out, the ceiling will come down, maybe a quicker way to die. Your choice. And don't you worry your pretty head. I saw you looking in that newel post. I know where the money and valuables are. I've watched you a lot, even through the front windows of the nursing home. I called you a couple of times, sure was fun to watch your reaction"

He pulled some twine from his pocket and tied my hands, twisting it around the post and back around my hands again several times. The twine was ragged, twisted from short fibers that tore the skin as he tightened it around my wrists. He'd been prepared for this. Had intended to do this all along.

"Where did you get that stuff? It really hurts and isn't necessary. I promised I'd not tell."

"Now darlin', you know I'd be petty stupid to believe you would keep that promise once I let you out of my sight. Now I'm going. It'll rain this afternoon, the clouds were rolling in as we walked along. You noticed? I thought so. I don't like water, as you know. So I'll be leaving."

"The flashlight. Can't you at least leave the flashlight?"

"Now, how could I see my way out of here without a flashlight? I'd like to leave it, but you can see I need it. You won't need a light for long. Nor will you be cold anymore."

"Phillip, please don't leave me here. If you must kill me, take me outside and shoot me. We're related, in a way. We've been friends for years. You don't just walk away from an old friend leaving her to drown horribly in this dark dirty place."

"You may be glad of the water, once I leave with the light and rats and spiders begin crawling over you. Well, gotta go."

"Phillip," I shrieked again and again. "Phillip, please don't leave me here."

The light had been gone for a long time, when I stopped screaming and began weeping silently, helplessly. There was no denying that Phillip intended me to die and enjoyed terrifying me. He'd not come back for me either, nor would he tell anyone I was here. There was no hope that either Randall, the sheriff, or Sergio would look for me down in the mine; even if I was missed before I drowned. My situation was hopeless. Only a miracle could save me, and miracles were fiction. My heart ached. There was no one to help me, no one to ease my passing, as Charlie had Molly's, no one to care that I died. Silent sobs shook my shoulders, as tears ran down my cheeks.

I felt something furry on my feet, stop and nibble at my toes. In front of me, two pairs of red eyes moved slowly forward. I stomped my feet and whatever it was fell off, the red eyes moved back a pace or two. Did the red eyes belong to rats? Hadn't I read somewhere that rats' eyes glowed red in the dark? Where was it? *The Pit and the Pendulum*?

"Oh God help me, I cried." My voice sounded raspy, hoarse from all the screaming. Cold, persistent terror crept over me, numbing me, freezing my mind. I didn't think of water pouring down the tunnel, I only thought of rats, thousands of hungry rats gnawing at my flesh. "I want to die. Please God, strike me dead, oh please," I wailed.

A part of my mind burned hot, a thought like spoken words entered my consciousness. "You will not drown. You will not die. These are only rodents. They cannot kill you."

Hope, there was hope.

"I will not die. You're just little rodents. You can't really hurt me. Besides all I have to do is get my hands out of this twine and I'll be out of here. Hear me?"

I pulled against the twine. The skin on my wrists seemed to split, but pain was not a problem. Waiting to drown was. I strained against the twine and felt the skin break. Stomping my feet and straining, I kept saying, "I will not drown, I will not drown, I will not…," But the twine held, if anything it was tighter than before.

Still, there was hope; I'd heard a voice that said I would not drown, so there had to be a way. The bandage scissors. They were in my pocket. If I could reach them, I could cut the twine and I'd be free.

I felt needle-like claws scratch my feet; tiny teeth nibbled my bloody toes. I screamed. I'd been still too long, and they'd come back. I stomped my feet, stomped them again and again. Finally, I saw the red eyes retreat, but not disappear. They were only waiting. I had to keep moving my feet.

Which pocket had I slipped the scissors into? Was it the right one or the left one? I rose up as much as I could and shifted the lab coat across my body. I pulled my hands down against the post and heard a rumble before I felt rocks tumble down. One struck my right foot before a second one fell on it pinning it to small sharp rocks. I sat back down and waited for the stones and pebbles to stop tumbling down. I held my breath waiting for the noise and the avalanche to end, either end or send a big enough one to knock me out, or kill me. Smaller sharp bits of stone cut my hands, sliced my face, and slit my scalp. Blood dribbled into my eyes and mouth.

Hadn't Phillip warned me? "If you pull against that post, you'll bring the whole ceiling down. That's a quicker way to die, of course. It's up to you," he'd said.

The spot in my mind burned hot again, and I heard, "You must help yourself before I can help you. You know what you must do."

"Who's there? Tell me what to do and I'll do it. I'll do anything to get out of here." There was no answering voice. I'd imagined the whole thing.

At least it was quiet now. There was no noise at all, and the red eyes were way back. Then I heard faint strains of music, just snatches of something familiar. Was Charlie near? If I tried to get out of these ropes would he lead me the rest of the way, either out of the mine, or away with him and Molly? I would try. "I'll try Charlie, I really will try. Just don't leave me."

The way I sat, the right coat pocket was in my lap. By raising my left knee, I could feel something solid, maybe the scissors. If I could only get my hands into that pocket, I'd get the scissors and cut the twine. My hands were pulled high up in back of me, if I could lower them maybe I'd be able to reach my pocket. I leaned forward and worked my hands to pull the knot down lower and lower. It took so long and was so hard to do, I had to rest and listen for the music. It was very still. I strained to hear. There was no music. Then from far away, a low muted rumble came echoing down the mine. The red eyes scrambled away. Then another rumble sounded from far away.

Thunder. Dear God, I heard thunder. The rats knew water was coming and the mine would flood and they left. I had to get out of here. I'd never get the scissors, no way could I reach into that pocket.

Desperate now, I pulled against the twine. I twisted and pulled. I felt the twine gave, but at the same time cut into my wrists. The whole mine seemed to convulse as rocks and dirt tumbled down. Another big rock struck my left foot and pinned it to sharp debris. I cried out in pain.

"This is just enough," I called out as though the mine was a living being. "It's enough pain and fear. I can't take anymore, do you hear? I'm going to get out of here and you just don't give me any more trouble."

Then it came to me. I'd pull the twine to the right and the beam would fall to the left. Wouldn't it? Well, it had better.

I pulled one last giant effort. The twine gave, my hands were free. I felt the blood oozing from my wrists, and my trapped feet felt warm and moist. They were covered with more blood. That would attract the rats. I had to move away, far enough away so the beam when it came down it would not strike me. I pushed and tugged at the rocks on my feet and they rolled off, slicing new cuts in my feet as they went.

The rocks above me had stopped falling and it was eerily quiet again. Again I heard a far away rumble that I knew was thunder. A pair of red eyes appeared above me. Then another pair gleamed over my head. They had found a way to higher ground to avoid the waters. Blood was dripping into my eyes. I reached into my pocket for tissues and found my little flashlight.

I pushed the button and light came, bright light. At least it seemed bright after the awful blackness I'd been in.

Now to make it out of here. Straight ahead, I thought. The light flickered. I turned it off, I'd have to conserve what battery power was left. I'd feel along the wall until I absolutely needed some light to get my directions.

I whispered a prayer, "Please God, lead me out of here."

I stumbled and fell. The flash rolled from my hand. "No. Oh no." Desperately, I felt around the floor. A short way ahead a soft glow winked. I reached for it, grabbed at it, picked it up. It was my little light.

I was back on my feet, but I'd lost any sense of direction I'd had, could only keep going. I came to a steep upward climb. Soft music began playing. It grew louder as I climbed. After a climb of several feet, the wall to my left fell away, and when I flicked on the light I saw I was standing on a ledge that led upward. A deep chasm was on my left. One misstep…

My light was blinking. It would fail soon, but I dare not turn it off now and risk plunging down the crevice. I crept steadily upward, my back to the right wall. Then the flashlight failed. I felt a drop of rain on my face. Not rain. Not now.

I sank down on the hard packed rock. Rain? I looked up. There was a dim, very dim light up ahead. *It had to be you*, came a soft refrain. I crawled on hands and knees upward until I pushed away a heavy lattice cover and pushed it aside before I pulled myself out through a grass ringed hole. A chimney. That's what Sergio had warned me about it, said not to step on it and fall down the chimney into the mine. It's for the mine's fresh air.

The music was fading. I heard angry voices, "She told me so. You shot my Juana, you left her for dead. She who never hurt anyone. I will kill you now. With my bare hands I will choke the life from you."

A grunt. "Not you, old man. You couldn't kill a flea."

Phillip. Sergio and Phillip. Phillip had a gun. He'd shoot Sergio.

I stood and tried to run, but I stumbled on my cut and bleeding feet and fell. Shoving aside bushes, I saw them. Phillip held his gun at Sergio's head.

"No," my voice was raspy, but Phillip looked my way.

"No," this time at Perro who charged toward the men.

Phillip's reaction was swift. He knocked Sergio down and turned the gun on Perro. She leapt at Phillip, knocking him down, his gun went arcing up the hill. Fighting for his life, Phillip jammed his elbow down Perro's mouth, and kicked his knees up in the dog's belly. Perro snarled her rage.

I reached the gun, picked it up and aimed it at Phillip. "Perro. Come here," I rasped, "Phillip, you're a dead man if you don't do as I tell you. Lay on your stomach, legs apart, hands over your head. Sergio come here."

Sergio stumbled to his feet. "Se, Patrona."

I held the gun with steady hands, knowing I would kill Phillip if he moved.

Then Randall and the sheriff were running up the hill. The sheriff handcuffed Phillip. Randall picked me up. I cried into his chest, "I'm so cold. So very cold."

"It's all over. You'll be all right now, sweetheart."

* * * * * * *

I was waiting on the sidewalk while Mama carried homemade soup to a sick neighbor across the street. I saw him coming. I saw him wave, smiling as he speeded up and the gray van swerved to hit Mama. I screamed and screamed, "Kassi, Kassi."

She was there, "What is it Nika? What?"

"It was Phillip. Phillip ran his van into Mama." I was crying and crying.

Kassi was crying too. “You just had a dream. It was you who nearly died today. Phillip who tried to kill you. I might never have been able to tell you I’m sorry for everything.“

Then Randall was urging me to lie down, soothing Kassi.

He said to me, “Do you remember Phillip driving the van that killed your Mother?”

“Yes, in my dream it was so clear.” I said.

“I’ll take care of it. You go back to sleep.” He said.

When I opened my eyes again, the floor lamp glowed and someone had lit a fire in my bedroom fireplace. Randall sat in the wing chair he’d pulled over to my bed and was holding my hand. “I’ve been waiting to tell you something.”

I’d never been so tired. “Tell me.”

“I love you Nika.”

“Yes,” I said, “I know.”

Chapter Twenty-two

Randall drove Timothy, Kassi and me to Molly's funeral held in a dark brick Episcopal Church, on a hill at the edge of Magdalena. Holy Trinity. I dressed in my black power suit, but navigated on crutches with my bandaged feet covered with gray wool hunting socks, supplied by Timothy. It was August and the sun was hot even at ten in the morning, but inside the little church, it was cool and peaceful.

When Timothy found out Tallulah's body was still lying in a morgue at the county jail, he asked that she be buried at the same funeral, a request everyone involved was happy to agree to.

The graveyard was a short walk from the church, and we followed the two coffins to the burial site and stood by for the commitment. At the end of the service, a family of mourning doves flew from the pine trees in formation over the caskets, and for a moment I could hear the sweet melody of, "It Had To Be You," floating after them. Yes, it may have been my imagination, but I wiped tears from my eyes.

After the final prayer, the priest, a man with gentile blue eyes and curly snow-white hair, gave me a rectangle of wood which held the image of a sad eyed woman holding an infant. "This is my attempt to copy a famous Icon. I've painted so many, my wife suggested I give them to mourners. I'd be pleased if you'd accept this one, which is my favorite."

The next milestone was Phillip's arraignment. During questioning, he began obsessing over his bad luck and admitted to driving the van into my mother and killing her. I could hardly accept it when he proudly told how his father had smothered Sapphira and Tony's two babies. "An courageous act of my father's to insure that I would be the only heir," Phillip said. He also admitted pushing Grandma, Dad and his father into the icy lake. I will never forgive him. He said he camped several miles down the road from Sappy's house, coming and going as he pleased in his father's old delivery van until losing the keys to the house and garage he'd had for years. He later found them on the floor of the van. For most of my testimony he sat with his head bowed, his hands clenched into fists.

Although I'd forgotten the *bums,* Randall reported that they were some kids who'd taken one of their dad's pickups and gone on a two-week lark. The dog was O.K. too he said.

Kassi had continued to work and save money for an education in restaurant management available at a school in San Francisco. One afternoon, she became serious and said, "Nika, how can I tell you, that I finally know what a brat I've been. How sorry I am, and how much I want to make amends."

"It's O.K., Kassi," I said, "You're no different than most teenagers, and I didn't know a thing about raising a kid. I skipped punishment so you'd continue to idolize me. Now I know, I'd rather have you as my friend and companion than anything else."

With that, she hugged me, "You're the best. Except for you, I'd be doing drugs or worse."

Timothy found me on the patio one day when he drove out to visit me. He was full of news. Tallulah's ranch was his, and his son-in-law, who would graduate from college mid-term, had accepted Tim's offer to manage it for eighty percent of the profit. He'd wanted to turn it over to them, but his son-in-law said it had to be on a business basis, or he wouldn't do it at all. He'd grown up on a ranch in western Nebraska and had brothers who'd help as well as his father, still actively running his own land. "Just think," Tim said, "I'll be able to see my new granddaughter anytime."

"Oh Tim," I said, "I'm so happy for you."

"It's all because of you," he said, his eyes moist with tears.

"Ah sure now, Timothy Ryan," I said responding by trying on his accent, "and you'd have done the same of me."

As he was leaving, he turned and said, "They're waiting to christen the wee one 'til they get here, in the old church up the hill. You'll come won't you?"

"That I will, Tim," I answered.

I was pondering Kassi's mid-September departure for college one day, while again sitting on Sappy's patio and thinking how everyone's life was coming together. Everyone's but mine. I shook myself and went for another cup of decaf coffee.

As I returned to my chair, Randall walked onto the patio with his brief case, a bag of wonderful fresh rolls, and a red velvet jeweler's box containing the biggest diamond I ever saw. When I started to protest, he held his hand up and instructed me to read an official looking paper, a prenuptial agreement, which said he had no claim on Sappy's fortune or property.

"Randall, we don't earn enough to keep up this ranch."

"Hear me out," he pleaded, "my grandfather made money, lots of it, in mining and land ventures. So much he set up trust funds for Dad, and when I was born, for me. I'm a T.F.K."

"A what?"

"A Trust Fund Kid." He smiled, "It put me through college and buys me BMWs. We've no money worries, none at all."

"But Randall, I've always earned my own way."

"It's simple," he said, "whatever I have or own is yours the minute we're married. Now, will you marry me?"

Marriage to a man who would forever manage my life? "Randall, you're very attractive, but..." the hurt was spreading to his eyes, and I hated to hurt this man.

"But what?" He asked.

"You have the most maddening way of directing my life. Telling me what to do. Don't you know that?"

"I'm just trying to take care of you," he said.

"That's just it," I said, "I want to take care of myself. I want someone who lets me make mistakes, but loves me anyway. I want to be my own person. Is that so hard to understand?"

Randall reached out to me, "No. No of course not, but if you let me make your decisions, you won't have to. Don't you see, when a guy loves a beautiful girl, he wants to protect her, make life easy for her."

I pushed his hands away, "It's called control, and if you tell me what to do, and it turns out badly then what? Will you say I didn't do it right?"

He was shaking his head.

"And if I make a decision or try something on my own that turns out all wrong, will you say, 'I told you so'?"

"No, I'd never," he tried to interrupt me.

"See? It'll never work. I've known it ever since I knew I loved you."

He drew me close to him, "There you see? You just said it, that you love me. And when two people love each other they can work out these small differences."

"They aren't 'small' differences. They're great big, huge differences, you just won't see it that way."

"I'll try. I'll try harder than anyone else ever tried in his life. Just give me a chance. Please," he said.

"You'll have to change a lot," I said.

"I'll change. A year from now you'll never know it's the same man, I'll have changed so much." He was wiping my eyes and kissing me at the same time. "Please say you'll marry me."

"Well," I said finally, "I suppose I will."

The next several minutes were devoted to his kissing me and slipping the ring on my finger. It was beautiful and sent flashes back to the lowering sun.

Did I have any doubts then? None. I was I love, and everyone knows how that is.

He asked, "Up to some company?"

Oh no, I thought, his parents. Now it starts. I fled to my room to wash my face, comb my hair, and apply a trace of lipstick. Taking a deep breath, I returned to the patio to find Tim grinning broadly and looking very proud. Juana, Sergio and their daughter were coming down the hill. And Clara was there.

"Now that we're all here," Randall said, "I want you to watch as both of us sign the document and then sign as witnesses."

We proceeded seriously and as the last of them signed their names, Clara brought out her Notary Public stamp and made it official. Only then did Sergio open a bottle of champagne and pour glasses all around for a toast.

We moved to the living room when Kassi joined us. Randall struck a match to the logs already laid in the massive fireplace. From somewhere, Juana served snacks fit for dinner and, as it grew dark, turned on table lamps until the room glowed.

Randall and I sat on a love seat, holding hands, nibbling snacks and sipping champagne. Tim's voice carried to us from across the room, telling a story, "Wanting to break Pat of his turrable drinking habit, his two friends lowered him into the open grave and waited for him to wake up in the morning…," The punch line was lost, but Clara's deep laughter wasn't. Looking as happy as I'd ever seen him, Tim immediately began another story.

Before she left for her doughnut shop, Clara came to me and said, "Love never dies, not ever. It's the only real magic, because you don't have to say it, those you love just know."

Somehow, I knew she was right.

Another thing I knew was that, although this wasn't a traditional family, this was a family. It was my family.

After she left, Randall poured me a second glass of champagne and as I sipped it, I heard the soft strains of, "It had to be you…". Molly and Charlie were not far away.

About the Author

Joan Monroe lives in Fort Collins, Colorado with her husband and their dog, a dingo mix named Cassie. She writes about her favorite fictional persons, RNs, the people who work with them and their patients.